DAMSELS JUST WANNA RUN

DAMSELS
JUST WANNA
RUN

Christopher Hall
aka Maxlex

Podium

Copyright © 2024 by Christopher Hall

Cover design by Andrew Clark

ISBN: 978-1-0394-6520-6

Published in 2024 by Podium Publishing
www.podiumaudio.com

Podium

DAMSELS JUST WANNA RUN

CHAPTER ONE

Back on the Chain Gang

TYLA

Something was different about today. Yesterday, another boatload of prisoners had arrived, the third since Tyla's arrival. Zamarrans, going by the darkness of their skin. A mix of boys and girls of about the same age as Tyla. Slavers liked their victims to be young. With no classes or levels, there wasn't much they could do to resist.

The new arrivals had acted much like everyone else. Fearful and subdued, they spoke quietly among themselves, and not at all to anyone else if they could help it. Nervous glances were cast at the reddish-brown skins of Tyla's Ett brethren and Tyla was the target of unabashed staring.

She didn't mind. The Zamarrans *were* invaders, but the bad blood from that was long since gone. They were neighbors now. *Greedy* neighbors that had to be held in check by the Ett Confederacy, but they understood boundaries.

The Elitrans did not. Or if they did, they did not *honor* them. They came as they pleased and took what they wanted. Now they had taken her.

Not for the first time since she was captured, Tyla cursed her luck. Her woodcraft was good enough to deal with either a sprained ankle or Elitran raiders. Both at once had proved too much for her. Now she was a captive, just like the Zamarran children who had huddled behind their walls for safety. This was her twelfth day of captivity. Three days on the boat, and nine days cooped up behind the bars of this cell.

Today was different, though. The guards were more alert, their ears flicking around at the slightest sound. Their fur was better groomed. They were waiting for something.

Sure enough, when the outer gate clanged open, what came through was not another small group of prisoners, but a well-dressed courl. Accompanied by a small coterie of humans and courls, he strode into the prison like he owned the place. All the guards stiffened to attention and faced him, so perhaps he did.

The cells that Tyla and the others were being kept in were large. Four people could sleep in relative comfort, and thus far that was the limit their captors had kept to. One of the walls was made up of iron bars, opening out onto a central octagonal area. It was into this area that the rich courl strode, without a care for the fearful gazes that came from seven other cells.

His fur was the most unusual thing about him. It was a rich, deep blue that shimmered in the lantern light as he moved. Tyla had never seen a courl with fur of that color and wondered if it was dyed. He was dressed in richly embroidered loose robes and his fingers glittered with rings.

Some of his entourage were carrying furniture: a desk, a chair, and a stool. These were placed in the center of the room, and he sat in the chair and started to peruse the bundle of papers that was placed on the desk. The stool was left alone in front of him.

After about five minutes of activity, during which he got his papers, his quill and ink, and his robes all arranged *just so*, he finally spoke.

"Greetings, slaves," he said, and Tyla was shocked to find that she understood him. Somehow, he was speaking the language of her tribe. From the shocked expressions on her fellow prisoners, they were all hearing something in their own languages.

To check, she sidled up to a Zamarran girl sharing the cell with her.

"What language do you hear?" she asked in the Tiatian Trade tongue. It wasn't officially spoken in the Ett Confederacy, but there were so many tribes and languages that it was often easier to speak the language of the invaders.

The girl jumped at Tyla's softly spoken words and stared wildly at her before returning her attention to the courl.

"My home tongue—I mean, Tiatian Trade," she murmured. "Does everyone hear something different?"

"Magic," Tyla muttered darkly. She stared at the courl. Her tribe did not countenance the practice, but she had heard that for a mortal to cast spells, they needed to be touching the corpse of a numenstone. Typically, mortals wore the large crystal around their necks, underneath their clothes. The courl's robes were so loose and layered that it was difficult to tell if there was a numenstone underneath them.

"Today," the courl went on, "you will be evaluated and graded, separated into lots based on that, in preparation for being sold."

He looked around to gauge everyone's reaction.

"For your own sake, I advise you to be cooperative." He smiled, showing his pointed teeth. "Let's start with the Zamarrans."

The cell next to Tyla was opened, and the first prisoner was dragged out. She was tall and slender, with dark skin and hair. She was dragged out to the center of the room, but instead of sitting on the stool clearly meant for her, she remained standing, her arms wrapped around herself, looking wildly around.

"Name?" the courl asked coldly. The girl looked at him but didn't reply.

He sighed. "Elira Thane," he said. "Herbalist, how troublesome. The first one off the rank has her second tier. No doubt that is why you thought to defy me."

"What?" Elira said, confused. "How do you know . . ."

"Do you think I could be an Evaluator without having an Identify trait? Foolish girl. Now you get to serve as an example."

He raised his hand and the girl started screaming. She stayed on her feet for a few moments, and then she collapsed to the ground, sobbing.

"No . . . no . . ." she cried. The Evaluator looked down on her.

"Just fear," he mused aloud. "All it takes to break someone. I could have used a different emotion, one that made you happy and cooperative, but this is more effective. Both on you . . . and everybody else watching."

He looked around at the other prisoners, emphasizing his point. "Now get up and sit down."

The girl's sobs stopped as quickly as they started. She whimpered as she got up and obeyed.

"Good," the courl said. "Do you speak Elitran?"

Elira shook her head. "No."

"You will refer to me as Sir, Master, or Evaluator when you respond to me. Do you understand?"

"Yes . . . Evaluator."

"Herbalism is a useful profession," the courl said. "You will need to learn more Elitran than the average slave does to be useful, and you will have to train more to learn the herbs that actually grow in the Empire. Are you willing to make that effort?"

When Elira did not immediately respond, his smile turned cruel. "Or, you can break your path and take Concubine. That profession requires much less effort."

"I . . . I don't qualify for that class . . . Evaluator."

The courl flicked his ears. "You will, once my men have taken their turns with you. No sense making you take Doxy when you can qualify for a Tier Two class."

The girl's eyes went wide with fear. Tyla sympathized. She would likely be making a similar choice very shortly.

"I—I'll work hard at being a Herbalist," Elira said quickly.

"A wise choice. Most of my men are courls, and while we enjoy sex with human women, we're just not . . . shaped right for it to be comfortable for *them*."

6   CHRISTOPHER HALL AKA MAXLEX

There was a murmur of laughter around the room from the guards.

He turned to one of his assistants. "Classify Lot One as containing skilled slaves and assign her to it. Next."

The second prisoner to be dragged out was a boy with curly hair. He was tall and heavily muscled, but natural strength was no match for a difference in levels. After a brief struggle, he went quietly and sat down on the stool.

"Name?" The Evaluator asked flatly.

"Galen Drakar, blacksmith's apprentice. Sir," the boy said.

"*Crafter's* apprentice," the courl corrected him. "Could only qualify for the more general version, I suppose. Level four. Hmm. I suppose it would be a waste not to make use of those levels. Very well, put him in Lot One."

The next prisoner was a girl, the youngest so far. She shied away from the guards' hands but sat on the stool without protest.

"I'm Cheia Lucina, I'm a baker's apprentice," she said nervously.

"You're not anything yet; you're too young. When you get your first level, take Doxy—or you'll be beaten until you do."

Ignoring her startled gasp, he turned to the assistant again. "Put Lot Two down as household slaves and assign her to it."

"She's too young for that!" the last person in the cell called out. It was a Zamarran woman, probably from the same village. She burst out of the cell protesting. The guards let her, probably because she was the next one due for processing.

"She is too young *now*, for the class, that's self-evident," the courl said. "She can't be more than a few months away, though, no?"

He gave the woman a smile that showed all his teeth. "She's not too young to service my men, however, should I deem it necessary."

There was another snigger amongst the guards. The Evaluator paused to let it die down and then continued.

"As a Tier One class, Doxy does not have the . . . *rigorous* requirements that Concubine does. So it shouldn't be necessary to damage the goods as long as her behavior is acceptable."

The woman stared at him. She stood with a certain poise and grace that wasn't doing her any favors. Nor were her indigo eyes, flashing with outrage. The Evaluator gestured for her to sit. She stood still for a moment but complied when the guards moved forward.

"Now," the Evaluator said. "Name?"

"Althea Selene," the woman replied sullenly.

"A common Server, level four," the courl said. "Good news! You'll be able to continue looking after your little friend, at least for a while. You can keep your class; it's harmless enough, and it will get you to Concubine sooner."

Althea protested, but he ignored her and addressed his assistant. "Make a note, she can start work before she's fully trained. Server doesn't directly lead to Concubine, but we can make sure she qualifies."

Tyla's cell was the next one opened, and Tyla was the first one brought out. The guards were much less lax with her; each of them grabbed one of her arms and forced her over to the stool. They must have known she had a Combat class.

She didn't resist them, which may have helped them relax their vigilance. They were taken off guard when she reached the stool. Instead of sitting on it, she hooked her foot under it as she approached, and kicked the thing straight at the head of the Evaluator.

He didn't blink. The stool stopped dead in midair, about a foot from his face. Tyla stared in shock as it fell down, clattering off the desk and falling to the floor.

"Tch," he sneered. "At least you didn't spill any ink. Well, if you won't sit, you can kneel."

At his words, the guards holding her forced her down, kicking her knees out from under her, and keeping her in an uncomfortable kneeling position. She struggled, but they were much stronger than her.

"We don't catch many of you," the courl mused. "The rarity value will make up for what will no doubt be a difficult training regime. Name?"

"Tyla Greenwalker," she said.

"How quaint. I don't recognize your class, some local specialty no doubt, but the Hunter part gives me a clue. What are your traits?"

Tyla paused, sensing a trap. She had never heard of an identification skill that gave up a person's traits, but they might exist. And he had magic besides. She elected to tell the truth.

"*Persistent Tracker* and *Silent Shot*," she admitted.

"Very wise," the courl said, grinning again. "You'd do well to forget you have those. They won't do you any good where you're going. Put her down for Lot Two."

Tyla narrowed her eyes. "I'm a warrior," she said coldly. "I'll kill any man that tries to touch me."

"Yes, yes, you're very fierce," the courl said dismissively. Tyla wanted to wipe the smirk off his face, but the guards kept their grip on her. "Unfortunately, your style hardly suits our janissary brigades. We've found slaves don't make for the best scouts, they keep on not coming back."

The laughter around the room indicated that this was a joke.

"And there is the matter of your rarity. A sad truth of this world is that when a man buys a woman solely because of that woman's rarity, the first thing he wants to do is stick his dick in her."

The joke was crude, and his leer was disgusting, but it was a hit with the guards.

"To that end, I'm afraid your current class won't do." He leaned forward, transfixing her with the gaze from his amethyst eyes.

"Break your class."

CHAPTER TWO

It's No Crime

Suliel didn't have a proper audience chamber; the castle wasn't big enough. Instead, the feasting hall was repurposed. The long table was removed, chairs were set to the sides for the audience, and the big chair was brought out.

Not a *throne*, though she'd called it that as a child. It was just a large chair, with a high back and elaborate armrests. The seat was a little too high for her to get on it easily. It was imposing enough, especially when mounted on its special dais. Only one step high, as befitted her rank as a Baron. One step more for Counts, another for Dukes, and only the King got to stand four steps higher than his supplicants.

Sitting on her chair, looking down at the room, she made sure everything was in place. Her people, her prisoner, and the lighting were all as she had requested.

The lighting was one of Kelsey's innovations. The men trained by her had fastened cables to the walls, leading from a large squat battery to the lights that ran along wall cornices. The illumination that they gave off was unique. Not the warm flickering of lanterns or torches, nor the cool blue glow of magic stones. It was bright and unchanging, but it was warm and the multiple sources lit everything from more than one direction, almost eliminating shadows.

It wasn't entirely flattering to have everything exposed under this glare. But Suliel wasn't trying to seduce anyone. *There are no secrets here* was, she hoped, the impression it gave. If nothing else, the unfamiliarity of it should put the judge off his game. She would need every edge she could get without her own support network being present.

<Is there any news?> she thought at Kelsey.

Kelsey sent back a feeling of amusement. *<You're lucky that dungeons seem to be built with an endless supply of patience,>* she sent. *<Otherwise I would have been driven mad by your constant need for updates.>*

Anton, Aris, Kelsey, and the two prisoners had left on their quest two days ago. They had delayed for a few days, picking up another level and a better understanding of Elitran, but Kelsey had advised against waiting for longer, as Anton was getting close to tiering up.

"You don't get a fancy new class for *planning* an epic quest," she had said at the time. "Ideally, you'd want to have finished it, but *starting* it has got to be worth something."

They had also hoped that delaying would mean that Anton was around when the judge arrived, which would have made things a little easier for Suliel. However, the judge had decided to take his time, pausing for almost a week at a village on the edge of Suliel's territory. Suliel's suspicions as to why were confirmed when he showed up with Suliel's mother.

After one last look around the room, she gave the nod for the judge's party to enter. They trooped in, the judge himself coming last as befitted his status.

Everything had been arranged in advance, of course. Suliel knew who was entering and what their roles were. Seats had been provided according to status. The judge was no supplicant to stand before her. He spoke for the King, and while he could not *order* her, his words had weight.

Three seats had been provided, one with a small desk for the scribe. Suliel had her own scribe recording the proceedings, but the judge's account would be the one that was reviewed by the King. The second seat was for Suliel's mother; she tested it for sturdiness before sitting down.

Suliel carefully did not let her annoyance show. It had been a thought only, and a petty one at that, to rig her mother's chair to collapse. Whatever satisfaction she would have gained would be more than made up for by the risk of the proceedings ending in a debacle.

The judge's apprentice and guards would stand behind him. He had arrived with two other servants. By mutual agreement, they would stay in the kitchen.

Finally, the judge himself took his seat. Suliel had seen him when he arrived. Then, he had appeared to be no more than an old man in plain black robes. Now, his plain robe had been replaced by an elaborately embroidered one, jet black with silver decorations. The cap that covered his head lent him an air of dignity, and his long grey beard was combed and shaped to look patriarchal.

Suliel inclined her head. "Welcome to my court, Judge Vadistock."

"Greetings to you as well, Baroness Anat. Shall we get started by elucidating the issues that bring us here today?"

Without waiting for her to reply, he rolled on, his words coming slowly but inexorably.

"One. The matter of your new class and the status of your rank. Two. The breach of hospitality that occurred between you and Lord Kinn. Three. The rift of trust between you and your mother, who sits beside me."

Suliel took a deep breath. "My class is not a legal matter, Lord Judge."

"Not as such, but it does lie at the heart of all the matters at hand, does it not?" the judge said. "I must say that I didn't believe it when they told me, but it turned out to be true. Whatever possessed you to take such a ridiculous class? Sovereign of the Crypts?"

Suliel looked at him as if he were mad. "It's an *epic* class," she said scornfully. "A *Tier Two* epic class."

The judge sighed. "Ah, the foolishness of youth. Grasping for power without a thought towards the consequences."

Suliel bristled but managed to hold back from saying anything that would prejudice her case. The judge's class was simply Judge. It *was* rare, but if he had made the effort while an Advocate, he could have qualified for a Unique variant like Impartial Judge or Fearless Judge.

"Of course, I thought about the consequences, but the King has no reason to be concerned," she said. "My title lays claim only to a crypt."

"And what crypt might that be, my lady? Could it refer to the nearby dungeon?"

Suliel hesitated before answering. There was no lying to a judge, she reminded herself. Not at her tier.

"It does," she admitted.

"You may have forgotten," the man said condescendingly, "but the dungeons are only *managed* by the local nobles. *Ownership* is held by his majesty, in trust for the people of this nation."

"The dungeon acknowledged *me*, not the King," Suliel snapped.

<You tell him!> Kelsey sent encouragingly.

Vadistock looked at her steadily. "That is quite the claim."

"Look at my class if you don't believe me. How do you *think* I came by it? The dungeon recognized me as the ruler of the territory it resides in. It is paying reparation for the deaths it has caused. It is a part of Kirido now."

Vadistock sighed. "Fortunately, I don't have to decide on this matter. It has been taken out of my hands."

He snapped his fingers, and his apprentice came forward, bearing a sealed document. He stepped up to the edge of the dais and offered it to Suliel, his head bowed.

Suliel had to get off her chair to accept it. She did so reluctantly. Even from where she sat, she could see the seal on it was that of the King.

It's my first time breaking one of these, she thought as she cracked the wax seal to open the document. Detaching it would have looked as if she was hoping to use it for later, which wasn't a good look in front of a judge.

"You're being summoned to court to answer for the unusual circumstances of your class," the judge said, saving her the trouble of reading it.

"I—Kirido is still recovering from the attack. I can't leave it right now."

"That has been accounted for. You have an entire month to finish matters here before presenting yourself."

Suliel's mind raced, looking for a way out, but there wasn't one. "Then . . . I would be glad to present myself to his majesty."

"Of course. As to the status of your rank, I had heard that you married against your mother's will."

"As is my right, now that I have reached my second tier."

"It is a sad thing when a mother cannot attend her child's wedding," the judge said. "I understand the rest of your family was not invited also."

"Circumstances dictated that we abandon tradition," Suilel said blandly. "The legal formalities were followed, of course." She gestured for the documentation to be brought forward.

"I . . . see." Vadistock started perusing the documents. "And where is Baron Nos?"

"Anton is on a quest to save those taken from the raid."

"A quest?"

"His class *is* Adventurer," Suliel said fondly.

"I see. Is he expected back before the month is up?"

"He only just left, so it isn't likely."

Suliel sent a thought Kelsey's way anyway. **<It's been fifteen minutes!>**

"Very well," the judge said. "If he should return, let him know that he is expected to present himself as well."

"Of course, I should be glad of his support."

"Hmm. My apologies for addressing you incorrectly Baroness Nos. Now, I see that he has left you with his full authority in his absence, so we can proceed with the other matters. The breach of hospitality with Lord Kinn—"

"We can hasten this if we hear from Lord Kinn at this time," Suliel interrupted.

"Oh? By all means."

Riadan stood up from his chair by the wall and stepped forward, placing himself between Suliel and the judge, but off to the side, so they formed a triangle. He bowed to both of them.

"I was entirely at fault," he said. "I take full responsibility for the events that occurred and have made a full and sincere apology to Baroness Nos for my actions."

"Riadan! You can't—" Lady Anat jumped to her feet, protesting, but she was quelled by an icy glare from the judge.

"How unusual," he said. "Has Baroness Nos demanded reparations of you?"

"Remembering the long relationship between our families, she was most forgiving. Some small payments must be made, trivial in scope compared to the severity of my crime. In addition, if Captain Oldaw feels that the impact on the Glimmered Lancers requires reparation, I would be glad to make it right."

"How noble," Vadistock said, with only the slightest touch of sarcasm. "If only all disputes could be settled so easily."

Suliel kept her face expressionless. It hadn't been at all easy.

"I've had a chance to go through the papers in Father's office," she said through the cell door. She'd sent the guards away and she was feeling a little nervous. The door was all that was standing between her and the man who had already imprisoned her once. Her chamberlain had assured her that it would stand up to the strength of a Tier Three.

"If I show them to the judge, then you will hang as a traitor . . . just as soon as they can get you back to the capital," she continued.

"You wouldn't vilify your own father that way," Riadan rumbled through the door. "You can't condemn me without implicating him."

"You think I won't?" Suliel said, her voice rising in both pitch and volume. "You might have noticed I have some problems at the moment! What better way to prove my loyalty to the King than to hand over my father and uncle as traitors? It takes care of two of my problems with one stroke!"

"You can't trust the King. If you've read your father's papers, then you know he's an impostor. He can't afford to have anyone around who suspects him."

"Maybe, maybe not," Suliel said tiredly. "I have only the word of Tikin that he's an impostor, and Tikin is not someone I feel a lot of trust for."

"I can confirm it's true."

"You're not on my list of trusted people either, *Uncle*!" Suliel cried.

"You're still not going to do it. You wouldn't have told me if you were."

"I don't *want* to do it, but I will. It's time for the Rose Circle to make me an offer."

"The Circle doesn't take well to blackmail, little Sue."

"The Circle will have to get used to it. It still wants the guns, right? Well, without me, there are no guns, so make me an offer, Uncle. Help me get out from under at least *some* of my problems."

* * *

"Well, this is good news," the judge said. "Should I understand that rapprochement includes the actions taken by your mother?"

"Indeed. She only took the actions she did because of encouragement from me," Riadan said smoothly.

"If Mother is willing to put the past behind us, then so am I," Suliel said.

The judge looked at Lady Anat, who was not looking pleased.

"I think . . . that Lady Anat will require a little time to process this turn of events," he said. "Perhaps it would be best if she was to return with me to the capital. Some time apart might seem in order, and you can meet again when you present yourself. Then mother and daughter can renew their bond under the watchful gaze of the King."

"As you say, Lord Judge," Suliel agreed.

CHAPTER THREE

Rock the Casbah

Anton knew he was out of his depth before the boat even docked. Rused was so large! And busy. While his hometown boasted a single pier to dock ships at, Rused had at least three—that he could see. With all the ships blocking his line of sight, there might be more.

The town was set in a natural harbor, the entrance of which was guarded by a military vessel. It looked completely different from the wide-bodied trading ships that Anton was used to. Even the raiders' ships had been rigged for sail and proportioned to carry as many men as possible. This was a galley, long and sleek. It looked dangerous even when it wasn't moving.

Unconcerned, the Kabimen had sailed their boat right past it. Anton had watched the soldiers on deck nervously, but they didn't seem interested in them.

"Told you it would be fine," the Kabiman captain said. "They don't bother traders."

"Makes sense," Kelsey mused. "If they did, they'd lose the trade."

The captain looked warily at her. The crew had started out liking her, but they'd gotten more nervous as the voyage progressed. Not sleeping for the three days of the voyage had worried them, but summoning some skeletons to bail water had really spooked them.

"They like money, same as anyone else," he agreed. "And sailors get levels quick. We're always sailing."

"True. Where should we be docking?"

She addressed the question to the two courls that were accompanying them, but it was the captain who answered first.

"Traders dock on the first dock, there." He pointed.

"Is that where we want to go?" Kelsey asked Kusec. He was huddled under a hooded cloak that Kelsey had provided, looking at the town nervously.

"That's fine, he said shortly. "As long as it isn't near there." He pointed to the third dock, lined with familiar-looking ships. "We don't want to get arrested for desertion."

"Is it really desertion, when you were captured?" she asked. "If you showed up, told them that you'd been captured, escaped, and made your way back here, would they take you back?"

"Maybe," the courl admitted. "Heck of a story, though, not sure if I could sell it."

Left unsaid was that he wouldn't be trying it without permission. When they were in the dungeon, the two raiders had felt that escape was impossible. Lacking hope, they hadn't tested the geas at all. That lasted until a short time after they set sail.

The plan had been simple: Toss the three adventurers overboard and then force the Kabimen to keep sailing for their destination. It had gone wrong the second they attempted it.

Kelsey had explained that the geas manifested differently for each person. For Anton, it was fear. For these two, it was pain. They'd cried out and dropped to the ground the moment they laid their hands on Kelsey, who just looked at them as if they were a particularly interesting species of bug. It turned out that she'd heard all their planning, and had just been waiting for them to try it.

"What have we learned?" she asked them when they recovered.

Kusec did most of the talking for the pair, even now that the group had a basic understanding of Elitran. He looked at his friend and then looked back at Kelsey.

"We won't try to escape, harm anyone, or alert the authorities. We'll obey any reasonable order from you three," he said sullenly.

"And you're free if we find Aris's sister or a year and a day has passed. Easy!"

Thinking back on it, that was probably when the Kabimen had started feeling nervous.

Now, knowing what they must be thinking, Kelsey grinned wolfishly. "Don't worry, boys; if we get lucky, we might find Cheia by the end of the week. Then you can go back to the warm embrace of your countrymen."

The two courls stared at her, but couldn't work up the nerve to glare. They bowed their heads and pulled their hoods over farther.

Docking looked tricky to Anton, but the Kabimen were professionals and managed it with ease. Kelsey smiled as they tied up and dropped some silver in the claw of the captain.

"You're staying here a week, right?"

"Aye. If the cargo we find isn't going your way, you'll make up the difference."

"Or find another ship," Kelsey agreed. "I'll let you know as soon as we find out."

The Kabiman nodded, and Kelsey lept up to the dock, joining the rest of her party. They were all looking around, Anton and Aris in wonderment, while the two courls were looking nervously around for threats.

One such threat was approaching now, walking at an officious pace.

"Are you the captain of this vessel?" the courl asked. He was tall, with chestnut-brown fur and amber eyes. He was dressed somewhat ridiculously to Anton's eyes, but he looked rich, and the way their two prisoners shied away from him made Anton think he was important. Something in the group's stance made him gravitate to Kelsey as the leader.

"Who's asking?" Kelsey asked nonchalantly. Anton frowned. Kelsey was better than him at speaking Elitran, but he wouldn't have made that mistake.

The man sneered. "Barbarians. You see this hat?" he asked, pointing to the elaborate three-pointed hat that he was wearing. "That means that I'm the harbormaster, in charge of these docks. I decide who gets to tie up, and who gets to stay."

"That does sound important," Kelsey agreed. "Maybe you can tell me something that's been puzzling me." She pointed to the next dock over. "How does a merchant get so rich he can afford a ship like that?"

The harbormaster looked over to where she was pointing and scoffed. "Fool! That's no merchant ship. It belongs to al-Zahar Pasha, an official of far more importance than any merchant."

The ship in question did look important. It was far larger than any of the other ships in the harbor, sporting three decks, one of which seemed reserved for oars. It was also rigged for sail, with two masts, and it had high fortified sections at the bow and stern. All of it was gaudily painted, and from what Anton could see of the furled sails, they seemed to have been dyed a rich magenta.

"Pasha? I haven't heard of that one," Kelsey replied. "Is that more or less important than the Bey what runs the city?"

"Ignorant naif," the courl growled. "This city is ruled by Nasira al-Qadir *Wali*, may he live forever. He governs the entire island but has deigned to honor this city with his presence. He has *two* Beys that head the military and civilian administrations."

"That sure is a lot of important people," Kelsey said. "How does the Pasha fit in there, then?"

"It's not comparable," the harbormaster said irritably. "The Pasha is from the Emir's court and isn't part of the city's administration. He is just here to oversee the harvest."

"That's a mighty fancy boat to haul some grapes," Kelsey observed.

"Not *crops*," the courl said, scandalized. "He's here to collect the dungeon core."

"Is he," Kelsey said, the friendliness dropping out of her tone. She took a long look at the other dock. Anton could make out a number of richly dressed people making their way off the boat. There were also a lot of guards.

"Kelsey . . ." Anton stepped forward, ready to intervene. Kelsey looked at him and smiled, but she didn't say anything.

"Now look, if you're the captain, I need to see your cargo manifest," the harbormaster said. Kelsey paused for just a second and then seemed to relax.

"Oh, I'm not the captain," Kelsey said easily, pointing out the actual captain. "That's him, we're just passengers."

The courl's eyes flicked to the captain, then back to Kelsey. "If you're looking to stay, the entry fee is three copper." He looked over at the hooded courls. "Two for Elitrans."

Kelsey handed over a coin. "Will these coins do?"

"Barbarian coinage," the courl sneered, as he examined it closely. "But overweight. I'll accept it," he admitted.

He pulled a small book out of his vest. "I'll need your names."

Kelsey grimaced, but gave her name, as did Anton and Aris. Their guides hesitated and eventually gave false names. Kelsey raised an eyebrow at that, and then led them down the dock, leaving the harbormaster to harass the captain.

"That was a risk," she said. "He might have had an Identify trait."

"More of a risk if our names show up in records," Kusec grunted. "You never know who's going to be cross-checking."

"Fair enough," Kelsey said, shrugging.

"What was that about a harvest?" Aris asked.

"I heard about it from Mel," Kelsey said shortly. "You want to fill us in, Kusec?"

Kusec looked at them warily. "You don't want a dungeon to grow too big, so once it reaches a certain level, it gets . . . harvested. There's always a demand for dungeon cores."

"Surely there's a lot more value in the loot," Anton said. "Yeah, another one would spawn, but you'd have to find it, that could take years."

"On the mainland, that's true," Kusec agreed. "They let those places go a lot longer. But here, and a few other places, it's different. This island is the only place for a hundred miles where a dungeon can spawn. Doesn't take too long to find the new one."

"How often do they do it, Kusec?" Kelsey asked, softly.

"*I* dunno. They level them up pretty fast, with ah . . . recalcitrant slaves." Kusec carefully didn't look at Aris. "If they can't be trained or they're too old to be . . . economic, they get fed to the dungeon. A year or two, I'd guess."

"A year or two . . ." Kelsey repeated, staring at nothing. "The fact that he's here—do you think that means it's happened?"

The two courls looked at each other and shrugged. "Maybe?" Kusec said. "Probably not, if he's just arrived. The way I heard it, he's the one that makes the decision, and the nobility are never quick about anything."

"Except collecting what they're owed," Erryan pointed out.

"Well," Kelsey said, "there's not much we can do about it right this moment. So for now, let's check out the market!"

"Can we find an inn first?" Aris objected. "We've been washing in salt water and sleeping on boards for three days. I want a bath."

"You got used to hot water real quick," Kelsey complained. "Where's your sense of excitement? We're a step closer to finding your sister!"

"You don't sleep at all, *or* need to wash," Aris countered. "And when you do, the salt doesn't dry on your skin!"

"Fine, fine. We'll look for one. Do you know a place?" she asked their guides.

Kusec shook his head. "We stayed at the barracks when we were here. We know the general area you want, though."

He started leading the group through the market. Anton swallowed nervously at the thought of merging with such a large crowd. The press of milling people was mostly comprised of courls and yellow-skinned humans. Other shades of skin were visible, though: darker, paler and even blue.

Anton started when he saw a man with four legs stride through the crowd. His head was adorned with four-pronged antlers, and there was a sword at his side.

A few moments later, he saw a small group of what had to be Scaled Folk. Anton had heard of them, and his parents had met some once, but they lived far to the west and rarely came near Kirido. They wore clothes, of course, so all he could see of their brightly colored scales were the ones on their hands and their elongated, flattened faces. Each person had a different color arrangement, just like his parents had said.

"It's nice to get out and see the world, isn't it Anton?" Kelsey said.

"It's different," he said, not sure if he agreed. "It's a *lot* of different."

"That's basically what growing is," Kelsey told him. "Experiencing a lot of different things. Kirido was a rut, and now you've jumped out of it."

"I liked it, though," he objected. "All my friends were there."

"You'll go back eventually, but first you'll make more friends and face new challenges. It's going to be exciting!"

She grinned at him.

"Excitement, adventure and really wild things. Did I promise you that?"

"No," Anton said. "Just to save me. I think I'd had quite enough excitement that night."

"No such thing," Kelsey demurred. "You'll see."

CHAPTER FOUR

Fall at Your Feet

K eep your hands on your guns, Aris," Kelsey warned. "Pickpockets might not know what they are, but that won't stop them from stealing them to find out."

"Pickpockets?" Aris asked.

"Thieves," Kelsey told her. "In a crowd like this, you can get right up to someone without them noticing and make off with their purse."

"How do you *know* that?" Anton asked. Kirido wasn't exactly crime free, but the thieves there mostly concerned themselves with evading the dungeon's traps. Stealing someone's purse wasn't going to work when everybody knew everybody else.

"Oh, I hear things around the place—Whoa!"

Kelsey's exclamation was due to the exact thing she was just talking about. Quick as a flash, a small figure had stepped in and made a snatch for Kelsey's purse. The quick flash of a dagger made sure that the strings didn't hold it. Before Anton could react, the pickpocket was already moving out of reach.

"After him!" Anton moved without thinking. The thief was already out of sight, hidden behind another passerby. If Anton didn't move fast, there would be no catching the pickpocket. Then Kelsey grabbed him by the arm.

"Hold up, there," she said.

"Why? Wait—" Anton said, as his thoughts caught up with him. *When did Kelsey start carrying a purse?*

"Don't want you getting too far ahead," Kelsey reminded him.

Then a bloodcurdling scream sounded. *Not* in the direction the thief had gone.

"Ah, that sounds promising," Kelsey said and started leading him towards it. The others followed, wondering what was going on.

"It's the handoff," she explained. "The guy that steals the purse doesn't keep it, he passes it off to someone else. That way, if you catch him, he doesn't have your purse, and you look like the bad guy. Depending on the sophistication of your pickpocketing ring, there might be a couple of handoffs. But sooner or later, someone's going to open the purse."

Most of the crowd was heading away from the screams, but Kelsey forced her way through to an alley, too narrow for stalls. It looked as if it was mostly used for waste disposal. Near the entrance, there was a gap in the crowd as shoppers diverted away from what sounded like a murder.

A few yards into the alleyway, a small figure clothed in rags was writhing on a pile of garbage, screaming her throat hoarse. One of her arms was clutched to her chest.

"Huh, she managed to get it," Kelsey noted as she approached. Anton didn't know what she was talking about until he noticed the crushed corpse of a palm-sized spider. A very familiar-looking corpse.

"Kelsey, what did you do?" he asked.

"Nothing . . ." Kelsey said innocently, fooling no one. She knelt beside the girl, pulling the girl's arm clear to examine it. There was a nasty-looking welt on it. "She just got bit by a spider is all."

"Leave her alone!" The voice came from the other end of the alley and belonged to the boy who had stolen Kelsey's purse in the first place. His drawn dagger and quick charge were something Anton knew how to deal with. Stepping past Kelsey, he intercepted the boy, grabbing the knife arm and twisting.

Kelsey didn't even look up. Producing a vial of ointment out of nowhere, she smeared it on the girl's arm. The girl tried to pull away, but Kelsey's grip was like iron and the girl's captured arm didn't move an inch. Once applied, the effect of the ointment was immediate. The girl gasped in surprise as the pain vanished, and she stopped thrashing about.

Kelsey looked up to see the boy that Anton had captured and grinned.

"Two for one!" she crowed. "Who knew fishing for thieves would be this easy?"

"What spider was that?" Anton asked. The boy was struggling in his grasp, but Anton kept a hold of him easily. Anton still wasn't clear on what was going on, but if the boy attacked Kelsey, he could get hurt. "No, what *venom* was that?"

"Serpent's Scourge," Kelsey said. Anton winced. Serpent's Scourge caused no lasting damage, but the pain it inflicted was extreme.

"Couldn't you have used the sleeping one?" he asked.

"That wouldn't have done us any good," Kelsey said. "How would we have found her if she just went to sleep?"

"Ah, Kelsey?" Aris said diffidently from the end of the alley. They both looked over to her. As they did so, a uniformed courl came around the corner.

"What's going on here?" he asked suspiciously.

"Oh there's no trouble here, officer," Kelsey said. She rose to her feet, still holding the girl's arm. Staring fearfully at the guard, the girl was forced to follow Kelsey as she walked towards him.

"This poor girl had the misfortune of being bitten by a spider," Kelsey said. "I happened to be passing by, and as luck would have it, I happened to have an antidote. Using it on the bite seemed like the decent thing to do."

"Did it," the guard said suspiciously. He looked at Kelsey and then frowned in confusion. "What about the other kid?"

"A friend of the girl. He was concerned that I might mean harm to the girl. My friend is making sure he doesn't do anything rash."

"Is any of that true, street rat? You being helped?"

The girl didn't seem inclined to answer him. Unable to escape Kelsey's grip, she had twisted her body to get as far away from the guard as possible. Now, she spat on the ground and cursed. Anton didn't know the words she used, but he tried to remember them for later.

The guard's face darkened and his hand went for the short club hanging by his side.

"Can I just say how much I appreciate you taking an interest in the welfare of those less fortunate?" Kelsey said. It was a long sentence for a short moment, but the guard was distracted by the handful of silver she was showing him in her free hand.

"What?" he said.

"Such concern for the less fortunate! It needs to be acknowledged," Kelsey said, jingling her coins. The guard looked at the girl and then back at Kelsey. Then he looked at the silver.

"Just doing my job, ma'am," he said, holding out his hand. Kelsey smiled and poured the silver into it. With one last glare at the girl, the guard turned his back and walked away.

"*Now* we can get an inn," Kelsey said. "These two will give me something to do while you're having a bath."

"What are you going to do with them?" Anton asked. Kelsey just looked at him and raised an eyebrow. Anton cursed. He'd lapsed back into Tiatian. They'd agreed to only speak Elitran where possible, accelerating the learning process.

Anton repeated himself in Elitran. The boy in his arms went still, clearly interested in the answer.

"We need to make contact with whatever criminal organization is in this city," Kelsey explained. "Where better to start than with a couple of pickpockets?"

"We ain't helping you, northie bitch," the boy said. "Anyone can see you're bad news."

"How rude," Kelsey said. "And after I helped your dear friend Leila? She was in quite the pickle."

"The spider was in the pouch!" the girl exclaimed. She'd been trying to pull away from Kelsey for the entire time of the conversation, but Kelsey's grip was unmoved. "You trapped your own bag!"

Belatedly, Anton thought to check the two of them with *Delver's Discernment*.

Leila Zafar, Level 0, No Class
Karim Bezirgan, Level 3, Thief

"You poisoned a *child*, Kelsey," he said with distaste.

"I'm old enough to cut you!" Leila retorted.

"Hey, she was the one who opened the bag after it was stolen from me," Kelsey said. "Blame him, he stole it."

"Bull!" the boy said. "There was money in that bag, I sniffed it out!"

"Oh sure, there was some silver in there," Kelsey agreed. "The guard has it now, so it all worked out for *somebody*."

"You gave away all your coin?" Karim asked doubtfully.

Kelsey blinked. "Oh, that was what you meant. You've got a trait for sniffing out coin? Nice. But I don't keep my coin where the likes of you can get it."

She winked a silver piece into existence. Karim started with surprise and stared at Kelsey intently.

"You see?" she said, making the coin disappear. "I've got plenty more where that came from, and a small amount of it could be yours, if you cooperate and tell us about how the underground works around here."

She gave him a wide, predatory smile. "Or, I've got more spiders, if you prefer."

"Kelsey," Anton warned. She rolled her eyes.

"Fine, fine, no spiders, no torture, just silver if—just silver. Anton, you make the deal."

"Fine, fine," Anton said, letting go of the boy. The kid stepped away from him warily but didn't go for his dropped knife. Anton picked it up and offered it to him.

"She serious about the silver?" Karim said.

The inn they eventually found had an attached bathhouse, but mixed bathing was absolutely forbidden. So Aris and the two courls had gotten to go, but Anton was stuck in Kelsey's room with her two informants. Aris had offered to take the girl for a bath, but the offer had been vehemently refused. Apparently, coming back to the Nest smelling of roses would seem as if they had spent their stolen money on smelling nice, instead of the food the Nest needed. A beating was sure to follow.

The Nest was an abandoned building where the twenty-some members of their gang lived, supervised by an older thief known as the Shrike. He was the one who took their money and brought them food.

"He takes all the money," Karim clarified. "And you have to hope it's enough for the food he brings, otherwise it's beatings."

"This guy's connected?" Kelsey asked. "He knows the people who run things around here?"

"Yeah," Karim admitted. "Sometimes he has us do stuff for the big gangs, take messages or watch a place."

"The Nest is just kids, right?" Anton asked. Kelsey gave him a look but didn't otherwise interfere. "What happens when you grow up?"

In truth, Karim couldn't have been that much younger than Anton. He'd clearly been working hard as a thief to get his three levels that quickly. Now he grimaced at a thought that was clearly bothering him.

"It gets harder, once you get a class," he admitted.

"Oh? I would have thought that the class made it easier," Kelsey said.

"Easier in some ways, sure," he replied, "But . . . the guards don't care about kids, no matter if they're thieves or not. But once you've got a level, there's a bounty if they catch you."

"They don't care about kids?" Kelsey asked. "I thought kids made the best slaves?"

"Not us street urchins. We make terrible slaves. We're dirty and scrawny and we steal stuff. They'll take us, but they don't *hunt* for us."

Kelsey chuckled, but Anton was still confused.

"Wait, why does that change when you get a class?"

"They got a use for us then—they can put us in the dungeon."

"A dungeon doesn't grow if it eats kids without levels," Kelsey told him. "You need a class to be good dungeon food."

The kid nodded, unaware of why Kelsey was snickering at Anton's repressed outrage.

"So that's . . . what happens to you? You get snatched off the street and fed to the dungeon?"

"Sometimes," Kalim said. "Sometimes you can find a place in a proper gang. Every now and then the Shrike goes on to bigger things, and a new Shrike gets picked from the older ones."

"Right," Kelsey said. "Back to the Shrike. Does he live at the Nest? Or do you know where we can find him?"

Karim looked at the small pile of copper coins and the single silver coin that Kelsey had placed on the table between them.

"You gonna talk to him, pay him to talk to the next guy up?"

"That's how it tends to work."

Karim scowled. "I might know about someone higher up."

Kelsey smiled and put another silver coin on the table. "Tell me more."

CHAPTER FIVE

That's the Joint

I don't understand," Aris said.

Kelsey looked at her. "I thought we went over this. We're going to see a man who knows the criminals of this city. What we want to do is going to be some kind of crime, and he should be able to point us towards the right *kind* of criminals for what we need done."

"I get *that*," Aris replied. "What I don't get is how this 'illegal gambling den' exists! If it's illegal, why don't the guards come and arrest anyone? It's not even hidden!"

"It's not like there's a sign saying 'illegal gambling den,'" Kelsey pointed out, looking intently at their destination. There was a sign on the door, but it was decrepit and damaged. The only letters that could be made out were "Hass . . . ar."

"But if even the kids know about it . . ." Aris protested.

"Well, it's bribery that does it," Kelsey explained. "Either lots of lower level guards are being paid not to report it, or a higher official is being paid to officially not know. Or both."

She stepped away from the corner they'd been hiding behind while Kelsey checked out the building.

"Or," she said, "they're good enough at hiding the illegal stuff that when the guards come, there's nothing to be found. "Let's go see."

She strode up to the guarded doorway confidently, Aris and Anton trailing behind. The courls had stayed behind on the off chance that there were military officials at the den. The kids had been set free once they had answered all the questions that Kelsey could think of.

The man standing guard was the very definition of surly. His dusky brown skin spoke of his mixed heritage, and his scowling expression hinted at his lack of educational resources.

"Hi there!" Kelsey said brightly. "I'm here to speak with Nazari."

The guard's scowl didn't change. "Who sent you?"

"No one. If you're asking who gave me the name, just a street rat. I find that coin makes a more effective introduction, don't you?"

A silver coin suddenly gleamed in her outstretched hand, Kelsey once again using her inventory to make it look as though she was using sleight of hand. Anton winced a little at the gleam. Karim had recommended they bribe the guard with copper, but Kelsey never seemed to mind overpaying.

The guard took the money, but he still glared at Kelsey suspiciously.

"Come on, I think you would have heard if the Bey had hired a northerner," Kelsey said.

The guard grunted. "Shows what you know. He hired a whole squad." He looked her up and down. "None of them were a girl as creepy as you, though."

"Olaf got hired?" Kelsey exclaimed. "What's the world coming to?"

"Who in the Hells is Olaf?" the guard asked.

"Oh, you know us northerners, we all know each other," Kelsey said. "Now are you going to let us in or not?"

"Fine," the guard growled. He opened the door. Kelsey walked inside, the other two following. The guard glared at them as they went by, but didn't make an issue of it. He then followed them inside, closing the door behind him and gesturing to another guard inside.

Ignoring the byplay, Kelsey stepped forward and was intercepted by two more guards. These two looked a little more professional. One was human, one was a courl.

"Weapons check," said the courl. Kelsey smiled and held her arms out to the sides. They gave her what seemed like a cursory glance and then moved on to Anton.

Against his instincts, Anton was only carrying a dagger. He hadn't wanted to, but they'd been told that larger weapons were forbidden. Looking around, he couldn't help but feel he'd made the wrong decision.

Kelsey's got my sword, he told himself. *I can be armed in a second if there's a need.*

The dagger must have passed inspection because the guards moved on to Aris without a word. Their silence didn't last long.

"What are those?"

"They're a class feature," Kelsey said blandly. "Your trait must be leading you astray if you think they're weapons."

"Let me see," the courl demanded. Aris shrugged and handed a gun over.

"I suppose you could use it as a club if you were desperate enough," Kelsey said. "Maybe that's why it triggers your sense?"

The human looked at her suspiciously, while the courl continued to try and figure out what the gun did. He managed to pull back the hammer.

"Careful," Kelsey said. "You could give yourself a nasty pinch if the hammer catches you."

The courl glanced at her with irritation, just as there was a loud Clack! Looking down, he saw that he'd found the trigger and caused the hammer to close. The gun, of course, was not loaded.

"Useless thing," he snarled and gave it back to Aris.

"If you say so," Kelsey said. "Now, can we get service at the tables, or do we have to go to the bar?"

The courl growled at the question. "Find yourself a table, someone will take your order," he said.

Kelsey slid into the booth, still grinning like a particularly pleased cat.

"You could have just stored her guns like my sword," Anton said. "Why go through all that rigamarole?"

"Pretty soon, the whole world is going to know about guns," Kelsey said. "There's going to be a very small window where you can get away with tricks like that, so let me have my fun while I can."

She passed two fast loaders surreptitiously to Aris. Aris looked apologetically at Anton, but dutifully reloaded her guns under the table.

"Now what?" Anton asked.

"Now, we take in the atmosphere and wait for this Nazari fellow to show up," Kelsey replied. She looked out over the room.

"Atmosphere?"

"Yeah. You've got a real wretched hive of scum and villainy here; you should be more familiar with them as an adventurer."

"The adventurers' tavern back home isn't so bad," Aris said. "It's quite clean and doesn't smell . . . smoky like this one."

Aris was referring to the fact that the tavern back home was lit, not with torches or lanterns, but with light-stones. Being a favored haunt of adventurers, it often picked up alchemical equipment as payment for drinking debts, and it could use light-stones.

There was another reason for the smoky atmosphere here, however. Roughly half of the occupied tables had some sort of smoking device. Tubes led from them that were occasionally sucked on by the people sitting at the tables. There was also a sectioned-off, raised area that was much smokier than the rest of the club.

The ventilation seemed designed to draw air to that section, rather than let the smoke escape, but there was a smell that underlaid the whole place. Anton and Aris weren't familiar with it, but Kelsey had a knowing grin.

They got served drinks. Almost none of the menu was familiar, but Kelsey was eager to try as many new things as possible. She ordered about half the menu, buying teas, liquor, and cordials. Anton and Aris looked over the offerings and ordered based on what looked good. Kelsey went over the entire lot and ended up ordering a pot of bitter brown sludge.

"This is *coffee*," she told them, using a different word from what the server had used. "Not as I'd like to drink it. Needs milk, and filtering. Bleagh."

"If you filter out the beans, you take out the flavor." The words were delivered with a silken voice from the courl that had just stepped up to the table. His fur was jet black, and he wore a dark velvet vest covered in intricate designs. His green eyes flashed as he looked down at them.

"That's your opinion," Kelsey said. "Just wait until I get an espresso machine working. Are you Nazari?"

"I was told you wanted to speak with me," the courl said. He didn't take a seat. "You are unusual, and you do have money, so that makes you worth a little of my attention."

Kelsey grinned. "I knew that the street rat wouldn't be the only one with a *Sense Wealth* trait," she said. "We need some work done, and we heard that you were the person to see about it."

The courl looked at Kelsey, evaluating her. Then he slid into the booth across the table from her. When he did so, a number of the patrons at the smoking tables started passionate discussions. A musician started laboring away on some kind of stringed instrument. It was a subtle change, but the quiet, lazy environment changed to something a little more lively.

"What kind of work," Nazari said quietly.

"I need to look at some documents in the Administrative Compound," Kelsey said.

The Administrative Compound was one of the three main government buildings in the city. The other two were the Wali's palace and the military headquarters. The Administrative Compound was technically the palace of the Bey of civilian administration. He did actually live there, but his living quarters were attached to an ever-growing hive of bureaucracy.

"What *kind* of documents?" Nazari asked.

"Slave auction records for the last three weeks or so," Kelsey replied.

Nazari flicked a glance at Kelsey's companions, taking in their dark skin. "That would only be the start of it then," he said. "Once you know where your merchandise is, you'll want to retrieve it."

Kelsey shrugged. "I wouldn't want to bother you with details until I know what I need."

The courl looked at her for a long moment. "I know a person who can give you the records," he said. "I can set up a meeting, tomorrow night."

"Sounds good," Kelsey said. "I take it he won't be bringing the documents to the meeting."

"No, you'll have to pay him before he takes any risks," Nazari said. "You can work out the details with him."

"And where do you take your cut?" Kelsey asked.

"From him," Nazari told her. "That's the tradition here. Expect him to charge accordingly."

"That seems fine," Kelsey said. "I'll be back then."

"Before midnight," Nazari cautioned her. "Some of us have to work in the morning."

"Sure thing," Kelsey said. "I'd take off now, but I haven't finished my coffee."

Nazari nodded and took his leave.

"Well, that seemed easy," Aris said.

"Seemed is the right word," Kelsey said. To their surprise, she switched to the Tiatian Trade tongue. "There's a few more complications, but let's not make a scene in Nazari's place. He'll probably want to track us down to where we're staying."

Mystified at what Kelsey meant, Anton and Aris just nodded. Kelsey finished her coffee, and they headed out. To the market.

Despite Kelsey's earlier words, she mainly seemed interested in shopping now. Coffee beans were a priority, but there were a lot of items that caught her eye. A general rule, Anton found, was that if he didn't know what a thing was, Kelsey did, and wanted it.

"A place like this, you expect to see someone demonstrating half a frog hooked up to a magic jar," she said at one point.

"Oh, you must have heard of Amel," the merchant whose stall they were at said. "No, they ran him out of town three weeks ago. He wasn't selling anything, just bilking the gullible out of their silver."

Kelsey laughed delightedly and went back to shopping. Finally, though, she seemed about done.

"All right, I think I've got this guy's patterns down," she said. "Let's grab him."

"No spiders this time," Anton said.

"Yeah, yeah, you guys can do all the work this time," she said. She led them back to an area of the market that they'd already gone over. "This alley looks good. Aris, if you stay around that corner, we'll lead him on. When a shifty-looking guy with brown hair comes around the corner, grab him."

"Are we allowed to just grab people off the street?" Aris asked.

"As long as no one sees," Kelsey said. "And if they do, and call the guards, we'll just bribe them. The guy is a thief; they're not going to care what happens to him."

"Don't they have a bounty on people they can feed to the dungeon?" Anton asked.

"Ooh, shoot, that might drive the price up," Kelsey agreed. "Let's just keep it quiet then."

They went around the corner, and it all went pretty well. The shifty-looking guy came around and Aris grabbed him.

"Hey! What do you think you're doing!" he yelled, trying to get free. He had the edge on her, Aris thought, but not by enough. He was still struggling when Anton arrived, leaping to the attack. One punch from her husband was enough to put the thief down on the ground, gasping.

"What . . . are you . . . doing?" he gasped. "This . . . is assault!"

"Stay down," Anton told him. To the quickly approaching Kelsey, he said, "I hope you know what you're doing here."

"Of course!" Kelsey said. "This guy was listening to our conversation. All we have to do now is make him tell us who he was planning on selling us out to."

CHAPTER SIX

Do You Really Want to Hurt Me?

T he first thing that Anton did was use *Delver's Discernment*.

Zaphar Alpashan, Level 15, Thief/Burglar

So he is a thief then, Anton thought. It made him feel a little better about hitting him. The man out-leveled him, but not by much, and both those classes were common. Anton probably had the edge on Zaphar in most abilities, except for Agility and Dexterity.

With that in mind, Anton grabbed the thief and hauled him up before the man could recover his wind. Zaphar tried to resist, but the difference between their strengths was just too great.

"This way!" Kelsey called, leading them into another narrow alleyway. She must have been spending some of her time while shopping scoping out the various small streets and alleys that made this place a warren. Anton supposed the knowledge was proving useful, but he'd prefer it if he never had to go down another one of these dirty and cramped streets again.

"This should do," Kelsey said. "Now, do you want to tell us who you were going to sell us out to? Or was the plan more of a general auction?"

"I wasn't!" Zaphar said desperately. "You've got the wrong guy!"

Kelsey rolled her eyes. "Right. We'll see if you change your tune once the spiders have had a little nibble."

"Wait, what—" Zaphar protested, but Anton stepped in, talking over him.

"No spiders, Kelsey."

She sighed in exasperation. "They'll only eat a *little* bit of him, Anton, he'll be fine."

"You can't torture some guy just because you think he was listening to us!"

"It's not torture, it's animal husbandry! Spiders need to eat too, you know."

"I know they're undead spiders, Kelsey, you're not fooling anybody."

Zaphar watched them both during this exchange, getting more and more nervous. Finally, he yelled out. "I swear! I wasn't going to sell you out! I was just trying to get some work without giving Rashaq a cut!"

"Is that so?" Kelsey asked. "Then why were you following us?"

"I needed for you to go someplace quiet before I made contact!" Pinned against the wall with barely any exertion on Anton's part, Zaphar screwed up his face in fear. "Yeah, the best place for that would have been whatever inn you were staying at. But you just kept wandering around the market, where anyone could get word back to Rashaq."

"Huh, that is a pretty good explanation," Kelsey admitted.

"I think you owe this guy an apology," Anton pressed. "We didn't need to hurt or threaten him after all."

"What? No way!" Kelsey blew a raspberry at the pair of them. "You've got to expect these sorts of misunderstandings when you're part of the criminal underworld."

"Uh, yeah, it's fine," Zaphar hastily put in. "No permanent injuries, just a few . . ." He winced. "Love taps. You're pretty strong, huh?"

"Sorry for hitting you," Anton said. "I was kind of following her lead."

"Yeah, yeah, I know how it is. How about letting me down now?"

"Not so fast," Kelsey said. "If you've got a pitch to make, you'd better make it now."

"Uh, no offense, lady." Zaphar looked at Kelsey warily. "I like money as much as the next guy, but I'm a lot less eager to work for you after all this. There's plenty of jobs out there that don't involve getting eaten by spiders."

"That's perfectly understandable," Kelsey agreed, stepping closer to Zaphar. He was already pressed against the wall, but Anton thought that the man was trying hard to go farther back. "But the thing is, you don't have any proof for that little story you spun, so if you *don't* have a pitch, well . . ."

"Ah . . . sure, sure, I see how it is." Zaphar swallowed nervously. "You know, I'm a lot more persuasive when I'm *not* stuck against an alley wall."

"I'll keep that in mind," Kelsey said.

"Sure, sure . . . so, yeah, Rashaq's got contacts in the administration, that's for sure. He can find a guy for you to bribe to get what you want. But those guys are *rich*. It's gonna take *gold* to get them to risk their asses. A *thief* will get you those documents for silver."

"*A thief?*"

"Yeah, before I would have been saying that I was the only one who could, but that would have been a lie. There's a few guys I know that could do a good job. I could put you in touch . . ."

"I don't think so," Kelsey said. "I don't want people knowing my business unless it's absolutely necessary."

"Course, of course. Don't worry about me, lady, I can keep my mouth shut!"

"One way or the other," Kelsey agreed.

"Why are you cheaper than the official?" Anton asked. "Seems to me that you're risking more."

"Thanks for noticing," Zaphar said. "Reason is, I'm a lot poorer than whatever Lala that Rashaq gets for you. I need silver to live, while he wants some gold so he can visit his perfumed courtesan a couple extra times."

"Ah, the injustice of poverty," Kelsey said. "Good news, though, Zaphar, you've got the job."

Zaphar somehow managed to slump against the wall when his name was mentioned. "You've got an Identify trait," he said.

"That I do," Kelsey said. "Is it a coincidence that you're sitting at the top of Tier Two, or is there some reason for it?"

"I'm holding on going up," Zaphar admitted. "Wanna see if I can qualify for a better Tier Three."

"Oh? Do you have something in mind?" Kelsey asked.

Zaphar grimaced. "That's not the sort of thing that people talk about," he said.

"That's a shame. I do happen to know of one that you might qualify for," Kelsey said. "Occult Larcenist."

"Sounds fancy," Zaphar said. "What's it do?"

"That's Risor's class," Anton said.

"Yeah, that's how I know about it," Kelsey said with a shrug. "I haven't read all those books on it like you have."

"How do you qualify?" Zaphar asked, trying not to look too eager.

Anton thought back to the description that he'd read. "You have to be a burglar and you have to have stolen something magical, from a wizard."

"Oh," Zaphar said. "That doesn't seem likely."

"Hmm . . ." Kelsey said. "Maybe, maybe not. We should talk more, maybe we can help each other out."

"There are others," Anton told him. "Thief paths weren't my main interest, but I should be able to remember some."

Kelsey rolled her eyes. "Ah, fallible memory. I don't miss it. If we really need to, I can get Suliel to check the book out and read it to us."

Anton blinked. Kelsey had been passing communications between the group and Suliel for the whole trip, but using her bond to read a book from all the way across the ocean seemed like cheating. However, Kelsey had moved on before he could say anything.

"So, Zaphar. You in? You going to help us out on this little heist?"

"Do I have a choice?" Zaphar asked.

"Yes," Anton said. He released the man and let him drop to the ground.

"Anton!" Kelsey protested.

"At some point, we're going to have to trust him," Anton said. "If we force him into it, then the first chance he gets, he really will turn us in."

"We have *options* in that regard, remember?"

"For someone who complains that it was used on you, you're awfully eager to use that *option*," Anton told her.

"Does this option involve spiders?" Zaphar asked nervously.

"No, it's . . . better not talked about here." Anton held out his hand. "So, seriously, are you going to help us? Kelsey does pay well, for all her faults—"

"I have no faults!"

"—so we can sort out remuneration back at the inn. Or you can disappear and forget you ever heard of us. It's not like we know this city well enough to find you."

"Actually," Kelsey put in, "I bet Rashaq could find him if we paid enough. We have his name after all."

Zaphar winced. "Yeah, yeah, that's true enough. I can hide, but I can't look for work while hiding. Guess the only thing is to prove what I said." He took Anton's proffered hand. "You just hired the best second-story man in Rused, Anton Nos."

"You have an Identify trait as well?" Anton asked.

"Nah, nah, I overheard you at the club," Zaphar said. "*Keen-Eared Lookout.* Saved my life a couple of times."

"I'm sure," Kelsey said. "Aris? How are we doing? Anyone paying attention to us?"

"I don't think so?" Aris said. She had been paying attention to the mouth of the alleyway they had ducked down. "There were a few people who noticed when we grabbed him, but they all left in a hurry."

"Good enough. Do you think you can take Zaphar here back to the inn? I've got one more errand to run. I'd send Anton with you, but . . ." She trailed off without finishing.

"Of course. I can do that. I think I've managed to keep my bearings, and Zaphar probably knows where our place is."

"Sure," Zaphar boasted. "Just name an inn and I can tell you how to get there, and whether your silver is safe."

"Great! We'll come running if we hear any shots, and if this guy runs . . . shoot him in the back."

"I'm not going to do that," Aris said.

"You can't do that, you've got no bow," Zaphar pointed out. "What level are you, anyway? You're way too strong for someone so young."

"Don't answer that," Kelsey said. "No point in revealing all our cards just yet."

Aris rolled her eyes. "I wasn't going to," she said. "I'll see you back at the inn."

"See you, then," Anton said, trying to keep the concern out of his voice. It was her first time in a city, the same as him, but he had to trust that she'd be all right.

Kelsey didn't waste any time looking back. She just strode off, clearly with a destination in mind.

"Where are we going?" Anton asked.

"The meeting place those street rats told us about," Kelsey said.

"Already? I thought we weren't going to need them again."

"Neither did I, but you never know how things are going to go. That's why I asked them where we could find them."

Kelsey *had* gotten directions to the Nest, but showing up there would probably lead to the kids scattering while someone made an ill-fated assault on the pair of them. The meeting place they'd arranged was a plaza, well populated with bustling cityfolk. Kelsey looked around when they arrived and spotted a likely target.

A hungry-looking kid was eyeing a street vendor selling some kind of meat on a stick. When they got closer, Kelsey tossed a copper coin so that it hit the ground behind the kid.

Whirling around, the child quickly snatched up the coin, even as he looked about for where it might have come from. His eyes quickly locked on to Kelsey, standing with another coin held out.

"I want to talk with Karim," she said. "Or Leila."

The kid nodded and held out his hand. Kelsey snorted.

"When you get back with him," she said. "I haven't got all day to play chase the beggar."

The kid grimaced but nodded and took off.

"I'm surprised you didn't offer him silver," Anton commented.

"We're in public view," Kelsey explained. "If I gave him silver, it'd be stolen from him before he got back to the Nest."

"Ah." Anton let the pause grow. They were standing against the wall of a building, out of the way. No one seemed to be paying attention to them. "Do you want to talk about the dungeon?"

"I want to save it," Kelsey admitted. "But I don't think I can. No matter what I do. If I was to raze this place to the ground, in six months, a year, they'd be back to *harvest* it."

"You can't move it?"

"Taking a core out of its dungeon is *what* kills it," Kelsey told him softly. "I can't put a living core in storage."

"How do you know?" Anton asked. As far as he knew, she'd never had another core to practice with.

"I asked Mel; she's had to deal with this a lot. And . . . she doesn't have any suggestions. Other than kill all the humans."

"You're . . . *not* going to do that, right?"

Kelsey snickered. "As if I could. Tier Three is pretty strong where we're from, Anton, but there are Tier Fours and Fives out there, maybe in this very city."

Anton felt a chill at the thought. "So we get strong," he said.

"I've stalled out, though," Kelsey said. "I made a mistake, back at the start, prioritizing safety over growth. I kept the rewards down because I didn't want to attract a lot of high-tier adventurers. But without a challenge, there's no growth."

"Couldn't you just increase the rewards?"

"I'm doing something different now, you might have noticed. I'll have to see how it plays out. Ah, here they are."

They were too small to be spotted in the crowd, so it seemed as though they appeared with a magic trick as the pair stepped out of the crowd. Kelsey tossed a copper coin to the boy who had fetched Karim and gave the boy himself a wicked grin.

"Good to see you again," she said.

Karim looked to be split between wary and hopeful. "There'd better be money in this, spider lady."

"Of course. Here, have a copper for showing up." She tossed the coin to him and he caught it out of the air, never taking his eyes off her.

"Now," she said, "there's two jobs I've got for you. First, I want to hire however many of you kids as it takes to watch a guy, day and night. How does twelve copper a day sound?"

"Sounds pretty good," he admitted. "He's going to be asleep a lot of the time, though."

"Then I want to know how loudly he snores," Kelsey told him. "He might be doing a lot of work at night, though, so keep an eye on him at all times."

"We can do that. Who's the guy?"

"Zaphar Alpashan. He's a burglar by trade."

"I've heard the name, not sure if I know his face."

"He's at my inn right now, so I'll get you an opportunity to see it. He's going to be working with us, so don't be surprised if you see him in our company. I need you to make sure he's not working for anybody else."

"Got it. What's the other thing?"

"I need a place where I can stash, say, thirty people without anyone noticing. An abandoned building like the Nest, or a warehouse I can rent with a landlord who won't ask questions."

"I can ask around," Karim said evasively.

"Take your time, and be discreet! I don't want everyone knowing where my new hideout is."

"Yeah . . . I can say we're looking to expand the Nest. What do you want a hideout for, anyway?"

"That's a question, kid." Kelsey tossed him another copper. "If you find a good place, I'll give you a silver."

"Sure thing, spider lady."

Kelsey smiled and clapped Anton on the shoulder. "Let's go back to the inn, show this guy what Zaphar looks like. I think my plan is starting to come together."

CHAPTER SEVEN

Escapade

A nton had some questions as they headed back to the inn. He didn't think Kelsey would want him talking in front of Karim about it, so he switched back to Tiatian.

"Thirty people is more than were taken, and didn't we figure that some of them would have been moved on by now?"

Kelsey looked at Karim, who had reacted to his speaking, but only to stare in confusion. If he was pretending to not understand, then he was doing a pretty good job. She shrugged.

"Yeah, but I figure we won't limit ourselves. It will be as easy to take whoever's locked up as it will be to find the ones we want and just take them."

Anton wasn't sure if that was true, but he didn't want to be the one to argue for leaving slaves locked up. Some impracticalities occurred to him, though.

"Our boat's not big enough for that many," he pointed out.

"Yeah, we'll have to get another boat," Kelsey agreed. "We were probably going to have to do that anyway. We don't really want to ferry around a bunch of teenagers while we look for the rest of the group."

"You just want to send them all back home then? Regardless of where they're from?"

"If they're from here, they can always stay," Kelsey replied. "If they're from the south, then we can take them along at least part of the way. If they're from the north, they can make their way home from there."

"You can't just dump them and expect them to find their way home," he objected.

"Suliel will look after them," she assured him. "Kirido needs workers, as much as it needs its children back. They can stay and work, or work enough to get passage home."

Anton nodded slowly. By this time, they were almost at the inn. Kelsey told Karim to hide and wait, and that Aris would come out with Zaphar after their meeting. She also arranged a time and place where she could give them their pay and get her reports.

Aris had, it turned out, made her way back without incident. Zaphar had joined the two courl prisoners in their room and was talking to them while they all waited for Kelsey to get back. The chatter sounded pretty friendly as they approached, but it stopped dead when Kelsey opened the door.

"Oh, don't stop on my account," Kelsey said brightly. "What were we talking about?"

Zaphar looked at her warily. "They—they were saying that deals with you come with a sting in them."

"True enough," Kelsey said. Anton came in behind her and shut the door. Walking over to Aris, who was sitting on one of the two chairs in the room, he smiled to see that she was all right. Smiling back, she jumped out of her chair and let him sit on it, taking her seat on his lap.

Kelsey took a seat on one of the beds, next to the courl whose bed it was. He made a face and switched to the other bed. Kelsey smirked at his snub.

"You'll make your deal with Anton," she told Zaphar. "He doesn't have the same impediment."

"How come we didn't get that option?" Kusec grumbled.

Kelsey raised an eyebrow. "This man, gentlemen, is a thief," she said, pointing at Zaphar. "He sneaks into people's homes, steals their most precious possessions and memories, and sells them to whoever will buy. Truly, he is a stain on humanity."

She paused, smirking, giving Zaphar a chance to look embarrassed. Kelsey wasn't done.

"You guys, though, I don't trust."

Kusec glowered at her but didn't respond. "You any closer to finding the girl?" he finally asked.

"Maybe! This guy's going to get us a look," Kelsey told him. "Let's move this into our room—we've got more chairs, and fewer surly courls."

Zaphar shrugged and followed them into Kelsey's room. The courls stayed behind.

"Why are they here?" Zaphar asked.

"To help us learn the language, and get us up to speed on how things work here," Kelsey explained. "They're almost surplus to requirements, but they can still be some muscle if we need it."

"Sure, all right, whatever," Zaphar said. "What do you need from me?"

"First off," Kelsey said, looking thoughtful, "We need a map of the compound, showing us how the buildings are laid out and what's where."

"I dunno about a map, but anyone can enter the compound," Zaphar said. "All you need is proof that you have business there. That guy you're gonna bribe can write a note saying he wants to see you, that'd do it. Or you could apply for a permit or something."

"They just let people in?" Anton asked. Zaphar looked at him nervously.

"Yeah, yeah. All the buildings *inside* are guarded. You need a pass or something for the building you want to get into. But just wandering around you can do, as long as you look like you know where you're going."

"All right, we'll check it out," Kelsey said. "Next, we'll need the interior layout of wherever they're keeping the slaves, and some idea of how many slaves there are."

Zaphar grimaced. "The one place where they're keeping valuable merchandise. Yeah, yeah, I can get that. Maybe one night to scope it out, and another to get inside. Wait, you mean the holding cells, or where the slaves that work there are kept?"

Kelsey grimaced. "The holding cells. Freeing every slave in the city is a little more than we're ready for."

"Sure, sure, I can get you that."

"Good. One more thing. Can you find out where this newly arrived Pasha is going to be staying?"

"That's easy," Zaphar said immediately. "Big shot like that, he'll be staying in the Wali's palace. But that place is bad news. They've got magic guarding it, as well as guards running all about the place."

"If you want a better class, you're going to need to pull off a flashy job," Kelsey told him. "What better job than stealing from the Palace?"

"Nah, nah, stealing from that place is suicide," Zaphar demurred. "You think getting me killed is doing me a favor? Hard, hard pass."

"We can come back to that later," Kelsey said. "Once you've got that building layout back to us, we're going to need to break in and steal those slaves."

"Sure, sure, but you know, I like to go for smaller stuff that's easier to carry. You got any idea of how to get them out? And how you're gonna keep them once you've got them?"

"A few," Kelsey said coolly. "But details will have to wait until we get more information."

"*That* part makes sense. The rest of it is crazy, but that part makes sense. So is that all you need?"

"For now. Why don't you talk to Anton about payment?"

Anton started as Zaphar looked at him expectantly. "Uh, name your price?" he asked. It wasn't as if Kelsey cared about expenses.

Zaphar blinked in surprise, but recovered quickly. "Two gold for the maps," he said, "and three gold if I get the details of the prisoners."

"I thought you said you worked for silver?" Anton asked.

"You said name your price," the thief said defensively. "Not like I want to work for you guys, so you need to sweeten the deal."

Anton wasn't sure if raising the price a hundredfold counted as sweetening, but he pressed on. "Why extra to count the prisoners? Won't you be taking the same risk going in to get the layout?"

"I'll have to go up to the cells and look inside," Zaphar said, shuddering. "Lots—Lots more risk."

"I guess that makes sense." Anton glanced at Kelsey, who didn't seem concerned. "All right then. Half now, half when the job's done?"

He was taken aback at Zaphar's sudden consternation.

"In the underworld, if you don't bargain, it makes them think that you plan to get out of paying by killing them when the job's finished," Kelsey said.

"Oh, what? We weren't going to—"

"That's *just* what a man planning murder would say!" Kelsey jumped in, laughing. "Don't worry, Zaphar, we're rich, so we don't care how much you charge."

"If you're that rich, why don't you just buy the slaves?" Zaphar asked.

"Well, you see, if you buy a slave off a slaver, he just goes and uses that money to get more slaves. And whatever it costs him, it's probably going to be less than you paid, so he ends up with more slaves than before. It just perpetuates the system."

"Stealing's better?"

"Yeah. You get the slaves and you keep your money. Free the slaves, and there's less of both in the system. The slaver has to spend more money getting more slaves, so it costs him. Cost him enough, and he drops out of the business."

"Sure, sure, I get it. You hate slavery then?"

"Don't most people?"

Zaphar shrugged. "Most poor people don't like it, sure. Rich folks, though, they never seem to mind too much."

"I guess we're just crazy rich folks then," Kelsey said, grinning.

"Yeah," Zaphar said, but he didn't seem happy to be in agreement. "Yeah."

"Is foreign coin fine?" Anton asked. "We've got plenty of gold, but it's not from here. Tiatian standard weight, even if it's not from the Empire's mint."

"Is that right?" Kelsey said. "I suppose I—er, I suppose it was copied from Empire coinage originally."

"A lot of dungeons do that," he told her. Whatever the coins were that were first lost in a dungeon, that's what they provide from then on. A place like this probably seeds a new dungeon with a set of coins."

"Standard or not, I don't want coins that mark me as connected to you lot. Can you change it first?"

"Sure," Kelsey said. "It will delay us paying you, though. Shall we say half after your recon, and the other half when you're done?"

"Sure, sure," Zaphar said. "Are we done then?"

"I think so. We're meeting Rashaq's guy tomorrow night, so make sure you get here before sunset. Aris can show you out."

Zaphar looked suspiciously at Aris, but she just smiled, so he shrugged and followed her. Anton had whispered to her earlier what she was expected to do, so she filled her role without asking any questions.

"I didn't see any sign of Karim," she said when she got back. "But I stayed with Zaphar until we stepped outside. He should have seen us."

"I guess we'll see tomorrow if he's good at his job or just slacking off," Kelsey commented.

"Are you really going to be fine changing your coins that quickly?" Anton asked.

"It's fine," Kelsey told him. "I got samples when we were out shopping, and I'm retooling the coin press now. I should have plenty by tomorrow."

"Samples of gold coins?"

Kelsey shrugged. "I swapped like for like with a friendly merchant. My—that is—*Tiatian* standard is a little heavier than theirs, so he came out ahead on the deal."

"If you're sure. How about sharing some details of this plan of yours?"

"It's still pretty shaky," Kelsey admitted. "Tomorrow, we need to find a boat with a . . . compliant captain. I doubt we'll be able to take them straight to the docks, so that hideout is a must. There are a few things we should go over in advance, though."

She pulled out a small metal box with a protrusion coming out of it.

"This," she said, "is a *timed detonator*. Uncharged, so it's safe. The unsafe version will destroy your hand if you're holding it when it goes off, or if it gets handled too roughly. So be very, very careful holding it."

She demonstrated its function. "You twist this, and the farther you twist it, the longer it takes before it goes off. You do not want to be near it when it goes off."

She handed it to Anton, who examined it in confusion. Now that he was holding it, he could hear a very faint ticking. The dial had markings and numbers that Kelsey told him represented minutes. Even as she explained that, there was a loud *clack* from the device, and the ticking stopped.

"There!" Kelsey said. "It's gone off, and you've lost your hand. And probably an eye, as close as you were to it. You lose, game over. Don't let that happen."

Anton shrugged and passed the strange device to Aris. She twisted the dial and listened to the ticking.

"Now this," Kelsey said, pulling another box out of the air, "is *teiantea*."

CHAPTER EIGHT

I'm Bad (Explicit)

Ugh, no more explaining!" Aris protested. "Can't we cover this some more tomorrow?"

"Sure," Kelsey said, clearing the table of the dangerous devices and materials she had been training them on. "Just remember, there *will* be a test on this."

Anton smiled. He'd always been the more studious one, and something about the things he had just learned seemed to call out to his class. Setting off explosives felt like something an Adventurer was meant to do.

"Let's talk about something lighter," he suggested.

"No, wait, there's something we *need* to talk about," Aris replied. "Kelsey, what did you think you were doing, poisoning that girl?"

"You threatened Zaphar with spiders as well," Anton recalled. "You can't do that!"

"Oh? Have I been *bad*?" Kelsey asked archly. "You'll have to punish me, then."

Anton narrowed his eyes. He knew what game Kelsey was playing; she called it "Good Cop, Bad Girl."

"If you've been acting out, just so we'd spank you . . ." he trailed off, trying to think of how to end the statement. They'd *not* punish her?

"It's not like that," Kelsey said quickly, dropping her affectation. "You guys, you live in a small community. Everyone depends on one another. Here, it's a dog-eat-dog world, and we're in the worst part of it. You've got to show these guys that you're someone to be afraid of."

"Dogs don't eat dogs," Aris protested, somewhat naively.

"Not in Kirido," Kelsey corrected her. "They don't get hungry enough. Here, it's so bad that everyone is a dog, scrambling to survive and desperate enough to do terrible things."

The pair looked at Kelsey doubtfully. She grinned back at them. "On the other hand, if it's got you all upset, I really could use a good spanking."

Anton and Aris looked at each other. He shrugged.

"Fine," Aris said. "But get the bathtub out, Anton needs to wash first."

Kelsey clapped her hands together excitedly and got to work. Aris had had a chance to use the bathhouse earlier, but Anton couldn't take Kelsey into the male baths. Not that she needed to bathe. Her skin didn't get greasy, her sweat was just clean water, and dirt was just another item that she could disappear into her Storage.

"How did you find the baths, anyway?" Kelsey asked as she filled up the large tub with hot water.

"It was a bit weird," Aris said. "I was a little worried that someone would think I was a slave, but most of the women using them were staff."

Kelsey stepped back from the steaming tub, waiting expectantly.

"Right," Aris said. "Clothes off, and get the suit out."

Kelsey grinned, disappearing her clothes in an instant. Then she handed a bundle of leather straps to Aris. Anton started undressing the slow way as he looked at the display in front of him.

Kelsey could have caused the "suit" to appear on her as easily as she disappeared her clothes, but putting it on was part of the ritual. Made of something that Kelsey called *synthetic*, it was less a garment and more a collection of straps attached to one another.

Putting it on was a complex task. Aris had done it before, but she still needed some guidance from Kelsey. Once it was done, Aris started tightening the straps that connected it all together. Kelsey's arms were pulled behind her back, and she was forced into a submissive kneeling position.

Leaving her behind on the floor, Aris walked over to Anton, sitting in his bath. *This* part Aris enjoyed. She wasn't much into this game, as either a submissive or a dominator. She had said that she could sort of see the attraction but didn't really feel it. That was about where Anton stood, though he did feel a certain frisson when taking the dominant role.

Suliel was heavily into it, at least when it came to what Kelsey called "beginner-level" play. The first time she'd seen the suit, she'd made a high-pitched keening noise, until Kelsey promised to make her one.

What Aris enjoyed was showing off her body to her man, and she was doing it now. Anton felt himself start to grow at the sight, as she slowly stripped out of her clothes and approached him.

"This is what good girls get to do," she said over her shoulder. Then she knelt down and kissed him.

They took their time. They hadn't had much opportunity for intimacy on the boat, and now they could make up for it. When they finally broke the kiss, Aris started washing the salt of Anton's skin, while he caressed her bountiful breasts. She didn't get in the bath, but she got plenty of water on her. It ran down her skin from his hands, dripping on the waxed wooden floor.

This was about getting clean, not sex, but Aris made sure to tease his member, just a little, as she ran her hands all over his body. There were giggles, groans, and more kisses. Throughout it all, Kelsey watched, bound and quietly whimpering.

When he was done, Anton stood up and stepped over to her, towelling himself off. Kelsey's eyes stayed fixed on his erection. Her intent expression was just as much of a turn-on as Aris's warm, still wet body, pressed into his side.

"You want this?" he asked.

She nodded eagerly. "Yes, please, master," she said. Even knowing that she was acting, Anton was shocked by the change in her demeanor.

He held it close to her face, close enough for her to smell it. He expected her to make a lunge for it, but instead, she opened her mouth and started panting. Feeling her warm breath on the tip of his member, he was tempted to let her start sucking it. But . . .

"No," he told her. "You're being punished."

"No! Please, master!" she wailed, but he ignored her. He pushed Aris over towards the bed, and she lay back, her legs spread.

"You've been a good girl, haven't you?" he asked.

"Oh, yes, reward me, please." Aris managed to say the lines without giggling, but she wasn't much of an actor. It didn't matter, though. Anton was eager to end his period of enforced abstinence, and his wife was ready and willing to sate him.

The cries she made as he plunged into her weren't faked, but they were enhanced a little for Kelsey's benefit. She was normally a little quieter. Anton found that her gasps of enjoyment were spurring him on to greater efforts.

Throughout it all, as the fervor of their lovemaking increased, Kelsey was left on the floor. "I'm sorry I was bad, master!" she called out. "Please punish me!"

Anton hadn't intended to leave her there the whole time, but he found himself quite unable to tear himself away from Aris until he finished. That round, anyway.

Lifting himself off her flushed and sweating body, he stepped behind Kelsey's still kneeling form. "This *is* your punishment," he told her. "No sex for you."

"Please, master, punish me properly!" Kelsey begged.

"Oh?" he asked. He bent and picked her up. The "suit" had a number of attached loops in strategic locations that made for convenient handles. Despite her strength, Kelsey didn't weigh more than a small woman, and he easily hefted her and carried her over the bed.

"What's the safeword," he asked.

"It's *pickle*," she told him. He couldn't see, but he knew she was rolling her eyes. She hadn't even told them about safewords until Suliel wanted a turn, and had always been dismissive about them being needed for her.

"Don't be like that," he told her. "Dying would be considerably more than an inconvenience if it left you halfway around the world from me."

He placed her on the bed, face down over Aris. He released her arms so she could support herself, but her legs were still kept bent. Her ass was raised into the air, her sex exposed. Anton ran his finger along it. As he expected, it was dripping wet.

Kelsey moaned at his touch, and Anton felt himself stir. Not for the first time, he admired the contrast of Aris's warm brown skin against Kelsey's cool paleness.

"Do you deserve to be punished, Kelsey?" he asked.

"Yes! I've been bad!" Kelsey replied.

"All right then," Anton said and brought his palm down on her ass as hard as he could. The crack of his hand against her skin was like a gunshot. Kelsey yowled, and he did it again.

"Harder!" she screamed. But Anton was hard again, so he shoved himself inside her instead.

It took a lot to hurt Kelsey. The gap between their strengths had closed, but she was still stronger than him. Tougher, too, but his *Stone Skin* made the difference. Without it, his slap would hurt him more than it hurt her.

Even so, he had to go all out before she felt it. As long as he wasn't using tools. Kelsey had suggested whips, studded paddles, and even knives, but he had to draw a line. It wasn't that Kelsey didn't know her limits. She *had* no limits. Even death was just another sensation that she was eager to try.

Since he was unwilling to provide her with that sensation, she had to settle for sex as rough as he was willing to grant. He slammed himself into her, alternating thrusts with slaps to her pale butt. He pulled on her hair, and Aris bit on her nipples. She screamed in release and begged for more.

"Yes! Yes! I'm—wait!" she yelled.

Anton had pulled out of her at the critical moment and plunged into Aris instead. She had recovered from the first round and had been getting thoroughly turned on by the intense lovemaking occurring above her.

Kelsey gasped in outrage but found herself being pulled down for a kiss by Aris. Anton slapped Kelsey's ass again but kept plunging into Aris's moist heat. Then he switched again, driving Kelsey into a frenzy.

Anton lost track of how long he'd been going for. He was pushing his enhanced stamina to the limit, he thought, as Kelsey finally came, screaming with delight. He switched back to Aris as Kelsey shuddered, squeezed between their thrusting bodies.

He finally exploded in Aris, setting her off again. With the release of his orgasm, he came back to himself, atop two naked bodies. Kelsey disappeared her bonds and rolled to the side. Anton burrowed in between them and relaxed in the afterglow.

Aris was the first one to drop off to sleep, exhausted. Anton was tired and sated, but he stayed awake for a little longer. Kelsey, of course, wouldn't be sleeping.

"Satisfied?" he asked her.

"It was pretty good," she said smugly. "You really went for it, this time."

"It seemed . . . a little different," he told her. "Like you weren't just after sensation."

"You could tell? How embarrassing," Kelsey said. She tried to look away, but he held on to her gaze.

"What is it?" he pressed.

"I suppose . . . I actually felt a little guilty this time."

"Over the spiders? That's great!"

"Not over the stupid spiders," Kelsey retorted indignantly. "Those thieves deserved everything they got. It was for giving up . . . on the dungeon."

"Ah. Did it help?"

"Well, it was a lot of fun," Kelsey hedged. "But . . . no. Even pain doesn't really . . . touch me when it comes from this body. It helped me forget, but not for very long."

"I'm sorry."

"Don't be. It's my fault I can't come up with a solution. It's just that . . . I've never had to give up before."

"Never?"

"I've lived a long life, down in that hole. I've had setbacks and failures, and I've gone down any number of dead ends that I had to give up on. But I always found a way to get what I needed."

"Until now."

"Yeah." Kelsey shivered in his arms. "That dungeon has never really lived, and now it's going to die."

"Don't give up, then." Anton wasn't sure why those words came out.

"As simple as that?"

"It seems a little silly telling you this," Anton said, "but that's part of the advice they give at the guild. If you give up, the Dungeon *will* kill you. Your only chance is to keep going, even if you don't see a way forward."

"You mean me." Kelsey snickered. "*I* will kill you, if you give up."

"I said it sounded silly," Anton said.

"No, it's good advice . . . for delvers. Maybe for me as well. That might be . . . what I needed to hear."

She wiggled out from under him.

"Get some sleep, Anton. I'll keep watch."

CHAPTER NINE

Watching the Wheels

MEL

Things were getting exciting again. Kelsey was starting up production lines that hadn't seen use for *years*. Not the stupid new ones that wove cloth or filled bottles. The fun ones. The *deadly* ones. Kelsey had spent a lot of time developing explosives, only to find that they were *too* effective. Once set in place, the danger that they represented settled.

Mel had tried to explain it to Kelsey, but Kelsey didn't understand *meaning* as Mel did. Danger was like a liquid. It pooled around the explosives, not in any physical way, but in an ever-accumulating reservoir of meaning. That was what people with a sense for danger detected.

Danger that came at someone's whim sent only the slightest scent ahead of it. Danger that wasn't complete was diluted by the possibility of survival.

Kelsey had rigged a tunnel to explode, the trigger being an electrical signal that she could send from outside of the magical interference that humans put out. The trap waited patiently for the delvers to find it. Its intent gathered and intensified the entire while.

The delvers refused to go anywhere near it. They felt it, as soon as they approached a certain point. Certain death, if they took another step. They looked for magic or mechanisms but found none. The wires and the charges were locked behind solid rock. And for all its wonderful effects, electricity wasn't magic.

So the delvers backed off. On the plus side, it gave Kelsey a chance to develop areas without fear of delver interference. The minus was that if Kelsey left the tunnel up too long, it would attract delvers of a high enough level to *survive* a tunnel collapse.

Eventually, Kelsey found the balance of risk and reward that kept the delvers coming but didn't attract the higher-level ones. Explosives weren't a part of that. Some of the lower levels, which humans didn't get to, were mined, but those charges had never gone off.

It was a shame. Mel had enjoyed watching the dynamite and the 2,4,6-Trinitrotoluene go off. She'd asked Kelsey why one of the names had numbers in it, but Kelsey had just said it was called something else.

Now the production lines were firing up again, but that was not what Mel wanted to talk about.

"Kelsey!" she said, pointing an accusatory finger. "You had sex again!"

Kelsey's mental avatar was currently sitting at the table she'd made near the secondary entrance. Two skeletons were standing next to her as some sort of honor guard. Now she looked at Mel and raised an eyebrow. "Uh, yeah? I know? I was there?"

"I thought you stopped!" Mel said. "You stopped for . . . a while." Time was a bit tricky for Mel, but Kelsey had definitely stopped for longer than a day.

"Yeah, we couldn't do it on the boat because those two kids were self-conscious about the Kabimen hearing. Or seeing. Honestly, it's not like those guys were interested. They don't even *do* internal fertilization."

"I thought you got tired of doing it," Mel said.

"Ha! As if I could get tired of sex!" Kelsey said, laughing. "I mean, you're not tired of it, are you? At least not once you get horny."

"I—" Mel started, and then stopped. She shouldn't be blushing. That was a physiological response, involving blood vessels that she *didn't have*. But embarrassment was an emotion that she could convey; that had *meaning*. So whether she was blushing or not, Kelsey could tell that she was embarrassed and Mel could tell that Kelsey knew. The feeling was excruciating.

"How did it go this time?" Kelsey asked innocently. "Did you try the self-care I taught you about?"

Mel stared, her horrified look caught by Kelsey's blandly interested one. Mel knew that Kelsey knew everything that went on inside her. They *pretended* that Kelsey only saw Mel when Kelsey's avatar was there.

Kelsey knew what Mel had been doing. She knew everything that Mel had tried and what effect it had had. She knew about every moan, every cry.

Kelsey was better at this game than Mel was.

"Yes," Mel finally managed. "It went . . . fine."

"Great!" Kelsey said with a friendly grin. "Just let me know if you want to keep doing it that way, or if you want some help."

Mel thought that the pause before she could respond went on for long enough that a human would have become worried. It *probably* didn't last the three million years that it felt like. Kelsey didn't let it worry her; she just waited patiently for Mel to respond. Dungeons were made to be patient like that.

"I will," Mel finally said.

"Great!" Kelsey said again. "Now, I don't know if you want to take off. I'm meeting Suliel down here, and I know you've been avoiding her."

"Meeting? Can she see this you, now?" Mel had, in fact, been avoiding Suliel. She had only seen her once before the human had taken a class that gave her *sovereignty* over Kelsey. That was . . . not right. Even if it was due to a class that the gods had made.

"Nah," Kelsey said. She pointed at the standing skeletons. "But she can see these guys. We're testing her new trait, *Bind Undead*."

"She's stealing your creatures now?" Mel gasped.

"Some of my Tier One skeletons, at least," Kelsey said. "Not like they're good for much. Things should get more interesting when she hits Tier Three."

"I suppose I should watch," Mel groused. "It's not like she's going anywhere."

"That's very mature of you," Kelsey said. "She's just about to arrive."

Kelsey looked over as the door started to open. She would, of course, have been aware of Suliel's approach through the previous two rooms.

Suliel entered the room, carefully and silently. The two skeletons noticed her as soon as she entered, rotating their skulls to face her. They didn't move to attack, though, no matter how much Mel willed them to.

The young noble was no doubt talking with Kelsey over the bond. That Kelsey now had a way of communicating that didn't include Mel was just one more reason for Mel to dislike the current status quo.

Suliel looked at the skeletons. They straightened to attention, not at the same time, but one after the other. Then Suliel looked right at Mel.

"What the!" Kelsey exclaimed. "She can see you!"

"What? What! *What!*" Mel yelled in fright. She started flitting around. As an immortal, immaterial creature, she had no instincts to flee, but the situation called for her to do *something*. Probably keep an eye on the dangerous invader from an unseen angle, but try as she might, she was unable to evade Suliel's gaze.

"All right, all right, calm down everyone. Suliel, it might be less confusing if you spoke aloud. That way we can stay on the same page. I presume you can hear Mel as well as see her."

"She's a witch!" Mel yelled.

"I heard *that*," Suliel said flatly.

"Great. Mel, stop flitting around before you work out how to injure yourself. You can hide behind me if it makes you feel safer."

Mel tried it, zipping behind Kelsey and grabbing on to her shirt. Then Kelsey spoke again, words of foul betrayal.

"Suliel, you still can't see me, can you?"

Mel froze in fright as Suliel answered. She was still exposed!

"No, I can see . . . it . . . just hanging from something? What *is* it?"

"This is Mel, my dungeon fairy. Mel, you can't just hide under the table."

"I'm not supposed to be seen by humans!" Mel called out. Kelsey didn't seem to understand the situation, which was about normal for her. "This is very bad!" she explained.

"Let's give her a bit of time to get used to the idea, shall we?" Kelsey said, taking a seat and gesturing for Suliel to do the same. "It might help if you didn't look directly at her."

"I still want to know what she is," Suliel said. "She keeps changing when I look at her closely."

"Don't do that!" Mel yelled from under the table. "No looking!"

"She doesn't have a material form," Kelsey explained. "You're seeing what I imagine her looking like, and I don't generally bother too much about consistency. So she changes."

"So a tiny, winged person with green skin is what you imagine a fairy looks like," Suliel said slowly.

"I guess? This must be a side effect of our link. I wonder if you can change what she looks like . . . can you imagine her with blue skin?"

"No imagining! No testing! No looking!"

"Maybe we should focus on what I actually came down here for," Suliel suggested.

"Oh, yeah, I almost forgot about that. You bonded them on sight, didn't you?"

"You can't tell?"

"I don't have my avatar here, so my link with them was broken when you entered the room. That they didn't attack you is a bit of an indication, but I think you might be seen as a part of me now, at least to my monsters."

The two skeletons suddenly saluted and then marched to behind Suliel's chair. They saluted again and stood at attention.

"You don't need line of sight?" Kelsey asked.

"No," Suliel answered thoughtfully. "I can feel a bond between us."

"Once you're out of the dungeon, that bond will probably need to feed them mana for maintenance," Kelsey told her. "It shouldn't be much for a couple of Tier Ones, but it will add up. We'll want to see if you can feed them from monster cores."

Suliel nodded. "The real problem is that they're only Tier Ones. They might startle the nobles at court, but they won't be a real threat."

"We'll get some more levels then! There's some stuff we can do. I'm training a squad right now. It won't be much, but they'll fight better than the average skeleton. Plus, you can arm and armor them with Tier Two equipment, or even Tier Three if you've got it."

"That would make them more dangerous," Suliel agreed. The skeletons stepped forward and put their rusted and chipped swords on the table. "I won't be needing these then."

"I'll take care of them," Kelsey promised. "You want to head up and start testing things out?"

"Yes, but what about . . ." Suliel pointed at the table, and the fairy hiding underneath it.

"You know what, let me talk to her while we work and you can meet her properly another time."

Suliel agreed and left, taking the two skeletons with her. Kelsey's avatar didn't follow her, but Mel imagined she was still conversing via the link. Her avatar stayed in the room with her, absorbing the swords on the table and giving her a disparaging look.

"Honestly, Mel, what was all that?"

"Humans aren't supposed to see me," she repeated sullenly. With no human to hide from, she flew out from under the table. "That's the *rule*, and more than that, it's how it's been for . . . a long time. A thousand years? A million?"

"Well, the rule has changed," Kelsey said. "Start getting used to it."

"It *hasn't* changed, you just cheated with that link of yours!"

"Did I?" Kelsey asked. "You're always saying, the gods get to do whatever they want . . . wasn't it a god that did this?"

"Maybe it was a bad god," Mel said. "Trying to get you in trouble with Riadi."

Kelsey's smile got a little colder. "If Riadi has a complaint, they can lodge it with my complaints department."

"I don't know what that is, and I don't think you have one," Mel said suspiciously.

"We'll find that out together, won't we? Anyway, Mel, I think you're missing the bigger picture here."

"What's that?"

"If Suliel can see you, she might be able to touch you," Kelsey said. "And if she can touch you . . ."

"What?" Mel asked. "You only touch me when you want to—" She cut herself off and stared at Kelsey in horror.

"You're getting it," Kelsey said happily. "Soon you'll be able to have your first threesome!"

CHAPTER TEN

If I Had a Boat

Y ou guys are going to find us a boat."

The two courls looked at each other, and then back at Kelsey.

"You already have a boat," Kusec said warily.

"We need a bigger boat, one that can carry more people," Kelsey explained. "One of those raiding ships would do nicely."

The courls' ears both flattened. "You can't steal from the Empire," Kusec growled. "Stealing slaves from private owners is a crime, but stealing a ship—"

"Relax," Kelsey said. "That's just to give you an idea of the size. We won't be taking your Empire's precious military hardware."

Her expression hardened. "Unless you can't find us a ship to buy, anyway. Well, rent, I guess. We need a crew to sail it, and that tends to go better if the captain owns the ship."

Kusec narrowed his eyes. "Where would you get a crew for a raiding ship?"

Kelsey shrugged. "I don't know," she said impatiently. "Which is just one more reason to make stealing from your Empire plan C, at best. So go out and find me a boat."

"We'll be seen if we go out asking questions," Kusec objected. "We're still deserters, remember?"

Kelsey waved her hands dismissively. "Just keep the cloaks up and avoid the military's dock. You'll be fine."

"What are you going to be doing?" the other courl, Erryan, asked.

"None of your business," Kelsey said flatly. She gave each of them a handful of copper coins. "For food and drink. Come back at sunset, or when you've found a boat. Get going."

The two courls tried to protest some more, but their winces of pain made it clear that Kelsey's last words had been an order. They took their leave, muttering to themselves.

"What are we doing?" Aris said when they were gone. "We're still waiting to hear back from Karim, and we won't be meeting Malik or that official until after dark."

"I've been thinking," Kelsey said. "And I think it's time we visited the dungeon."

"What do you mean, we can't?"

The courl guardsman showed Kelsey his teeth. Anton wasn't sure if that was supposed to be a friendly smile. It didn't *look* friendly.

"You're not locals," the guard said. "You're not slaves from any of the farms, you're not farm owners or workers. You're foreigners."

"Well sure, but you let us into your city without any fuss."

The guard shook his head. "Foreigners are allowed into Rused, to trade. There's only two reasons for foreigners to get out onto the rest of the island. One is to try out the dungeon, which isn't allowed. And the other, well, some fools like to try their luck out there as bandits, preying on the farmers and such. Needless to say, that isn't allowed either."

"Wow, that's so racist," Kelsey said, shaking her head. "We just wanted to take a walk through the picturesque countryside."

"Too bad."

Kelsey frowned. "I don't suppose we can alter your attitude with a little silver, can we? We'd be back by sundown."

"Maybe if you *weren't* coming back," the guard said. "We get off shift in two hours, so it'll be a different bunch on the gate when you come back."

"So? I've got enough silver for them as well."

"Or," the guard said, "they can take your silver, arrest you, and report *us* for letting you out in the first place. Then they'd get *our* silver as a reward."

"How mercenary." Kelsey made a face. "Are all of the guards like that?"

"Enough that I don't want to take a chance on who comes after me. You'll need to take your walk inside the city."

"So what do we do now?" Aris asked.

"I guess . . ." Kelsey started to answer, before losing herself in thought. "I guess we tour the inside of the walls, see if there are any blind spots."

"To climb over?" Anton asked. "I don't think there will be anything we can use in daylight."

"Maybe not," Kelsey agreed. "We might have to head out after dark. I don't like the delay, though."

"We could probably get some kind of a pass to let us out?" Anton suggested. "At the administrative compound."

"Bad idea," Kelsey said. "We don't want anyone knowing we were out there. If we bribe some guards to let us out, we can count on them to keep it quiet, but issuing a pass gets us all sorts of attention that we don't want."

They started walking along the inside of the wall. This wouldn't have been possible in Kirido. There, buildings had been built right up against it, saving on the construction costs of one wall. Here, there seemed to be a rule against that. There was a road that ran all around the city, and no buildings, except for the gatehouses, approached too closely.

"Nice discipline," Kelsey said, reluctantly approving. "Makes it hard for us, though."

"We can probably get over the wall without getting stopped," Anton said. "I saw a few places that are pretty far from a guard post. But . . . not so far that they won't notice us. Maybe if there's no moon. The thing is, a lot of guards will have *Nightvision*."

"Getting spotted by the guards isn't exactly conducive towards a leisurely midnight stroll to the dungeon," Kelsey agreed. "We need to *coordinate* our bribery."

"With who?" Aris asked.

"With ourselves. We need to be able to reassure the guard that lets us *out* that the guards who will let us *in* are equally corrupt. That means knowing the guard schedules, and knowing the guards."

"But we don't know any of that," Anton objected.

"I know," Kelsey sighed. "So, *again*, we're going to have to consult with an expert."

The two courls were waiting for them when they got back.

"That was quick," Kelsey said.

"Not that many big ships in the harbor," Kusec said. "And most reputable captains took one look at us and shooed us off."

"These cloaks make us look shifty," Erryan put in.

"Only because you've got something to hide," Kelsey said. "But you *did* find a *dis*reputable captain?"

"We found one," Kusec agreed. "Didn't *speak* to him, but we asked around. Everyone thinks he's crazy, no one will give him cargo. But he's rich, and he owns the ship, so he just sits in port waiting for someone crazy enough to hire him."

"If he's rich, can't he just buy his own cargo and sell it?" Kelsey asked.

"Don't you need to have a merchant class to make that work?" Anton asked. "He's probably got a ship-sailing class."

"Anyone can buy and sell, Anton," Kelsey said. "There's a trick to buying low and selling high, but it's a skill, not a trait."

"Reckon he's short on crew, for a ship that size," Kusec said, answering his mistress's earlier question. "The merchants hate him as well, so they might not be willing to sell him bulk cargo."

"Wow. Crazy, lacking a crew, and the merchants all hate him for some reason. You really found a prime candidate here."

Kusec shrugged. "You want someone who won't ask questions carrying a bunch of escaped slaves, you don't have a lot of options."

"I suppose not. You know where we can find him?"

They all looked down at the boat tied up on the docks. It was much smaller than what they had been promised.

"This is the tender that takes supplies out," Kusec said to Kelsey's raised eyebrow. "Anything else that approaches is likely to have shit thrown at it."

"Charming," Kelsey said. She looked at the crew of two courls. "And they'll take us to the ship?"

Kusec shrugged. "They'll need paying."

Sailing out into the harbor, the crew were soon able to point out their destination. It was a big ship. Anton estimated that it was about twenty-five yards long and held three or four decks. The three masts rose up from the deck like withered trees, devoid of sails. There wasn't any movement to be seen from it as they approached, but Anton felt they were being watched.

It was just Kelsey, Anton, and Aris on this trip; the courls had been left to go back to the inn. The tender was small enough that it was cramped with just the five of them. The sail took up a lot of room.

"Ahoy the ship!" the male crewmember called out. There was no reply.

"He's in a mood again," the female crewmember said. "Do you want to try again later?" She had been introduced as Setana and had light brown fur, with a dappled pattern that made it look like sand.

"Nah," Kelsey said. "Let's see him at his worst. Can you get on board?"

"*We* can," the Setana said. "We left a rope." She pointed to the stern, where a thick rope dangled in the water.

"That's fine," Kelsey decided. "Anton can climb that and pull the rest of us up."

The two crewmembers looked at each other. "Captain won't like that," the male said. He was called Rashid, and his fur was a mix of grey and greyish-blue. He was distinguished from any other courl Anton had met by the long strings of beads he had wrapped around his neck and arms.

"That's fine," Kelsey said. "Since I'm paying you for this trip, at least while we're on this boat, I'm the captain."

There was a pause, as the two looked warily at her. Sensing the tension, Anton thought to size them up.

I really should have done this earlier, he thought to himself.

Setana Sandwhisper, Navigator, Overall Level 21, Deckhand/Sailor/
Navigator
Rashid Stormcaller, Weatherwitch, Overall Level 18, Deckhand/Sailor/
Weatherwitch

Anton wasn't familiar with the classes, but they didn't sound like combat-oriented paths. The moment passed, though, and the two sailors relaxed.

"Fair enough, but don't blame me if you get a bucket of shit thrown at you," Rashid said.

"Bring us alongside, then," Kelsey said grandly. She pulled out a bundle of rope from under her seat and handed it to Anton.

Spider Climb made short work of the walls of the ship. It was the first time Anton had been able to test his new trait by climbing more than a few yards off the ground. Clambering onto the main deck, he looked around warily but didn't see any sign of a captain. He lowered the rope.

Aris was stronger than she used to be, but she wasn't used to climbing a rope. It was quicker for him to pull her up. He was fairly sure Kelsey was perfectly capable of pulling herself up, but she seemed to want him to do it, so he obliged. The crew were just as good climbers as he was. They tied the tender up to the ship and swarmed up the dangling rope, but they offered him no help getting the others up.

"Permission to come on board?" Kelsey asked as she clambered over the railing.

"Yeah, sure, whatever, welcome aboard," Setana said unenthusiastically.

"Great! So where's this captain, then?" Kelsey asked.

Setana shrugged. "This way," she said and led them under the raised half-deck.

"Captain! Got some customers for you!" she called, banging on the first door they came to. She paused to listen and then banged on the door again. There was the sound of a muffled voice.

Just as she was about to bang again, the door was flung open, and the courl behind it was revealed. Resolving to get better at doing this, Anton immediately used *Delver's Discernment.*

Farid al-Nazari, Ship's Captain, Overall Level 26, Midshipman/Bosun/
Ship's Captain

"Customers! Clients, you mean! Honored clients! You never said we had clients on board!"

The courl that came out of the cabin might have been dignified, or even imposing at one point. His brilliant green eyes and jet-black fur made for a striking image. But the way he was slumped against the doorframe, the way his richly colored silk tunic was now . . . richly discolored, painted a different picture.

As green as his eyes were, they looked dull when they looked around him blearily. Slowly and not at all surely, they focused on Anton. It took a moment, but a frown started to form on the captain's face.

"Bah! Who let monkeys on board the ship?"

"Oh great," Kelsey said. "He's crazy, racist, *and* he's drunk."

CHAPTER ELEVEN

Big Ship

I'm not drunk! You're drunk, you albino monkey!" Forcing himself upright with sheer outrage, the captain's sway gave away his lie, as did the pungent smell wafting off him. He had about a foot of height on Kelsey, and he glared down at her angrily, jabbing his clawed finger in her face.

"Umm, maybe we should do this when the captain's feeling better," Setana said.

"No no, I *love* making deals with drunk people," Kelsey said. Then she called out to the captain, speaking loudly and slowly. "Hey, Captain! We want to charter your ship! I'll give you a cask of wine if you agree!"

For just a moment, the captain's ears perked up. Then he frowned. "Do you take me for a fool? Charter a ship for a cask of wine?"

"Fine," Kelsey sneered. "*Two* casks."

The captain's ears went flat with rage and he charged at Kelsey, only to stumble when she stepped to the side. He snarled and whirled around, but by that time Anton was able to get between them.

"Stand down," he grunted, grabbing a hold of the captain's wrists.

It irked him a little, to protect Kelsey like this, but Anton was afraid that if she actually felt threatened, she'd pull out a gun.

And the captain was strong. Stronger than Anton, maybe stronger than Kelsey. He easily pulled out of Anton's grip and gathered himself for another attack.

"Captain, no!"

"She's a *paying* customer!"

The two crewmembers intervened. Despite the cramped quarters, they effortlessly wove around the captain and interposed themselves between Anton and his opponent. Between them, they managed to push the captain back into his cabin.

"Sorry, he's normally . . ." Setana trailed off, searching for the right word.

"Able to hide his bigotry?" Kelsey finished for her.

Setana stared at Kelsey with her mouth open, trying to find the next thing to say.

"Why don't you take a look around the ship?" she finally managed. "Rashid can show you around. I'll get the captain . . . presentable, and you can talk in a bit."

"Sure, sure," Kelsey said. "Have fun with that."

This was only the second ship that Anton had been on. It was bigger than the one that he had sailed here in and . . . that was the limit of his knowledge.

"Crew quarters holds ten," Rashid said. "With a full crew, that leaves two cabins free for passengers."

"Where are the rest of the crew?" Kelsey asked as they poked around one of the empty cabins. It was pretty cramped, a narrow room with bunk beds on one side and enough room to stand on the other. It was a sight more comfortable than their trip over here. Then, their quarters had been a corner of the partially filled hold, their beds a choice of sacks of flax or a hammock.

"Not much call for them, if we're just sitting in port," Rashid said uncomfortably. "If we get hired, we should be able to fill the slots without trouble."

"You two are the only ones with hard-to-find skills?" Kelsey asked. "Weatherwitch and Navigator, those sound like rare classes."

"There's plenty of other skills needed, for a ship like this, but they're not hard to find," Rashid agreed. "Let me show you the hold."

There were actually two holds. The one they were looking at had trapdoors in the ceiling and the floor, allowing cargo to be lowered straight into the lower hold.

"How many passengers can the ship hold?" Kelsey asked, looking around.

"Four? Or do you mean if we refitted the holds for passengers?"

Kelsey nodded. "Can you hold this here?" she asked Anton. Anton did as she indicated, holding the end of the metal ribbon that she had produced against the wooden rib that held the ship's hull in place.

"Go on," she told Rashid.

"Well, it would depend on how you fitted it out," Rashid said, looking at Kelsey's activities curiously.

She had moved across the hold, the ribbon stretching out behind her, seemingly infinite in length. Anton realized there were markings on the ribbon, and that she was measuring distances.

"Is that a magic item?" Aris asked, curious as well.

Kelsey grinned. "No, it's just rolled up tightly. Rashid?"

"I don't know what to tell you," he said. "Nobles would want the place fitted out, I doubt you'd fit four of them in here. Slavers, they pack them in, so maybe fifty, just lying about on the deck."

"I see," Kelsey said, continuing to measure things. "So there's no standard fittings? You'd have to get carpenters in and build everything?"

"Of course," Rashid said. "If that's what you're after, it would take weeks just to get the designs made and the materials in."

She continued measuring the distances between everything in the hold. Aris and Rashid watched, while Anton helped her by holding one end of the measuring tape, as she called it.

When she was finally done, she directed Anton to release his end of the tape. When he did, the ribbon whisked itself back into its container.

"Are you sure it isn't magic?" Aris asked.

"Just a spring," Kelsey answered, handing the box over. Aris quickly realized that she could pull the tape out about a foot or two, and then release it, allowing it to zip back into the box. She laughed delightedly.

"Let's go measure the second hold," she told Rashid, who was casting envious glances at Aris.

"Your boat is shit, and we probably don't need it," Kelsey said. They were all sitting down at the one table large enough to seat six people, in the ship's galley. The captain had wanted to negotiate in his cabin, but there was only room for two.

Kelsey continued. "Half your rigging is missing, you have no sails, and nowhere near enough stores of food—of anything, really, except for alcohol—to feed the number of people we want to transport. And you'd need a refit to hold them all in comfort."

The captain's eyes bulged with rage, but Setana restrained him with a touch on his arm.

"All the sails and the rest of the rigging are in storage," Setana said. "The captain has a trait from his bosun days, *Shipshape*, which keeps items stored in his hold from decaying. They're still going to be in good shape. We can load food and water at the same time as we load passengers; there's not much point in doing it before."

"What sort of people are you carrying, and where?" the captain asked demandingly. "You all look far too shifty for this to be a legal cargo." He twisted his lips into a snarl that showed his teeth. "Illegal people can only mean slaves, and I won't have slaves aboard my ship."

Kelsey raised an eyebrow. "I would have thought you approved of slaves."

"Ha!" the captain snorted. "Because I hate you monkeys? That you would think that just shows your lack of intelligence."

"Captain . . ." Setana pleaded, "Can you not insult our clients?"

"Hmmph," was the captain's disgusted reply. "Let me tell you, ever since the Empire started bringing in you monkeys as slaves, things have been going downhill. Laziness and greed have been choking the productive courls of our nation. The foul blot on the honor of our glorious race needs to end!"

"Okay, I wasn't expecting that," Kelsey admitted. "But don't you guys have humans that aren't slaves?"

"Bah! To compare the citizens of the Empire to the barbarians that we dredge up from the northern coasts is an insult! They may be able to breed with you lot, polluting the purity of their race, but there is a wide gulf between a productive citizen and a barbarous brute like yourself."

"You're concerned about the purity of a different—no, wait." Kelsey shook her head. "Let's not go down that rabbit hole. You might go for this then: We want to transport a group of ex-slaves back to the country they came from."

"Ex-slaves? You mean stolen slaves."

"Call it what you like," Kelsey said. "How does that fit in with whatever passes for values in that head of yours?"

The captain paused, pondering the notion with a frown. Meanwhile, Setana and Rashid looked at each other. "This sounds dangerous, Captain," Setana said. "Maybe we shouldn't . . ."

"Ha! A good idea from a monkey? What is the world coming to?" the captain said loudly. "Yes . . . why didn't I see it before? They need to be shipped back to where they came from, to go back to squatting in their squalid little hovels . . . and you're going to *pay* to accomplish this?"

"If we can come to an agreement, sure," Kelsey said, bemused. She shared a glance with the dismayed crewmembers. "Are you two good with this?"

Setana sighed. "We're with the captain. And at least this is a job. Just how illegal is this going to be?"

"Do I look like an Elitran magistrate?" Kelsey asked. "Pretty illegal, I guess. But it's fine. We're not going to get caught."

"Are you sure about that?" Rashid said. "It just takes one person to blab to the authorities and we're all in the pit. Just how many people already know about this?"

"About this boat?" Kelsey asked, "Just the two courls you met earlier. Don't worry, they're not going to snitch on us. Now, let's talk terms."

"Uh, Kelsey," Anton interjected, "shouldn't I be the one making the deal?"

"Not this time," she said. "Since we won't be able to go with them, we're going to need a little extra assurance that they'll follow through."

"You needn't worry about that," the captain said stiffly. "We are all courls of honor here."

"That's great," Kelsey said. "And no, I'm not worried about that at all. You see, I've got this little condition, or maybe you'd call it a curse . . ."

"That went surprisingly well," Kelsey said as they walked off the docks. "I mean, considering how crazy he was, he seemed remarkably competent."

"I'm still not sure about entrusting the people we rescue to him," Aris said. "He didn't seem like he'd treat them well."

"He won't go back on the terms of the deal," Anton said. "He can't."

"Now we have to source ourselves some supplies as well," Kelsey said. "I suppose we can leave that to the boys to do tomorrow."

"It's almost sundown," Anton pointed out. "We should see if Zaphar is back."

Zaphar *was* back, and he had maps.

"It's an octagon, you see?" he said, pointing out the features. "Seven big cells, and one passageway out. That goes right through the guardroom."

"And that's the only entrance?" Kelsey asked, poring intently over the map.

"Well, there's a skylight over the central area. The glass on one of the windows is loose . . . now," Zaphar said smugly. "You could pull someone up through there, but it won't be quick. Or quiet."

"How much noise would it make to pull someone up?" Kelsey asked.

"The window's too short to just stand in the frame and pull them up directly," Zaphar told her. "You've got to stand back and pull from the side. The rope rubs against the window frame, and that makes noise."

Kelsey hummed to herself. "I could make a pulley that sat on the frame. That would make it easier, and quieter. How many people?"

"I couldn't get too close," Zaphar cautioned her. "It's a big open area, and the moon lights it up a bit too much. I got a look though. There's three in this cell, eight in this one, and nine in this one. All the others are empty."

"Why do it that way?" Aris asked. "Why not split them evenly?"

"Probably sorting them," Kelsey replied. "If they cleared a bunch—our bunch—out before we arrived, this might mean that they've had three shipments in since then. Each ship's cargo goes to a different cell until they get a chance to sort them out."

"One crew only brought in three girls?" Anton asked. "Should we ask Kusec if that's common?"

"Nah," Kelsey said. "The less those two know about our operation, the happier they'll be. We can get the details from Rashaq's man."

"I should get going then," Zaphar said nervously. "If you'll pay me, that is."

Kelsey rolled her eyes and pulled out two gold coins. Zaphar examined them closely and bit them both before putting them away.

"So trusting," Kelsey said. "Stay here, though. I'll have the inn send up some food. This official that we're meeting might have come prepared with the information we need. In which case, we'll need to plan our next move."

CHAPTER TWELVE

Everyday I Write the Book

The underground casino was a lot busier at night. There was *sort of* a crowd outside. Not a line, not a group of people, but several small groups of disreputable-looking people were gathered in the general vicinity of the entrance. Close, but not close enough to be lit by the lanterns above the entrance. As the trio approached, Anton saw one group go up to the door and speak with the guards.

Anton could feel the eyes on him as they approached, but Kelsey ignored them. She also ignored the group arguing with the bouncer, brushing them aside as if they were nothing.

"We're expected," she said.

"Hey! You can't do that—" the courl she had just shoved yelled. Then he stopped, his outrage diverted in mid-rant, as the guard nodded and opened the door for Kelsey. "You're letting her in? Do you know who I am?"

Anton glanced at him as they moved past. He was wearing silk, but no rings, and his sword looked pretty basic.

Steel Sabre, Weapon, Good Quality, Tier 1

The courl himself wasn't much more impressive.

Nazim Alpash, Law Clerk, Overall Level 4, Law Clerk

"You're Tier One?" Anton snorted. The courl was clearly older than him.

Nazim drew himself up to reply, but the door closed behind Anton before the Law Clerk could come up with something.

Inside, it was much more crowded. The quiet and casual air of the place during the day was gone, replaced by a bustling crowd of richly dressed people, looking far too eager to join the games that were on offer. Everyone was drinking and speaking too loudly, and only the ubiquitous guards kept things from getting out of hand.

Once inside, they were handed over to a different pair of guards. "If you'll take a seat, the boss will be ready for you in a bit," one of them said. He took their weapons, at least the weapons that they had been carrying. Kelsey had their real weapons in her storage, but Anton and Aris had carried some basic swords, just so that they wouldn't be walking the streets unarmed.

The guards led them to a fairly small table. Given how crowded the room was, though, the fact that it was empty was fairly impressive. Anton looked around, but he couldn't see anyone who looked as though they had just been evicted from their seats.

"Stay frosty," Kelsey said. "We're going to be waiting here long enough for him to make his point that he's important, and we're not. He'll probably try something to make you lose your cool."

"Why would he do that?" Aris asked. "Aren't we here to make a deal?"

Kelsey waved her hand vaguely. "It's a criminal thing," she said. "He needs to establish that he's the one in charge. Making you lose your cool means that he managed to control you, at least a little bit."

"Oh," Aris said. "I should have asked before, but what's cool, and how do I lose it?"

Anton had been wondering the same thing, but it was generally easier to just shut up when Kelsey used terms he didn't know. Kelsey chuckled.

"Um, I guess *composure* would be the proper word?" she said. "Like, he's going to do something to make you upset, or angry."

"So anger is hot, and cool is the opposite of that?" Anton asked.

"You got it, daddy-o," Kelsey said, smirking. Anton felt his face get hot. This was why it wasn't worth asking about her weird terms.

A guard stepped up to the table. "The boss is ready for you now," he said.

They all followed the guard to a back room. Here, the tables were more widely spaced. The players looked richer, if not any less desperate. The guard led them up some stairs, to a balcony that overlooked the gaming area. There were a few nooks set up here, and the guard led them to the largest of them.

Rashaq Nazari was waiting for them. The booth boasted a wide banquette, padded with leather, that wrapped around the three walls. It was deep enough to let the crime lord lean back and rest his feet on the low, ornately carved table that occupied the center space.

Anton remembered his resolution.

Rashaq Nazari, Fixer, Overall Level 24, Laborer/(broken) Merchant/(broken) Fence/Fixer

Anton blinked at the list of broken paths. There was a story there, of how he went from Laborer to Merchant . . . probably a grim one. The courl himself had his arms draped around two women, one on each side. They were curled up next to him, leaning into his embrace.

One of the women was a courl, with fur as black as Rashaq's but with brilliant sapphire-blue eyes. She was dressed in brightly colored silks that wrapped around her, revealing more than they covered. Her legs were drawn up underneath her, allowing her to show off her delicate silver ankle bracelet.

Sylara Veleska, Courtesan, Overall Level 19, Doxy/Concubine/Courtesan

The other was human, a girl not much older than Anton, with golden skin and lustrous ebony hair. Her eyes were a warm brown, and her dress, a thin silk shift that clung to her skin, was a cascade of midnight blue, adorned with delicate silver embroidery that shimmered in the half-lit gloom.

Amina Deshara, Courtesan, Overall Level 18, Slave/Concubine/Courtesan

Both of them stared at the group with fixed smiles and guarded eyes. Both of them wore unadorned silver collars.

"Won't you sit down?" Rashaq said, nodding to one side of the nook. "Our other guest should be arriving shortly."

"Classy," Kelsey said, taking her seat. "You brought your sex slaves."

The easy smile on Rashaq's face flickered. "Crude," he said. "As befits barbarians. This is my casino, why wouldn't I bring my girls here?"

Sitting down next to Kelsey, Anton kept a hold of Aris's hand. Amina's skin was too light to be Zamarran, and Aris wouldn't be able to see the path of the slave girl. Still, Rashaq had made it obvious what the girls were.

Just keep your cool, Anton reminded himself. The girls didn't look scared, or mistreated. He wasn't here to save every slave in the city. He looked over at Aris and she seemed to be following Kelsey's advice. Then he looked over at Kelsey and his blood ran cold.

She was smiling. It wasn't a fake smile, or a forced one. It was the same grin that she'd had when the Baron had told her that she was going to be tortured.

Anton remembered what she'd said earlier. *If you buy a slave off a slaver, he just goes and uses that money to get more slaves.*

Anton had a feeling that Rashaq Nazari now had a very limited time to buy any new slaves.

"So where is this guy?" Kelsey asked.

"It takes a bit of effort to drag him off the tables," Rashaq said. "Here he comes now."

Anton looked over and widened his eyes in surprise. Courls weren't normally *fat*.

Zephyrion Kaldoran, Administrator, Overall Level 18, Clerk/(broken) Law Clerk/Administrator

The courl that waddled over was richly dressed, but he was also the fattest courl that Anton had ever seen. He hadn't thought they could get fat.

Taking a seat opposite them, Zephyrion accepted the large bag that one of the guards was carrying for him. He looked over at his customers, panting a little, as if the trip up the stairs had been too much for him.

"Now that we're all here, we can get started," Rashaq said. "On my right is Kelsey, who's looking for some information, and on my left is my dear friend Zephyrion, who can tell you what you're looking for."

"Records, yes?" Zephyrion said, his eyes gleaming with avarice. "Of incoming slaves and their deposition? I have the records you'll need," he said patting the bag beside him.

"Great!" Kelsey said. "I hate wasting time. We're going to need you to find a slave called Cheia Lucina and tell us where she, and everyone that came in with her, went."

"A-bup pup up!" Zephyrion interjected. "We need to determine a price, first. Five gold."

"Did you lose all your money in the casino, or do you have a particularly bad drug habit?" Kelsey exclaimed dramatically. "I can hire someone to steal the damn book for five silver!"

"Hmph! Even if they could get past the matchless security of the Administrative Compound, they wouldn't find it! It's safe here with me." Zephyrion patted the bag next to him smugly.

"Oh, in that case, five *copper*, for someone to mug you when you leave, and they get to keep everything else on you," Kelsey sneered.

"Now, now," Rashaq interjected as a massive frown formed on Zephyrion's face. "I don't know how you do things in barbarian lands, but here, I won't have threats made against my dear friends. Zephyrion is protected, coming and going from this place."

Kelsey's smile got wider. "You think you can—"

"Kelsey!" Anton interjected. "Stay frosty. Daddy-o."

She looked at him incredulously and then burst out laughing.

"Spoilsport," Kelsey complained. "But a good point, I suppose."

She turned back to Zephyrion. "*One* gold."

Eventually, they settled on three. Only then did Zephyrion take out a large ledger.

"A slave called Cheia Lucina you say?" He pored through the entries. Anton would have preferred to read them for himself, but Kusec and Erryan hadn't known the written language to teach it to them. From the intent way that Kelsey was staring at the ledger, Anton thought that might change.

"Ah, here we are, from about a month ago," the fat official said. "Cheia Lucina. Arrived with fifteen others. They were processed and auctioned off about three weeks ago."

"Where did they go?" Kelsey asked. The courl scowled but turned back to his book.

"They were split up into four lots, and combined with other intakes," he said. "One lot was sold to Dragan Vorin, two went to Zaraq Malik. The final lot was . . . oh, I see. Since there were only three of them, they were held back for further training."

"How much training do you need to be a sex slave?" Kelsey asked.

"Very little," Zephyrion said, leering. "Since those three were deemed to have worthwhile skills, they were held back for language training. Doxies can pick up the language they need on the job, but skilled workers have more complex language needs."

"All right, read out each of the names in the lots," Kelsey said.

"Do you need something to write this down?" Rashaq asked.

"Nah, I've got an excellent memory," Kelsey said. Zephyrion read out the names. When he was finished, Kelsey's face fell.

"There are two missing," Anton said. He pulled out their list to be sure. "Dendany and Edary."

Zephyrion went back to the ledger. "They're not listed here," he said. "They must not have made it. It's not unusual to lose a few on the trip."

Anton clenched his fist. He wanted to smash the official in his stupid uncaring face, but he found Aris was holding on to his arm.

"Sorry, Anton," Kelsey said sympathetically. "It happens. I'll let Suliel know."

Anton nodded, not trusting himself to speak.

"So where can we find these two merchants, Dragan Vorin and Zaraq Malik?" Kelsey asked.

"Oh, they would have left with their purchases," Zephyrion said airily. "They could be anywhere; the Empire doesn't track merchants."

There was a crack. Everyone looked towards the source, which was Kelsey's hand. At some point, a bone, a rib bone from the look of it, had appeared in her grip. She had just snapped it with her fingers. As they watched, she let one half of it drop to the table. Bracing the remainder against her four fingers, she pushed with her thumb, eliciting another sharp *crack*.

"Could you be," she asked, "a little more helpful?"

Zephyrion stared at the shattered bone. "Ah . . . well, they have offices here? Agents? I'm sure you could ask them where they've gone?"

"That's great," Kelsey said. "Where can we find them?"

"There, there should be an address listed . . ." Zephyrion started leafing through the start of the ledger. "Ah, here they are."

"Fantastic," Kelsey said.

CHAPTER THIRTEEN

Northwest Passage

W hen Zephyrion had gone, Rashaq ordered drinks for the table. "We still have business to discuss, yes?"

Throughout the previous discussion, his hands had not left his women alone, stroking and caressing them gently. Now Amina had to lean forward to pick up her master's drink and hold it to his lips.

Kelsey watched him steadily, her face showing no emotion. "I suppose we might," she said. "What did you have in mind?"

"You are clearly planning to steal some of the Bey's valuable property," Rashaq replied. "You have enough muscle for such a job, I think, but you'll need more than muscle to succeed."

"Oh?" Kelsey said, smiling. "How would you go about such a job?"

Rashaq cocked his head as if considering. "Hmm. Bribery and violence, I should think. Someone with knowledge of the guards could tell you who could be bribed to create a hole in their pattern of coverage."

"If there's a hole in the net, do we even need violence?" Kelsey asked.

"Of course!" Rashaq exclaimed. "The guards at the door won't take a bribe. No guard is going to accept a bribe that gets them fired—or executed. You will have to . . . take care of the *actual* guards. The bribes just ensure that no one discovers you, until it is too late."

Kelsey nodded. "The guards will have the keys to the doors and the chains."

"Most likely. If not, copies can be made, for a price."

"That would leave us outside of the compound, on the run in a strange city with a bunch of ex-slaves," Kelsey pointed out. "What then?"

"You'd need a safe house where you can lay low until the hunt dies down. Once things are quiet, you can get them on a boat, perhaps the one you came in on."

"They may not be inclined to wait around for us," Kelsey said. "We might need to make other arrangements."

"I'm sure that's achievable, with enough gold to lubricate things," Rashaq purred. "Shall I start making inquiries?"

"Not yet," Kelsey said. "I want to focus on our exit route first. The alternative arrangements I have in mind involve getting the slaves out of the city."

"Out on the island?" Rashaq frowned, considering. "Clever, but I think impractical. There are a few beaches and bays suitable for a quiet pickup, but they are watched."

"Why don't you let me worry about all that," Kelsey said confidently. "What I want to know is if there's a way out of the city that the guards don't know about."

"There . . . is," Rashaq said slowly. "You'll have to negotiate passage with them, and I don't think you'll like their prices."

"It can't hurt to ask," Kelsey said.

"I suppose so. For one gold, I'll give you directions and an introduction."

"Sold!" Kelsey said, putting a coin down on the table. "For now, hold off on that other stuff until I know when we're ready to do it."

"They won't keep those three in there for long," Rashaq warned.

"I know," Kelsey said. "I'll get back to you just as quick as I can."

Once back at the inn, Kelsey sent Zaphar on his way with some silver and some instructions.

"Nice work there, keeping your mouths shut," she told her companions.

"I didn't understand a lot of what was said," Aris said. "Are we going to have Captain al-Nazari pick us up from offshore? Because it sounded like . . ."

"His ship is way too big to escape notice," Kelsey agreed. "No, most of what I said in there was a lie."

"Why? Aren't we working with him?"

"A guy like that, you're only working with him until he sees more money in selling you out," Kelsey explained. "Right now, he thinks he can still get money off us, but once the job is done . . ."

"We'll leave and he won't see us again?" Aris asked, confused.

"No, that's when he turns us in for the reward," Kelsey corrected.

"So we want him to know as little as possible about what we're actually doing," Anton finished. "The less he knows, the less he can tell the authorities."

"Couldn't you just keep him quiet with a deal?"

"He'd never accept it, and he'd know something was up if I tried," Kelsey said sourly. "*And* he'd probably find a way to wiggle out of it. Now get some sleep, you two, it's a big day tomorrow!"

* * *

"I think this building should be condemned." Kelsey spoke with a flat even tone. "There's serious metal fatigue in all the load-bearing members, the wiring is substandard, it's completely inadequate for our power needs, and the neighborhood is like a demilitarized zone."

"It's free, though," Anton said. Aris started to speak up, no doubt about to ask what Kelsey was talking about, but Anton touched her on the arm and shook his head. It wasn't worth it.

"Oh, in that case, we'll take it!" Kelsey said. To whom, Anton wasn't sure. The reason it was free was because there wasn't anyone to sell it to them.

The kids had scouted the place through a narrow second-story window, but Kelsey had just pulled the boards off the door.

"If someone comes to ask us what we're doing, or the guards come and arrest us for breaking in, then it's not the place we're looking for," she'd said. Anton had looked around, once everyone had gone inside, and the street had stayed deserted. If anyone was watching them, they were staying hidden.

"We're going to have people staying here?" Aris asked, coughing a little at the dust that was being raised.

"Just for a little while," Kelsey said. "It needs cleaning but it seems basically sound. You did good, kids!" she called out to the second story where the kids were stomping around.

"Pay 'em and then get 'em out of here," she said to Anton.

Anton nodded. Officially, he was the one who had made the deal with them. He sent them on their way with a few extra coppers. Once they were gone, Kelsey slammed the door closed.

Then she summoned a grinning skeleton. This one had a leather satchel, jammed full of strange tools, hanging off its shoulders.

"Get to work securing that door," Kelsey said. The skeleton saluted and went to work.

"We'll need some bedding and supplies, but the curly boys are seeing to that," Kelsey said absently.

"You haven't called them that where they can hear, have you?" Anton asked. Kelsey grinned but kept her eyes on her skeleton.

"No," she said. "I wouldn't want them to get all catty."

Anton sighed. "Where did you pick *that* up from?"

"It's a fairly easy jump to make," Kelsey said, raising her eyebrows. "They call you monkeys, you call them cats."

"*I* don't, I was raised better," Anton said. "And they called *you* a monkey."

"I can hardly blame them for a case of mistaken identity. I *look* human, after all. I'm taking offense on your behalf, though."

"Just save it," Anton said. "I'm pretty sure Captain al-Nazari is essential to your plans. I can ignore a bit of name-calling without stooping to his level."

"Ha! That's what you forget! As a dungeon, my natural level starts underground."

Faster than Anton would have thought possible, the skeleton was done with the door. With a bow and a flourish, he presented two keys to Kelsey.

"Nice work, Handy-bone," she said, dismissing the monster. She tried the key in the newly installed mechanism. With a loud *clunk*, the bolt slid into place. Grinning, she twisted it again, and the bolt slid free with a slightly different sound.

"Let's go," she said. "We've got at least one more appointment today."

"This," Kelsey said, waving a piece of paper in front of the hole in the door, "is either an introduction from Rashaq Nazari or an instruction from him for you to kill us. I don't know which, I can't read your language yet."

"We don't work for Nazari," the man behind the door growled.

"Whew! That makes me feel a lot better about handing it over, let me tell you," Kelsey told him.

It took a moment for the man to think that one through, then he cursed ruefully. "Just give it here, then."

Kelsey pushed the paper through the hole. There was a pause before the man spoke again. "You're Kelsey?"

"Yep!"

"Whadda you want?"

"You want me to talk business on the street?"

There was another pause. "No," the man finally admitted. "You'd better come in."

"Everyone is so friendly around here," Kelsey noted as the door opened. "Do you think they'll serve us lunch?"

"I doubt it," Anton said wryly. Judging from the glare that the human behind the door gave her, he was right.

Behind the door was a small room with chairs, a table, and two humans. Neither of them looked particularly rich. Or clean.

"So Nazari told you about us," one of the men said.

"That he did. He told us that you have a way past the wall. Does it get much use? I wouldn't have thought there'd be much call for smugglers if the bays are being watched."

The two men looked at each other. "We do all right," one of them said.

"Not like it used to be, though," the other admitted.

"Well, I want to use it, and not just the once," Kelsey said. "I'm prepared to pay, of course."

The two men looked the group over greedily. *Smugglers*, Anton thought, *probably have a way to identify the value of gear.*

"One silver per person that goes through. One way," one of them said.

Kelsey shrugged. "Anton?"

"One silver for all three of us," Anton countered. Kelsey shot him a surprised glance, but he didn't want these two taking advantage of them.

"Done," was the quick response. Anton winced. It sounded as if he'd overpaid.

Kelsey put a silver coin on the table. "There you go, now let's get moving."

The two men looked at each other. One of them shrugged. "This way, he said."

He led them into a room farther back. Pushing aside a ratty cabinet revealed a hole in the floor.

Kelsey pulled out her torch. To the two smugglers' consternation, she shone the light down the hole.

"Nice work," she complimented them. Disdaining any attempt at climbing, she stepped off and let herself fall.

Stepping up to the hole, Anton looked down. There was a wooden ladder affixed to the side of the hole, and a pool of light, about twelve feet down from Kelsey's torch, helpfully pointed back to illuminate the entrance.

"Come on in, the water's fine!" she called back.

Anton shrugged and started climbing down. Aris was next, and one of the smugglers followed after.

"This way?" Kelsey asked facetiously. There was only one way to go. She led the way; the tunnel was too narrow to pass easily.

"Why did you make a tunnel under the wall?" Aris asked the smuggler. "It seems like a lot of work for not much reward."

The man shrugged and didn't answer. From the front of the line, Kelsey called back.

"Whenever there's a wall, there's always a secret way around it. That's just human nature."

"I don't think that's true . . ." Aris protested.

"There was one in Kirido, wasn't there?"

"You mean *your* tunnel?"

"Kelsey just used the one that was there already," Anton told her. "It was a secret tunnel from the castle, to the town and to a cave in the cliffs."

"Suliel's dad knew about it, but he didn't write anything down about it," Kelsey said. "Who made it might stay a mystery."

"No talking when we're under the wall," the smuggler said. They travelled the rest of the way in silence.

After a longer journey than Anton had expected, they emerged into a cave.

"I was wondering why you were willing to do this during the day," Kelsey said. "I'm impressed."

"Just make sure there's no traffic on the road when you come out, and you'll be fine," the smuggler muttered. "They can't see you from the wall."

"Nice. How do we get back? Just come back through the tunnel and knock on your floor to let us back in?"

"It takes one of us to open the ends," the man said, glowering at her suspiciously. "I'll wait here for you to come back."

"Well, we won't be back until sunset," Kelsey said, "So feel free to head back inside and wait in comfort."

She poked her head outside of the cave and then strode out purposefully. Anton and Aris followed in her wake

"Bye, Mr. Smuggler," Aris said as she left.

CHAPTER FOURTEEN

Ain't No Half-Steppin'

Anton wouldn't have thought there was anything unusual about the fort if it weren't for the fact that it was the destination that they had been seeking. As soon as it came into view, Kelsey pulled them back, off the road, and had them climb a nearby hill. Now they were all on their bellies, looking at their target.

"How do lens flashes work again?" Kelsey muttered to herself. "If the sun is . . . there . . . and those guys are . . . we should be good." Pulling out some kind of device, she held it to her eyes and looked through it at the fortification.

Anton and Aris looked at each other. "What is that?" Anton finally asked. He kept his voice low, even though the guards manning the fort were far too far away to hear.

"Gimme a minute," Kelsey murmured, focusing on the fort. "I should have made more than one of these, but it's finicky work and monsters don't have much use for them."

Still curious, Anton used *Delver's Discernment.*

Binoculars, Tool, Excellent Quality, Tier 3

Kelsey continued to stare into the device, before finally rolling over and offering it to Anton.

"Here, your turn," she said. "Hold it to your eyes and turn the wheel. If the picture gets more blurry, turn it in the other direction."

Anton did as she said. To his surprise, a closer view of the fort jumped at him through the device.

"It's a double telescope?" he blurted. He'd heard of telescopes. The texts he'd read weren't sure if they were magical or not, but this device was definitely not. Though how they were Tier Three items *without* being magical was beyond him; he couldn't detect any mana running through them.

"Get a good look," Kelsey said, "and then pass them to Aris."

When they had both examined the fort carefully, Kelsey had them scoot down off the crest of the hill.

"I don't like the size of the place," she said pensively. "They had two guys on the gate, and one on the tower. If they're running four shifts a day, that means they just need twelve men. Courls, that is."

"Right," Anton said. Math wasn't his strong point, but he could manage that much.

"That place can hold a lot more than twelve men," Kelsey said. "I'd say fifty?"

"Maybe they sometimes have more people there?" Aris suggested.

"Maybe," Kelsey agreed doubtfully. "At least it looks quiet now."

She made a face as she thought about it, but then seemed to come to a decision.

"Okay, team," she said brightly. "We need to get in there and access the dungeon. They won't let us, so we need to kill them."

"Wait, what?" Anton said.

"They're the enemy, Anton," Kelsey said, looking at him with a serious face. "The same army that you faced on the wall. I'm not going to tell you that they're all evil and need to die, but these guys are in our way, and we can't afford any witnesses."

"That doesn't make it sound less like cold-blooded murder," Anton objected.

"It's killing in defense of others," Kelsey insisted. "As soon as Lord High Mucky-muck finishes drinking the palace dry, he's going to come up here and kill this dungeon. We need to do something before that."

Anton wanted to argue with her. The idea that this dungeon had been fed slaves and other criminals for all the years that it had been alive revolted him. But it wasn't like *it* had had a choice. Part of him wanted to argue that dungeons weren't *really* people, but he couldn't deny the evidence in front of his eyes. Still . . .

"No witnesses, though? We don't need to kill everyone to get inside."

"Any witnesses, any account of what went on here, is going to make it much harder for us to pull off our next heist. The less that the Bey or whoever is in charge of hunting us knows, the better."

"So no quarter given," Anton said slowly. *Just like the wall.* Except they had taken captives back then, hadn't they?

Thinking back to the wall brought up another objection. "Are you sure we can do this? Three of us against twelve, and they out-level most of us."

"Ah, that's because I haven't told you my cunning plan," Kelsey said. "It won't be three against twelve, it will be one against nine!"

"Pretty sure that's worse, but go ahead and explain it," Anton said glumly. Without even asking, he knew that he was going to be the one.

"Step one," Kelsey said. "Aris takes out the visible guard from here, with the rifle."

"Are you sure you can do that?" Anton asked his wife. She nodded.

"I killed that noble before, and before then I shot some of the guards," she said. "It's not as bad as hacking at zombies."

"In a perfect world," Kelsey said, "they would just all swarm out looking for the shooter and Aris could just cut them down. However, we live in a sadly imperfect world, so they'll probably just hole up in the fort where we can't get to them. So!"

She held two fingers up.

"Anton and I are going to get close to the fort before Aris starts shooting. Close enough to run through the gate before the reinforcements start to close it."

"That leaves two of us against the nine we think are inside . . . You're not going to fight them, are you?" Anton asked.

"I don't get experience from this avatar, remember? It'll be a massive waste if I join in. I *will* watch your back and keep you out of trouble, but the main event is all yours, kid."

Anton glared at her. "And what if there really are fifty guards in there?"

"Then we run, and Aris picks them off as they chase after us," Kelsey said placidly. "That's what we do if you can't handle a mere nine guards as well."

"There's no way that I can," Anton said bitterly. "Nine guards! Probably Tier Three as well."

"You won't be fighting them all at once," Kelsey pointed out. "They'll be off-duty, maybe unarmed. Some of them will even be asleep. At the start, at least."

She smiled wickedly. "They won't know what hit them."

I can't believe I'm really doing this, Anton thought as the pair of them trudged up the road to the fort. The courls manning it were not particularly alert, but they didn't have to be to note the approach of the two attackers. Anton had been close enough to hear the warning that was shouted down from the tower, but as they approached closer, the guards did not appear too concerned.

They weren't leaning against the wall anymore, but they hadn't taken any basic precautions like closing the main gate. Anton had his sword sheathed and wasn't presenting a threat, and Kelsey looked like a harmless unarmed woman. Looked like.

"Dungeon's closed!" one of the guards yelled out to them. Anton looked at Kelsey, but she elected to keep walking calmly. The guards watched them approach.

When they were close enough to speak instead of yell, Kelsey addressed the guards.

"Gate's open, though," she pointed out. It wasn't a particularly clever response, but it let them get a few paces closer.

"Breeze keeps it cooler inside," the guard explained. "Doesn't mean you can come in." They both raised their spears meaningfully.

From a far-off hill, there came a loud *crack*, made softer by distance.

"What was that?" one of the guards asked. Anton held his breath. There was a soft clatter from the tower.

"Dunno. You see anything?" he called up to his compatriot. No one answered, and he had just long enough to frown before the *crack* came again. There was a pause of about a second before the bullet smashed into his face.

"What was that? What did you do!" the remaining guard yelled.

"What? Us?" Kelsey said theatrically, raising her hands. Anton couldn't bring himself to act, knowing what was going to happen next.

They had stopped at the first shot, that having been Aris's signal that moving closer would block her sight lines. The last guard yelled for backup and pointed his spear at them, but he didn't come closer. He had only a few seconds to live.

This isn't a fight, it's an execution, Anton thought as the third guard fell.

"Let's go!" Kelsey called and broke into a run. Anton followed, hoping that she'd remember that he was supposed to be taking the lead.

As if listening to his thoughts, Kelsey stopped suddenly as soon as she got through the entrance. When Anton joined her, he too stopped, jolted by what he saw.

The fort looked larger because much of it was empty space. A large interior courtyard, partially roofed over, occupied at least half of the volume enclosed by the fort walls. A building at the back was probably where the occupants lived. Anton could see some uniformed courls coming out of it now, pulling out weapons.

Chained to the posts that held up the roof of the courtyard were a dozen slaves.

"Worry about the combatants for now, Anton," Kelsey said, giving him a slight push. Knowing she was right, he ignored the surprised stares he was getting and charged towards the courls.

He triggered *Leaping Attack* as soon as he was in range, long before the courls realized he was a threat. With the momentum of his leap behind it, Chainbreaker sliced through the courl's armor and continued on into his stomach. It stopped on his spine, but Anton was pretty sure the courl was dying even as he pulled out Chainbreaker and moved on to his next target.

This one managed to get his sword in the way of Anton's strike. He was faster and more agile than Anton, but Anton had a few advantages. Courls were renowned for their agility, not their strength or speed. Anton was tough, and he had both *Stone Skin* and heavier armor. He thought he had the measure of the courl's blade, but he checked to make sure.

Standard Elitran Short Sword, Mark IV, Weapon, Good Quality, Tier 2

Anton left an opening. It was a real opening, but it was also a trap. When the guard's sword flew, Anton took the blow. It hurt, but he was ready for that. The actual damage done was minimal as the sword glanced off Anton's layers of protection.

Shocked at the lack of effect, the guard hesitated. Anton didn't. Chainbreaker made short work of the guard's neck.

Anton moved inside. He could hear movement from farther in the building, but his next opponent was racing into the room right now. Theoretically, a short sword had an advantage in such cramped quarters, but the guard was panicked, unsure of what was going on. He yelled at Anton, but to Anton's surprise, he couldn't hear what was being said. All he could hear was the sounds of the wall. The shouts of the enemy, the screams of his friends.

The sounds of his family dying.

The next thing Anton knew, he was standing over the dead body of the courl he had just been facing, breathing heavily.

"You all right?" Kelsey asked from behind him. "You got a little heated there."

Anton looked down at the courl, and then back at Kelsey. "I'm fine," he said.

"You want me to take the rest?" she asked.

"What about the waste?"

"Losing you would be a bigger one," she said. "Whether it's to a wound or something more . . . psychological. The next lot should be easier, but a bit more more . . . morally challenging. Some of them are probably still putting on their pants."

"I'll give them that much time, at least," Anton told her. "But my parents always taught me that fighting fair was for sparring and tournaments."

A little while later, Anton went back to the gate and signaled for Aris to approach.

You have reached Level 9.
Please allocate free Ability point.

Dexterity, Anton thought. It was his lowest physical ability, and courls were just too hard to hit sometimes. A number of the guards had managed to slip around his guard and get a blow in. None had beaten his defenses, but Kelsey had had to shoot one of them.

With a few free moments, while he waited for Aris to arrive, he glanced over his status.

Anton Nos, Adventurer, Level 9
Overall Level: 14
Paths: Delver/Adventurer
Class: Adventurer
Strength: 17
Toughness: 21
Agility: 17
Dex: 16
Perception: 15
Will: 13
Charisma: 10
Traits:
Delver's Discernment
Leaping Attack
Stone Skin
Uncanny Evasion
Sense Mana
Spider Climb

Looking back, he saw that Kelsey was going through the bodies, touching each one with her foot, and making it disappear. By the time Aris jogged up to the gate, Kelsey was almost done.

"So!" Kelsey said, coming up to the pair with a bright smile. "What are we going to do with the slaves?"

"What do you mean?" Anton asked.

"No witnesses, remember?" Kelsey asked.

CHAPTER FIFTEEN

It's Tricky

I got a level!" Aris called out as she approached. Then, as she entered the compound, she looked at her two companions staring at each other. "What's wrong?"

"They're not witnesses!" Anton finally managed to stutter. "They're victims!"

"They can be both," Kelsey said, shrugging. "Use your head, think it through. What are we going to do with them?"

Anton looked over at the slaves, chained to posts. Kelsey had slipped into Tiatian, no doubt deliberately, but from the intent stares he was getting, some of them spoke that language.

"We'll free them," he said slowly. "The boat can hold that many extra. Didn't you say Kirido needs more people?"

"More *workers*," Kelsey said disparagingly. "This lot are slaves at the end of their working life. I doubt they can even make it back to the city. Except for this guy."

She pointed at a dark-skinned human who was following their conversation. Unlike the others, he wasn't just shackled to a post. His arms were manacled behind him and he had more chains linking his legs. His face had been recently tattooed with an ugly design featuring lots of sharp angles.

"What's your story?" Kelsey asked, going up to him without fear. Anton thought to check his status.

Tavik Aissi, Level 8, Slave, Helot/Slave

Helot hadn't been included in Anton's education on classes, but from context, he guessed it was the Tier One version of Slave. Tavik was older than Anton, his low level was probably an indication that he was a poor slave.

Now he glared down at Kelsey.

"I killed my master and got sent here," he said in Tiatian. "Short story."

"It sure is," Kelsey chuckled. "You've got some muscles on you, but you don't have much in the way of abilities. How'd you manage to kill him?"

"Her. Gained her trust and killed her while she slept."

Kelsey smiled. "Was that why they gave you that tattoo? To make sure no one ever trusted you again?"

Tavik shrugged. "Didn't tell me why."

"What will you do if we set you free?"

Tavik gave her a long look. "Whatever you want?" he said hesitantly.

"Do we look like we're in the market for slaves?" Kelsey asked with a grin.

"Maybe not," Tavik conceded. He glanced over to the empty space where Kelsey had vanished a slain guardsman, then over to where Aris and Anton were quietly talking. "Never seen anyone like you."

"Whadda ya think, Anton?" Kelsey asked, turning around. "He seems fine to me."

"We're freeing them, all of them," Anton said firmly.

Kelsey shrugged. "Just remember, this means we're going to have to kill the guys manning the tunnel."

"What? Why? Can't you just pay them the extra?"

"I *could*," Kelsey said disapprovingly. "But if I did, the first thing they'd do is go running to Rashaq for another payday, and let him know what we did."

"That doesn't sound so bad . . ." Anton said.

"Oh, but it is," Kelsey insisted. "Remember, we want him to think we're taking the slaves *out* of the city. Bringing a whole bunch *in* will make him start to think we're lying to him."

"We *are* lying to him."

Kelsey rolled her eyes, "And that's exactly why we don't want him to think that."

"Excuse me, master, mistresses." The voice that interrupted them was female and laced through with pain. Anton looked over to see it came from one of the slaves. She had the bronze skin tone of a native Elitiran, and unlike most of the slaves, she had remained seated while they stood nervously.

"If it's all the same to you, I'd rather not go on another journey," she continued.

Kelsey wandered over to stand over the elderly woman. "You know why you were brought here," she said.

The woman nodded. "To be fed to the dungeon. It's not such a bad end. I've been in pain for so long . . . at least it will be quick."

"Can't we heal her?" Aris asked. "We have potions."

Kelsey shot Aris an incredulous look. "If you knew what those things cost," she muttered. Nevertheless, she knelt down and started examining the old woman.

"No can do," she said after a tense silence. "She's fractured her leg, and it's healed badly. Constant pain, more if she walks."

"That sounds about right," the old woman agreed.

"For a potion to work, you'd have to break the leg again, possibly a couple of times, in just the right places," Kelsey explained. "I could do it back home, maybe, but the shock of that, plus the shock of the potion, would kill her for sure."

"Oh," Aris said. "So there's nothing we can do?"

"A mage could do something if he had the right magic for it," Kelsey said. "They have better options for healing. Same goes for a cleric with a high enough level."

"Then we could—" Anton started.

"We're *not* going to find a cleric willing to help an escaped slave," Kelsey snorted. "Much less a mage. Those guys are all going to be rich and connected to the government."

"It's fine," the woman said. "I've been expecting this for ages."

"If you don't want the experience—and if you haven't checked, this girl is level twenty-six—we can always give her to little sis," Kelsey said.

The woman chuckled. "That level might sound impressive for a slave, but my decrepitude outpaced the gain from levels long ago."

Anton stared, trying to figure out what Kelsey was talking about. *Little sis.* "You mean the *dungeon*? That's not better!"

"Oh, master, it is, truly." The old woman smiled up at him ingratiatingly. "For an end . . . it really is all I seek right now."

"So how many of you want the same thing?" Kelsey called out to the rest of the group, who stared at her with suspicious faces. "Just so you know, the other option on the table is smuggling you into the city and then take you by ship to Zamarra, where you'll be free, if penniless."

"So we get to starve?" one of them asked.

"I'm sure we can . . . hang on a minute." Kelsey held up one finger and there was silence for a few moments. "It seems we'll be able to implement some sort of program for broke immigrants. It will help if you have some sort of skill that you can use or teach, but no one will starve. Is that all right, Baron?"

She glanced back at Anton, and he caught himself from looking around to see who she was talking to.

"That's fine," he said. "I'm sure we can afford it with you helping."

"Fantastic," Kelsey said. "So, whadda you say, big guy? You ready for a trip to Zamarra?" she asked Tavik.

"Better than here," he agreed.

"That's good enough for me. Anton, can you give me a hand here?"

Kelsey produced the same pair of oversized shears that she'd used before. This time, she had Anton use them, cutting them near the pillar while she held the chains tight.

Bolt Cutters, Tool, Excellent Quality, Tier 2

Anton had seen the bolt cutters at work before, but he still marveled at how easily they sheared through the hardened iron without any magic. Tavik was impressed, too. Not just by their action, but by how Kelsey had made them appear out of thin air.

"Who *are* you people?" he asked, eyeing Kelsey warily.

Kelsey smiled. As soon as the chain was separated from the column, she made it vanish, taking with it the collar around Tavik's neck. Then she touched the shackles on his arms and legs, making them disappear as well.

"Just a group of footloose vagabonds, travelling the countryside, looking to do a good deed," she said. "Now, who wants to go to Zamarra?" she asked the main group.

The slaves discussed it among themselves as they were freed by the pair. One of them was deaf, and it took a while for them to understand the offer.

In the end, it was only the crippled Elara who insisted on being taken to the dungeon.

"Are you sure about this?" Anton asked. "It won't be painless. Whatever monsters the dungeon has are going to cut you up until you die."

"Oh, I can help there!" Kelsey said. Producing a small glass bottle, she handed it to Elara. "Pop a few pinches of this into your hand and breathe it in. You'll be out in no time and won't feel a thing."

"Wait," Anton said. "Don't you have numbing poisons as well? Couldn't they help deal with her pain?"

"They're poisons, Anton," Kelsey said patiently. "They're not meant for long-term use."

"This is fine, master," Elara said. "I'll take it just before I shuffle in."

"Take it now if you like," Kelsey said. "We can get you into the dungeon; we'll be making a visit before we leave."

"Then master, mistress, I will take my leave." Elena bowed her head and limped a little way away. The other slaves clustered around her, saying goodbye.

Anton took Kelsey aside. "I'm not happy with this," he whispered.

"It's her time," Kelsey said placatingly. "She'd never survive the trip back, and at least this way she goes out peacefully and usefully. More to the point . . ."

She called Aris over to join their little huddle. "Are you guys going to be okay with killing those smugglers?" Kelsey asked.

"I don't *like* it," Aris said, frowning. "But I can see the sense. They *are* criminals, after all . . . but are we any different?"

"We're righteous crusaders," Kelsey assured her, "forced into violence in order to bring about a greater good."

"I wish you believed that," Aris said, rolling her eyes. "But I do want to save these slaves. All of the slaves."

"There's a limit to how many we can rescue on this trip," Kelsey told her. "Baby steps."

Aris and Tavik fed and watered the prisoners while Anton and Kelsey looted the place. Kelsey seemed intent on taking literally everything that wasn't nailed down. Every barrel, every chair, every *bed*. Anton even caught her eyeing the window frames speculatively.

"Do we really need a barrel of . . . whatever that was?" he asked as she vanished another small barrel he'd handed her.

Kelsey held up a finger for a second. "Nails," she finally said. "No, we don't need it, but it won't go to waste. More to the point, the Elitrans won't have it."

"Is that really important?"

"When they come out here to find out what happened, they'll find all the bodies, all the slaves, all the supplies gone," Kelsey explained. "They'll be distracted by having to resupply this base from scratch, but more importantly, this will look as though they've been raided by a large, professional force."

"Maybe they'll think the dungeon did it."

"I doubt it. Monsters are mindless once they leave the dungeon, remember? If I'd been able to gather resources from outside, Kirido would not be the size it is today."

Anton shivered at the reminder that Kelsey had been an *entirely* malevolent force for most of her life. As opposed to a *partially* malevolent force now.

"So why is that important?" he asked.

"If they're looking for an army, they won't be looking for little old us," Kelsey said smugly. "And we get all this stuff!"

"The supplies, at least, will come in handy," Anton admitted. "Even if it's mostly meat."

"Obligate carnivores," Kelsey said thoughtfully. "It's like they're *trying* to be the bad guys. But they brought some bread for the prisoners. We just need to find some vegetables and it won't be a bad diet."

They made their way back to the courtyard. All the slaves were slowly eating the bread and meat that had been provided. Except for Elara, who was laid out on the ground.

"The powder . . . uh, worked," Aris said, gesturing towards her.

"Of course it did," Kelsey said. She knelt down beside Elara and retrieved the bottle clutched in her hand. Putting the old woman's arms on her chest, Kelsey slipped her hands under the unconscious figure and lifted her easily.

"Let's go say hi to the dungeon."

CHAPTER SIXTEEN

Graceland

The dungeon was locked up in the fort's basement. They'd found it when they were looting the place and had left it alone, although Kelsey had taken the iron gates that locked it off once she realized they could be detached from their hinges.

Now they approached with Kelsey carrying Elara in her arms. Knowing he needed to practice with this sort of thing, Anton activated his *Sense Mana* and looked at the dungeon entrance in a way he'd never bothered to do for the dungeon he'd grown up with.

He could see the demarcation between the dungeon and the outside world. A thin eggshell of magic, it offered no resistance to Kelsey's entrance, swirling around her like water and then reforming. The faintest touch of mana escaped as it did, dispersing behind her like smoke.

Anton followed Kelsey, creating his own puff of escaped mana. Once he was inside, he could see a faint residue of mana all around. It seemed to be disturbed by his presence, as small distortions rippled away from him. What effect that had, he couldn't say.

After some roughly carved steps down, the passageway extended on, sloping gently downward. It looked like a natural cave, the walls rounded as if carved by water. The tunnel was, however, completely dry.

"Let's just go in until we see some monsters," Kelsey said. "Then we'll leave Elara and back off."

"I still don't like this," Anton protested.

"If you've got another workable idea, I'm listening," Kelsey said. "Just think of it as being part of the cycle of—oh, hello."

"What?" Anton said, but Kelsey was looking at a patch of thin air.

"You must be the dungeon's fairy," she said. "Do you know Mel? Hey, don't—"

She grinned at Anton. "She handled that about as well as Mel did, when she found out that Suliel can see her."

"Suliel can see Mel?" Anton asked, confused.

"Yeah, I think it's due to the link we have," Kelsey said. "Though why I can see this dungeon's fairy . . . I was hoping that I'd feel some sort of connection that we could talk through, but no luck so far."

"You can't talk to the dungeon through the fairy?"

"I *could*, if she hadn't taken off." Kelsey shook her head. "Maybe she'll get over it."

"So you came down here not knowing whether you'd even be able to talk to the dungeon?"

"Worst case, I can just say stuff and she'll hear me. It would be nice to have some feedback, though."

They only had to take a few more steps before Anton could hear the shuffling of monsters. Frowning at his lapse, he quickly drew Chainbreaker.

"Don't charge them," Kelsey warned. "It won't be a problem if we kill a few, but that's not what we're here for."

"I don't want to drop my guard before we come up against unknown monsters," Anton replied, his eyes intent on the corridor up ahead.

"Geez, they're only going to be level two," Kelsey told him. "I have doubts they'll be able to finish off Elara here."

At that moment, the monsters came out of a side passage that branched up ahead. They were small, less than half Anton's size. Their elongated faces were scaled, and they carried daggers, holding them as if they were swords.

"Ah. Kobolds," Kelsey said disparagingly. "Well, it's *a* choice."

Ignoring the small humanoid lizards' approach, she took a few more steps forward and then laid Elara on the ground. She was more gentle with the action than Anton had expected.

"Right, and one more parting gift," she said. A crate appeared under her outstretched hand. "Let's back off."

Despite Kelsey's doubts, the kobolds did not have any difficulty in driving their rusty knives into Elara's unconscious body. It delayed them, though, long enough for the pair to back away, and then get out of the dungeon entirely. It took all of Anton's willpower to not rush in and try and save her.

"We'll need to give her a bit of time to process all that," Kelsey said. "Particularly if she really is just a child in terms of development."

"How long?" Anton asked curtly. Kelsey glanced at him but didn't say anything at first.

"About a minute," she said finally, "if they're on the ball. We'll give them that long, just to see if they are."

Anton nodded. The minute passed in awkward silence.

When they returned to the tunnel, the box and Elara were gone, with not even bloodstains remaining.

"Good, good. Nice hustle," Kelsey said. "But we're not done yet. Why don't you boot that fairy up here, so we can talk?"

The dungeon sent kobolds instead. Just as before, they charged up the passageway, waving their knives furiously. This time, though, Anton didn't hold back.

Three swings, three severed heads, three small bodies slumped to the floor. Kobolds moved faster than zombies and probably didn't need to be decapitated like zombies did, but that was how Anton had been trained.

"Don't *make* me come down there," Kelsey threatened the ceiling. "I'll—ah, there we are. Mel says hi. Do you want to tell me your name?"

Kelsey was talking to the air again, so Anton settled down, trying not to listen too closely to the one-sided conversation. It took a long time for Kelsey to explain that she was a dungeon, and longer still to explain the change in this dungeon's circumstances.

Then she got to the gift.

"Is that really a good idea?" Anton asked with alarm. "I thought you said explosives were dangerous!"

"That's kinda the point," Kelsey said. "I'm not sure if it will work, but it should prove a nice surprise for those core-stealing bastards."

"But you said she was a child!" Anton's knowledge of explosives was, at this point, entirely theoretical. But Kelsey's warnings had been graphic and detailed.

"She'll be fine, as long as she keeps them away from her core," Kelsey said dismissively and went back to telling the dungeon fairy how to trigger a detonator. From the sound of it, Kelsey wasn't relying on the explosives she supplied, confident that the dungeon would be able to make its own using magic.

Another pack of kobolds arrived during the discussion, making for a welcome distraction for Anton.

Then Kelsey was waving the empty air goodbye, and they exited the dungeon, leaving Anton's doubts behind them.

"How's everything been going up here?" Kelsey asked Aris.

"Oh, fine," Aris replied "I think we're ready to go, but I'm not sure that everyone is going to be able to make the trip back in one day."

"No worries," Kelsey said. "I've been thinking about that, and working on the solution!"

She led them all out into the courtyard.

"Unfortunately, my Dungeon Inventory space isn't big enough to do this in one go," she said. "So some assembly will be required."

With those words, she made a strangely shaped metal box appear on the ground.

"You should be able to lift this, Anton, can you give it a go? Just from here," she said. Anton shrugged and complied, lifting up the front of the box so she could attach some wheels to it. Then the back, so the entire contraption could rest on the oddly bulbous wheels.

"Now we attach the cabin . . ." Kelsey muttered as she went about her business. The work proceeded quickly, as every part and tool she needed appeared in her hand or at her feet. Soon, she had assembled two more strange carts, clearly intended to be towed behind the original device. They were narrower than the carts Anton was used to, with two rows of seats facing away from each other.

"These are a variant of the trolleys we're using to cart stuff around Kirido," Kelsey confided to Anton. "All aboard!" she called out to the group. "Next train to Rused, leaving now!"

With a bit more chivvying, everyone got aboard the vehicle. Aris had to ride on the trailers, while Anton got the dubious honor of riding in the front with Kelsey.

"But how does it go?" he asked. He'd already figured out that Kelsey wasn't going to magic horses—undead or otherwise—out of the air to pull it.

"It's a *kind* of magic," Kelsey said. She pushed a button and a horn sounded out of nowhere. "Toot toot!" she called. Then she pushed a pedal with her foot, and the train started moving.

Anton already knew it wasn't magic. He could *see* magic, and he couldn't see this. "How?" he asked again.

"I know, right?" Kelsey laughed as they picked up speed. "Magnets! How do they even work!" Soon they were moving as fast as a galloping horse, but so smoothly and silently that they could still talk easily. The Elitran road was better than the ones they had back home, but the strange wheels seemed to eat up every bump on the road, turning it into a gentle nudge.

Eventually, Kelsey's delight in the fact of their own motion eased, and she thought to respond to Anton more seriously.

"Really," she said, "It's just like a water pump, or a lever. There are certain physical principles, which, if you know what they are, you can leverage to do stuff."

"That makes no sense," Anton complained.

"Well . . . you know about levers, right? When you jam your sword into a lock to open it. That uses a physical principle that allows you to apply more force than you otherwise would. In this case, to my poor locks."

Anton rolled his eyes. "You use a dagger, not a sword," he said. "But all right."

"In this case, the principle is that if you have a magnet in a rotating electrical field, it provides a mechanical force that you can use to turn a wheel," Kelsey said, as if that explained everything.

"I don't know what any of those things are."

"A wheel?" Kelsey asked raising her eyebrows.

"I know what a wheel is," Anton said. "But an electikal field? A magnet?"

"Electrical," Kelsey corrected. "Electricity is what lightning is made of, and magnets are what make a compass work. But all you really need to know is that both of them are in there." She pointed at the box in front of them. "Doing work for us."

"I still don't understand."

Kelsey shrugged. "This sort of knowledge . . . it's built on other knowledge, brick by brick. That's why it would take too long to explain. All you need to know is: Pedal makes train go faster."

She twitched her foot, adding a bit of speed.

"Button makes toot toot sound," she said, sounding the horn again.

"And wheel changes the direction." She didn't demonstrate this one, but Anton had already figured out the connection.

"What if I *wanted* to spend the time to learn all this?" Anton asked.

"You could, but you'd have to take time away from adventuring," Kelsey pointed out. "I don't want to Obi-Wan Kenobi you, but we really do need you grinding levels as fast as you can."

"Obi-Wan Kenobi?" Anton asked despite himself. Kelsey grinned, then put on a distressed expression.

"Help me, Obi-Wan Kenobi, you're my only hope!" she said, raising the pitch of her voice. Then she laughed at the expression on his face.

"That doesn't explain anything!"

"Fine." Kelsey rolled her eyes. "Obi-Wan was a guy, and he was the only hope for a particular princess, just like *you* are the only hope for Cheia. Does that spell it out for you?"

"So I'm like this Obi-Wan guy, is what you're saying."

"Yeah. But I didn't want to put a bunch of pressure on you is all. Breaking these slaves out, chasing after those merchants on the mainland . . . it's a big ask, but we can take it one step at a time. One level at a time."

Anton stared forward down the road.

"Did Obi-Wan ever have to kill some smugglers, just so they would keep quiet about what he was doing?"

"Oh sure," Kelsey said. "He was killing criminals all the damn time."

CHAPTER SEVENTEEN

Kill the Poor

s there really no other way?" Anton asked at the last minute. Their group was huddled just a little way from the cave. Kelsey's strange cart had been vanished away, and the group of freed slaves was just waiting for the way to be cleared.

Kelsey gave him a serious look.

"If you're just feeling squeamish, I can take care of it for you," she said. "But if you're not cool with it at all, we can go over the options again."

Anton hesitated. He *didn't* want to spoil their chances of rescuing his fellow villagers. Kelsey's other suggestions for getting the former slaves back into the city had ranged from unlikely to horrifying.

"I could do it?" Aris suggested. "It might be easier, with guns?"

"It's not the same," Anton said, swallowing. "I know you've killed people, but they were all at a distance. It's different when they're in front of you."

"If you say so," Aris said doubtfully.

"Why me?" Anton asked rhetorically. Then, more seriously, "Why *are* you letting me make this decision, Kelsey?"

"Hmm?"

"I can see how impatient you are," Anton said. "Those guys are just another tick on your checklist. So why are you waiting for me?"

Kelsey shrugged. "I don't have a stake in this, remember? This is *your* quest. I'm just tagging along to keep you happy."

"Is that really true?" Anton asked. "You went to all this trouble, just to keep Aris and me happy?"

"It hasn't been a huge imposition," Kelsey demurred. "And I got to go out into the world, see new things. I'm pretty happy with how it's turned out."

Anton's eyes narrowed with suspicion. He was getting better at reading Kelsey. "You're not telling me everything."

Kelsey raised her eyebrows. "I think," she said gently, "that you're distracting yourself from the hard decision at hand. It's almost sunset."

"Fine," Anton said. She wasn't wrong. He gave his mind one last chance to come up with another plan but drew a blank. "Let's go."

The longer shadows of the dying day made the cave harder to find. Anton started to turn back, thinking that they might have missed it, but Kelsey kept him going, sure of her navigation. When it finally appeared in front of him and he stepped inside, one of the smugglers was waiting for him.

"Where's the other one?" the man asked.

"She'll be through a bit later," Anton said grimly. "Can we get through?"

He held up a silver coin.

The man brightened at the sight and hastened to collect his earnings. "Yeah, go on through," he said, gesturing at the back of the cave.

To Anton's surprise, the man followed him into the tunnel.

"You're not waiting for Aris?" he asked.

"I'll leave the slab open," the smuggler grunted, tapping a slab near the entrance that did not look at all moveable. "Ya need me to signal the other end to open."

Kelsey gave him a significant look, and Anton forced himself to relax. Kelsey had warned him to make sure both ends of the tunnel were open before he struck.

"It'd be a bit embarrassing if we killed those guys and then didn't have any way to open the tunnel," she'd said.

This time, Kelsey pulled out her torch and used it to light their way through the tunnel. Their guide looked at it suspiciously.

"Get that in the dungeon, did you?" he asked.

Kelsey looked at him. "Dungeon's closed," she said mildly.

The man snorted. "Didn't come out with it, must have picked it up from somewhere," he pointed out.

Anton knew the truth was different. She hadn't shown it before, because she hadn't wanted word spreading about her "technology." Now that the smugglers were—

Anton paused his thought as it ran to an uncomfortable place. Being *silenced* had a better sound to it than being *murdered*. He went with that.

Now that the smugglers were being silenced, Kelsey was being more free with what she showed them.

The smuggler wasn't done, though. "What else didya get?" he asked.

"Nothing," Kelsey said. "Certainly not a whole pile of gold. Or gems."

Anton looked back at Kelsey and saw the grin on her face. *We already have to kill these guys, does she have to mess with them as well?* he thought.

Then they were at the ladder, crammed into the small open space around the shaft. The smuggler pulled a rope that Anton hadn't noticed before. Looking up, he saw that it ran through a smaller hole that had been drilled into the cave's ceiling. The smuggler pulled it three times, paused, and then twice more.

After a short pause, there was a grinding sound from above. The smuggler licked his lips nervously.

"I reckon," he said, "you should be paying a tax on what you took out."

"That wasn't what we agreed," Kelsey said. "And we didn't take anything out."

"Right," the man said, but Anton could tell from the tone that the man didn't believe her.

"We paid for passage, and you won't be getting a penny more. Go on up, Anton, I'll be right behind you."

Anton felt a twinge of fear from his geas at the thought of leaving her behind, but the shaft wasn't that long. He nodded and started climbing up.

He was about halfway up when he heard a scuffle below.

"Hey! Hands off the merchandise, buddy!"

"Jeb! These guys are loaded. Grab that one when he comes up! I've got the girl!"

Oh. That was what she was doing, Anton thought. He felt like such a fool. Looking up, he saw the unwashed criminal was sober enough to produce a dagger at his compatriot's words.

"Jus' come on up, kid, nice and slow," the smuggler said.

Kelsey would be fine, Anton thought. She was probably waiting for him to get to the top before she made a move. He should go up and secure the exit. Attacking a man at the top of a ladder you were climbing would have been foolhardy for most, but Anton wasn't everybody.

He stepped off the ladder and braced one foot on the side of the shaft. An awkward pose for most, but Anton had *Spider Climb* to ensure his footing. He drew a dagger of his own. Quarters were going to be too close to easily use Chainbreaker.

The man above frowned at his lack of compliance, but Anton was a bit too far away for him to fear. He was well out of range.

"Give it up, kid. You're not gonna—"

Thanks, Kelsey. Having them try to rob us does make it easier, Anton thought. *Leaping Attack.*

He shot out of the shaft like one of Kelsey's bullets. His target was surprised, but he already had his dagger out and pointed at his enemy. He barely had to move to skewer Anton.

Uncanny Dodge.

Anton twisted in midair, curving around the man's stab. His own dagger buried itself in the man's stomach.

There was the distinctive sound of one of Kelsey's "silenced" guns from below.

Anton's leap didn't take him entirely out of the shaft, but his feet clung to the sides, and he was able to easily scramble out. The smuggler offered no further resistance, dropping his dagger and clutching at the one that Anton had left in him.

"Sorry," Anton said. The man had tried to rob him, but that thought only helped with Anton's guilt. It didn't erase it. He picked up the man's dagger. It was Tier One trash.

"Sorry," Anton said again. He finished the man off with a thrust to the chest. *I never even found out his name.*

"You all right up there?" Kelsey called out from below.

"Yeah."

"Well, throw that guy down here. I'm all finished as well."

Anton sighed. He recovered his dagger and sent the corpse back down to Kelsey. Then he stopped fighting his fear and let it take him back down.

The body was already gone by the time he arrived.

"Did you secure the building?" Kelsey asked.

He shook his head. "Too nervous," he replied.

Kelsey looked up the shaft speculatively. "It should be fine, if we're quick," she said. "Let's get the others."

It was a short walk from their hiding place to the cave, and from there into the city, but some of the ex-slaves didn't find it easy. Kelsey provided a pair of crutches to the lame one, but the ladder was too much of an obstacle for some of them. Two of the older slaves weren't able to grip the rungs strongly enough to support themselves. One of them kept forgetting what he was doing and stepped off the ladder.

Kelsey took it all in stride. She produced a rope and harness, and she and Anton hauled up the ones who weren't able to make it on their own.

"Now," Kelsey said, once they were all gathered in the smuggler's front room, "you can't go out looking like that. It's twilight, so no one is going to see you clearly, but people will notice a bunch of raggedy-ass ex-slaves shambling along. First thing, did everybody take new classes?"

There were murmurs of assent around the room. Anton knew that while he could see the entire path of a person he identified, most identification traits only showed the current class.

"Anybody get anything interesting?" Kelsey asked.

"I got Murderous Lover," Tavik said. "I . . . didn't take it, though."

Anton wondered who would take a class that advertised such a horrible crime. It was probably a Rare one though, so maybe some might be tempted.

Other than Tavik, no one had anything to report. Tavik had taken Warrior, going back to Tier One, and others had managed to find their way into various crafting classes. Kelsey waited patiently for them all to finish reporting.

"Okay! Next is disguises." She started handing out robes to each of them.

"These are mostly hooded, but some of you can get away without wearing hoods, and if we were *all* hooded, it would look like I was starting a cult."

"Will they fit?" Enara, one of the recipients, asked.

"Yep! The one I'm handing you is sized for you, so no swaps."

"Did you make all of these?" Anton asked. In the glare of Kelsey's torch, now held by Aris, he could see that the robes were varying shades of brown, grey, and deep blue.

Kelsey winked at him. "Courtesy of the Boneworks Clothing Emporium," she said. "I knew we'd need them, so I took some approximate measurements, and my boys have been working on them all day. No mass production here, it's all artisanal."

Murmurs of appreciation were coming from the group as they each tried on their cloaks. Some of them needed help with even the most basic of tasks, but they all appreciated the clothes once they were on.

"So soft!"

"So warm!"

Anton wasn't sure what the cloaks were made of, but it certainly seemed of better quality than what slaves normally wore.

"Should we wait until it's darker before leaving?" Aris asked.

"Nah, this is the right time. There's still a little natural light, and people are going about, headed off to dinner parties or the entertainment district," Kelsey said. "Our cloaks will fit right in."

It proved to be so. Tavik helped them shepherd the group to the safe house, managing to avoid being accosted by any random guards. The house was still as they had left it, and Kelsey's newly installed key got them in the front door.

Producing more water and cold rations, Kelsey urged them all to eat more, and then rest for the night on the simple woven pallets that she provided.

"You'll stay here for tonight and tomorrow," she told them. "The night after that, we'll get you loaded onto the ship and heading back to Zamarra."

Anton frowned. "We still have to get the others," he said.

"Yeah," Kelsey replied. "We're doing that tonight."

CHAPTER EIGHTEEN

Burning Down the House

O kay, here's our map of the city," Kelsey said. She laid a large piece of paper down on the table. Anton, Aris, and Zaphar looked down at it. They had left the slaves to rest for the night and had met back up at the inn.

"Where did you get this?" Anton wondered. The map had a curious look to it. Some of the areas were detailed, while others were just sketched out. The Administrative Compound was quite detailed and included all the details that Zaphar had given them.

"I've had a draftsman skelly sketching according to my instructions since we got here," Kelsey said.

"Um, excuse me, but what does that mean?" Zaphar asked.

"Draftsman? It's a fancy word for someone who draws. I don't know what the word is in Elitran."

"No, no. I mean, yes, I did not know that word, but the whole statement, it makes no sense."

"You don't want to know," Anton butted in, stalling Kelsey who was already grinning.

"That's probably true," Kelsey agreed. "If you learn too much, we might need you to . . . commit more fully to our little endeavor."

Zaphar rolled his eyes. "I'm already . . . I've already committed crimes, you know? I stand to lose my life if we're caught."

"Even so . . ." Kelsey said meaningfully.

Anton cleared his throat. "It's more to do with how you get five more questions every time Kelsey answers one. Just let it go."

Kelsey cackled. "It's a fair cop, but society is to blame."

"If you're done teasing the new guy, can we get on with . . . whatever this is?" Aris asked.

"Sure thing!" Kelsey said brightly. She pointed at the map. "Here is where the prisoners are being kept. There are locked doors here, here, and here."

She pointed to inside the building, the front of the building, and the front of the compound.

"And there are guards here,"—she pointed at the front of the prison again—"here,"—she swept her finger over the interior of the compound and finally pointed at the front gate—"and here."

Anton looked at Zaphar, who nodded in confirmation.

"Now," Kelsey continued, "the plan Rashaq was trying to sell was that we bribe most of the guards but take out the ones guarding the actual jail."

Zaphar nodded again. "That way he gets—gets rid of a few honest guards."

"Exactly," Kelsey said. "Then the bribed guards look the other way as we make our way out of the compound with just the three slaves we're looking for. We head down to the docks and sail away."

"You think he's going to tip off the Bey and there will be guards waiting for us at the docks," Anton said.

"And aren't we going to take *all* of the slaves?" Aris asked.

"Yeah, we won't be following his plan," Kelsey said. "We're going to take *this* route instead."

She ran her finger from the back of the prison, through the back of the compound, and into the city. She stopped right about where their safe house was.

"There are two high walls blocking that route," Zaphar objected. "There aren't any gates to pass through."

Kelsey grinned. "Where we're going, we don't need gates," she said. "Let me tell you what you're going to do."

"This would be so much easier if we had remote detonators," Kelsey muttered. "Relying on timers is a little nerve-wracking."

"These aren't remote detonators?" Anton asked softly. It wasn't as if they were supposed to detonate up close; Kelsey had been most particular about that.

"These are *timed* detonators," Kelsey explained. "A remote detonator, I could just push a button and have it go off when I wanted. I've not been developing wireless as fast as I could have, though."

Anton didn't respond, focusing on seating the charge firmly into what Kelsey had called "the goop." The sticky, soft substance hardened quickly and left the charge sticking to the wall.

"Up until recently it was so much easier to just run wires to anywhere I might want to send a signal," Kelsey explained. "I thought that I could wait until I got transistors before really developing that, but they've proved . . . difficult."

She knows I haven't the faintest clue of what she's talking about, right? Anton wondered. He was pretty sure that some of her words weren't even in a language he was familiar with.

Kelsey handed him another packet of goop. He frowned a question, and she held up a small metal barrel in answer.

"Stick this next to the charge," she murmured. "It'll give it an extra *boost*."

Anton shrugged. He wasn't sure why the charges at *this* end of the compound, which Kelsey had described as diversionary, would need an extra boost, but it was her plan and they were her devices.

Moving quietly to avoid the patrol, they found another secluded corner to place a second set of explosives, before moving over to the prison.

"Fifteen minutes to go," Kelsey said. "Nice timing."

Aris was waiting for them in the hiding place they'd scouted earlier.

"The prisoners are still in the cells we thought they were," she reported. "So I set the charges where we discussed."

"Zaphar is in there?" Kelsey asked. Aris nodded.

"Then all we have to do is wait," Kelsey said. "Ten minutes."

They waited nervously, the tension not at all lowered by the occasional time report from Kelsey.

"Thirty seconds," she finally said. "Keep in mind that no mechanical device is perfect; they might be off by a few seconds. Twenty . . . fifteen . . . ten . . . five . . ."

The *crump* of the first detonation startled the two humans, even though they'd been expecting it. They couldn't see the results, but the warm glow of firelight spread across the compound.

Two of the four prison guards ran across their field of vision, heading towards the explosion.

"Not ideal," Kelsey admitted. "But that was why we had the—"

The *crump* of another diversionary explosion cut her off. Shouts were beginning to sound from the other end of the compound. No further guards ran out, though. Kelsey *tsk*ed.

"No big deal, I guess. There's only two left. Now cover your ears and open your mouths."

Kelsey had mentioned this before, and she was following her own instructions, so Anton and Aris went along with it, still not entirely sure if she was joking or not. The thunderous noise and crashing shockwave that hit them as the charge placed on the wall went off disabused them of the notion.

"Another one?" The guard came around the corner and stared at the hole in the compound wall. Anton would have rated the wall to stand up to at least a few blows from a siege weapon, but a single explosion had punched a hole so big that three people could walk through it.

The guard stared at the hole, ignoring the trio. To be fair, Anton and Aris were staring at the hole as well. Kelsey had to give Aris a little shake to snap her out of it.

"Aris? Shoot the guard, would you? I think we can stop worrying about making noise."

Aris blinked and then remembered that they were on a schedule. She looked over at the guard and drew her pistol.

"*Sure Shot*," she whispered as the gun fired. The guard gave a short, guttural scream, and fell to the ground.

Knowing there was another one, Aris lifted her sights slightly. Sure enough, the final guard came around the corner, attracted by the sound of his partner dying.

"*Sure Shot*," Aris said again, and another guard fell.

She stared at the fallen courl, and the hands that had been so steady under the influence of her trait started to shake.

"You were right," she whispered, "It is different when it's close."

Anton had been broken out of his trance by her first shot. Now he stepped close and embraced her.

"Very touching," Kelsey said, "but we've got one minute more before the final charges go off, and the shockwaves were a *little* more powerful than I thought they'd be. We should move off a little."

She chivvied them around the corner, out in the open if anyone had been watching. From here they had a good view of the fires that had been started.

"A diversion?" Anton exclaimed. "Kelsey, you're going to burn the city down!"

"That would be a good diversion . . . but I don't think it will come to that," Kelsey said.

Aris put her guns away and returned Anton's embrace. They both watched the chaos unfolding for another moment.

"Okay, hands on ears again," Kelsey said. This time the shockwave was much reduced.

When they went back around the corner, they found the damage to the walls was just as extensive. The cells containing prisoners had been opened to the air. It took a little while for the captives to stumble out. Zaphar dropped off the roof before they managed to collect themselves.

"They can . . . they can just walk out?" he said, stunned at what had happened.

"Elira!" Aris called out to the first person to poke their head out of the prison. She was stepping gracefully over the rubble when she heard Aris's call and twisted her head to see Aris running towards her.

"Aris?" she asked. "What are you doing here?"

"Looking for you, silly," Aris said, catching the girl in an embrace.

"Aris? Anton?" Another voice called out as Galen stumbled out of the hole. The burly blacksmith's apprentice looked shocked, probably as much from their presence as their sudden release.

More reserved than Aris, but still glad to see his childhood friend, Anton stepped forward. "Galen," he said, emotion choking him.

"What? How?" Galen said as he stepped out. "What's going on?"

"We came to rescue you. All of you," Anton said. Galen's face fell.

"A lot of us got taken away," he said. He looked guiltily over at Aris. "Cheia . . ."

"We know," Anton assured him. "We've got leads on where they went, and we'll be chasing after them."

"Assuming we get out of here, that is," Kelsey put in. She clapped her hands loudly. "Okay, anybody who wants to go back to Zamarra, let's get moving! That distraction won't last forever!"

"Who is *she*?" Galen asked. Anton sighed.

"It's a long story," he said.

With a bit of shouting and shoving, Kelsey got them all moving. Both the captives from Kirido and the other recently taken slaves. Most of them were from nearby countries like the Ett Confederacy and were quickly promised that they could either live free in Kirido or find their way back home from there.

All of the captives had simple metal collars to show their status. Kelsey quickly took care of this before they left, grasping each one and making it disappear. If her pale skin and strange manner weren't already making people ask questions, that would have.

"Not the time!" was her answer to most queries. "We can explain things once you're all safe."

Too slowly for Anton's liking, but reasonably quickly, the group got organized and started heading out, led by Aris. Kelsey hung back at the rear, and Anton was forced to join her. She called Zaphar over.

"Well, kid, I guess this is where we part ways." She dumped a small stack of gold coins into his hand. He goggled at it.

"This, this is more than we agreed."

"I know," Kelsey said. "I want you to think about how lucky your big score was, and not anything like following us to find out where our safe house is."

"Oh. Then this, this is goodbye?" The thief sounded disappointed.

"'Fraid so," Kelsey said. "Unless . . . you were interested in making more of a commitment?"

"What do you mean?" Zaphar asked cautiously.

"We've got other places to go after this, more slaves to free. We could use a good cat burglar. If you come with us, you'll get more money, more chances to feel good about yourself. And you'll get some answers to all those questions you've been holding back."

"I—I—" Zaphar stammered. He looked at Anton's confused face. "This is . . . one of those situations where I have to decide right away?"

"Yep. You walk away, and if we see you again . . . did you see what Aris did to those guards?"

Reminded, Anton glanced back and saw that Kelsey, at some point, had disappeared the bodies. Another mystery for the authorities to solve, he supposed.

"I did," Zaphar said slowly. "Answers, you say?"

"Like Anton said, I can't promise you'll like them," Kelsey answered, grinning.

"I think . . . I think I need to know them, regardless," Zaphar said. "I'll come with you, if you'll have me."

CHAPTER NINETEEN

Buy Out the Bar

Come tomorrow morning, you guys are done," Kelsey said. "I don't need anything more from you, so you can just hang out here until then. That's also how long the rooms are paid for, so after that, you're on your own."

Kusec glared down at the pale girl. "You *were* the ones who hit the Administrative Compound," he said slowly. "Everyone's talking about it."

"I couldn't possibly comment, but I'll remind you that talking about your suspicions is forbidden, under penalty of pain, for another twenty-four hours."

Grimacing at the memory, Kusec shook his head. "You won't get away with this," he stated. "That ship is big and fast, but the Navy's ships are faster. They'll catch you."

"Thanks for the concern," Kelsey said, grinning. "I'll take it under advisement."

Turning on her heel, she strode out of the room, Anton at her side. Entering her room across the hall, they almost ran into Aris, packing up the rest of their gear.

"Got everything? Then let's go," Kelsey said.

"This room is a lot more comfortable than the other place is going to be," Aris said mournfully.

"Don't worry, we won't be staying there for long," Kelsey assured her. "But we're wanted criminals now. We can't be too easy to find."

"I thought you said the authorities wouldn't know who did it?" Anton asked.

"The authorities no, but Rashaq must have a few ideas," Kelsey said.

The city was as bustling as ever. The only sign of the attack last night was the presence of additional guards, scowling suspiciously at the passersby.

"This isn't the way back to the other—the safe house," Aris said.

"No, we've got a few errands to run," Kelsey said. "We need to pick up some supplies, and we need to chase up those other merchants."

Anton frowned. "Rashaq was there when we got those addresses," he said. "We should probably stay away from them if we want to avoid Rashaq."

Kelsey grinned a tight little smile. "I never said we were avoiding Rashaq."

The first address went without incident. Posing as an interested buyer, Kelsey managed to get the city where the merchant (and her wares) could be found. The second shop was also proceeding to plan when Anton, keeping watch outside, noticed something concerning.

"Mistress," he said. Both he and Aris were posing as slaves, wearing recycled slave collars from the outpost. He hadn't thought it would work, as both of them were not dressed in anything like a slave. Kelsey had said, though, that as long as the collars were visible, no one would see anything else.

Now she looked to see what he was pointing at. Two large courls had stopped outside. They were barely visible from inside, but the flow of traffic had given them a wide berth, attracting Anton's attention. Kelsey just smirked and finished up with the merchant's clerk.

"You can take those off now," she said as they stepped outside. Anton and Aris pulled their collars off with some relief. They looked solid, but Kelsey had rigged them to come apart with a firm pull. They got a few stares from the crowd and concerned frowns from the thugs that had stepped in their way, but Kelsey ignored the looks, and Anton followed her lead.

The thug's face twitched, trying to hold two thoughts in his head at the same time. He *wanted* to ask about the collars, but that *wasn't* why he'd been sent. It only took a second for duty to win out over curiosity.

"Boss wants to see you," he finally said.

"That would be Rashaq, I take it?" Kelsey said easily. When they nodded, she smiled. "Let's go, then, we wouldn't want to keep him waiting."

One of the thugs led the way, while the other fell in behind the group, keeping watch. Anton thought to use *Delver's Discernment* on the two of them.

Yusuf Kaya, Level 14, Cudgeler, Brawler/Cudgeler
Emre Efe, Level 18, Warrior/Enforcer/Bonecracker

He was slightly out-leveled, but they weren't great classes. Anton thought he could probably beat them on most abilities, except for Agility, which the courls were famous for. It would help if he had a weapon, but Kelsey was holding on to it for now.

He held on to Aris's hand, for reassurance. She gave him a nervous smile in return.

Kelsey was looking at everything except their guards. She was looking in all directions, even spinning around and walking backward for a few steps. It made the thugs nervous, but she didn't try to hare off, so they slowly relaxed.

Anton knew better than to ask what she thought she was doing.

Then they were back at the casino. Since it was still early in the day, the place was deserted except for Rashaq's staff. They were led inside without any fuss and directed to sit in a booth. One of the thugs stayed to watch them while the other went to get the boss. They weren't kept waiting for long.

"Emre, why is this one still carrying her weapons?" was the first thing he asked. Emre shrugged.

"They're just those weird club-daggers, boss," he said. "Didn't seem worth it."

Rashaq scowled. "What weapons were the others carrying?" he asked.

"Nothing," Emre stated confidently. "Well, just the knives."

Rashaq stared at the man. "We know she can make money appear out of nowhere," he said. "You think she can't do that with weapons?"

Emre shrugged again. "I don't know what you want *me* to do about that," he complained. "Besides, isn't that why you've got all"—he waved at the dangerous-looking people around the room—"that?"

"What's all this talk of weapons?" Kelsey asked innocently. "Surely you don't suspect us of perpetrating violence?"

Anton was glad they hadn't been served drinks. He would have choked on his.

Rashaq glared at her. "I *know* you hit the Compound."

"Wow," Kelsey said. "That would be pretty impressive if it was just little old me. I heard it was a squad of mages."

That had, in fact, been one of the wilder rumors that they'd heard on the streets. Another was that the Tiatian Navy had shown up and the attack was from their siege weapons, fired *over the island*. Rumor was getting pretty wild.

"Don't play me for a fool," Rashaq spat. "The prisoners you came for are gone, and *nothing else is*. I don't know how you managed it, but unless you pay up, you're going straight to the Bey as a goodwill gift."

"Gosh, I thought we had a better relationship than *that*," Kelsey said. "Didn't we pay you all that money?"

"I made some money from you," Rashaq allowed. "But when you start to disrupt the city, you make yourself more trouble than your gold is worth."

"So you don't want my gold?"

"Let's see just how much of it you have," Rashaq growled. "If you want to get out of here unharmed."

"Well, that is very intimidating," Kelsey said agreeably. "I think I've got something here to satisfy all of your concerns, though."

She held up one hand, and a small, round object appeared in it. Not entirely round—there was some kind of . . . lid, perhaps? Held in place with a pin attached to a ring?

"What is that?" Rashaq asked suspiciously, echoing Anton's thoughts.

"In the words of my people, it would be described as . . . *Duck under the table when I throw*," Kelsey said, switching to Tiatian as she pulled the pin out.

Either Rashaq spoke Tiatian, or he reacted to the sudden looks of alarm on Anton and Aris's faces. He stepped back with a shout. It didn't do him any good, though; Kelsey had already thrown the object.

Her enhanced strength meant that even though she was just using her wrist, it was a good throw. Not a fast, flat throw meant to hit someone hard. She lobbed it, as high as the ceiling allowed, over the heads of everyone gathered around the table.

Anton couldn't see where it went, since he had ducked down, but he was pretty sure it landed behind the bar. He became *absolutely certain* of that a second later, when the bar exploded.

If the smoke, fire, and noise of the explosion weren't enough, the weapon turned half of the bar into flying splinters that shot out at everyone in the room. For most, they were an annoyance. Some unlucky few were injured. All of them, though, were instantly, completely distracted.

Kelsey shot up from her seat. Using one leg, she *kicked* the booth's table at Rashaq. One hand dropped Chainbreaker in Anton's lap.

"Time to grind out some XP!" she shouted.

Rashaq gave out a cry of pain as the table hit him, but he didn't go down. The table dropped down, revealing his bloody, angry face.

"Get—" he yelled before he was interrupted by Aris's gunshot. He twisted out of the way when he saw her aim at him, and the shot took him in the shoulder.

Anton rushed out of the booth, Chainbreaker in his hand. He needed to establish a front line, allowing Aris to fire freely. Emre was the closest, already bringing up two batons to block his strike.

Kelsey cackled and threw another of her . . . things towards the entrance. This one didn't explode but started spewing out a thick black smoke.

Emre managed to block Anton's strike but got an alarmed look on his face when he saw how deeply Chainbreaker cut into his weapons. Batons were supposed to be a good defense against swords, but everything was relative. A Tier One or Two wouldn't be good for long against the Tier Three sword.

Aris fired again, forcing the thugs to hold back. Rashaq wasn't down, but he had pulled back. Anton could hear him shouting for medical attention, for crossbowmen, and for everyone to just kill them already.

Kelsey threw another smoke weapon to the opposite corner of the large room. Now everyone was being hemmed in by two walls of slowly advancing, choking smoke. Anton felt a chill. It looked as though Kelsey had a *plan*, which was much more frightening than her acting up randomly.

The thugs were pressing forward more desperately, encouraged by the smoke and Rashaq's shouting. That just made them better targets for Aris to pick off, as they tried to get past Anton.

He was fighting two of them now, but Emre had reached the limit of his weapon's durability. This time, when he blocked Anton, the sword cleaved through the baton and sliced through the bone of his arm. Emre screamed and fell back, freeing up space for another grim-faced enforcer.

Anton was hard-pressed, but his opponents so far hadn't been very skilled. He was able to keep them at bay without using any traits. Stuck where he was, guarding the approach to Aris, he couldn't use his favorite trick, *Leaping Attack*, but between his armor and *Stone Skin*, the thug's blunt weapons were having trouble damaging him.

That changed when his latest opponent dived under his guard, in what looked like a suicidal move. Just before the man hit the ground, his twin dagger blurred, changing to an upward trajectory, headed right for Anton's stomach.

Uncanny Dodge, Anton thought desperately, triggering the trait. His body performed its own unnatural gyration, twisting out of the way of the daggers—and right into the club swing of his other opponent.

Anton gasped in pain at the blow, but it didn't feel like anything was broken. The man with the daggers had collapsed on the ground, his chance lost. Anton brought up his sword for a return blow at the cudgeller and stomped on the face of the dagger-man. Another shot from Aris dropped a man trying to flank him.

Then the smoke was almost upon them. Anton's opponents started coughing and fell back. It put them deeper in the smoke but out of range of his attacks. Before Anton could start choking, Kelsey stepped up next to him.

"Here, put this on your face," she said, her voice muffled through the mask she was wearing. An identical mask was being held up in front of him.

Kelsey guided the mask on and then deftly fastened it. He looked over to see that Aris was already wearing her mask.

"What now?" he asked.

He couldn't see Kelsey's face, but he knew she was grinning that wide crazy grin.

"Now?" she said, "Now we teach these low lives the meaning of regret."

CHAPTER TWENTY

Which Way Does That Old Pony Run?

ARIS

They ran out of the building coughing from the smoke, just like the noncombatants (and a few of the smarter combatants). Kelsey had confiscated their masks just before they left, and the sting of the acrid smoke made Aris feel sorry for those who'd had to breathe it all along.

Kelsey was coughing now, just like them, but Aris was pretty sure she didn't need to breathe and was just doing it to allay suspicion. She focused on clinging to Anton so that they didn't get separated in the press as they made their way away from the building.

A crowd was already forming, mixed between gawkers and the start of a bucket brigade. Aris was surprised to see such public-mindedness in this rundown part of town, but she supposed that no matter where you lived, you didn't want to see your house burning down.

Their efforts would be wasted. Kelsey's strange weapons had made thick, choking, smoke but no fire. Probably not dangerous in small doses, but anyone who was caught in it would make it a priority to get *out*. They didn't stop moving until they'd moved well away from both the gawkers and the people fleeing.

"I think he got away," Kelsey said, disappointment coloring her tone. "I'm pretty sure I winged him, but I didn't see him when we were getting out."

"Does it matter? We got away unhurt." Aris said. Anton had done an amazing job of keeping the thugs away from them, which had let Kelsey and herself deliver a devastating hail of fire. She'd even made a level.

You have reached Level 7.
Please allocate 2 free Ability points.

There was no trait to choose this time, so she just accepted the level and put her points into Dexterity.

Applying Benefits for Level 1
Toughness + 1
Agility + 1
Dexterity + 1
Perception + 1
Willpower + 1
Free points assigned to: Dexterity

She quickly checked her status, while Kelsey lectured them on how to crime.

Aris Lucina, Original Gunslinger (Level 7)
Overall Level: 12
Paths: Scullion/(broken), Original Gunslinger
Strength: 9
Toughness: 10
Agility: 14
Dex: 14
Perception: 20
Will: 18
Charisma: 11
Traits
Eye for Freshness
Heat Resistance
Sonic Resistance
Sure Shot
Trick Shot

"It's not great, because he knows at least *something* about us and what we're doing. He's probably going to run to whoever is in charge of law enforcement . . . at which point we'll find out *what* he knows."

"Maybe you shouldn't have engineered that confrontation, then," Anton said. Aris could hear worry in his voice, but also a bit of smugness at the thought that Kelsey might have made a mistake.

"Kelsey didn't engineer that, though," Aris pointed out. "He dragged *us* off the streets."

"She knew that he would, though," Anton explained. "And that he'd try to lean on us."

"Really?" Aris asked, looking at Kelsey. "They were tricked?" Now she did feel bad for them. She'd thought that she was fighting in self-defense, but it didn't feel as pure now.

"I'm not as good a shot as I thought," Kelsey said, pouting. "I do well enough on the range, but in actual combat . . . Aris makes this look too easy."

Aris frowned. By now Aris knew Kelsey well enough to know that a lack of an answer *was* an answer, just not the one you wanted.

"Don't feel too bad for them," Anton reassured her. "They *were* all trying to kill us, and the only one that was tricked was Rashaq. And *he* got away."

"Don't remind me," Kelsey said sourly.

Aris thought about it for a bit. "Then shouldn't we warn Captain Tkukkuk? He brought us here; he's sure to be associated with us."

"We can have one of the urchins pass him a message," Kelsey said dismissively. "We already cut the cat brothers loose, so the only things we have to worry about are our safe house and our contract with Captain al-Nazari."

Aris gave Kelsey a reproachful look. It seemed to her that a warning to a friend that they might be arrested was the sort of thing you delivered in person. It *was* a risk though, so she let it go.

"Let's go then," Kelsey said. "We need to get back to the safe house, and we need to make extra sure that we aren't followed."

They hadn't been gone long, but the derelict house was already showing improvements. Debris had been gathered and thrown in the backyard. Some of the stored water and the slaves' old clothes had been used to clean the floors.

Most of the former slaves were resting on the bedding that Kelsey had supplied, but a few of them were waiting around impatiently.

"Finally! We were getting worried," Galen said when they entered. "Is everything all right?"

"Everything's fine," Kelsey assured him. "Work on your patience, though; we're not doing anything until night falls."

Galen looked at Kelsey doubtfully but sighed in frustration when Anton nodded in agreement.

"I was stuck in that cell for so long, and now I'm just waiting in a room that isn't much better," he complained. "I just want to *do* something."

Kelsey raised an eyebrow. "Sure," she said. She produced a device that looked a bit like Aris's guns. A closer look, and Aris realized that she'd actually seen it before, when the skeleton had installed the new lock on the door.

"Get some practice with this," Kelsey said. "It's called a drill, but you'll be using it as a screwdriver."

The gun-like bit was attached to a large box with a flexible cord, and Kelsey showed him how to carry it with a strap over his shoulder. Then she gave him some "self-tapping screws" and told him to try them out.

"There's got to be something in this scrap heap that you can fix with a screw," she said, "and there'll be more work for it on the boat."

Some of the younger slaves expressed interest in the tool and came over to see what Galen was doing. She left them to it, going over to where Anton and Aris were sitting.

She sat down next to them, cross-legged with her back to the wall.

"Now," she said, "we just have to wait and see if Karim sells us out."

"You seem pretty calm about that possibility," Aris said.

Kelsey shrugged. "He got a taste of what it's like to cross us," she said. "And we've been feeding him and his crew plenty of cash. Rashaq is looking pretty weak right now, so I like my chances."

"Not so much that you didn't try to kill Rashaq," Anton pointed out.

"Eh, I took my shot. You can't win them all," Kelsey said.

Aris waited with the ex-slaves near the docks, while Kelsey and Anton met with the ship's crew. Galen, Tavik, and she had the job of guarding the group while they waited to get on the boat.

They were hiding in an alley fairly close to the tavern where the meeting was, so she could see that the crewmembers were upset when they came out. Anton looked concerned, while Kelsey seemed entirely free of worry as she waved them to approach.

"What's wrong?" she asked.

"They haven't got all the new crew that they need," Kelsey said. "It's fine. We should probably take a day or two to get the place shipshape."

The female courl—Setana—glared at Kelsey. "You can't do work on the ship if we're not there, and if we *are* there then we can't recruit."

Kelsey waved dismissively. "We'll work something out," she said. "Lead on."

Setana didn't move immediately. "You've got supplies arranged for all these . . . humans?" she asked. "I don't see any barrels of water."

"It's all arranged," Kelsey said reassuringly. "Let's get moving."

It was tense, moving through the streets at night. Aris didn't know where an attack might come from, and *everyone* on the street took note of the large group moving together. What people thought of them, Aris wasn't sure, but the suspicious glares did nothing to calm her nerves.

Despite all that, they made it to the dock without incident. The ship's . . . tender, Aris thought it was called, was tied up, ready to go.

"Two trips," Setana said, looking at the group. "And you're in the first group," she said, looking at Kelsey. "Captain will want a word."

"Looking forward to it," Kelsey said, rolling her eyes.

That meant Anton was going as well, of course. Aris needed to stay back and guard. She watched as the boat was loaded up with the less physically capable former slaves, and then watched as it sailed into the darkness.

There were a few lights out on the harbor, but even with her improved Perception, Aris couldn't tell one ship from another. She hoped the crewmembers knew where to go.

It was a long wait in the darkness. It wasn't totally dark. There was a lightstone, affixed to a post, high up on the end of the pier. It stopped boats from running into the structure, she supposed, though why they were sailing at night, she didn't know.

Three docks over, it looked as if someone was preparing to sail at night. *That* dock was all lit up, with Elitran soldiers moving around in a purposeful fashion. Soldiers all seemed to do that, Aris had found. She wondered if there was a trait that they all shared that did that.

She watched them in fascination until she was startled by a voice.

"Ahoy, land lubbers!" It was Rashid, the other crewmember. The boat had returned and she'd missed its arrival.

Aris felt the blood rush to her face. She was supposed to be on watch, but she'd let herself get distracted.

"What's going on over there?" she asked, trying to cover her lapse.

Rashid looked over and frowned. "They're getting the *Prowler* ready to leave, he said."

"At night?"

"Maybe . . . maybe they just want to be ready to leave at dawn. A lot of logistics getting a ship that size ready."

Aris could see what he meant by the size of the ship. It was even bigger than the one that had guarded the harbor when they arrived. It looked as though they had to load it with a lot of sailors and soldiers . . . and slaves to pull the oars as well.

"Anyway, none of our business," Rashid said. "Get your people aboard."

Getting everybody moving was complicated enough that Aris forgot about the other ship. Soon enough, they were moving through the darkness, heading for the tiniest of lights, shining over the water.

"Did everything work out with the captain?" she asked.

Rashid shrugged. "The thing about the captain is, he likes having a chance to shout."

"He's happy, then?" Aris had known a few shopkeepers like that at home. She had avoided them when she could.

"Not really," Rashid said, "He's lost track of what he should be shouting about."

Aris giggled. Kelsey was like that.

"That storage device of hers," Rashid said wonderingly. "Do you know how big it is? I've never heard of anything like it."

"Oh . . . I'm not sure if I should say," Aris said. Then again, it wasn't as if Kelsey was hiding the ability. "I'm not clear on how storage devices work, but they're like an invisible box that you can take stuff out of?"

"That's the basics of it," Rashid agreed.

"Well, Kelsey's isn't like that. It's more like a . . . tunnel? A short one, but it goes somewhere else. And she's got people there, on the other side, putting stuff in and taking stuff out."

Rashid whistled softly. "That's still quite the item," he said. "You people really are more than you seem, aren't you."

"That's a fair statement," Aris said. The dark bulk of the ship was coming up, the light they were seeking rising higher as they approached. "You should keep that in mind."

Rashid gave her an uncertain look and then busied himself tying the tender to the ship and arranging for a sling for the passengers.

Aris watched with interest. When they'd arrived before, they'd had to climb up a rope, but many of the passengers weren't capable of that, having bad hands, bad eyes, or just general weakness. For them, a counterweighted sling had been set up, allowing Rashid to pull them up to the ship, one by one.

When it was her turn, she took the sling, just because it looked fun. It wasn't. During the day, maybe, but tonight she couldn't see anything, and she just swung about dizzyingly as she got hauled up.

Anton helped her out, and she clung to him until the world stopped moving. Not that it *did* stop. They were on a ship, and the waves, gentle as they were, never stopped. But it was nice to hold him.

He let her hold on as long as she liked. They only broke off when Kelsey approached.

"Listen," she said without preamble, "I think there might be a problem."

CHAPTER TWENTY-ONE

Fight the Power

Y ou noticed the ship, right?" Kelsey asked.
"Of course," Anton said. It was easy to know what ship she was talking about. There were other ships in the harbor, either tied up or anchored, but they were all slightly less black smudges in the night, their positions marked by a few lanterns that did nothing to illuminate them at this distance. There was only one ship that was well-lit, the military ship that was being loaded.

"Take a closer look," Kelsey invited, holding up her strange spyglasses. Anton took them and held them up to his eyes. He remembered how to turn the wheel for clarity.

"What am I looking for?" he asked.

"See if you can find the captain," Kelsey replied.

Anton did as she said, scanning over the busy workers, looking for someone important. It wasn't easy holding the glasses steady with the motion of the water underneath him, but he was getting the hang of it.

He found what he was looking for, on the raised platform at the rear of the ship. The courl there was dressed more importantly than the others. On impulse, Anton triggered *Delver's Discernment*, just to see if it would work through the glasses.

Orhan al-Demir, Level ???, Admiral, Midshipman/Reckless Pilot/Ship's Captain/Admiral

"I can't see his level!" he blurted out.

"Thirty-six," Kelsey murmured. "Well into Tier Four. You haven't found it yet, though. Keep looking."

Confused, Anton looked around the Admiral. When he saw what Kelsey was talking about, he swore. It wasn't the Admiral, it was who he was talking to.

"Kusec and Erryan," he spat. The two ex-prisoners were talking animatedly with the Admiral. It looked as if they were under guard, but the Admiral was listening to them.

"I didn't think they had it in them," Kelsey admitted. "They must have found some way around the geas."

"Or just bore the pain," Anton suggested. "It looked like it hurt, but it wouldn't necessarily stop someone from talking."

"I really didn't think I was going to see them again," Kelsey mused. "But the game's up now, so we're going to have to take steps."

"That ship isn't coming for us," the captain put in, coming up to them. "There's no need for all those supplies, just to take a jaunt across the harbor."

"Not *just* us," Kelsey agreed. "My guess is this is a response to the attack on the dungeon garrison."

The captain blinked. "There was an attack on the dungeon garrison?"

"Haven't you heard?" Kelsey asked with a smile. "It's the talk of the town, let me tell you. They'll be looking for a large force, the kind that can strip a fort bare and leave no corpses behind. That's the sort of force that comes in by boat, so they'll be going around the island, looking for signs of a landing, and checking to see if their patrols are still in place."

"Have you heard anything about this?" the captain asked his crew. They shook their heads.

Kelsey continued as if he hadn't spoken. "That *would* have been the plan. Now they've been told that the source of all their problems is on this boat. They'd be remiss if they didn't at least *check*."

"I still want to know—fine." The captain checked himself. "They'll come aboard for a search. I presume you don't have papers for any of these slaves."

"*Former* slaves, and no, no papers," Kelsey said. "Feeling like giving us up?"

Captain Farid looked at Kelsey warily. "I'm not one to go back on my word. And you've as much as told us that we *can't*. I'll take your passengers to Zamarra. I can't help you if the *Prowler* comes after us, though. I can't run faster than it, and I can't fight it."

Kelsey nodded. "Do you think they'll come at us tonight?"

"Not unless we run," Farid said. "Boarding is a nightmare in the dark. They'll stay put until first light unless we give them a reason to leave."

"Right. Then we've got tonight to get this ship ready.

"I'm still short on crew," Farid objected.

Kelsey shrugged. "You'll have to make do with what you've got. Some of your passengers are able-bodied—teach them how to be sailors. Right now, though, we need to outfit this ship!"

"Do what you like," the captain said. "Just don't put holes in the hull. No matter how it would light up the place." He looked over to his two lieutenants. "You'd better unpack the sails."

Outfitting the ship, it turned out, meant installing bunk beds. Kelsey had been directing her skeletons to turn out sections of steel frames that could be bolted together and then attached to the walls by the "self-tapping screws" that Anton had seen before.

At least Anton thought they were steel frames. They seemed remarkably light when he was fitting them into place.

"They're actually aluminum tubing," Kelsey said. "Hollow on the inside, and made of a lighter metal than steel that doesn't rust."

"It's not steel?" Anton asked, following almost nothing of what Kelsey had said.

"Nope! I imagine that the Empire will have some *questions*, if they can catch us, and they look closely at the hold." Kelsey giggled at the thought.

"About that *us*," Anton said. "I didn't think we were going back in the same ship as these guys?"

"That was the original plan," Kelsey agreed. "It's been updated a bit since then. We'll still be making our way south in a separate boat, though."

"*What* boat?" Anton asked.

"You'll see," Kelsey promised. "First, though, we have to get *this* ship ready."

"Fine. But do you have to hum that annoying song?"

Kelsey looked offended. "A construction montage has *got* to have the proper background music!"

She launched into another rendition. "Badap ba dum dum! Dum dum dum. Badad up pada dum! Dum dada dum."

"I don't know the original song, but I'm pretty sure your tone is off," Anton said.

"Well, music was never my strong point," Kelsey said.

It took them all night, but they got the ship ready to run. First light found most of the passengers fearfully packed away in their beds, with just a few of the able-bodied ones joining the crew making ready to set sail.

Kelsey, Anton, Aris, and Zaphar were down on the tender.

"You *can't* have the tender," the captain had said. "That wasn't part of the deal."

"I'm not going to take it," Kelsey had assured him. "The next bit needs to be done closer to the water."

Anton was used to Kelsey's surprises by now, but he didn't quite know what to make of the tightly wrapped bundle she made appear. Then she undid the straps and unwrapped it, revealing . . . nothing? The wrapping was the point, apparently.

Kelsey had them spread it out on the floor of the tender, like a tent that had yet to be raised. Then she attached something she called a compressor. It made a low growling noise, quite unlike anything Anton had heard before.

Anton didn't know why it was called a compressor when what it did was make things bigger. Perhaps the tent was the result of the compressor's action, and now Kelsey was undoing it?

However it worked, they all watched in amazement as the tent swelled and grew and turned into—

"It's a boat!" Anton said, surprised despite himself. He'd known that they needed a boat, and yet . . .

"Yep!" Kelsey said. "Help me get it in the water."

The new boat was surprisingly, ridiculously light. Despite being big enough to hold six people, it didn't weigh more than the original tent. This, Anton felt, *had* to be magic.

Kelsey got into the boat first and busied herself placing boards in critical locations. A solid floor, seats . . . and a sturdy construction at the back. Meant to hold the heavy-looking object that Kelsey produced. She attached it to the side and lowered part of it into the water.

"All aboard that's coming aboard."

Anton felt it as soon as he stepped aboard. It was just a trickle of experience, far less than he'd gotten from the recent fight. It seemed that transporting slaves, even if it was illegal, was just logistics. Getting into this boat, whatever Kelsey had planned, was going to be an *adventure*.

Shouts came from above, yelling that the *Prowler* had left its dock and was headed in their direction. Anton swallowed his nervousness and helped Aris down into the boat. Zaphar jumped down nimbly on his own.

"Right!" Kelsey called up. "We'll distract them, and you clear out once it's clear that they're not paying attention to you."

"Stupid monkey!" the captain called back. "How are you going to distract them with a tiny boat when you don't even have any oars?"

Kelsey grinned. "This is going to be fun," she told the others in the boat with her. "Everyone sit down and grab on to something."

Then she pulled a string out of the . . . thing at the stern.

It was similar to the compressor, the noise that it made. Where the compressor had growled, though, the unnamed thing *roared*. Anton gripped the side of the boat harder, which was just as well as the boat started to *move*.

It started at what Anton would consider a normal speed. They slipped out from behind the tender, and Anton had time to look up at the gawping faces of

Captain Farid and his crew. Then Kelsey made the boat roar again, and they took off. Fast and getting faster.

"Not bad, eh?" Kelsey yelled over the roaring sound.

They were going to reach the *Prowler* in minutes, Anton realized. He tore his gaze away from the laughing Kelsey and looked forward.

Their approach had been noted, he saw. People were pointing at them. They were probably yelling as well, but he couldn't hear. It wasn't long before bows were brought out, and the soldiers started shooting at them.

As soon as she saw that, Kelsey made the boat turn in a wide circle. Arrows flew down, roughly where they would have been if they kept going straight.

"We don't want to get too much closer, we're not made for taking arrows!" she yelled.

"Is this really going to distract them enough for our ship to escape?" Anton yelled back.

Kelsey grinned in response. "Glad you asked!" she said. A big metal object appeared in her hand. It was heavy, enough to make Kelsey strain to hold it one-handed.

"Grab the handle," she yelled. Anton did so and grunted as he felt the weight for himself.

"Put it in the water. Point that end at the Prowler. Press the button on the handle. Then let go."

Anton held back from saying "What?" The instructions were simple enough; they just made no sense. That was normal for Kelsey, though. The increased tingle of experience he felt when he took the item was sign enough that following the instructions would have *interesting* results.

Not expecting enlightenment, he used *Delver's Discernment* on the item.

Mark 3 Torpedo, Weapon, Average Quality, Tier 4

Anton blinked. Once again, Kelsey had managed the impossible. Tier Four? For an average-quality item that wasn't even magical? Just to be sure, he used his *Sense Mana* on the thing and confirmed it. No magic.

"Get ready!" Kelsey called. "I'll take us in on another run."

There was nothing for it but to follow her instructions. He leaned over the side with the weapon, hanging onto the seat. He felt Aris grab his arm, and turned to meet her concerned gaze.

"It'll be fine. Probably," he yelled. He put the torpedo in the water.

It was much easier to hold once it was submerged. He didn't know how that worked, but it was probably deliberate. It was harder to aim, though. The water wanted to snatch it away, and it took all his strength to keep it pointed in the right direction.

"Hurry up!" Kelsey called, "Gonna have to turn soon."

With a last grunt of effort, Anton pressed the button. The next part was "let go," but it wasn't necessary. The torpedo tore itself out of his hand, travelling even faster than the boat.

"Whooo!" Kelsey yelled and turned again. Anton could see a white line of bubbles headed straight for the *Prowler*.

Arrows were coming uncomfortably close, and Kelsey jinked back and forth, making them a harder target to hit. They didn't have to wait long, though, before their own strike hit home.

The explosion ripped a massive hole in the side of the *Prowler*. It went below the waterline and was big enough that Anton could see, even at this distance, the devastation he'd wrought across at least two decks of the massive military ship.

"Nice aim!" Kelsey yelled. She pulled them away from the ship and reduced their speed.

"You never intended to distract them, you always meant to sink them," Anton realized, now able to speak normally.

"Yeah, but who would have believed me if I'd said that?" Kelsey said. "It should be clear sailing now, except . . ."

She looked over at the *Prowler*, puzzled.

"Why isn't it sinking?" she asked.

CHAPTER TWENTY-TWO

Kiss Off

W hy isn't it sinking?" Kelsey asked again. Anton didn't know. They were a fair distance from the warship, but even from here, he could see the gaping hole.

He didn't know, but he could guess. "The Admiral must have a trait that keeps his ship afloat," he speculated.

Kelsey looked at him in consternation. "That's *cheating*," she protested.

"Maybe you could hit him with another one?" Aris suggested. Kelsey immediately looked guilty.

"You don't have another one?" Anton asked incredulously. "What if I'd missed?"

"You weren't going to *miss*, Anton," Kelsey said. "You had a single shot, one chance to save us all. There's no way a hero would miss that shot."

"I'm not actually a hero yet, you know, just an adventurer," Anton said. That wasn't quite true. Firing the torpedo had put him over the edge. He could feel his final Adventurer level waiting to be accepted. Now was not the time, though.

"Also, this *wasn't* our one chance," he said, pointing at the ship still stubbornly remaining afloat. "We still need to figure out what to do about that thing. Tell me that wasn't *why* you only made one."

"It's not like *you've* brought a bunch of anti-ship weapons to the table," Kelsey snapped. "Those things count as Tier Four. I can't just magic them up, I have to build them the hard way."

"Even so," Anton said doubtfully. He'd seen just how much Kelsey liked to overprepare.

"And," Kelsey continued, "I've only been working on torpedoes since we started this sea voyage. Not a lot of point to them until then."

"What about the earlier versions?" Anton asked. "That was a Mark Three, right? What about the Mark One and Two?"

"The Mark One showed a *distressing* tendency to explode when you put it in water," Kelsey said. "And the Mark Two wouldn't swim straight."

"Um," Zaphar said. "I hate to interrupt, but the warship is getting closer."

They all looked. It was missing some of its oars, but the *Prowler* was indeed heading straight for them, seemingly unslowed by its damage.

Kelsey cursed and started up the engine again. "At least we got its attention!" she yelled.

Zaphar said something that Anton couldn't hear. Probably something about that being a mixed blessing, at *best*. Either Kelsey could hear him, or she guessed what he was saying. She grinned back at him but then turned to Anton.

"Anyway, the thing is, I *do* have another one," she shouted. "It's just that we need it for *that*."

She pointed and Anton was reminded that the *Prowler* wasn't the only warship on the island. The galley they had passed going in—or another similar ship—had been anchored out past the entrance of the bay. To get out of the harbor, they would have to pass quite close to it.

Anton swore. They'd attracted *that* ship's attention, too. Whether it was a communication from the flagship or that they'd noticed Kelsey's small boat buzzing across the bay, Anton couldn't say. Its oars were moving and it was turning to meet them.

"What's the plan?" he shouted. It looked as if Kelsey was headed straight for the second galley.

"Just before we get into arrow range, you fire the second torpedo," Kelsey yelled. "Whether it sinks or not, they should be distracted enough for us to slip by."

That didn't sound like much of a plan, but it did mean that he had a few moments before he had to act. A perfect time to accept his new level.

> You have reached Level 10.
> Please select a new Trait.
> Available Traits: Finish the Job, Divine Action, Irresistible Blow,
>   Impenetrable Defense, Disarm Trap, Unwavering.

Anton swallowed. He knew what all of these traits did, of course. *Finish the Job* wasn't always available on the main Adventurer path. It typically activated after you died, keeping you moving until you finished whatever it was you set out to do. You *could* still live if you got healing before that point. Few did.

Anton wondered if the reason he'd been offered it was his experience on the night he met Kelsey. He knew what it was like to strive beyond the bounds of what his body was capable of. Regardless, he wouldn't be taking it. It was powerful, but it was only useful after he was dead.

Divine Action was more tempting. It could only be used once a day, but it guaranteed success on any one thing he tried to do. It would come in handy right now.

Irresistible Blow and *Impenetrable Defense* were your standard capstone skills. They weren't actually undefeatable, especially when going against higher tiers, but they were very hard to defeat. *Disarm Trap* was from the lower levels and wasn't a serious consideration.

That left *Unwavering*.

A Hero can't let her fears stop her.

That had been a favorite saying of his mother. *She* hadn't been afraid on the wall. Her last actions had been to see to Anton's safety.

Unwavering selected.
Applying Benefits for Level 10
Strength + 1
Toughness + 1
Agility + 1
Dexterity + 1
Perception + 1
Please allocate free Ability point.

Anton put the extra point in Strength. He was getting closer to Kelsey's strength, he could feel it.

"Head's up!" Kelsey called. She had the second torpedo ready for him. He lifted it more easily now. He'd thought that *Unwavering* wouldn't be immediately useful, but he'd been wrong. He could feel the trait flowing through him, strengthening his resolve. He'd done this before, he could do it again.

He took the weapon and moved to the front of the boat. This time, he thought to use *Spider Climb* to attach himself to the deck as he leaned over.

The warship was ahead of them. It was headed straight for them, but it was already starting to turn. They would be in arrow range soon, and the archers could only fire so many from the front of the boat. Far better to give them a volley from side on.

Turning side on gave Anton a better target as well. He held on until he saw a ranging shot come down ten yards in front of them. They'd cross the line in seconds.

He pressed the button and yelled for Kelsey to turn. She did so, instantly, forcing Aris, the only passenger without *Spider Climb*, to hang on for dear life. Fortunately, she had him to cling to.

They watched the thin white line head for the galley as Kelsey brought the boat around in a circle. They were trapped between the two galleys now, and arrows were beginning to splash down nearby. In a few minutes, the *Prowler* would catch up to them.

Before that, though, the torpedo found its target. The explosion was devastating. The galley, while almost as long as the *Prowler*, had fewer decks. The explosion ripped through all three levels of the warship, at a point around a third of the way back from the bow.

"Whoo hoo!" Kelsey yelled. "Stay afloat after that, I dare you!"

She completed the circle they were moving in so that they were back to heading right at the stricken galley. They were in arrow range now, but the sailors had more pressing concerns.

Over the shouts and screams of the sailors and the crackling of the fires started by the explosion, came a loud *crack*. To Anton's astonishment, the warship split into two pieces. Both of its ends rose up in the air, the hole from the explosion plunging into the depths.

All of the sailors were screaming now, scrambling up the steeply slanted decks or climbing into the rigging to get farther away from the churning waters that the ship was disappearing into. Anton could feel the experience from the deaths flowing in. He took a moment to confirm that his footing was secure and there were no immediate threats. Then he focused on his level.

You have completed Level 10.
Please select your new Class.

Anton looked through the list of available classes. Hero was there, of course. So was Wandering Hero and Noble Hero, two variants. They were all Unique classes. Travelling to another country must have qualified him for Wandering Hero, and Noble Hero must have come from his title, even if he hadn't been recognized by the King.

Heroic Marine wasn't one that he'd heard of, another variant of Hero, probably. There were a few others that looked interesting.

Dungeon Companion (Tier 3, Unique)
Requisites: Relationship with Dungeon Avatar
Ability Improvement: 8 points per level. STADPWC

He resolved to never, ever, tell Kelsey about that one.

Guardian of the Crypt (Tier 3, Epic)
Requisites: Completed Adventurer, Relationship with Dungeon Avatar
Ability Improvement: 9 points per level. STADPWC (2 Free)

That was better than Dungeon Companion, but it still tied him a little too closely to Kelsey for his liking. Was that unfair? He was *married* to the Sovereign of the Crypt, so it wasn't just Kelsey that he'd be guarding.

He wasn't sure and he was running out of time. There was one other epic class, though.

Heroic Liberator (Tier 3, Epic)
Requisites: Completed Adventurer, Rescue at least 10 slaves, Feel the sting of captivity
Ability Improvement: 9 points per level. STADPWC (2 Free)

He liked the sound of that. That class probably got experience from freeing slaves, which he should be doing a lot of in the immediate future.

Heroic Liberator selected.

He returned his attention to the battle. Kelsey was cackling as she swung the boat around the sinking ship.

"If we're lucky, the big one will stop to help them," she yelled. "We just—" she looked around wildly. "Where's—"

Aris was the one to point their ship out. Ignored in all the fuss, it had quietly slipped out of its berth and was heading north. It was still in the bay, but not for much longer.

Kelsey frowned. "I guess we should stick around to make sure no one follows them," she said.

Anton nodded absently. He had a few other concerns.

Applying Benefits for Level 1
Strength + 1
Toughness + 1
Agility + 1
Dexterity + 1
Perception + 1
Willpower + 1
Charisma + 1
Please allocate free Ability points.

Anton chose Strength again. He checked his Status. His progress had been so fast, it was ridiculous.

Anton Nos, Heroic Liberator, Level 1

Overall Level: 16
Paths: Delver/Adventurer/Heroic Liberator
Class: Heroic Liberator
Strength: 22
Toughness: 23
Agility: 19
Dex: 18
Perception: 17
Will: 14
Charisma: 11
Traits:
Delver's Discernment
Leaping Attack
Stone Skin
Uncanny Evasion
Sense Mana
Spider Climb
Unwavering

"Um," Aris said. "That big ship, the *Prowler*? It's definitely still following us."

Kelsey cursed. "We'll just have to keep avoiding it then. Hopefully, none of the other ships will be able to get underway quickly enough."

As they skidded across the bay, Anton realized there was something he could test out. His *Delver's Discernment* was supposed to give extra information when he reached Tier Three. He was at a higher level as well, which meant he might be able to . . .

"Kelsey," Level 28, Necropolis, S: 21 T: 18 A: 20 D: 17 P: 23 W: 24 C: 19

I can see her level! was the first thing he thought. Then, *her abilities really are terrible.*

Terrible was a relative thing, of course. Kelsey's abilities were about on par with his, now. But he was level sixteen, and Kelsey was level *twenty-eight.* They were both Tier Three, but there should have been a vast distance between them.

Anton reminded himself that there was much more to Kelsey than the base abilities of her avatar. As long as she could pull Tier Four weapons out of nowhere, she was going to outmatch him. But it didn't make a difference to the feeling that started to well up inside him. For the first time since the raid, he felt as if the irresistible currents of Kelsey's agenda weren't able to hold him anymore. He wasn't on dry land yet, but he was swimming.

I'm a hero, like you both were, he thought. *I'm going to make you proud.*

CHAPTER TWENTY-THREE

The Boy in the Bubble

I think the hole's getting smaller," Aris shouted, peering over Kelsey's shoulder. They were running out to sea, pursued by the apparently unsinkable *Prowler*, and she had to shout over the sound of the engine.

Anton couldn't be sure, but he thought she was right. It was hard to tell from this distance, and the bouncing of the boat made it impossible to train the spyglasses at the oncoming vessel. Kelsey had been confident that they could get away, but . . .

"It shouldn't be able to go that fast!" she complained loudly.

Anton shrugged. There were plenty of explanations for that: high-leveled rowers or another trait of the Admiral. Going faster seemed like a fairly obvious thing for a captain to have. The staying afloat with a big hole in the side was much more impressive.

It looked like their captain had a similar trait because his ship had also been quick to move once the way was clear. It was just a dot on the horizon now, and Anton was starting to harbor hopes that they'd make it.

"Well, it is!" he shouted back.

"What—what are we going to do?" Zaphar called from the front of the boat. He had been pretty quiet during the adventure thus far, but things had quieted down a little.

"I dunno, I guess we keep running out to sea. It's not faster than us, just not slow enough for me to lose them. At this rate, it will still be in sight when it's time to refuel. They'll be able to catch up, and we'll start all over again."

"Is it safe, to take such a small boat on the open sea?" Zaphar asked.

Kelsey got a thoughtful look on her face. "Probably? I'm not sure what the issues are with small boats. Lack of propulsion and supplies are the ones that come to mind, and we've got that sorted."

Zaphar didn't look at all reassured, so Kelsey kept on.

"Look, we'll be fine. This hull is buoyant enough to float even if it fills with water, so no storm is going to sink us. We can just tie ourselves on and we'll live through it. In fact, maybe going through a storm will dissuade our stalker."

She adjusted the angle of their travel.

"It looks like one's forming to starboard; we'll go through it and lose them."

"Unsinkable, remember?" Anton reminded her. She scowled in response.

"We don't know that," she said. "It might still be worth trying."

"We don't want to go in there!" Zaphar shouted urgently, looking ahead of them.

"We'll be fine; a little rain never hurt anyone," Kelsey said.

"You don't understand, it's *green*!" he yelled.

Anton looked at the trembling thief. They were all wet from the spray of their passage, but he cut a particularly bedraggled figure. Anton and Aris's clothes were rugged, made for the outdoors and for protection. Zaphar's shirt and pants were made of the thinnest and cheapest cloth available, and they clung to him now, as though he were wrapped in a wet sheet.

Kelsey's strange clothes didn't seem to get properly wet at all.

"Well, whadda ya know?" Kelsey drawled. "You're right!"

Anton looked. There *was* a greenish tinge to the center of the swirling clouds, one that was steadily growing more intense.

"What does that mean?" Kelsey asked. "Some kind of superstorm?"

Zaphar shook his head. "I've heard stories, from the sailors," he shouted. "Sometimes, when it's crowded on the waters, a green storm will come. It *takes* one of the ships, and then it goes away."

"Takes? You mean, like, sinks?" Kelsey asked. Zaphar shook his head again.

"Just *takes*, is what they said. They never saw those ships again."

Kelsey narrowed her eyes and muttered something that Anton couldn't hear.

"Well, that changes everything!" she exclaimed. She adjusted their course again. *Not* away from the storm, Anton was alarmed to note. Instead of skirting the edges, they were now headed straight into the center.

"What are you doing!" Zaphar yelled. He twitched, caught between two different urges of self-preservation.

"It's fine, I think I know what this is!" Kelsey called.

"Are you sure?" Anton shouted.

"Not really, but if I'm wrong, just consider the logic!" Kelsey called. "If it takes the *Prowler*, we're golden!"

"What if it takes *us*?" Zaphar yelled shrilly.

"I wasn't planning on coming back to this podunk town, anyway!" Kelsey cheerfully yelled back.

Anton opened his mouth to say . . . something, but he was interrupted by a voice that cut through the engine noise, despite being spoken in a normal conversational tone.

"Well spoken!" the voice said. The voice was coming from a direction that Anton couldn't quite describe. It wasn't from the front, the back, or the sides. He could turn his head that way, though, to see who had spoken.

It was a green man. His skin was green, his hair a darker green, and his eyes were glowing emeralds. He wore a light green shirt with a fancy cut and darker green pants. His shoes were of green leather and pointed.

He was all of three feet tall.

"Oh, thank goodness," Kelsey said, cutting the engine. The sudden silence seemed deafening. "I was worried we'd have to make it all the way into the storm before you showed up."

"Since you were so good as to accept my invitation, it would hardly do for me to keep my guests waiting," the green man said.

"You move pretty quickly," Kelsey said, flicking a glance at Anton. "I don't think he transitioned more than an hour ago."

"Not as quickly as you, it seems," the green man said sourly.

"Kelsey, do you . . . know this person?" Aris asked.

"Kelsey is, you might say, a colleague of mine," the green man answered before Kelsey could speak. Kelsey shrugged in response.

"I'll take the compliment, but there's a wide gap between us and what we can do," she said.

"One that you seem to be in the process of surmounting," the green man said. "You've taken risks, but they seem to be paying off for you."

"Thanks," Kelsey said wryly. To Aris, she said, "I met someone like this a while back."

"Did they give a name?" the green man asked.

"No," Kelsey replied. "I got the impression that they were a 'no names, no pack drill' kind of person."

"Very wise of them. I believe I'll be following their example."

"What do you *want?*" Anton asked, his mind reeling. A colleague of Kelsey's? What could that mean? Kelsey had referred to another dungeon as a *sister*, but she'd clearly felt herself to be superior to it.

"What do I want? Why, merely to make a deal," the green man said.

"Like Kelsey did with Anton?" Aris asked. The green man winced.

"Exactly like that," he agreed, "But it seems that option has been taken off the table."

"Kelsey's geas," Anton realized. "It's because she's an outsider. Like a demon or a fae." He glanced over to Kelsey, sitting calmly by the motor. "She'd be a lot more worried if you were a demon, so you must be—"

"Indeed, you've reasoned it out. No need to use the word, it isn't one that I'd choose."

"All right?" Anton said, confused by the request. "But why do you want a deal with me?"

"Wanted, is the right word here," the green man said.

"I don't think our goals are incompatible," Kelsey said quietly. The green man shot a look in her direction.

"I can't bind myself to him like you did," he said. "Pull him from two directions and he'll split himself. Then neither of us will get what we want."

"There's still the possibility of a token," she said. "And of course . . ." She nodded at the other two people still in the boat.

"Companions on the journey . . ." the green man said. "You haven't . . . no, I see. Well, perhaps there is room for some benefit here."

He turned back to Anton. "A deal," he said. "I can grant much, but only for the right price. It must be fair."

"You don't want ordinary things, I guess," Anton said slowly. He looked over at Kelsey, but she shook her head.

"They hate it when people hand-hold," she said. "I guarantee you that you'll get better terms if I don't say anything."

"Quite," the green man said wryly. "You are correct, I do not want ordinary things. From you . . . perhaps the grief you hold for your family?"

"What?" Anton exclaimed incredulously. "You can *take* that? You *want* it?"

"Yes, to both questions," the green man said. "I won't be *feeling* it, of course, just contemplating its beauty. Such a strong, pure emotion. And, I think, you would be happier if you didn't have it, yes? These feelings, they wear at you. Better to trade it for something nice."

"Like what?" Anton asked.

"Hmm . . . let's see. You are seeking your sister-in-law, cruelly taken from her home. How noble. I could aid you, send you to the next city that is your destination. All it would cost is something you don't need."

"I . . . don't know," Anton said. If he stopped grieving for his family, would he still be himself? Or someone else? He looked over at Aris. The look of concern in her eyes settled it for him.

"No," he said. "If you want something out of the ordinary, how about this?"

He held up Chainbreaker. As a Tier Three magical item, it was the most unusual thing that he had.

"How disappointing," the green man said. "Humans never let go of the things that are holding them back." He looked at the sword. "This isn't bad," he admitted. "It has a *history*, despite someone's attempt at filing it clean."

"No apologies," Kelsey said. "I thought he was going to use it, not stick it in a museum. Speaking of which, don't you need that, Anton?"

"You're still holding on to my father's sword," Anton said. "I can find myself another Tier Three eventually."

"Quite so! I feel that even higher tiers will be in your future," the green man said. "It's a deal!"

Then he turned to Aris.

"You . . . she may not have made a deal with you, but she's got her claws in, nonetheless. Let me take a look at that gun of yours."

Aris hesitated, but she pulled the gun out of its holster and held it out. "Do you want to trade for my weapon, too?"

"Oh no," the green man exclaimed with distaste. He picked up the weapon and held it in front of his face. "It's an ugly machine for killing, and *new* besides. It has no story. The lives that it has taken don't speak to me; they still don't know how they died."

"Uh, sorry. Why did you want it, then?"

"So that I could offer you *this*," the man said. He handed Aris her gun back and then made another gun appear in his hand. It gleamed silver, the handle a pale ivory with a golden design inlaid.

Aris gasped at the sight of it. Anton tried *Delver's Discernment*.

Eclipse Whisper, Weapon, Perfect Quality, Tier 4, Enchantments: Final Darkness, Silenced

"Show-off," Kelsey snorted.

"It's something, isn't it? I'll wager you've never seen a Tier Four item before," the green man said. "And it can be yours for . . . let's say, the love of your husband."

"Wait, what?" Anton exclaimed. He started to stand up.

Suddenly Kelsey was beside him, holding him down.

"Settle down, big man," she said. "Have some faith."

She stepped aside to let him see that Aris was shaking her head. "It's amazing," she said, "But I can't give Anton up, not for anything."

"Too bad," the green man said. He threw the gun up into the air and it turned into glittering dust. "It was a long shot, but I had to try. You don't have anything else that interests me."

Anton felt something unclench in his chest. He scrambled over to give Aris a hug. She accepted it with a surprised laugh.

"Now," the green man said, ignoring Anton. He turned instead to Zaphar. "That just leaves you."

CHAPTER TWENTY-FOUR

What Was It You Wanted

Me?" Zaphar asked nervously. "What about me?"

The green man examined the thief closely. "Yes, yes, I can work with this. Not too much in the way. As a consolation prize, he will do."

"I don't mean to tell you your business," Kelsey drawled. "But if you operated somewhere people *lived*, you might get more action."

"Valid," the green man agreed. "But there are other considerations. People are so *annoying*."

"True enough," Kelsey admitted. "Present company excluded, of course."

The stranger laughed. "Indeed! Present company very much excluded."

He turned back to the bedraggled thief.

"Now you . . . you have no grand dreams, no important mission. A shame. But you are young yet! Still seeking. On the cusp of your third tier, but holding back for a better class. I approve!"

"I'm sorry, I don't know what you're talking about," Zaphar said.

"Why should you?" the green man asked. "You should be able to understand this, though: You want a better class."

"Doesn't everyone?" Zaphar asked, shifting uneasily on his seat.

"There are some that are happy with what life brings them," the green man replied.

"Maybe rich folk and nobles are happy with the classes they get, but everyone I know had to settle for a rotten common class."

"How tragic," the green man said, without any emotion. "I can offer you better."

"A class? You can do that?" Zaphar asked incredulously.

"Indeed! There is very little that I cannot do," the green man said proudly. "Here, then, is the deal I propose. I will help you on your path, and you will show me where I need to go."

There was a weight to the words when he said them, which made Anton jump. He looked over at Kelsey, reminded of when she had first spoken to him.

I was delirious at the time, but did she sound like that?

Noticing that he was looking at her, Kelsey shrugged.

"That's what it's like when you do it *properly*," she said, explaining nothing.

Zaphar was just as confused. "I don't know what that means," he objected. "How am I supposed to do that?"

"Don't worry about it," the green man said. "Just stick with these three, and you'll get where you're going. Is that fine with you?" he asked Kelsey.

"Sure," she said lazily. "Glad to have you on board."

Anton wanted to warn Zaphar about accepting vague deals, but he was stopped by Kelsey's earlier warning, as well as her relaxed attitude. Looking back, was he really upset by what the deal had brought him? Kelsey had shackled him, true, but she had dragged him out of a dark place. She'd earned a little of his trust.

"Does this mean that you'll be coming with us?" Zaphar asked.

"Oh, no no no," the green man said. "My colleague rightly chides me for my isolation, but I can monitor your progress from here."

"I'm not sure I like the sound of that," Zaphar muttered. "Can you at least tell me what class I'd get? Will it be Fine? Or Rare?"

"That, I can't say," the green man said. "Only that it will be acceptable to you."

"How can you know that if you don't know what it is?"

"I don't *select* the class," the green man replied. "But if it wasn't acceptable to you, the deal would be imbalanced and wouldn't be accepted."

"And why say it like that? Why not just say you'll get me a new class?"

"You may need some additional help along the way," the green man admitted. "The phrasing gives me some latitude to help you as needed."

"I guess I can't say no to a better class, whatever the price," Zaphar said. He looked over at Kelsey. "You were *talking* about getting me a better class . . ."

Kelsey held up her hands. "Hey, we'll do what we can, regardless of how this turns out. But you should know that anything I can do is going to be strictly inferior to what this guy can do."

"Quite so," the green man preened. "So, do I have your answer?"

"Yes," Zaphar said. Anton felt a sizzle in the air somewhere. Then Zaphar gasped.

"It's Unique!" he exclaimed.

"Take it," the green man purred.

If you knew the moment, you *could* see when someone took a new class. The difference was almost imperceptible, but it was there. Anton used *Delver's Discernment*.

Zaphar Alpashan, Level 16, Fae-Touched Rogue, Thief/Burglar/Fae-Touched Rogue
S: 4 T: 17 A: 24 D: 27 P: 17 W: 10 C: 7

"Welcome to Tier Three," the green man said. "And with that, our business is concluded."

He snapped his fingers, and everything went black. Anton couldn't see the sea, the boat, or even his companions. Just as he was starting to panic, the blackness disappeared and they were on the sea once more.

The sea was there, the sky was there, but it was an entirely different coastline that loomed ahead of them. Anton could just make out the tallest towers of what must be a coastal city.

"That went well, don't you think?" Kelsey asked.

Kelsey hadn't wanted to just sail right into the harbor like any other boat, and Anton had agreed. Her main concern had been about showing off her technology, but Anton's concern was that, sooner or later, word would come from Rused about a small, strange boat that had tried to sink the Admiral's flagship. Kelsey might have disappeared the boat by then, but it would still be a trail that the military could follow.

Kelsey's next idea had been to find a ship out on the water, hijack it, and then sail that ship into the harbor. Anton had vetoed that plan. Kelsey had argued, but Anton wasn't willing to execute a crew of fishermen just to eliminate witnesses. He might have felt better about a military patrol ship, but that seemed as if he would be biting off more than he could chew.

"In any case, none of us know how to sail a boat or crew a galley, so the whole idea is flawed," he'd said, and that was the end of it.

That left landing in some uninhabited place on the coast and walking to the city.

"This would be a lot easier at night," Kelsey complained. "Instant travel is so inconvenient."

Anton just shook his head. With Kelsey's spyglasses, it wasn't that hard to find an unoccupied beach. They may have been noticed by other ships coming in, but their strange craft was quite low to the water and moved quickly. No one, Anton thought, came close enough to identify them.

Anton had wondered about how they were going to land. Regular ships needed to tie up to a dock. Kelsey just ran the boat up onto the beach, timing it so that they rode a wave most of the way in.

"Whoo! Let's go back and do it again!" she cried when they'd stopped moving.

"No," Anton said. He pointed at the boat, now resting on the sand. "Are you going to dispose of that?"

"Yeah, let's give that a go," Kelsey said. She unscrewed something on the side, and there was a hiss as the boat started to shrink and collapse on itself. They all watched in fascination as the structure that had supported them in the water turned into a complicated blanket.

Kelsey picked up the engine and made it go away. "Just fold this up as best you can," she said. "We need to squeeze it into as small a volume as we can."

It wasn't as easy as she made it sound. The boat wasn't completely deflated. Pushing in on one part made another swell up. Trying to get the whole thing within an invisible box of uncertain dimensions was a challenge that tested the patience of all four of them.

Finally, they managed it. The mess disappeared with a slight pop, and everybody cheered.

"Right!" Kelsey said. "Who wants some dry clothes?"

With barely a flicker, she took her own advice and replaced the clothes she was wearing with something similar. The top this time was an eye-searing blue.

Zaphar gaped in surprise. "Did you—were you just—" he said. He clammed up and looked embarrassed when Kelsey looked at him.

"Can we get some privacy before changing?" Aris asked.

Kelsey looked at her scornfully. "Don't be ashamed of that body, Aris! Glory in it!"

"I'll pass, thank you," Aris said. "Our clothes are just a little damp, they'll dry on the way. I'd rather change clothes after a bath. A proper bath," she added, forestalling Kelsey. "Not one on a beach."

"Fine!" Kelsey said.

"Ah, actually, I'd like some new clothes," Zaphar said. They all turned to look at him, and he took a step back nervously. "Unless it's going to cost me my soul or something."

"No soul required!" Kelsey said brightly. "Consider it a gift."

She paused and then brought out a bundle. "See how that goes," she said. "I've been trying some Elitran fashion with the fabric I bought in Rused."

"Thanks. I, uh, don't mind undressing on the beach, but do you all have to watch?"

"No," Anton said. Taking Kelsey by the shoulders, he turned her around. She didn't resist, but she did pout at him. He followed suit, and Aris did as well. "Just let us know when you're done."

It felt strange, standing on the sand with the only sounds being the wind, the waves and the rustle of clothing.

"I'm done," Zaphar said. They all turned around to see what looked like a normal Elitran.

"Huh," Anton said. "I felt sure that she'd do something weird."

Kelsey snorted. "I dressed the both of you, and you don't look weird!" she said. "If you want to dress like me, you have to ask nicely."

"I'm glad that I'll never need to know what that entails," Anton said seriously. "Do you want to think, maybe, about dressing more normally in *this* town?"

"I'll think about it," Kelsey said. "I get that you're worried about word spreading, but . . . I just gotta be me, you know?"

"I had gotten that impression, yeah," Anton said wryly. "Aris and I might want to see about dressing to fit in, too. The only armor I've seen so far was on soldiers, but there must be a style that suits the local adventurers."

"The style's wrong, but you look like foreigners anyway," Zaphar told them. "You might as well dress like one."

They started talking about clothing options as they set off towards the city, with Aris and Zaphar holding the conversation up. It mostly went over Anton's head, and Kelsey got shot down whenever she made a suggestion.

"Have you a plan for entering the city?" Zaphar asked after they'd been walking a while. Unoccupied beaches were not to be found *near* the city.

"Do we need papers or something?" Kelsey said.

"I can't think of any other somethings that would do," Zaphar said. "We need papers."

"You don't have any papers," Anton said.

"Yes, I had no right to leave Rused," Zaphar told them. "Under normal circumstances, I'd have to get papers if I wanted to go somewhere by ship. It would have been expensive."

"What would have happened if we'd arrived by boat?" Kelsey asked. "Just pay to go in, like it was at Rused?"

"Rused is on the frontier, so travellers are expected," Zaphar said. "I don't know what the rules are here."

He looked forward to the city walls rising up ahead of them. "I don't even know where we are."

"I'm not one hundred percent sure," Kelsey said, "So I'll leave off guessing until we find out. All we really know is that it's the city where Cheia ended up."

Zaphar didn't say anything for a long moment. "It seems," he finally said, "like a lot of trouble to go to for one captured villager."

Kelsey grinned. "Try telling that to her sister," she said, pointing out the glare that Aris was giving him.

"Ah, sorry, sorry, I didn't know," Zaphar said quickly.

"But it's not just Cheia," Kelsey continued. "There were a bunch of these guy's friends in that other boat. A bunch more with Cheia, when we find her."

She clapped Anton on the back.

"And now we've got ourselves a Heroic Liberator!" she crowed. "Gonna be freeing slaves left and right! Yessiree!"

"You made Tier Three?" Aris gasped.

"You're a Hero?" Zaphar exclaimed.

Kelsey ignored them both. "It's too bad, though, that we went for Cheia first. I would have preferred to pick up the ones earmarked for fighter school. I'm worried that this lot are all going to be dead weight for the next stage."

CHAPTER TWENTY-FIVE

Say No Go

TYLA

Cheia got her first notification two weeks after they left Rused. They took her that night. Tyla held her as she cried, afterwards. All of the girls had gotten a lot closer over the last few weeks of captivity. The distinctions of tribe and country didn't seem to matter as much anymore. By that time, they were off the boat and living in a new city that they didn't know the name of.

Sex was a constant part of their lives now. Their bodies were doled out as a reward to the guards and the guards in turn were used as a punishment. Uncooperative girls were given to the worst guards, the ones who would hurt them if they didn't comply. It didn't take them long to learn the rules. Once they did, though, they found themselves in competition with each other. Whoever pleased Master Malik the *least* would find themselves with the worst of the men in his employ.

It was different for Tyla, for reasons that Master Malik was happy to explain. He was pleased by the fact that she already spoke Elitran and often came to talk to her. *At* her, might be a better phrase for it.

"Your buyer," he told her, "will want something exotic. A savage elf, fresh from the wilds! There are some that would prefer we left you entirely untouched, but the majority . . ."

He didn't bother finishing the sentence, but Tyla was already aware of the cruel logic that overlaid their lives. Doxies got experience from sex, and Concubines were worth more than Doxies.

"So," her owner had continued, "if we cannot provide a client with your first blood, we can at least provide them with an *unbroken* savage. They will enjoy breaking your will, training you into an obedient plaything."

That was the reason why, of all the girls, only Tyla was not forced into sex. Not directly. She just wasn't allowed to eat if she didn't spread her legs. She always got the gentlest of the guards as well, a young man with an earnest expression who always backed off if she told him no.

The bastard would apologize afterwards, which made Tyla burn with an anger that she couldn't express. Even if she did release her rage, her fists couldn't do anything against his much higher Strength and Toughness. If she'd had a weapon to even the odds, perhaps . . .

Even her ineffectual flailing would mean that she went without food for another day. Despite the pain, regardless of the injury to her dignity, she made herself accept it. A level was a level, after all, and she needed them as much as her master wanted her to have them. A poor ability progression was better than none at all.

The traits helped. They were geared towards helping a woman survive this life she'd found herself in. From what she'd heard, the Tier Two Courtesan class was more oriented towards pleasing her clients, but the base class was all about her survival.

Tyla wouldn't have turned down *Danger Sense*, even as a hunter. She was hoping to escape before she got to level four, but *Disease Resistance* was another generally useful trait that was commonly offered at that point.

For now, all she could do was bide her time and wait for a chance. For what felt like the hundredth time, she reviewed her assets. Aside from the clothes on her back, she just had herself.

Tyla of the Padascar Tribe (Doxy Level 2)
Overall Level: 6
Paths: Padascar Hunter (Broken) / Doxy
Strength: 10
Toughness: 6
Agility: 6
Dexterity: 11
Perception: 13
Will: 7
Charisma: 7
Traits
Persistent Tracking
Silent Shot
Danger Sense

She was stronger than all of the other girls, but she wasn't strong enough to bend bars or snap the collar around her neck. Surprisingly strong for a girl was all it amounted to. Her Dexterity was better, perhaps enough to pick a lock, if she had a tool, or any skill with such things. Or she could use it to steal a knife, perhaps? They kept her away from knives, feeding her only meals that could be eaten with a wooden spoon. She resolved to practice keeping a spoon concealed, in hopes of replacing it with a weapon.

Her best ability was her Perception and it would surely come in handy. She just had to stay alert for her chance.

Today was the first special day. They were going to be shown off to prospective buyers. Master Malik urged her not to get her hopes up, reminding her that it would take time for word to spread about the "special jewel" that he had available. As if Tyla should be *eager* to be sold. She didn't manage to smile, but she nodded along with his words as if they meant something.

The reason for the occasion was that the other girls had learned enough Elitran to obey basic commands. They were being shown off, too, but with a much greater chance of actually being sold. The night before had been tense. No one knew if they'd see each other again. Hugs were exchanged and tearful goodbyes were made in case they didn't get a chance later. Tyla cried as much as any of them. She had been separated from them by her race, but they were all slaves in the end.

When they had been sold to Master Malik by the Empire, they had been walking pieces of meat. Stripped naked and paraded before the cold eyes of the merchants, who had cared more about the documents describing them than the actual people who stood there.

Tyla had expected more of the same, but this was *retail*. Master Malik wasn't selling meat, he was selling the dream of . . . well, Tyla didn't want to think about what he was selling, when what he was *really* selling was her.

In any case, the experience was very different. All the girls were dressed up. They weren't wearing very *much*, but what they were wearing was of the finest quality. Makeup had been applied by the professional artist that Malik kept on hand. Another slave, of course.

Tyla had been given a dress to wear that was supposed to be like what she wore back home. She hadn't been consulted. Instead of leather trousers, protective and easy to move in, she had been given a leather skirt of impossible thinness. It was cut tightly enough to be hard to move in, and it was short enough that it would ride up if she tried. They had carefully cut the hem to make it look as though it had been raggedly made with a stone knife.

Her makeup was also designed to enhance her supposed ferocity. Like all the girls, she had been thoroughly cleaned before dressing. Now she was made up with streaks of fake dirt and a hint of blood going across her face. Her nails were painted red to imply, she had been told, that she had just buried them in the entrails of some beast.

It was all so very fake. Tyla would have just rolled her eyes and laughed at the absurdity of it, were it not for the fact that the intended result of all the artifice and frippery was her sale to some new master. Who would, presumably, rape her until she was a properly tamed savage.

It made her so angry she could spit. Spitting was forbidden, of course, but Master Malik was very pleased with the furious glower that she couldn't seem to get rid of.

"Very savage, darling," the elegantly dressed courl said sardonically. "You've gotten it exactly right."

Tyla tried to focus on the opportunity. There had to be one. They hadn't left the compound, but they *had* been released from their cell. House slaves were running around, preparing for the event. Additional staff had been brought in, there were even a few early guests hanging around. The guards had too much to look out for. They must, inevitably, start losing track of things. All she had to do was make sure one of those things was her.

She started pacing, testing the limits of her leash. She encouraged the other girls to do the same.

"Separate out," she said softly to Cheia. "Don't move in a group. One of us might get a chance."

A chance for *what*, she didn't say. She didn't know. She just knew that there had to be something, and moving around was better than staying cooped up in a cell. Which was an excuse she used when she was challenged on why she was moving around so much.

Her newly extended range was not *greatly* expanded. There were three connected rooms where they were being prepared. Combined, those rooms had seven more doors that she wasn't allowed to go through. Five of those doors had guards. Three of them had guards on her side, and the other two had guards on the *other* side, keeping people out. That still worked for keeping her in, however. Those doors weren't supposed to be opened.

The two remaining doors were being used by servants. There wasn't a guard on either side of them, but there was a guard in the *room*. Guarding a different door, but he could see the room clearly and warn her off if she got near the forbidden door.

Tyla glared at the guard. She was allowed to do that; it was in character. It wasn't very effective, though. He was one of the bad guards, the ones that the girls wanted to avoid getting given to. He ignored her glares with the equanimity of someone who knew nothing she could do could hurt him.

The moment, when it came, was the smallest of things. Two servants came through the forbidden door, laden with snacks destined for the guests. They both had their hands full, so one servant held the door open with his back, while his companion came through. At the same moment, someone tried to open the door behind the guard.

"Hey, back off buddy, you've got the wrong door," the guard growled. The person on the other side tried to say something, but Tyla wasn't paying attention. The guard had turned around, and the way through the door was clear. She made a dash for it.

The servants shouted in alarm as she ran past them, but there was no way they were going to stop her. The guard, of course, would be after her, but he was going to be delayed by the person at the door. Maybe only for a moment, but that might be all she needed.

She quickly took in the new room. More servants, no guards, three doors, all of them open. All the servants were looking at her, but she didn't stop. She picked one of the doors and ran for it. She didn't have time to be sure, but it looked as though there was natural light behind it.

Stepping through, she saw that she was right. There were people and things in here, but there was a shout from behind her and she didn't have time to pay attention to them. The only important thing was that this room was on the edge of the building, and it had windows. Wide open windows, the shutters flung back to let the breeze in.

They were up a level, she knew, but she had grown up in the forest. More specifically, she had spent a lot of time in the treetops. She knew how to take a fall. She didn't pause at all and ran for the windows.

The guard hadn't been delayed much at all, and his next shout came from within the room she was in. She was already leaving though, leaping through the window. Wherever it led, it had to be better than here.

Ironically, she wasn't terribly worried about being caught. She didn't want to be, of course. She would be punished. But she thought that Master Malik would be pleased by the confirmation that she was still untamed. The guard might hurt her, bringing her back in, but he would avoid *damaging* her if at all possible.

Assuming that she didn't damage herself, that was. She rolled into a clumsy somersault, hoping to get her legs under herself before she hit the ground. She was a bit more agile now than she had been back in the forest, but she'd never been very good at these kinds of aerial maneuvers.

She managed well enough. It was fortunate that she landed on a manicured lawn instead of a wall or hard stone pavement. She tumbled to absorb the impact, as she'd practiced back home. The breath was knocked out of her, but she didn't think she'd broken any bones. Success!

The guard following her was more cautious, more deliberate, but also a lot more sturdy. He looked out the window and saw her, picking herself off the ground. He looked at his landing spot and casually jumped down, absorbing the shock by just bending his knees.

Tyla didn't have time to watch his performance, though—she was already running. She was still in the compound, she didn't know where she was going, and there was a guard on her tail.

The end of the chase was easy to predict. Tyla was pretty pleased to have gotten as far as she did. She'd found a small shed with a low roof that butted up against the outer wall. It took her only a moment to clamber up on the roof and slip over the wall.

It was a moment that she didn't have. The guard leapt onto the shed, catching up with her just as she was about to leap down. Freedom—so tantalizingly close—was snatched away from her, as the guard grabbed her by the back of her shirt and threw her back down into the compound.

The wind was knocked out of her, *again*, and all she could do was glare up at the guard as he looked down at her. Then, from far away, there was a loud *crack*, and the guard's face became a bloody mess.

As Tyla watched, stupefied, the guard slumped down and fell, landing on the ground next to her with a muffled *thud*.

A strange, pale-skinned girl poked her head over the wall.

"Hey," she said, as Tyla gaped at her. "You want to get out of here, or what?"

CHAPTER TWENTY-SIX

Sludgefeast

SULIEL

I don't think Anton will be back before we have to present ourselves to the King," Suliel said. She spoke aloud, preferring to use her voice, rather than using the bond directly. There was no one around to hear her speak to the empty air. The reply came instantly, as if Kelsey had already thought about this.

<Yeah, once the captives were split up, the chance of rescuing them all and getting back in time started to get very remote. We could still make it if we headed back right after rescuing Cheia's group, but I haven't brought up the possibility. Do you want me to?>

"Anton wouldn't abandon his fellow villagers," Suliel said. Kelsey already knew that, it was why she hadn't brought it up.

<He might, if you needed him.>

A little thrill ran through Suliel at the thought of Anton dropping his quest just because she needed him, but those were the thoughts of a child. Anton *should* come back, Suliel knew. From the perspective of a ruler, the few missing children weren't that important. Not compared to meeting their king with the survival of the barony on the line.

Anton didn't see it that way, which was why he was a hero, and she was a sovereign.

"I don't *need* him," she lied. "We'll just have to make preparations assuming his absence."

<Fair enough,> Kelsey said. *<I've got a hundred preparations ready to go, and they're getting ripe.>*

"Of course, let me gather the troops."

Suliel headed down to the courtyard where the new unit was waiting. Twenty men, all armed with the new weapons that Kelsey had provided. They were sharply inferior to the guns that Kelsey had provided Aris, but Suliel found it hard to complain about the favoritism shown to her fellow wife.

They saluted her as she came up. Some of them had the sharp, practiced salutes of a trained soldier; others were more ragged. She had scraped together these twenty men and women from wherever she could find them. Some had already been her soldiers; some were adventurers attracted by the higher pay and the possibility of a better class. A few of them were spare cousins, lured away from the small estates that surrounded the town.

All of them had trained with the new weapons, but training did not qualify one for a class. You needed to use them, and that was what they were here for.

Suliel returned the salutes and nodded to the ones she knew personally. "At ease," she said. "We're moving out to the dungeon."

Her horse had been made ready and was being held by the stablemaster. He would be coming with them, to take care of the beast when the firing started. Kelsey had asserted that horses could be made accustomed to the noise of guns. She didn't have any ideas of how that could be done, but she had offered, if Suliel was to supply her with a horse, to make a special undead mount for her that would not spook.

Suliel had passed on the offer—horses were too valuable to sacrifice. They didn't live forever though, so Kelsey might be getting a horse at some point.

The current plan to accustom the horse to gunfire was to have it nearby during the exercise—preferably without Suliel sitting on it.

She led the troops forward at a walk. They weren't going far, not even all the way to the dungeon. About halfway up the hill, a short wall had been erected. It was about three feet high, not a serious defense, just something for her troops to kneel behind.

Most of the trees between here and the dungeon had been cleared. There had been a pressing demand for wood, and Suliel planned to have a lot more traffic going between the two foci of her domain.

<I think we're ready for you,> she sent once her forces were in place.

<Roger Wilco,> Kelsey replied as she often did, with nonsense words in some made-up language. *<First wave on its way.>*

It took a few moments for the zombies to appear, and Suliel started to worry that they'd been turned around. Then the first of them hove into view.

<Second wave going out . . . now,> Kelsey said.

Suliel could tell the moment that the first zombie caught sight, or scent, of the humans below. It gurgled something and picked up speed. The others soon followed. Suliel felt a chill at the sight of the ten zombies shambling towards them. She had heard about the terror Kelsey had caused, releasing a cellar full of the monsters in the town.

She reminded herself that these were the weakest of Kelsey's monsters. Just fodder, there to be killed. The outbreak in town had scared a lot of people, but no one had *died*. A person of average strength could club a zombie to death with an improvised weapon.

Still, she felt a mixture of disgust and fear at the sight of the shambling horrors approaching. The soldiers in front of her stayed calm, holding their fire until the right moment.

Suliel had imagined that the best tactic was for each soldier to fire when they were ready, but Kelsey had off-handedly mentioned the devastating effect of volley fire. So that was how they had trained.

"Steady . . . steady . . ." the sergeant called in a low voice. "Ready . . . and fire!"

Ten rifles roared as one. They weren't perfectly synchronized, but they were close enough that the sound of them merged into an extended rumble of thunder. Seven of the zombies fell to the ground.

"Switch!" the sergeant called, and the front line switched their rifles with the soldier behind them. The rear echelon started reloading, while the front line started to aim.

Suliel glanced over at her horse. He was being held in a bear hug by her stablemaster. She wasn't sure which of them had the wilder eyes.

"Fire!" the sergeant called again. The remaining zombies dropped as the guns rang out again.

This time, there was a short pause before the sergeant called for the switch. The guns were still being reloaded as the second wave came into view. This had been planned for, though, and there was enough of a gap between the waves for the front line to get ready to fire.

The front ten would be the only ones to get new classes today. Kelsey had only been willing to "waste" one hundred zombies at a time, and they thought it would take ten kills for each soldier to get a new class. It wouldn't work out evenly, but enough of them should qualify. Those who missed out could do a dungeon run. Avoiding that duty made for an excellent incentive to get a class today.

Kelsey continued to release waves of zombies, and they continued to be cut down by volley after volley. There was a longer gap after the fifth wave, to check and clean the guns, but they were soon back to it.

Even the noise became routine after a while. Her horse seemed to have calmed somewhat, though her stablemaster was still calming him.

Eventually, the last wave was called, and it was time to tally up the rewards.

Suliel listened intently as each soldier called out what they had qualified for. Everyone seemed to have qualified for Musketeer, while only a few had qualified for Rifleman.

Original Rifleman and Original Musketeer were snapped up as soon as they realized that those classes could only be taken by one person. Suliel couldn't blame them for instantly snapping up a Unique class. But even the standard versions were Rare. She wondered how long it would take for them to become more common, and what would happen to those who held them when the downgrade happened.

"I want you to take Musketeer," she announced once she'd gleaned the details. "That seems to be the one made for operating as a unit."

An army wasn't going to turn away a Swordsman, or an Axeman, but what it wanted were Soldiers. Classes of that type held traits that helped the user to fight in a group. Traits that supported their fellow soldier, traits that helped them understand and carry out orders . . . as well as the traits that helped with combat.

"You can choose otherwise if you wish, of course," she added. Attempting to force someone to take a class rarely worked out well, and Suliel didn't want to be that kind of tyrant.

Once she released their attention, the small crowd quickly erupted into excited discussion as people debated their choices, and commiserated with those who hadn't had a chance to qualify yet. Suliel backed off to consider what they'd learned.

<So some of them managed ten kills, but Musketeer only needs six. But it requires an Acknowledgement of Authority?> Kelsey mused.

<That's normal for Soldier-type classes,> Suliel sent silently. <Well, not the kills; normally you just need to have held a Warrior-type class.>

<So I only need to send six waves next time?>

<Eight,> Suliel sent firmly. <We don't want anyone missing out next time, and that's still a reduction. Hold on a moment—>

She interrupted herself as her sergeant approached.

"What is it, Thurom?"

"My lady," he said, bowing his head. "I just noticed that I qualified for a new class myself. Drill Sergeant, Third Tier, Rare."

<Oooh, sounds like he's got a lot of yelling in his future,> Kelsey put in.

"What does that have to do with guns?" Suliel asked them both.

"I don't know, my lady," the sergeant answered. Kelsey's answer was slower and more considered.

<I don't really know either . . . in movies—uh, stories—the drill sergeant was the guy that whipped the new recruits into shape. Sounds like something you'll need.>

Suliel nodded slowly. "I'd advise you take it then,"

Thurom grimaced. "I don't much like the idea of starting my third tier over again, my Lady. I held some hopes of reaching Tier Four before I retired."

Suliel nodded. "It's your choice," she said, "But your current class is Fine, is it not? You don't want to overlook a chance at an upgrade."

She thought to check him with *Nobility's Privilege*.

Thurom Avist, Level 20, Parents: Alive and in Domain, Married with two children, Loyal, Sergeant

"You'd only have to redo five levels," she said. "I know Kirido has been a bit of a backwater where nothing happens, but that's changing. I predict that there will be many opportunities to gain experience in the near future."

<I wonder if that's your version of the old Chinese curse,> Kelsey mused nonsensically as Thurom nodded thoughtfully. *<"May you have many opportunities to gain experience.">*

<I have no idea what you're talking about,> Suliel told her.

She got only giggles in response, which was about what she'd expected. Ignoring it, she addressed her soldiers once more. They didn't notice her at first, but Thurom bellowed at them to pay attention. Nodding her thanks, she started a short speech.

"Well done everyone! I've got two more things to tell you, and then you can have the rest of the day off to celebrate your new classes!"

The cheers were muted, because Thurom was glaring at them, but they were there.

"First of all, the Adventurers Guild will pay silver for any details of a class that isn't in their books. Needless to say, it's first come, first paid."

A quiver ran through the unit as they all realized what that meant. They were going to be racing back to town.

"Second of all, there are a hundred zombie corpses dissolving uphill. Some fraction of them will have mana crystals, which the guild will also pay silver for. Probably about thirty?"

Now they were torn. Should they run uphill or down?

"My lady," Thurom said in a pained voice. "They're not supposed to be running around town with their rifles."

"That's true," Suliel agreed. "You'll have to check your equipment in before you can go crystal hunting *or* report to the guild."

"Yes, my lady," Thurom said. "All right! Back to barracks, quick march!"

Suliel stayed where she was and watched them head back to town. Her horse had calmed down, so she mounted him and sent the stablemaster back as well.

<I can have the next batch ready in three days,> Kelsey told her.

"We'll be ready," Suliel said.

CHAPTER TWENTY-SEVEN

She's Out There Somewhere

They are being *tediously* anal about this," Kelsey griped.

Zaphar frowned in confusion. "I'm not—I'm not sure what buttocks have to do with the situation?"

Kelsey looked at him blankly for a second. "Oh!" she finally said. "Bad translation. There was an old, influential guy who attributed every problem a person could have with how they were toilet trained."

"Toilet . . . trained?" Zaphar asked.

Anton sighed. Eventually, Zaphar would learn not to go down the rabbit hole.

"You were probably too young to remember," Kelsey explained, "but at some point, you learned to defecate in a hole and not in your pants. That's toilet training."

"I see . . . but how does that relate to our situation?"

Kelsey sighed. "To say that someone is anal is to say that they are overly fixated on what comes out of their arse. As shown by their fixation on *other* things, like properly regulated wall patrols."

"So . . . they are anal because they are doing their job properly?" Zaphar asked. "It seems a little rich for a thief to expect that the way in will be made easy for them."

"There's no reason for it, is all!" Kelsey exclaimed. "We're in the heart of the Empire, probably. There shouldn't be any external enemies that they need to worry about."

"There are always threats for walls to guard against," Zaphar replied.

"Bandits, covert raids from other governors . . ." He gestured at the group of them. "Extraordinary intruders."

"Even if that's true," Kelsey groused, "It doesn't mean that I have to like it."

Anton could agree with that, at least. They'd hoped to slip over the walls of whatever city was ahead of them once darkness fell, but the soldiers that manned the walls were not being cooperative. The top of the wall was well lit with the illumination reaching to the ground in many places. Guards kept up a constant patrol every half hour.

It wasn't perfect. Anton thought there were a few gaps where Zaphar or himself could sneak through. Dropping a rope and hauling up Kelsey and Aris, though . . . that would take too long.

"We need a distraction," Kelsey mused. "And I think I know just the thing."

"We're not blowing up the wall," Anton said immediately.

"I like the way you think, Anton, but you're right."

Kelsey grinned at him. Anton grimaced, which meant that his worst idea *wasn't* the worst idea that *she* could come up with.

"I don't think you could?" Zaphar put in. "The city walls are much thicker than the buildings you—" He broke off as Aris gave him a gentle cuff.

"Don't *challenge* her, you idiot," she told him.

Kelsey's grin grew wider. "Well, if there's that much demand for it, I might reconsider. But we don't know if word about us has made it here, and we don't want to tip our hand this early."

"So what's your idea?" Anton asked, dreading the answer.

"You're gonna love it," Kelsey told him.

"I hate this idea," Anton told Kelsey. The pair of them were alone in the darkness, a little way from the wall. Zaphar and Aris were waiting in position.

"You're just saying that to be hurtful," Kelsey said. "If you had a better idea, you would have said it by now."

"What if we carried you over the wall?" Anton tried.

"Zaphar can barely carry the rope I gave him; he's not going to be able to carry a person while climbing. And you can't carry the both of us."

"Isn't summoning monsters really costly, though?"

"Eh, zombies are as cheap as they come. And I overbudgeted for Suliel's thing. She's not going to need as many zombies as I thought."

Anton took a moment to worry that Suliel was getting far too comfortable with undead monsters. Kelsey took advantage of the pause to summon her first zombie.

"Look," she said as it stumbled away. "There's no one out here; they must not let anyone build outside of the walls. These guys are going to smell the soldiers on top, they're not going to go anywhere else."

"Can they climb the wall?" Anton asked. Kelsey shrugged.

"I'm not sure," she said. "This many, they might be able to clamber over themselves to get there. Doesn't matter, though, they're not going to be a problem for trained soldiers."

She kept summoning zombies. One after the other, they all shambled away, toward the city. Shortly after she stopped, they heard a shout coming from that direction.

"Just the thing," she said smugly, "that will keep them heading in that direction."

Anton had to lead Kelsey back to the place where they'd decided to cross. Kelsey needed to keep her gaze fixed on the backs of the shamblers, to make sure they remained on target. Once there, he gazed despondently at the empty section of wall above them.

"Come on," Kelsey said. "It won't last. As soon as they recover from the shock, they'll send someone to check the rest of the wall."

Anton nodded and took the rope she gave him. Climbing the wall, swiftly and silently, was easy enough thanks to *Spider Climb*. Kelsey wasn't as graceful, but she could pull herself up the rope almost as fast as he could pull her up. The street behind the wall was well lit, but it was empty, so he lowered her down. He tossed her his end of the rope, and she disposed of it before it fell to the ground.

A neat party trick, he thought as he made his way down.

"No shots fired," Kelsey said when he rejoined her. "So I think they must have had just as easy a time. Let's go."

They both headed off in the appropriate direction. Anton was only barely paying attention; his thoughts were on something else.

He'd rejoined her. Standing on the wall, with her at the bottom, had been about as far as he'd managed to be from her since she'd put the geas on him. Not the absolute farthest, but close to it. And he'd felt . . . not *nothing*. He'd felt a twinge of unease, but his heart hadn't started beating faster. The cold sweat hadn't chilled his skin.

It had to be the effect of his new trait, *Unwavering*. Anton had hoped, but this was the first chance he had to test it since the sea battle. It seemed . . . promising. He grinned to himself as they met up with the others.

"So what's the plan now?" Aris asked quietly.

"We need information first," Kelsey said. "First, what city are we in? Then, where can we find the slaver who has Cheia?"

She looked at Zaphar. "Since you're the local, we'll have you do most of the talking," she said.

"If the goal is not to arouse suspicions, perhaps I should not ask those questions?" Zaphar protested. "What city am I in? How does one not know that?"

"I'm sure we can find someone whose opinion doesn't matter," Kelsey dismissed. "A drunk or a beggar or someone."

"You said you had some idea, at least," Zaphar countered.

"Fine," Kelsey allowed. "We were planning on finding Cheia in Denasti, held captive by a courl called Zaraq Malik."

"That's something to work with," Zaphar said, nodding. "So, when I was on the wall, I saw more lights in . . ." He cast about, trying to orient himself. "In that direction, I think. It was probably the entertainment district? We can probably find someone to ask questions of there."

"Sounds like a plan," Kelsey said. "We can also find an inn to use as our base of operations."

"Sure, sure," Zaphar agreed. "But, but if our purpose is to avoid attention . . ." he trailed off nervously.

"What?" Kelsey asked.

"Dark-skinned humans are common enough, at least they are in Rused," Zaphar said. "Pale-skinned ones like you, though . . . are not."

"You get travellers from the north, though," Kelsey said.

"I have seen them," Zaphar admitted. "They, they do not wear what you wear, though."

Kelsey glared at him. "I'm not going to wear sealskin leather and polar bear fur, thanks."

"No, no!" Zaphar said, raising his hand in surrender. "Perhaps something more . . . local? That covered your skin?"

There was a tense moment of silence, which was finally broken by Kelsey.

"Yeah," she said. "I could probably do something like that."

"What!" Anton and Aris chorused.

"Right back at you," Kelsey said, scowling at them. "What's your problem?"

"You could have worn normal clothing all this time," Anton lamented. "People thought I was crazy for associating with you."

"Well," Kelsey said reasonably, "all of those other times, I *wasn't* trying to stay unnoticed."

Without any fuss or fanfare, a garment of deep blue cloth appeared around her. Anton was sure that it had a name in Elitran, but the closest he could come to it was a robe.

Kelsey tugged a fold of cloth over her head, concealing her features. The long sleeves of the robe allowed her to hide her hands.

"Will this do?" she asked. "It's basically the same as what I made for the slaves."

Zaphar nodded vigorously. "Yes, yes, that will do nicely! As long as you do not speak, people will think you are a rich lady who has hired me to ask questions. If you two walk behind her, no one will look twice."

"Back to being a slave," Aris groused.

"No, no—I mean, seem to be, yes." Zaphar spluttered.

"This won't last," Kelsey promised. "Once we've got the information we need, we'll act. Incognito will go out the window shortly after, I suspect."

"Let's get going then," Anton said.

It took a little while to walk to the entertainment district, as Zaphar called it. He found someone to confirm that the city was, in fact, Denasti. Kelsey had an address for Malik, so they agreed to leave chasing that lead until the morning. They moved on to finding an inn to stay at.

"Not this one," Zaphar said of the first one they tried. "The cloth of your kaftan is too fine for a low-class dive like this."

"But I like low-class dives," Kelsey protested. "Did I make this thing too well?"

Anton looked at her inquiringly. "You've always stayed at the best inns available before," he said.

"Well, yeah, but low profile, remember?"

"I'll find something," Zaphar said.

"Something with a bath," Aris insisted.

They eventually found a place that suited them. Three bedrooms, linked by a common room for dining and discussions.

"Cozy and private," Kelsey had said of the arrangement. "I like it."

Now, with Aris taking the first bath, they started making plans.

"Once we find out where this place is," Kelsey said, "we're going to have to scope it out. That's going to be on you," she told Zaphar.

He nodded. "I'll be able to sneak in the next night and get an idea of where everything is," he said.

Kelsey shook her head. "Yeah, we'll do that, but we're going to have you go in during the day."

"I'm not . . . I don't think I can sneak in during the day," Zaphar said cautiously.

"You won't be," Kelsey said. "Remember when I said you were going to be doing the talking? We're going to dress you up like a rich person and you're going to go in saying you want to buy some slaves."

"Ah . . . I'm not sure I'm suited for that? I don't—I'm not the right sort?"

"You'll be fine," Kelsey said, dismissing his concerns. "Unless you think I should do it?"

She probably *could* do it, Anton thought. Her Charisma was as high as the rest of her abilities, which explained how she was able to bull her way through social situations when everything about her screamed to run away.

Zaphar was not so lucky. Anton used *Delver's Discernment* to remind him of what the thief's Charisma was.

Zaphar Alpashan, Level 16, Fae-Touched Rogue, Thief/Burglar/Fae-
Touched Rogue
S: 4 T: 17 A: 24 D: 27 P: 17 W: 10 C: 7

He had the worst Charisma out of the whole group. Of course, that meant that he was easily convinced to do the job.

"Yeah fine, whatever," he said, caving to the pressure.

"Don't forget the escape plan," Anton said. "We won't have a fae to get us out of trouble this time, and there are sure to be more Tier Fours in this city."

"Yeah," Kelsey agreed. "We should ask around about those. I'm not too worried, though."

She grinned evilly. "We've got a city full of slaves and a Heroic Liberator at our disposal. This city won't know what hit it."

CHAPTER TWENTY-EIGHT

Fashion

The next morning, they started work on Zaphar's disguise. Anton was a little surprised that Kelsey didn't just use her own resources, but she had her reasons.

"We want him to look like a local," she explained, "and I don't know if local fashions here are the same as Rused. Plus we need someone to fix his hair."

"Fix? What needs fixing?" Zaphar asked.

"I'm not sure . . . well, apart from everything," Kelsey told him. "Everywhere does hair differently, so we'll need an expert local to make sure you fit in."

"*Does* hair?" Zaphar wondered. "I've always just cut it with a dagger when it got too long."

"I didn't want to say anything, but that has been *painfully* obvious since I first met you," Kelsey said. Zaphar shut up after that.

Anton wasn't entirely sure it wasn't all just an excuse for another shopping trip. As she'd done before, Kelsey roved through the market, alert for any kind of unusual merchandise. She tweaked her own disguise, purchasing a shawl for additional concealment and a sash to go around her waist. She also picked up a string of beads for no apparent reason other than she liked the look of it.

Anton tried not to stare too hard at the sight of the non-human races that lived in the town. Due to its proximity to the great plains of Elitra, Denasti was home to large populations of Grasswhisperers and Plainsrunners. Anton had seen the vivid green hair of a Grasswhisperer in Rused, but this was his first time seeing a Plainsrunner, and he had to work hard not to stare.

It was his first time seeing an intelligent being with four legs. Anton watched out of the corner of his eye as a small pack (or herd?) of them trotted down the street, their horns jutting up above the crowd. Like the humans of the plains, they had been conquered and folded into the Elitran empire, but unlike the humans, they hadn't worked their way into the inner sanctums of power.

Somewhere in all of this, they managed to see to Zaphar's makeover. Washing had been taken care of back at the inn, but now he was properly shaved and his skin anointed with properly masculine oils and scents.

Aris had pronounced them "stinky," which had put paid to any thought of Anton following the local customs.

Zaphar's hair had been professionally, or at least expensively cut, and was now curled into little ringlets, held in place by some concoction that Kelsey was weirdly happy to call "product."

They had also made some modifications to Anton's outfit. After asking around, Kelsey managed to find a place that was selling higher-tier armor, and Anton selected a pair of linen pants. They swished loosely around his legs distractingly, but they were Tier Three, giving him more protection than the heavier leather pants. They talked about strapping on some metal plates, but since getting *Stone Skin*, Anton hadn't felt the need for heavier armor. Mobility and speed were the touchstones of his fighting style, and he didn't want anything that would slow him down.

"Shouldn't we get you a Tier Three sword as well?" Aris asked.

"I'm fine with Dad's old sword," Anton demurred.

"Yeah, that's for the best," Kelsey agreed. "Armor and equipment you can just buy off the rack, but a hero's sword needs to be more personal."

Anton gave Kelsey a wary look. "You're not wrong. I *do* want to keep using Dad's sword for personal reasons . . . but it sounds like you mean something else."

Kelsey shrugged. "Don't get me wrong, we'll upgrade you eventually. But it'll be like Chainbreaker was, taken off of your enemies, or inherited from a mentor or something."

"Captain Oldaw wasn't really my enemy, though," Anton pointed out. "I fought two nobles that day, and he wasn't one of them."

"Yeah, I'd say that was why it didn't stick," Kelsey agreed. "I tried to make it a bit more thematic, but I couldn't change the enchantments, so there was only so much I could do."

"Are you mad that I gave it away?" Anton asked curiously. "It got us away from that ship, and got us to here."

"Eh, we could have gotten out of that some other way," Kelsey waved dismissively. "I'm not mad, exactly, I'm just a little miffed that I didn't get the sword right."

"I'm hearing it too, now," Aris put in. "What does 'getting it right' *mean*?"

Kelsey looked at the pair of them, and then glanced over at Zaphar. She sighed, a slow hiss of escaping air.

"Eahggghh . . . I'm not really ready for this. There are rules, you see."

"What sort of rules?" Aris asked.

"Oh, there are lots. You know a lot of them already, the ones that apply to, well, mortals. You can't fly, you have to eat, you die. How you get traits and so on."

"I heard that Skytenders can fly," Anton interrupted. "They live farther east, but I was hoping to see one . . ."

Kelsey glared at him. "The mortal rules aren't the point," she said. "The point is the *immortal* rules."

"Anton's not immortal, so I still don't see what it has to do with us," Aris said. "For that matter, as worried as you are about dying, I'm not sure that you should be using the word for yourself."

"I don't age, so it sort of works," Kelsey said mildly. "And as for Anton . . . some of the laws that apply to . . . higher beings also apply or interact with heroes."

Aris looked at Kelsey suspiciously. "What . . . sort of laws?" she asked slowly.

Kelsey shrugged. "I dunno." She held up her hands in the face of the pair's instant protest. "Not all of it, not enough of it. And what I *do* know, I'm not prepared to say."

She glanced over at Zephar. "You never know who's listening, you know?"

Zaphar frowned. "You're keeping secrets from my . . . er . . . patron?" he asked.

Kelsey snorted. "I don't know if you were paying attention to that conversation on the boat, but both of us were trying to imply a lot without saying a damn thing. Neither of us trusts the other worth a damn."

"But you'll still work with him," Anton said.

"Well, sure. I'm pretty sure our interests are aligned. As long as he feels the same way, we can work together."

"But you don't want him to know what your interests *are*, because they *might* . . . clash." Zaphar mused.

"Yeah. Of course, your nameless patron is the least of my worries. I'm much more worried about who *else* might be listening in."

"Other fae?" Anton guessed. "Demons?"

"Sure, but that's not who I was talking about," Kelsey said. "For now, let's get back to shopping."

Aris was the final one to receive a makeover. Kelsey was reluctant to compromise or modify Aris's "look", for reasons she was unwilling to explain. But they managed to find a lighter long coat that was more suitable for the warmer weather and matched whatever arcane requirements that Kelsey was working under.

Eventually, she declared they were ready. Or at least that Zaphar was.

"I'm to go—to go in there on my own?" he exclaimed.

"You're just buying a slave," Kelsey told him. "Not even that, you're just looking. There's no reason to send a whole party in for that."

"Just one of you could come? You could come?" he asked.

Kelsey shook her head. "If I go, then Anton has to go, and if either Anton and Aris are there, the presence of some armed Zamarrans might raise their suspicions." She looked over at the two of them. "You don't look very much like slaves," she said.

"Thanks," Aris said cooly.

"Actually," Anton said, "since I got my *Unwavering* trait, I've been managing the geas a lot better. I bet I could handle staying out here while you went inside."

"Really," Kelsey said, her face expressionless. She gave him a long look without saying anything. Then her face cleared. "That's great! We'll have to test it in a bit."

She turned back to Zaphar. "You're still going in alone."

"But why?" he wailed.

"Aside from the fact I don't want an armed Zamarran reaching his limit and running in after me; if you go in alone, you'll get more experience."

"Experience? This isn't a break-in."

"And you're not a Burglar anymore. I'll bet a gold coin to your copper that you'll get experience from this."

Zaphar looked at her pleadingly, but Kelsey was unyielding.

"Fine," he said. Collecting himself, he stood up straight in a passable impression of a rich man's demeanor and marched off towards the shop.

Finding it had not been a problem. They'd been able to get directions, and there was a sign on the front door. Slave traders needed business, after all.

Kelsey watched Zaphar disappear into the shop.

"So, *Unwavering*, huh?" she said.

"Are you angry?" Anton asked.

"Hmm, no," she replied. "I mean it's a *little* hurtful that you want to spend some time apart after all we've been through, but I get it. And it's better if we can split up from time to time."

"It doesn't . . . entirely negate the geas, from what I've felt," Anton said.

"It wouldn't," Kelsey agreed. "We'll test it later . . . the important thing is that you stick around, not that we're in each other's pockets all the time. Just—" She stopped herself.

"Just what?" Anton asked.

"Just—remember when I said that the geas was *managed*?"

"I never heard that," Aris said. "Managed by who?"

"Dunno," Kelsey replied, "But I also told you that it used fear because that was the most effective method, for you?"

"Yeah, you—wait." Anton felt a chill come over him. "You mean that if it becomes *less* effective, it will change?"

"I can't say for sure," Kelsey said "I've never had it happen. But that's what I think."

"I guess there's no getting away from you then," Anton said. He tried to inject some despair into his tone, but Kelsey wasn't fooled.

"Best buddies forever!" she said, lightly punching him in the arm.

They had to wait a little longer for Zaphar to come back out and make his way over to them.

"I didn't see any of them," he said. "There's a big auction in two days and the new arrivals are being prepared for that."

"Prepared how?" Aris asked anxiously.

"Uh . . . teaching Elitran and . . . and advancing in their class," Zaphar replied.

"What class do slaves have?" Aris asked.

Anton frowned. He'd never considered the question. There was at least one Slave class wasn't there?

"Uh, everyone at the auction will either be Doxy or Concubine," Zaphar said. "There are some Courtesans in the place, but none of the new ones have . . . been around . . . long . . ." He trailed off, looking at Aris's face. "Sorry," he added.

Anton put his arms around her and she buried her face in his chest.

"They wouldn't . . . she's my little sister. She's too young . . ."

Kelsey took a step closer and laid a comforting hand on the young girl's shoulder. "The world is a terrible place, Aris," she said. "Let's burn it all down to the ground."

In the moment, Anton could only agree. He kept his mouth shut, though, because Kelsey didn't need any encouragement to produce wide-scale devastation.

"Two days then," Kelsey said briskly. "We'll send you in tonight, get a look at the place."

Zaphar nodded. "Their security is good," he said. "I doubt I'll get inside any of the buildings, but I should be able to find out where they're keeping the captives."

"Next order of business is securing our escape route," Kelsey said, "Except for—did you get experience for going in?"

"I did actually—why are you holding out your hand?"

"We made a bet, didn't we? You owe me a copper!"

"I never actually agreed to that bet. Wasn't it just a figure of speech?"

"A welcher, eh?" Kelsey poked her open palm at him aggressively. "Don't you know, in the criminal underworld, there's no one more despised than someone who doesn't pay his debts?"

"Fine, fine," Zaphar said, reaching into his money pouch for a coin. "You are made of money, why would you care about a single copper?"

"It's not the money that's important," Kelsey said. She took the coin and held it in front of her face, flipping it over so that she could see both sides.

"This is about me being right."

Giving the coin a long final look, she made it disappear.

"Come on guys," she said. "We've got a lot to do before we can rescue Cheia."

CHAPTER TWENTY-NINE

How Soon Is Now?

C an't we go in tonight?" Aris asked. "Cheia is just in there!"

"Now, now." Kelsey took Aris's arm and walked her down the street. She switched languages to Zamarran. "We need to have a plan."

"Just go in there with explosions and guns and get her out," Aris muttered, following Kelsey's lead with languages. "Those walls don't look any tougher than the ones back in Rused."

"Absolutely," Kelsey promised. "And this time, as we leave, I'll drop a horde of hungry undead. They'll scour the compound clean of life and then burst out into the city, devouring all in their path."

"Um, I don't think that last bit . . ." Aris objected.

"I can see it now," Kelsey said. "Shambling over the piles of corpses, blood running through the streets . . . until some Fourth Tier comes along and puts an end to all the fun."

"What?" Aris asked.

"What's worse is that if we're still around at that point, he'll find and put an end to us as well," Kelsey said morosely. "People get so moralistic over a mountain of bodies."

"I can't imagine why," Anton said sardonically. Zaphar was just looking at them, unable to follow the conversation.

"That's why we need a plan," Kelsey said firmly, switching back to Elitran. "We need to know how many people we're taking, we need a place to take them, and we need a way to get them home."

"Is it not the same plan as before?" Zaphar asked once he was included again. "An abandoned house, and a hired ship?"

"Maybe," Kelsey said. "I don't have any other ideas right now, but that plan has a few problems."

"What problems?" Anton asked.

"For one, this town is much more well-ordered than Rused was. I don't know if we'll be able to find a neighborhood where we can move into an abandoned house and not attract attention. For another, we're not on the edge of the Empire anymore. Once Captain al-Nazari got over the horizon, he was off the map. *We'll* have to sail up to and *past* Rused before we get to that point."

"But," Aris protested, "it's only two days until the auction. Do we have time to make a new plan?"

"Don't worry about it," Kelsey assured her. "If the auction gets held, we'll attend and make note of who buys her. It will actually be easier stealing her from her new owner."

"Them," Aris said, frowning. "I want to save Cheia, but I can't abandon the rest of them."

"Sure, sure," Kelsey agreed. "We can track them all. Now, let's head down to the docks to see what our options are."

They spent the rest of the day walking the docks, with Kelsey getting more and more frustrated. When they got back to the inn, she was quietly fuming.

"Not a hint of impropriety!" she exclaimed. "Not a sniff of anything untoward!"

"You said it was a well-run town," Anton pointed out. The four of them were eating their evening meal in the shared room.

"No town is *that* well-run. Some of them must be smuggling things. The problem is that none of them are willing to tell a stranger that."

At issue was that none of the ship's captains were willing to take on passengers who didn't have travel papers. Kelsey had hinted at more money in return for less checking, but none of them had taken the bait.

Kelsey looked at Zaphar speculatively, and he sighed. "It will take more than a few days to find and gain the trust of the criminal underworld here," he said. "And you've got me scouting the compound tonight."

Kelsey nodded her reluctant agreement. "I do have some ways that might get us in contact with them sooner, but in this town, they might get me arrested."

"No getting arrested," Anton insisted. He didn't want the deaths that would cause on his conscience. Kelsey stuck her tongue out at him but didn't protest otherwise.

"We could buy a boat," she said thoughtfully.

"How would we crew it?" Anton asked skeptically.

"I've lowered the water level on the Sunless Sea," Kelsey said as if that answered him. Everyone looked at her, puzzled, but Zaphar was more confused than the rest of them.

"What is the Sunless Sea, and how do you change the water level?" he asked, but Kelsey ignored him to answer Anton's unspoken question.

"Enough to put a boat on top of it," she said. "And train some Skeleton Sailors."

"Monsters crewing the boat? *Monsters?*" Zaphar asked. He'd absorbed the idea that Kelsey was a dungeon, but he hadn't really accepted the reality of it.

"They'd be terrified," Anton pointed out. "*I'd* be terrified. How do skeletons know how to sail?"

Kelsey waved a hand vaguely. "The magic takes care of things like that."

"You'd still have to get out of the harbor," Zaphar said. "The harbormaster, I think, will want to check your papers. *He* might have some objections to skeletons crewing the boat. If not the harbormaster, then the Navy might intercept. *They* would surely sink us on sight."

"Hmm," Kelsey pondered. "If we had a deck-mounted machine gun we could sweep their decks . . ."

"I thought you didn't want to get chased all the way to Rused," Anton interrupted. Or risk running into another Tier Four."

"Point," Kelsey admitted. "Maybe we could distract them with something. If there were a lot of people leaving, or unrest in the streets . . ." She trailed off in thought.

"Zaphar," she said eventually. "Tell me about healers and priests in the Empire."

"Those are mostly the same thing," he replied. "There are alchemists and physicians as well but they are more expensive. From what I hear, often less effective."

"Go on," she said.

"Well . . ." Zaphar said doubtfully. "Alchemists have potions that can make you heal quicker, and antidotes to poisons. Physicians can stitch you up and set broken bones and such, but they don't have magic."

"They have traits, surely?" Kelsey asked.

"Not magic ones. I think they get supernatural skill ones?"

Kelsey nodded. "What can they do about disease?" she asked.

"Not much, but I think they can stop themselves getting it," Zaphar replied. "For disease, you want a priest . . . the right priest."

"What gods are good for healing?"

"Well, the human and courl gods, of course. Tiait and Kait."

It was the first time that Anton had heard the name of the God of Courls, and he was surprised by how similar it was to the God of Humans.

"Kait can't cure humans, though, right?" Kelsey asked.

"They can, actually, although word got out that the trait was called *Tend Prey*, which didn't make them more popular."

Kelsey snorted but kept her focus. "Who else?"

"There's a God of Medicine, isn't there? I don't steal from temples, it's unlucky. There was one time there was a plague ship, and they sent priests of Denem in."

"God of Trade, eh? Inutan was one of his, she was pretty versatile . . ."

Kelsey trailed off in thought again. Eventually, she returned her attention to the others.

"I think I've got the start of an idea, but it will take more than a few days to get started," she said.

"Then we could look at getting, what did you call it, a safe house?" Anton said. "Hide out in there until we have a boat ready."

"Yeah," Kelsey said slowly. "This time, we should go legitimate. Get a warehouse and kit it out, smuggle people in secretly and stay hidden for a while."

"You probably need residency papers to buy a warehouse," Zaphar said.

Kelsey growled. "I really wanted to avoid dealing with criminals this time around," she said.

"Sure, sure," Zaphar said nervously. "I should get going on that compound reconnaissance, right?"

He left hurriedly. The rest of the group talked among themselves, brainstorming ideas until Kelsey called a halt.

"Get some sleep," she told the other two. "I'll stay up to meet Zaphar when he comes back."

From Aris's sudden case of the giggles, Anton knew that he wouldn't be getting sleep immediately.

"You're not coming?" he asked. Kelsey raised an eyebrow and he felt heat come to his face.

"I mean—I'm just used to—"

Kelsey cut him off with a smile. "Treat it like a test of *Unwavering*, and see how long you can stay in a different room from me."

"Right." Anton nodded. Being on the other side of a door was especially challenging for his geas because he didn't *know* how far away Kelsey was. "I'll see you in the morning then," he said awkwardly.

Aris dragged him towards the bedroom. "This will be the first chance we get to be alone since this all started," she giggled. Anton didn't contradict her. He was fairly sure that Kelsey's senses were up to listening through the door.

The door closed behind them, and Anton felt a twinge of the old fear. It didn't control him now, so he took hold of Aris and kissed her.

"You'll have to distract me from the geas," he said.

"I can do that," she eagerly replied.

Kelsey had breakfast ready for them when they got up. She'd drawn up a map of the compound from Zaphar's description, and now they went over it with the others.

"Guards are all around," Zaphar said. "Stationary posts at these six positions, patrols around the wall, and also inside the compound."

"Inside?" Aris asked.

Zaphar nodded, tracing the routes he'd seen the guards take. "I think to catch escaping slaves," he said. "But it works for trespassing thieves as well."

"They didn't catch you, though," Kelsey pointed out.

"I'm good," Zaphar boasted, "But they did limit me. I couldn't spend as much time as I'd like looking through windows, and I couldn't get into most of the buildings at all. All the windows are barred, even the higher floors. The only exceptions were the gardening shed and the stables."

"So you don't know what's inside the buildings?" Anton asked.

"Some," Zaphar said. He pointed out each building as he spoke of them. "The front entrance, it has a small showing room and a reception area for customers. This I have seen. That is only half the building, though, so I suspect there are offices and a waiting area for slaves before they are brought out."

"The main building?" Kelsey asked.

"The bottom floor is entirely open, and double height," Zaphar explained. "I think that is where they will hold the auction."

"This," he said, tapping a mid-sized building on the map, "is where the slaves are being kept. There is a walkway that leads from this building to the second level of the main one."

"The second level?" Aris asked, confused.

"Yes. They must prepare the slaves for auction, yes? They do that upstairs and then bring them down. The third floor, I think, is living quarters for the family. This building, a barracks for the guards, and this building is quarters for the house slaves."

Kelsey asked a few more questions as the rest of them ate. Once they had finished, she rolled the map up and made it disappear.

"Right," she said. "Let's see if you need papers to buy a boat."

They did not, as it happened, need papers to buy a boat—at least the kind of boat that was available.

"It's much smaller than the other one, isn't it?" Aris asked hesitantly.

Assuming she was talking about the tall ship captained by al-Nazari and not Kelsey's small bucket of insanity, Anton had to agree. The court selling it did not.

"It's a big ship!" he insisted. "Coastal Trader. Good hull, lots of storage. Come take a look!"

They did so, Kelsey showing more enthusiasm than the rest of them. It was, Anton had to admit, bigger than the fishing boats that frequently docked at Kirido. There was a single hold, a cavernous dark space accessed by a small hatch at the front and a large hatch in the middle. There were cabins above the deck, room enough for four, or eight if everyone shared a bunk. There was the deck.

And that was it.

Kelsey dropped down to inspect the hold. There was a small splash.

"It leaks?" Aris asked.

"All ships leak," the courl salesman said. "It's unavoidable."

Kelsey poked around the hold for a bit. Anton could see her shining her torch around. Finally, she jumped up and hauled herself out of the hatch, disdaining the use of the rope ladder.

"I think we're interested!" she said brightly. "Why don't we talk price?"

"Of course, of course," the courl said. If he noticed, as Anton did, that Kelsey's boots were completely dry, he didn't say anything.

Just before they got off the ship, Kelsey took a look out over the harbor. She frowned and paused for a longer look.

"What's wrong?" Anton asked. She grimaced.

"Look," she said. "Recognize that boat?"

Sailing into the harbor was a large gaudy boat that looked as if it was about to capsize. Anton couldn't swear he recognized it, but he'd only ever seen one boat that looked like that.

"That's the Pasha's boat, sailing in from Rused," Kelsey told him. "If news hadn't already arrived about our activities there, it just did."

CHAPTER THIRTY

Paid in Full

It's not a problem," Kelsey said confidently. They were back at the inn, and able to talk privately. Anton and the others had held back while they were in the shipyard, but they could speak up now.

"How is it not a problem?" Anton asked. "If there needs to be an inspection before the ship leaves, they're sure to notice all the freed Zamarrans onboard. And they'll be checking for papers as well!"

"Hmmph," Kelsey grumped. "Don't need papers to buy a ship, but you need them to sail out on it? Bit of a bait and switch, true. But it doesn't matter."

"Why not?" Aris asked.

"Due to a cunning plan . . . that is not yet fully formed." Kelsey paused and looked thoughtful. "Or, we could just *forge* some papers."

"I thought we weren't enlisting the underworld this time around," Anton said doubtfully.

"We don't need to," Kelsey said smugly. "I'm a dab hand at forgery myself, or at least my Scriving Skeletons are."

"You can't read Elitran, though," Anton pointed out. "Isn't that necessary?"

"Hmm, hang on," Kelsey said. After a brief pause, she pulled a piece of paper out of nowhere and gave it to Zaphar. "Is this legible?" she asked.

Zaphar looked doubtfully at her, and the paper she offered him, but took it. "This . . . this is good paper," he said wonderingly.

"Thanks, I made it myself."

"As for the writing . . ." Zaphar looked at the words and sighed. "It says that Anton is a mean poopy head. He's lucky he's so hot."

Kelsey nodded. "That is *exactly* what I wanted to write," she said.

Anton rolled his eyes, not just at Kelsey's pettiness, but at the ridiculousness of what she could do. "So, *you* don't read Elitran, but your skeletons do? How does that work?"

Kelsey shrugged. "I don't make the rules," she said. "The skeletons can write, so they can write any language that I can speak . . . even if I don't know the letters."

"Can they read as well?" Zaphar asked.

"Yeeeaaaah, sort of," Kelsey said. "They don't *speak*, so getting information out of them is hard. The link gives me nonverbal impressions . . . which isn't always reliable."

"You'll need more than that for forgeries, though," Zaphar pointed out. "You need to know *what* to write, and you'll need inks and a seal . . ."

"You can help with that," Kelsey said. "You can break into the office of whoever issues these papers and get me some examples to work off."

Zaphar drew in his breath nervously. "Maybe. *Maybe* I could get some papers. But steal a seal?"

"You don't have to *steal* it," Kelsey said. "I can give you something to take an impression of it and make my own from that."

"Even so," Zaphar said. "It will likely be locked up tight outside of office hours."

"You can't crack a safe?" Kelsey asked. "Wait, we are talking about a safe, right? You have those?"

"We do, and I can't," Zaphar agreed. "I just sneak in and steal things."

"Well . . . maybe I can reverse engineer it from the impressions it leaves," Kelsey said. "We'll workshop it."

The next item on Kelsey's agenda was renting a warehouse. This turned out to be much harder than it had been back in Kirido. There, Anton had known just about everybody, and a few questions had identified who was looking to sell out and retire after the raid.

It was much more complicated here. Fortunately, they had Zaphar to do the actual talking. As a native Elitran, he could at least pass for a local. And his recent makeover made him appear respectable. All that meant, though, was that the merchants he talked to were *willing* to talk to him. Useful information was much harder to come by.

If there was an informed person who kept track of which merchants had spare warehouse space, no one was willing to direct Zaphar to them. Nor did they keep tabs on the business dealings of their neighbors, or so they claimed. Zaphar was reduced to wandering the warehouse district, going from door to door, looking for a seller.

"This isn't working," Kelsey groused after two hours of this. "We've found *three* likely prospects, but not a hint of who to talk to!"

It turned out that warehouses that suited their purpose, i.e., unused and far away from well-trafficked areas, often lacked a conveniently available owner. There wasn't much reason to stay near an empty warehouse, after all. Nor were their neighbors much help in tracking down the owners. Two of the warehouses they had found had neighbors that yielded a first name for who they *thought* might own the building. Nobody was able to say where these people were to be found.

"Maybe we should check out the taverns where merchants gather?" Anton said.

"Worth a try," Kelsey agreed. "If that doesn't work, we can try burning one down and see who shows up."

"Then . . . there wouldn't be any warehouse for us to rent, though," Aris said.

"True, but I'd feel better at least," Kelsey said. "Let's try the taverns, though."

Asking questions in taverns did not prove any easier. It was more comfortable, though, than trekking from door to door. And it was, eventually, successful.

"Warehouse space, you say? I might have something available." The portly middle-aged man ran his hand through his thinning hair.

Zaphar glanced at Kelsey for reassurance but pushed on with his script without any help from her.

"We're not looking to share, we need a building of our own," he said firmly.

The man nodded. "I've some product there, but it can fit into other stores," he agreed. "If the price is right."

Zaphar didn't know what the right price for warehouse space was, but he knew haggling. He let the man suggest a price and then made a counteroffer for a third of that. Anton watched as the thief bargained the merchant down to half of his initial suggestion.

Anton didn't think that the price actually mattered, but it would have looked suspicious, and not very merchant-like, if they hadn't tried to find a bargain. From the way Kelsey stayed silent through the discussion, she felt the same way.

The discussion finally reached the point where an inspection of the premises was in order. It was late in the afternoon, but there was still daylight, so they headed out immediately. Kelsey's eye twitched when the merchant led him to one of the properties they'd already marked as a prospect. The merchant next door had given the owner's name as Fari. The man in front of him had given his name as Farid al-Darim, so that might not be incorrect, but would have made finding him based on that difficult.

"You see! Everything is as I described," al-Darim declared, waving at the cavernous darkness. Zaphar and Kelsey shared a look. Anton was *pretty sure* that both of them could see in the dark.

"I think we'll need a little more light to see," Kelsey said mildly.

"Of course! A lantern is kept . . . near . . . here," al-Darim said, fumbling near the door. He did manage to find and light a lantern and he was soon shining it about the place. As he'd said, there was a small stack of crates sitting in the middle of the place, but it was otherwise empty.

"How soon can you get rid of those?" Zaphar asked.

"I can have those removed tomorrow," the merchant assured him. "I can get the contract ready by then and we can probably get it registered after lunch."

"Registered?" Kelsey asked. Something in her voice made al-Darim look at her nervously.

"Well, yes, all lease and purchasing contracts need to be registered with the central administrative bureau . . ." he said, trailing off as he looked at Kelsey. He swallowed as Kelsey took a step forward.

"Don't you think," Kelsey purred, "that it would be better if we kept this contract informal?"

"That's, ah . . . very irregular," he said. He took a step back as Kelsey kept moving closer, but there was a limited number of steps he could take before his back was against the wall.

"Of course," Kelsey said, "we'd be willing to pay, say, fifty percent more for the convenience."

"That's ah . . . very tempting, but it's *technically* illegal, so . . ."

"And if central administration didn't *know* about it, you wouldn't have to report it on your taxes, would you?"

Kelsey had the man backed up against the wall, despite not having come closer than a yard of him. Anton wasn't sure how she was doing it. Her body language wasn't threatening, and her voice sounded as pleasant as he had ever heard it. It must be something to do with the way she was staring at the merchant.

At the mention of taxes, the merchant's face became a little more calculating.

"That . . . but it wouldn't work, you see. You'd have to report this place as your place of business, and they'd need to see how it is you're able to trade from here. They'd notice the discrepancy."

"Ah, but we won't be trading from here," Kelsey said.

"You won't?"

"We're not merchants. We just need this space, and some privacy, for our own purposes."

"Oh, that's . . . fifty percent, you say?"

Kelsey smiled and turned around to face Zaphar. With a wink, she handed over a leather bag, heavy with coin, while her body blocked al-Darim's view. "You can work out the final details with Zaphar."

"So, we've got a ship and a warehouse," Kelsey said. "I feel a plan coming together!"

"We don't actually have a ship," Zaphar pointed out. "You didn't finalize the deal."

"There's no point in paying docking fees for longer than we need to," Kelsey said. "I've got some upgrades in mind for that ship, but the ship can belong to the shipyard until I'm ready to start work."

Zaphar nodded. "So my next target . . . do you know where the documents are produced?"

"Ah, no," Kelsey admitted. "The central administration that Farid mentioned?"

"Maybe," Zaphar agreed. "I don't know where that is, though. I could ask around, but it would look a little suspicious if I did so after the place closed."

"Get some rest then," Kelsey suggested. "We've got that auction tomorrow; you'll want to be at your best."

"Are . . . we even going to do anything at the auction?"

"Take notes on the buyers at least," Kelsey said. "And be ready if there's an opportunity."

Zaphar grunted acknowledgement and turned to go to his room. He paused at the door.

"By the way, I felt some experience accrue when I dealt with al-Darim," he said. "I'm not sure why."

"Preparations for the heist," Kelsey said. "Your class is about bigger, more complicated ways to steal things now. We should get you trained on safecracking when we get the chance. That enhanced hearing of yours will help a lot."

"It will? I don't see how," Zaphar said. "Speaking of my enhanced hearing, I would like to get some sleep tonight, and this room is only separated from mine by two walls and an open room."

It took Anton a moment to understand what Zaphar meant. When he did, he felt the heat rise in his face. From the mortified look Aris got, she understood as well. Kelsey just grinned.

"No promises," she said. After Zaphar closed the door behind him, she looked at the other two.

"So . . . I guess there weren't any anxiety-related performance issues?"

"Not last night there weren't," Anton muttered. "I didn't realize he was—"

"He wasn't here last night, remember?" Kelsey said. "He didn't get back until the two of you were fast asleep."

"Oh," Aris said. "Now I feel embarrassed *and* dumb."

"You'll get over it," Kelsey chuckled. "The thing is, he's gone down to get dinner now . . . but they'll still be serving it for at least one more hour. So if you want to get some *actual* private time . . ."

"We could . . ." Aris said. "I mean . . ."

"Or if you're hungry, we could eat now and Zaphar can stay in the common room for a couple more hours . . ." Kelsey slyly suggested.

"I'm . . . not that hungry," Anton said slowly.

CHAPTER THIRTY-ONE

Girl on a Road

Anton woke to the smells of breakfast.

"Wakey wakey, eggs and bacey!" Kelsey called out. She'd brought food up to their rooms. There wasn't any bacon, but there were eggs, turned into an omelette and wrapped around some kind of vegetables that Anton wasn't familiar with. The food had been very strange since they'd arrived in the Elitran Empire, but Anton hadn't been raised to be a picky eater. Kelsey was delighted by all the new things to try.

"This tahini is to die for," she said, waving a piece of flatbread at him. He wasn't sure if tahini was the sauce or the bread itself.

"Did someone die for this?" Zaphar asked, stumbling out of his room.

"Of course not," Kelsey scoffed. "Breakfast is included in the cost of our rooms."

Anton elected not to say anything. Aris was the last to join them. Now that she didn't have to get up before dawn every day, she made a point of luxuriating in a late rise any chance she got. Not to the extent of missing breakfast, though.

She scowled at the food that Kelsey had brought up. "Bread isn't supposed to be *spicy*," she declared. She sat down and started to eat anyway.

"It's flatbread, it's different," Kelsey said brightly. "It'd probably do well as a pizza base, and they've got tomatoes here . . ."

"What are we doing today?" Anton asked, mostly to save the cooks downstairs from being bullied into making one of Kelsey's ideas.

"Well," Kelsey started, as she took a spoonful of the sauce and started spreading it on the bread, "Zaphar here is going to attend the auction, take note of who's buying, and get a closer look at their security from the inside."

"Is that all?" Aris asked. "Shouldn't he be sneaking in somewhere to set them free?"

"That would be suicide," Zaphar told her.

"Weeeellll," Kelsey said. "Truth be told, I'm hoping that either Zaphar's class or his patron will give him a nudge towards some sort of scam or heist that he can pull off. You can't count on someone's whims like that, though. Anyway, we're not ready to take in a bunch of freed slaves. That's what we'll be doing, getting that warehouse habitable."

"I won't have backup?" Zaphar exclaimed at the same time as Aris burst out with, "We're not coming with them?"

Kelsey tutted at them both, but Aris would not be denied.

"How is he going to know who Cheia is? He's never met her!"

"She looks like you, doesn't she?" Kelsey asked. "I think he'll figure it out. More to the point, *you* look like *her*, so what do you imagine the slavers will think if they see an older version of their captive wandering around the grounds?"

Aris stubbornly didn't answer, but Kelsey just stared inquiringly until Aris gave in.

"They'd think that I was here to rescue her," she admitted.

"Yeah," Kelsey agreed. "Let's not make the slavers right about *anything*, is my motto."

"Still," Anton said, "we can't just leave him to go in alone. What if something goes wrong?"

Zaphar nodded in furious agreement. Kelsey rolled her eyes.

"Fine," she said. "We can wait outside, just in case. We can use the time to test how far we can separate now."

It turned out that the distance was quite far. There was a spike of fear, a big one, whenever Kelsey went out of sight, but after that, Anton couldn't tell how far she was, and hence how much he should be panicking.

He was trying to judge how long he could keep this up when he heard the gunshot. His anxiety instantly spiked, but it was a different kind of fear. The only other person who could make that sound was standing right beside him, so Anton's immediate thought was, *Who has Kelsey shot?*

It was ironic, he thought as he started running, that being tied to Kelsey had made her less of a danger to others. Now his freedom had resulted in someone's death, and Anton could only hope that it was justified. He could hear shouts and the sound of people running, but he didn't see anyone as they ran around to the back of the compound.

When the pair of them rounded the corner, he saw Kelsey, helping someone down from the compound wall. Not Cheia, he saw immediately. This was . . . an elf? What was a scantily clad elf maiden doing in Elitra? It took a moment for him to realize that he had a way of getting *some* information.

Tyla of the Padascar Tribe, Level 6, Elf, Doxy, Padascar Hunter (Broken)/ Doxy
S: 10 T: 6 A: 6 D: 11 P: 13 W: 7 C: 7

Anton focussed on the (Broken)/Doxy part. *So another slave, then? Escaping? What—*

"What's going on?" he said, shoving his thoughts aside. "Who got shot?"

"He's on the other side of the wall," Kelsey said. "He seemed bad, so . . ."

"He was bad," the elf agreed. "I need to run—can you hide me?"

"Of course we can!" Kelsey agreed. "Aris, can you take her to our inn?"

Before Aris could reply, Kelsey looked at Tyla critically. "Here," she said, pulling a long piece of cloth out of nowhere. "Wear this."

"Can't I stay here for Cheia?" Aris asked.

Tyla wrapped the cloth around her like a cloak. That wasn't how the people here wore it, Anton knew, but it did cover her up. She made sure to drape it over her head, covering her pointy ears.

"Sorry," Kelsey said, "but we need to get this girl out of here, and I need to stay. Zaphar's gotten into trouble."

"How do you know?" Anton asked.

Kelsey grinned and pointed. From somewhere in the compound, a thick plume of smoke was rising up, high enough to be seen over the wall. The shouting, Anton now realized, wasn't as far away as he thought. It was just muffled by the high wall.

"Trouble's there," Kelsey said. "If Zaphar's not in the middle of it, he may have to hand in his class."

"Cheia . . ." Aris said softly, looking at the smoke.

"You look like her," Tyla said suddenly. "Are you her sister?"

Aris looked at the elf, surprised. Then at Kelsey, who was making shooing motions.

"We can talk about it at the inn," Aris said. "This way."

"We should get moving, too," Kelsey said. "Let's head around to the front entrance, see if they're evacuating."

There was a crowd of people leaving the estate. They were milling around uncertainly, but there was no sign of panic.

"Probably not sure if the auction's been called off or not," Kelsey mused. "Oooh, check out that one. The big courl with the blue sash."

Anton did what she said.

Salim al-Kadir, Level ??, Courl, Champion of Denasti, Scion/Duellist/ Champion/Champion of Denasti

S: ?? T: ?? A: ?? D: ?? P: ?? W: ?? C: ??

There was a salty iron taste in his mouth. "I can't see his level," he admitted.

"Forty," Kelsey said idly, as if it were *nothing*. "Pulling off a heist with him in the room must have netted Zaphar some very tasty experience."

"We're not going after him, though . . . right?" Anton asked uneasily. They were a fair distance away, but he worried that the courl might be able to hear them.

"Not directly," Kelsey agreed. "Not unless he ends up buying Cheia. But if we fail badly enough, he'll come after *us*."

Anton resolved that whatever happened, they had better not fail that badly.

"So what now?" he asked.

"I'm taking notes," Kelsey told him. "These guys are important people, but most of them are merchants or officials. There are some Tier Threes, but they don't seem like people we need to worry about."

Anton nodded. "But where's Zaphar?" he asked.

"Good question," Kelsey answered. "They're not evacuating the servants and slaves, so the fire can't be too bad."

She frowned. "Unless it *is*, and they don't care . . . but I don't see any of the family out here either."

"So what's going on? And why didn't they send anyone to investigate the gunshot?"

Kelsey chuckled. "They don't know what it *is*, still. And that dead guard fell down inside the compound, so that's where they're looking for the killer. I wonder if they're blaming the missing girl?"

As they watched from a distance, a pair of guards came out of the front gate. They escorted a richly dressed courl with auburn fur, who came out to talk with the guests individually. The first person he went up to was the Tier Four Champion, al-Kadir. He had no reaction at all to the exaggerated bows and gestures of respect. Once he had heard her out, he turned and left.

The other guests were mostly more receptive. A few were angry, but most seemed to be accepting of the apologies.

"Let's get a little closer," Kelsey suggested. "I might be able to hear what they're saying."

Since al-Kadir was gone, Anton felt a little safer about approaching. They moved forward, trying to seem like a natural part of the crowd. As a dark-skinned Zamarran and a pale northerner, though, they did stand out. When people started giving them confused looks, Kelsey shuffled them to the side a bit, closer to where the servants of the guests were patiently waiting for their masters to be done.

"What it looks like, basically," Kelsey murmured as they sidled away from the arrogant gazes. "Apologies for the disruption, promises of a new auction next week. Nothing about who was responsible, though."

"Do you think they captured him?"

Kelsey hummed with thought. "A few of these people are officials. Some might be judges. I don't think the Malik family is authorized to take justice into their own hands. I might be wrong, but if they captured Zaphar, they'd have to hand him over to the authorities. And with the authorities *right there*, they'd do it immediately."

"So . . ."

Kelsey hummed again. "Aris isn't going to panic if we take a while getting back, is she?"

Anton thought about it. "She'll want to talk to Tyla about Cheia for a while. If she gets worried, she'll leave the elf hidden at the inn and come looking for us."

Kelsey nodded. "If we can keep a lookout, we can intercept her before she does anything silly."

Anton gave her a look. It wasn't Aris who had shot a guard for no reason at all. Kelsey ignored him.

"Here, take this," she said, handing Anton a gun.

He took it. "It's smaller than Aris's," was all he said.

"Don't worry, it doesn't make you less of a man," Kelsey said. "It's a simpler design, with only two shots. I know you'd rather use your sword, but if you use that, I'll know you're in trouble. Just fire it in the air if you have to."

Anton nodded. "Got it. Fire it if I need you."

"I mean if either of us sees Zaphar, or gets a clue as to what's going on, we should find the other one," Kelsey clarified. "But you know how it goes. Emergencies happen."

With the crowd dispersed, it wasn't as easy to hang around the compound unnoticed. Kelsey took the front, tucking herself into a small corner where a gatehouse jutted out from the wall of the property across the street. It concealed her from half of the road, and some ornamental shrubbery did a decent job of hiding her from the rest.

Anton found something similar around the back, but he needed to climb to reach his spot. An accident of construction where a tower rose up behind a wall had left a small ledge fifteen feet up where he could perch. He was quite visible if anyone looked at him, but lines of sight were blocked from most directions, and people rarely looked up.

From here he could see into the compound, at least a bit. There were a fair number of people running around, but the fire appeared to have been put out. Eventually, the excitement seemed to die down.

Kelsey had warned him that they might have to wait until after dark for Zaphar to show himself. There was still no sign that the Malik family had caught anyone, so he was still hopeful.

Nonetheless, it was a relief when he saw a dark figure pop up on the roof of one of the large buildings, about an hour after sunset. He couldn't make out the details, but the lone figure moved with the easy grace that Zaphar did when he was on a job.

Anton could have sworn he was invisible in the darkness, but the figure seemed to catch sight of him, and headed his way, jumping lightly from one roof to another.

Anton jumped down from his perch, as the figure approached the wall. Coming closer, he could see that the figure was, indeed, Zaphar. He looked exhausted.

"Nice work," Anton said. "Let's collect Kelsey and get back to the inn."

Zaphar nodded silently and let Anton lead him around to the front. He waved to Kelsey from a distance, and she came trotting up.

"You made it!" she said brightly. "Was it fun?"

Zaphar stared at her. "No. It wasn't." He pulled out a ring of iron keys from his shirt and tossed them to Kelsey.

"What happened?" Anton asked. Zaphar tried to glare at him, but he seemed too exhausted to muster the energy.

"I hate my life," he said. "I hate this class. I hate this city, and I hate my patron."

CHAPTER THIRTY-TWO

Testimony

TYLA

It was all very strange. Tyla had *expected* to be caught and dragged back to her pen. At *best*, she had thought that she might manage to make it to the street. She would be penniless and barely clad, but she would be free for at least as long as she lasted. Instead, she was wrapped in expensive cloth while eating meat and greens wrapped in a spiced flatbread.

Tyla's mind mulled over the inexplicable events that had led to her current circumstances. First, there was the way that the guard had died. There had been a noise, but no other sign of a cause.

That stank of magic, as far as Tyla was concerned. True, she didn't know of any spells that made a head explode, but spells could do many things. She was certain that she hadn't heard of every kind of spell. Magic meant a mage, and mages were a threat.

At least they were back home. Mages came to the forest looking for numen-stones. The tribes protected them as best they could, but they had failed many times as the dark-skinned humans pushed the forest back.

Tyla wasn't sure what to make of a mage being here, though. If they were after numenstones, they were far away from her forest. Any numenstones here were not hers to claim.

The second strange thing was the pale-skinned woman who had beckoned her over the wall. Tyla had heard that humans that pale lived far to the north. If that was where the woman was from, she was far from home indeed. Was she the mage? Had she come all this way to plunder the southern lands for numenstones?

The third and most inexplicable thing was that Cheia's sister was here. Cheia had spoken of her family, and her sister was supposed to be a baker's apprentice, like Cheia. The woman who had led her away from the slaver's compound and brought her to this inn did not seem like a baker's apprentice. She smelled of smoke and iron, and her long leather coat seemed too heavy to be anything other than armor.

And yet . . . she looked like Cheia. She was called Aris, which was the name that Cheia had used for her sister. And she was anxious about her sister.

"You've seen her recently, right?" Aris asked. "How was she?"

Tyla considered the question. It seemed a strange one to ask, but Tyla thought that might just be her perspective.

"She is fine," she tried. "As well . . . as can be expected."

"Then, is she . . . has she . . . did they . . . ?"

Tyla gave Aris a blank look. It wasn't *supposed* to be blank, but in this moment, blank was suddenly all she had.

"One gets used to it," she said. "Most of the guards are not cruel."

"Oh!" Aris exclaimed, her face falling into dismay. "You—you were as well . . . I'm sorry."

Tyla nodded. The woman had nothing to apologize for, but it felt nice to hear it. That seemed to have killed Aris's appetite for questions, so Tyla asked one of her own.

"Why are you here?"

Aris smiled weakly. "Isn't it obvious? We're here to rescue Cheia. Oh, and all of the rest of you, as many as we can. But mainly Cheia."

Tyla nodded again. That was indeed obvious. Cheia had often expressed her hope that her family would come and rescue her. Most of those dreams had featured her sister's boyfriend, rather than her sister. He was an adventurer, apparently, the child of two Heroes. Those three had often been mentioned when she talked of being rescued.

Tyla had asked the wrong question. "*How* are you here?" she asked.

Aris smiled, more warmly this time. "That's . . . a really complicated story," she said. "It started when . . ."

By the time Aris had finished her story, the sky had gone dark, and Tyla's mind had gone blank again.

A numen?

She was still processing the implications when the rest of the party returned.

"All hail the conquering heroes!" the pale one, Kelsey, said cheerfully on entering the room. She had a cask of wine tucked under one arm.

Tyla quickly rose from her chair and went down on one knee in front of Kelsey. She bowed down low, one hand across her chest. Kelsey blinked.

"Aw, no need to bow! I might have helped you out, but only a little."

"Ah, no," Tyla replied, still with her head bowed. "I *am* grateful, but this is the respect due to a numen, according to the traditions of my tribe."

"A what now? Please, get up, you're making it weird. Or wait—maybe it's because everyone else isn't kneeling! Give it a go, guys, let's see how it feels!"

The dark-skinned man—Anton—snorted and spoke up. "We won't be doing that," he said firmly. "Please. Stand up. Kelsey doesn't require that sort of thing."

Reluctantly, Tyla got to her feet. Anton nodded at her. "I'm Anton," he said. "This is Zaphar, and you seem to know who Kelsey is."

"Now, what's all this about a numen?" Kelsey asked.

"Numen . . . are the spirits that live in the Great Mazes in the depths of the forest," Tyla said uncertainly. "They come from numenstones, and there are stories that say that the greatest of them can take on a physical form."

Kelsey smiled smugly. "You see, Anton? I'm the *greatest*. Hang on, let me chat to Mel about this."

Despite her words, Kelsey did no such thing. Instead, she got them all seated around the main table and cracked open the cask she had brought.

"We're celebrating a successful mission," she said when Aris questioned why she was serving drinks. This time it was Zaphar who snorted.

"Okay!" Kelsey declared after they all had a cup. "So according to Mel, elves are the *best*. They still keep to the old ways, or pretty close. They honor dungeons, live in harmony with them, and they never, ever, try to kill them."

"Why didn't you know this before?" Anton asked.

"Mel never mentioned it," Kelsey said. "In fairness, I don't get out much, so there wasn't much of a need."

Tyla bowed again. "Then, wise one, will you aid me?"

Kelsey raised her eyebrows. "I mean, sure? We'll help you get at least part of the way home. Worst case you'll have to make your way home from this guy's town, but I think the elven tribes are sort of on our way?"

"Ah . . . what I mean, wise one, is that numen are our guides on the path and the source of all the classes, so I was hoping you'd know why I can't go back to my old class."

Kelsey shrugged. "Beats me," she said. "And knock it off with that wise one stuff. I'm just Kelsey."

"Actually, I might know," Anton said. "You're talking about Padascar Hunter, right?"

Tyla looked at him and nodded.

"That sounds like a local class," he continued. "They still work outside of the local area they were created for, but they can only be taken if you're in the territory of the . . . group that caused it to exist."

"So . . . I can't take it until I return home?" Tyla asked.

"That's right," Anton said. "I wouldn't recommend sticking with Doxy, but perhaps there's something else you could take until then?"

"Nothing that appeals," Tyla said sourly.

"Actually, I might have an idea on that front, but I need to think about it," Kelsey said. "Don't make any hasty decision tonight."

"You have an idea," Anton said. "One that helps?"

"Am I not the Guide to the Path? Am I not the Way?" Kelsey said loftily.

Anton looked over at Tyla. "Great," he said. "There'll be no living with her now,"

Kelsey gasped and pointed at him.

"What?" he asked.

"You know what you did. Admit it!"

"I have no idea what you're talking about," Anton said. "Are we going to listen to Zaphar's story now?"

"Yes! I mean, No! We can't until you admit it!"

"Admit what?"

Kelsey scowled. "Fine. Tell the story," she said to Zaphar.

Everyone looked at Zaphar expectantly, including Tyla. Now that she was looking at him, he seemed familiar.

"Fine, fine," the young man said. He looked into his cup as though it held his next words, then took a long sip of it.

"It all started when I got hit on by Soraya Malik," he stated.

"Malik?" Anton asked. "Isn't she a courl, then?"

"*Yes*. Yes, she is," Zaphar said. "So, no, I don't know what she was thinking. Maybe she likes humans? Her father trades in them, after all. Anyway, she saw through my disguise."

Zaphar paused and looked thoughtful for a moment. "I think that was what attracted her to me? The fact that I wasn't a rich person there to buy slaves was interesting. She flat out told me that I was an impostor and asked me what I was doing there."

He took another long sip from his cup. "And then *he* told me to tell her the truth."

Kelsey cackled. "I *knew* he wouldn't be able to resist meddling," she said gleefully.

"Are we talking about the fae?" Anton asked. Tyla's eyes widened. Aris had *mentioned* a fae, but Tyla had thought that she was exaggerating.

"*Yes*. So I told her, and she offered me a deal. If I disrupted the auction, she'd see to it that I got what I was here for. At which point, she left me alone to "do my thing." And thank Anyn for that.

"I went back to my original plan and tried to find a way into the rest of the building. Everything was guarded, but *he* told me the exact timing to open one of the doors—"

"That's where I saw you!" Tyla exclaimed. "You were the one who distracted the guard."

Zaphar blinked at her owlishly, making the connection. "You were a pretty good distraction as well," he said. "The guard chased after you, and I just slipped in behind."

"Smooth," Kelsey complimented. Zaphar scowled.

"I'd much rather do that sort of thing when there's no one in the house," he said. "Anyway, they were too busy chasing you to notice me, and he told me what to steal to make a distraction."

"What was that?" Kelsey asked.

"Some makeup that was on the table; they had a ton of it," Zaphar told her. "Two lanterns' worth of oil, all mixed up in a bucket."

"This stuff burns?" Tyla said, alarmed. She had forgotten about the powder they'd daubed her with almost as soon as she put it on.

Kelsey came up and licked her finger before dragging it across Tyla's cheek. She stayed quite close and as she brought her finger back into view Tyla saw the powder stuck to Kelsey's finger just disappear.

"Hmm," Kelsey said. "Low purity long chain polymer, probably natural in origin. Some sort of tree sap? Dried and ground up . . . It's not *particularly* flammable, but it would make a lot of smoke if it did burn."

"It did," Zaphar confirmed. "I put it in a closed-up room so the smoke could build up before they found it . . . and so I wouldn't be *there* when they found it. After that, it was just running and hiding."

"Aw, don't leave it at that," Kelsey said. "There must be some amusing bit where you hid in the slaves' changing room and they hid you under a pile of their underwear."

"If there were any stories like that," Zaphar said stubbornly, "then I will take them to my grave. It was very stressful, though. Eventually, Soraya found me."

"How?" Anton asked.

"She walked around alone, in the deserted parts of the house, jangling those keys," Zaphar said. "I thought about *not* contacting her, but she was going to attract attention to me before too long."

He pointed at the keys, or rather, at Kelsey, who had made the keys disappear. "Those are supposed to be the spare keys for everything. From the outside gates to the slave quarters. It should only be a day or two before they're missed."

"Nice," Kelsey said. "But the most important thing . . . did you get a level? What trait did you get?"

Zaphar looked at Kelsey for a long time, and Tyla thought that he wasn't going to answer. *She* wouldn't have answered, if Kelsey hadn't been a numen. Coming from a mortal, the question would have been rude.

"*Glamoured Disguise*," he finally said. "It changes my identification information to match the disguise I'm wearing."

"Nice," Kelsey said, grinning. "We'll make a face character out of you yet."

CHAPTER THIRTY-THREE

Lion's Den

They weren't ready for this. The hideout hadn't been outfitted, and the ship hadn't been bought yet, let alone made ready. Their newest member hadn't even chosen a new class yet. Kelsey had acknowledged all of that, but she insisted on making the raid tonight.

"If there's a small window of opportunity before they realize these are gone, then we've got to take it," she said.

"But, but, for our hand to be forced like this, you do not think it's a trap?" Zaphar asked. He was Anton's only ally in arguing for delay. Both Aris and the new girl were in favor of going in as soon as possible.

"Eh, if it is, it's the sort of trap that just brings more opportunity," Kelsey said cryptically. That didn't reassure Zaphar at all, and it even made the girls more cautious. Nervous or not, though, Aris was intent on rescuing Cheia, and any doubts that Tyla had were assuaged when Kelsey brought out her new equipment.

Tyla's outfit was a simple leather jerkin worn over a thick cloth shirt. Leg protection was leather trousers and boots, and her arms were sheathed in leather bracers and vambraces. Anton recognized it as a common style in Kirido, although it wasn't normally dyed black. That was probably a Kelsey addition. Delvers came in all sorts, though, so Anton couldn't swear to it.

When it came to weapons, Tyla had been pleased to receive a pair of daggers as sharp as they were wicked-looking. She was less pleased with the bow Kelsey offered her.

"This is a . . ." she said a few words in her own language. "Very bad bow."

Kelsey sniffed. "I don't see the skeletons complaining."

"Like they can," Anton put in. "Don't you have adventurer equipment?"

Kelsey shrugged. "I don't get a lot of bow-users, and those that I do get tend to stay in the back and run away when things get dicey. Besides, it's a stick with some string, how good can it get?"

"It's dry," Tyla explained. "Not bendy enough, and not strong. No power, will probably break before too long."

"Skeletons don't have long lives," Kelsey said. "I do have this . . ."

She caused . . . something . . . to appear in her hand.

"What is *that*?" Tyla asked, asking the question everyone was wondering.

"It's a bow!" Kelsey said. "An experimental one." She took an arrow from Tyla's quiver and placed it in the device. Now that she was drawing it back, Anton could see that it did kind of look like a bow. But it was metal and it had spikes coming off it, and wheels . . .

With a grunt of effort, Kelsey drew the device back to full extension and released the arrow, aiming at one of the room's support beams. There was a *thwock*, closely followed by a *thunk* as the arrow embedded itself in the beam.

Anton stared. The arrowhead had been almost two inches long and he couldn't see any sign of it.

"Rated for twenty strength," Kelsey said proudly, "But I can dial it down if you like."

"I think . . ." Tyla said, trailing off as she looked at the arrow. She went over and tugged at it, but it was stuck fast. "I think I would like to try it sometime, but I won't be ready to use it by tonight, even if we had a place to practice."

"Fair enough," Kelsey said. She made the device disappear and produced a small saw which she used to cut the arrow shaft flush with the beam's surface. "Wouldn't want to lose our deposit."

Now Anton, Kelsey, Aris, and Tyla found themselves standing in front of the back gate to the Malik estate. This late at night, there were no guards outside, just a featureless slab of iron-reinforced wood.

Kelsey stepped up and squirted a few drops of silencing oil in the lock and on the hinges. Then she stepped back and waited for the rest of them.

The keys they had been given included the ones for this gate, of course, but guards were wandering about the grounds. Avoiding them would take timing, which was why Zaphar had snuck in. He would open the gates when the time was right.

They didn't have long to wait. There was no sound as the gates opened; the line of dim light from the other side was the only sign that Zaphar had completed his task.

"That was quick," Kelsey murmured.

"I didn't see any sign of guards," Zaphar whispered. "I think something is wrong."

"Hmm," was all that Kelsey said. The moonlight was bright enough for them to make their way to the slaves' quarters. It was locked and dark, but its door opened easily enough to one of the keys. Zaphar gasped at what he saw inside, but Kelsey just hummed and stepped inside. She pulled out a light-stone, and the rest of them could see what Zaphar saw.

The room was arranged with a long, wide corridor stretching from the door to the other side of the building. It was lined with bars so that the guards could easily see into the cells when there was light. Kelsey's stone shone into the nearest ones, and Anton could see that one side was a cell with two beds, both occupied, while the other had four beds.

Of more immediate concern were the two male humans stretched out on the floor. Their uniforms and weapons made it clear that these were the missing guards.

Kadir Beyazit, Level 12, Human, Enforcer, Warrior/Enforcer
S: 20 T: 15 A: 11 D: 17 P: 2 W: 7 C: 4
Murat Osman, Level 18, Human, Guard, Warrior/Soldier(broken)/Guard
S: 23 T: 20 A: 15 D: 15 P: 8 W: 2 C:8

They're alive, at least, Anton thought.

As they were taking that in, light bloomed at the far end of the corridor. The door to one of the farthest cells opened and a courl stepped out and started walking towards them.

"You took your time," she said haughtily. "I thought I was going to be waiting all night."

Kelsey grinned and stepped forward, but Tyla was faster. The elf dashed the few steps it took to get to the guards and dropped to the floor next to one. She did it so smoothly that Anton only noticed that her arm was locked straight and her dagger was in her hand at the last moment. The dagger slid into the man's chest, Tyla's full weight behind it.

The unconscious man jerked and coughed up blood.

"What are you doing, you monster!" the courl—Anton supposed that she had to be Soraya—yelled.

Kelsey took no action, but Anton stepped forward. She was clearly going to kill the other one if she was given the chance. Tyla ignored the courl yelling at her to turn and say just one word.

"Rapist," she said.

"That doesn't mean you can—" He took another step forward, but he felt a hand on his arm, holding him back. He looked back to see Aris, struggling to speak.

"Cheia," was all she managed to say.

Meanwhile, Soraya was still speaking. She had been walking swiftly forward, but she had paused to keep a safe distance between her and the murderous elf.

"Don't be ridiculous," Soraya said. "They had permission from father, it wasn't rape. They—"

She broke off as Tyla put her knife through the throat of the other guard. Anton felt Aris bury her face in his back.

"That's a pretty bold statement to make in front of someone who just killed two people who raped her," Kelsey said with amusement. "I'm really warming to this girl, but you, you've got some moxie."

"Just this one," Tyla said, pointing to the one that she had cut the throat of. "The other raped other girls."

"You're Tyla, aren't you?" Soraya said. "The savage elf who escaped. I had no idea you were *this* savage."

"Any day you learn something new is a good day," Kelsey quipped. She tossed the ring of keys over to Anton and nodded at the cell doors. Then she turned back to Soraya. "So let's learn why you're here."

Soraya didn't reply directly. Instead, she stared at Kelsey with her eyes narrowed. "Why doesn't my *Dealer's Insight* work on you?" she asked.

"Maybe it's broken," Kelsey suggested impishly.

"Don't be ridiculous," Soraya sneered, but she looked at the others anyway. "What is . . . a Gunslinger? And a Heroic Liberator? Are you going to just let that savage get away with murder in front of you? Is that heroic?"

"Maybe not," Kelsey agreed. "But it was very liberating. You know, the tree of liberty is watered with the blood of slavers . . . or something like that."

Soraya took a step back. "I don't like your tone."

Anton had turned to the cell doors. While he tried the keys, he used *Delver's Discernment* on the sleeping forms.

Seren Kaelith – No Levels
Thalindra Mirelle – No Levels
Seraphina Moonshadow – No Levels
Morwyn Elariel, Level 5, Human, Doxy, Scullion (broken)/Doxy
S: 2 T: 6 A: 9 D: 5 P: 11 W: 5 C: 9

He knew three of these. From the name, Seraphina was probably from the Confederacy that lay west of Zamarra. Finding the correct key, he unlocked the door and moved to the other side of the corridor, to the room with two.

Althea Selene, Level 7, Human, Doxy, Servant (broken)/Doxy
S: 2 T: 4 A: 11 D: 7 P: 6 W: 11 C: 13
Syrena Nael, Level 7, Human, Doxy, Server (broken)/Doxy
S: 10 T: 6 A: 9 D: 4 P: 12 W: 7 C: 11

Meanwhile, Kelsey was still talking. "Worried about your own life? How about it, Tyla? This girl on your list?"

"No," the elf said, but from her tone, Anton wouldn't swear she was telling the truth. There was some anger there.

"Well, of course not!" Soraya declared. "I'm not worried, I was just put off by that display of savagery! Really, there was no need for it."

"Well, if that's what's bothering you . . . here."

Glancing over at Kelsey, Anton saw that she'd removed the bodies. Shaking his head, he kept going.

Elowyn Nyx – No Levels
Cheia Lucina, Level 2, Human, Doxy, Doxy
S: 6 T: 3 A: 9 D: 5 P: 4 W: 8 C: 11
Elysia Thalor, Level 4, Human, Doxy, Servant (broken)/Doxy
S: 10 T: 5 A: 8 D: 5 P: 8 W: 3 C: 7

"Aris!" he hissed urgently, even as his heart fell to see Cheia's class. She hurried to his side, and he pointed out Cheia's bed.

"Cheia!" she called softly, shaking the girl. "Cheia! Wake up!"

"Sis?" Cheia mumbled. "What are you doing here?"

Anton left her to it. There were still doors to open.

Aurora Silverbrook Level 5, Human, Doxy, Server(broken)/Doxy
S: 6 T: 9 A: 6 D: 1 P: 8 W: 5 C: 9
Lyra Emberleaf Level 3, Human, Doxy, Hunter(broken)/Doxy
S: 8 T: 5 A: 8 D: 3 P: 9 W: 6 C: 11

"So now that's out of the way, are you going to tell us what you came here for?" Kelsey said, with a hint of impatience.

Soraya didn't seem inclined to move on. "You—you have a *storage device*? Is that why I can't—is it a magical item that's shielding you?"

"Soraya!" Kelsey snapped. "In a few seconds, slaves are going to be *waking up*, and I'll be too busy to talk to you. So get it *out*, girl."

"Fine!" Soraya said. "If you don't have *time* for a proper conversation. In exchange for easing your way into this little heist, I want you to take me with you."

"Why?" Kelsey asked.

"Why? Because in order to put a damper on the *appalling* marriage Father is trying to foist on me, it has become necessary for me to disappear for a while."

"I meant, why should we?" Kelsey said. "I don't know if you do a lot of these crime deals, but it's customary to make the arrangement *before* you pay the other party off. We've already got what we want."

"What! Where is your sense of gratitude?"

"Same place as those corpses," Kelsey said, grinning. "So, have you got something for us, or are we going to get rid of the witnesses?"

"Well, I—" Soraya paused. "If it's *absolutely* necessary, I can give you thirty percent of the ransom."

CHAPTER THIRTY-FOUR

West End Girls

W hat ransom?" Kelsey asked.

"I left a note in my room," Soraya said loftily. "Ransacked it as well so it looks like someone kidnapped me. Then I gave the guards some drugged wine and waited here for you."

"*You* wrote a note," Kelsey said. "I don't suppose that your father knows your handwriting?"

"I thought of that, of course," Soraya sniffed. "I wrote it with my off hand, and in blood, so he knows it's serious."

"Wow, you really have thought of everything," Kelsey said with what Anton recognized as fake enthusiasm. She turned to him and asked, "It sounds like a good deal! We should go for it, don't you think?"

"Please tell me you're joking," Anton said. He snatched the light-stone from Kelsey's hand and stalked the rest of the way down the corridor, looking for more slaves. Soraya flinched away from him as he went past.

"We have enough to worry about without taking on a passenger who . . . she's one of the enemy!"

The rest of the cells were empty, though Anton noted that the cell that Soraya had walked out of had two leather travelling cases in it. Walking back, he saw that Aris had, with Zaphar's help, been quietly waking the slaves and getting them ready to go.

"Oh well," Kelsey said. "I guess you'll want to kill her, then."

"What? No!" Anton protested. He was just drawing near Soraya as he spoke and she flinched away from him again.

"You can't—do you know who I am?" she squeaked. "I was given to believe that this was a *heist*, not a murder spree!"

"Zaphar's new," Kelsey said wryly, barely keeping laughter in check. "I do apologize if he's given you the wrong impression of how we do things here."

She looked over at Tyla. "What about you, kid? You want to go for the trifecta?"

Tyla had been looking at the space where her two victims had lain, with a disturbed look on her face. Now she looked up, at Kelsey and at Soraya.

"No," she said. "Maybe her father, but not her."

"Looks like it's up to you then, Anton. Make it quick, for her sake."

"I'm not going to murder her in cold blood," Anton told Kelsey firmly.

"We can't leave any witnesses, remember?" Kelsey said in a singsong voice. "I *suppose* we could tie her up and take her with us, but that seems like a lot of extra effort for someone who's *asking* us to take her with us."

"Fine!" Anton exclaimed. Soraya yelped and ducked away from him. "She can come," he clarified, glaring at her.

Kelsey clapped her hands. "Yay! We'll have such fun!" she said. "We'll braid each other's hair, and I can scratch you behind the ears."

"You will not," Soraya said, instantly regaining her composure. "I am *not* a cat. And I will only reveal the contact method if I am well treated."

"Hmm. We'll discuss the ransom later," Kelsey said. "For now, let's get on with the rescue. Sandal pack!"

She produced a bag which she handed to Aris that turned out to contain a bunch of sandals. Aris started handing them out to the captives, who had no shoes.

"Where did you get the leather for those sandals?" Anton said suspiciously. He knew Kelsey was a cornucopia of numerous goods, but there were some things that she was short of.

"They're not made of leather, they're *synthetic*," Kelsey said, handing him one for closer examination. Sure enough, the soft flexible material they were made of was like nothing that Anton had seen. It didn't seem that it would be as comfortable, or as long-lasting as leather, but it would do for one trip.

"I assume," Soraya said haughtily, "that you have transportation waiting outside? Can one of you carry my luggage?"

Kelsey raised her eyebrows. "The thing about that," she said, "is that *someone* forced us to do the heist while we were still in the surveillance phase. So we didn't have anything ready. You'll be walking, like the rest of us."

"Walking? Are you joking? How far is your secret hideout?"

"Yeah, about that," Kelsey said sourly. "That's not exactly ready either, but we'll have to make do. And you can carry your own luggage."

It wasn't easy getting eleven traumatized girls and one entitled courl across the city without being seen, but they managed it. It helped that most of the girls knew Anton and Aris, which made the rest of them willing to trust them. There was also a bond that had formed between the girls that extended to Tyla and helped them work together. Scared and confused as they were, none of them wanted to put the others in danger by bolting or crying out.

Rather than travel in one big group, they split up into four, each one led by either Kelsey, Anton, Aris, or Tyla. Zaphar scouted ahead.

They left behind a bloodstained flagstone, and not much else. The girls had gathered their meager belongings and Kelsey had looked speculatively at the bedding they were leaving behind before making it disappear.

"Waste not, want not," she had said. They had even taken the soap from the washroom. It was of surprisingly good quality. Taking the chamber pots as well seemed like a step too far to Anton, but Kelsey declared that "All biologicals are good biologicals," and ignored him.

Kelsey had also disappeared Soraya's luggage, once it had been made clear that the courl couldn't carry both bags for anything like the distance required. Soraya hadn't seemed happy about that, as Kelsey had been noncommittal as to whether Soraya would get her luggage *back*.

After all the hurried organization, carried out in hushed voices and urgent whispers, the trip back was something of an anticlimax. Anton was finally able to relax when he led the last group into the warehouse. Kelsey slid the door shut behind him and unveiled her light-stone.

"This is not a suitable place for habitation," Soraya declared as soon as the light level was sufficient for her to examine her surroundings. "It's cold, it's drafty, there are no beds. There is no water for washing and no way of disposing of—"

"Yeah, yeah, keep your pants on," Kelsey said, then winced. "Okay, poor choice of words there," she said, glancing at the girls. "Let's start with some chairs, and a meeting."

"Chairs! Of all the things—" Soraya shut up as Tyla pulled her dagger out and glared at her.

"Quiet when the numen is talking," Tyla said.

"Thanks, Tyla!" Kelsey said brightly. "Now, chairs . . ."

True to her word, she started handing chairs to Anton, Aris, and anyone else close enough. Somewhat bemused, they placed them down in a rough double semicircle facing the center of the room.

The four walls and the warm magical light were helping the girls to relax, to believe that they were really free. A murmur spread through the room, as girls started talking to each other, or their rescuers.

"I can't believe you really came for us," Althea said to Anton, hugging him. A lot of the girls from Kirido wanted to hug him, or Aris. It made Anton a little uncomfortable. All of the girls were *prettier* than he remembered, which reminded him that Doxy gave a strong boost to Charisma.

"A lot happened," Anton said. "But we're going to do our best to get us all back."

"All right, everybody!" Kelsey announced. Enough chairs had been produced for everyone to take a seat. Feeling shy, Anton took a seat in the second ring. Aris sat next to him.

"Hello, everybody," Kelsey said. "I'm Kelsey. No need to introduce yourselves, I can see all of your names."

She ran her gaze over the nervous faces in front of her. "Now, I'm sure you've got a bunch of questions, but I'll just give you an overview of our plans, which are still in a very nebulous stage. We have a boat, we're going to get you on it, and we're going to head back to Kirido. I'm open to making stops farther west, for those of you who come from there, but I have assurances from Baron Anton there that you will be welcome to make new homes in Kirido if you so desire."

There was a muted uproar as every girl from Kirido squeaked or squealed some variation of "Baron Anton?" Anton felt even more uncomfortable as they all seemed to be focusing on him.

"It's a long story," Kelsey said, talking over the interruptions. "You can hear it later. Right now, I want to discuss something important. Classes."

She had the girls' attention again.

"Now, some of you are thinking that you want to go back to your original class. Anton, can you tell them how that works?"

Anton cleared his throat as all the girls looked at him again. "Um, if you go back to a class you partially finished, you start at level one and you don't get any benefits until you regain levels to the point you stopped," he said. "It's not that bad since you're all Tier One, but it takes a while to get back on track."

"I don't care, I'll earn the levels back," Elysia spoke up. "I *liked* being a servant to the Baron, so I'll go back to that. If, um, you'll have me, Lord Anton." She fluttered her eyelids at him.

"Oh, ho!" Kelsey exclaimed. "Before this goes any further, I'd like to let you know that Aris is a *lot* stronger than she used to be. And there are other options than going back. Combat options."

"If I go back, I'll be a Hunter again," one of the Confederacy girls, Lyra Emberleaf, said. "That's a Combat class."

"Pff, bows," Kelsey said. "I'm talking real weapons here. Aris, come to the front."

Aris did so, and drew one of her pistols.

"This," Kelsey said, pointing at the gun, "is a boomstick!"

"Don't be crude," Aris said. "It's a pistol," she told the group. "It's a deadly weapon that fires bits of metal at high speed. It can kill Tier Two warriors with a good hit."

There were murmurs of surprise and astonishment from the group.

"Have you killed anyone with it, sis?" Cheia asked.

Aris grimaced. "I've already lost count of the people I've killed with it," she said.

"Now, these are available to those who want to fight for the cause," Kelsey said. "The problem is that they are very loud and need room to practice with, which we don't have. And getting the class that goes with them . . . Anton?"

"If they kill just one person or monster, they can get Warrior," he said. "For a Tier One specialist class? Probably five kills with the weapon."

"That's a lot of kill experience going towards Doxy," Kelsey said. "It's wasteful."

"Can you supply bows as well?" Lyra asked. "I think I'd like to go back to Hunter."

"I can, but you're not allowed to get sniffy about the quality," Kelsey said, looking at Tyla. "It's a stick with string."

The girls started discussing things among themselves. Four of them were too young to have classes.

"Do we have to fight?" Seraphina, one of the younger girls asked.

"Nope!" Kelsey said brightly. "Kirido needs lots of young workers with different classes, so if you want to hold off, there will be plenty of craft classes to take. We might be able to start you off while we're waiting here if there's anything you're interested in."

"Is one of those pistols available to me?" Soraya asked.

"Don't be silly, you're the hostage," Kelsey said. "You're lucky you're not being tied up."

In the end, only Lyra and Elysia elected to switch back to their old classes. The rest elected to wait for either weapons training or Kelsey's vaguely specified "vocational training."

"Is the pistol what you had in mind when you said you had a special class for me?" Tyla asked when the hubbub had died down.

"Noooo . . ." Kelsey said. "When I said *special*, I meant it. Let's get everyone set up with the basics, and then we'll talk."

CHAPTER THIRTY-FIVE

In the Stone

TYLA

The people had need, and the numen provided. That was how it worked in the forests of the elves, and that was what Tyla saw now. The numen—Kelsey—made bedding for the women appear out of thin air. It *looked* like the bedding that they had just stolen from the Malik compound, but comments from the women indicated that it had been cleaned, thoroughly.

"If there's one thing I have plenty of, it's steam," Kelsey said cryptically. She summoned lightweight—at least to Anton and herself—partitions that fastened together ingeniously to form private sleeping spaces for everyone. It wasn't long before the women returned to the sleep that their rescue had interrupted.

Tyla held herself apart from the activity. There was a bed here for her, but Kelsey had said that they would talk later. She watched the body that the numen had formed carefully. Numen could be capricious and cruel at times, and Kelsey certainly showed signs of that. Tyla watched Kelsey closely, seeking hints as to how she should be properly appeased.

Eventually, later arrived.

"So, do you know of any other dungeons—I mean, numen—that have avatars like me?" Kelsey asked, sitting down in front of Tyla.

Tyla shook her head. "No, they were all killed when the first Dark Humans came."

"All of them? From Anton's lot?" Kelsey asked.

"She must be talking about the Forerunners," Anton said, joining them and taking a seat of his own.

"I never took you for a history buff," Kelsey said. She narrowed her eyes, staring at the space between them.

"It's not history so much as stories," Anton replied. "The guild doesn't just have books on classes and monsters, you know."

"Fair enough," Kelsey agreed. She summoned one of her partitions and handed it to Anton. "So who were the Forerunners?"

Anton stared at the panel he'd been given and held it awkwardly. Kelsey produced some kind of post and attached it to one corner. "Well, you know that Zamarra is a colony of the Tiatian Empire, right?"

"I know you came from far away," Tyla said. "A place to the east."

Kelsey attached another post to another corner.

"Yeah, that's the Empire," Anton said. "A long time ago, our ancestors came here, looking for a place to carve out kingdoms for themselves, out of the reach of the old Empire. A lot of the kingdoms on the north coast of the Sea were founded that way."

"And these ancestors were the Forerunners?" Kelsey asked. She attached a third post to a third corner and then pulled the panel down so that the three posts were standing on the floor.

"No," Anton said. "The Forerunners were from before that. There was . . . a war? I've heard it was called the Unification War, and after it was over, there were several very powerful fighters left with nothing to do."

"Normally what would happen then is they would start carving out their own kingdoms and you'd need another Unification War," Kelsey said. She attached the final leg to the table and moved it so that it was standing between the three of them. Then she sat down again.

Anton shrugged. "*That's* history," he said. "The stories I read didn't touch on why the Forerunners didn't seek to rule. The tales just said they came here, to the wilderness, looking for challenges."

"The Dark Ones slew everything in their path," Tyla said. "None could stand against them. And when the strongest of us had fallen . . . they left. When your people arrived, we thought them more of the same, but they were . . . lesser."

"They went back to the Empire," Anton explained. "Boasted of their victories. My ancestors were the ones who heard about lands where all the big threats had been wiped out and decided to form an expedition."

"Nice and opportunistic," Kelsey said wryly. "But we've gotten away from the main point, which is dungeons with avatars."

"I know of none still existing," Tyla told her. "The ones who were slain were all very old. I don't think that a numen has formed an . . . avatar, as you call it, for over a thousand years."

"That's a long time!" Anton said, startled. "The Forerunners would have been three hundred-something years ago."

Tyla nodded. "My grandfather was alive to see them," she said. "For older events, we have tales passed down. I don't know *why* the numen stopped making bodies, only that they did."

Kelsey nodded. "That's a shame. I would have liked someone to talk to, you know? But that's not what I wanted to talk to you about."

She waved her hand, an all-encompassing gesture at the space around them. "We're all in this together, you know? Us and the girls and you. Even Soraya."

Tyla nodded. She shared neither blood nor tribe with those here, but she had grown close to the girls, and she understood the necessity of banding together against a greater enemy.

"But some of us," Kelsey continued, "are more *in this* than others. The core group: Anton, Aris, Zaphar, and myself. And I want you to be a part of that."

"Why?" Tyla asked.

"I like to think I have an eye for talent . . . and you've got it," Kelsey said. Anton snorted in response.

"This is because she murdered those two guards in cold blood, isn't it?"

"Not *just* that," Kelsey objected. "Speaking of which, do you still have a problem with the way she did that?"

"I—" Anton looked awkward. "I don't like it, but I guess I can understand why she did it."

"It *was* wrong of me to kill those men," Tyla put in. "My . . . hasty actions put the *operation* in danger." The Elitran word *operation* was new to her, but she had heard Kelsey use it several times, and she was a fast learner.

Kelsey shrugged. "It's not much of a plan if it can't take a few speedbumps along the way. You're fine. Right, Anton?"

"You mean, am I fine with her joining our group?" Anton asked. He looked at Tyla, really looked at her. His eyes met hers and she felt, for the first time, that he might be something more than a skilled fighter.

"Just . . . no more murders, all right?" he asked. "Not prisoners or unconscious people."

Tyla nodded. "It was cowardly of me," she admitted. "They were higher-tiered and warriors. If they had been awake, I would not have been able to kill them."

"Nothing cowardly about that," Kelsey said. "You see your chance, you take it, is what I say."

Anton sighed. "Just . . . try to do better in the future. And speaking of better, you might as well accept that level. The experience isn't going to go anywhere else."

Tyla scowled. "I don't want another level of Doxy," she complained.

"A common class is still a class," Kelsey said. "It may not be much, but not much is better than nothing."

Tyla's scowl grew more fierce, but she had to admit that it was true.

You have reached Level 3.
Applying Benefits for Level 3
Dexterity + 1
Willpower + 1
Charisma + 1

Checking her status, she could see that it left much to be desired.

Tyla Greenwalker of the Padascar Tribe (Level 3)
Overall Level: 7
Paths: Padascar Hunter (Broken)/ Doxy
Strength: 10
Toughness: 6
Agility: 6
Dex: 12
Perception: 13
Will: 8
Charisma: 8
Traits
Persistent Tracking
Silent Shot
Danger Sense

Getting the *Danger Sense* trait from Doxy had been the *one* benefit that she had gained from the situation. A trait that was generally useful instead of one tailored to her doomed fate. Tyla was determined to get out of the class before it gave her another trait.

"So you said you didn't have any good classes to go to," Kelsey said.

"No," Tyla agreed. She checked again. "I already had Warrior and Hunter. Now I have . . . Throat-Slitter, which seems to be some sort of criminal class. It's a better grade, at least."

Anton nodded. "I know about it," he said. "It's not nice, but it leads to Assassin, which . . . still isn't nice, but it's a Rare class."

"Mhm-hmm," Kelsey said. "I think we can do better than that." She placed a glowing crystal sphere on the table.

Tyla stared. "Is that . . . you?" she asked, astounded. "I thought . . ."

"No, I'm pretty much immobile," Kelsey confirmed. "This is a dead dun—numenstone that I took off a wizard."

"It's dead?" Tyla asked. It didn't *look* dead.

"It still produces magic," Kelsey explained, "but whoever was living in there before is gone now, as far as I can tell."

"You're not sure?" Tyla asked. Kelsey frowned.

"My own magic is sharply limited when it comes to this particular topic," she admitted. "I did some experiments and they found no sign of life . . . but I'm a bit dubious about relying on them. Mages have probably got better tools for this, but their incentives are all in the wrong direction."

"Why are you showing me this?" Tyla asked.

Kelsey laughed, a short guffaw of genuine amusement. "*That's* why," she said. "Girl, I'm offering you this. *Touch* this, and you get offered a spell-casting class. *Take* this, and you'll be able to cast spells."

Tyla stared at Kelsey for a moment, not able to process what she was saying. Anton filled the gap in the conversation.

"I thought you hated mages for carrying around the corpses of your sisters?" he asked.

"Don't worry, Anton, we're still best buddies forever!" Kelsey assured him. "I thought about offering this to you. A Heroic Sorcerer would have been pretty neat. But . . ."

She trailed off, looking at Tyla, who was still staring at her. "It didn't feel right," Kelsey said. "This does. She has a respect for cores that goes beyond what you've learned, or even my knowledge. I feel like this is more respectful than just leaving the thing sitting in an alcove for the rest of my life."

Tyla regained her voice. "It is forbidden," she said. "Elves are not permitted to take up numenstones and use magic."

Kelsey shrugged. "You're a long way from home, and this is a . . . numen? Numen spirit? Telling you that it's fine. That's gotta overrule what the elders say."

"Even so, I would not be able to return home after such a sin," Tyla said doubtfully. "I would not be welcome in my own tribe."

"We have a lot of things we need to do before going home," Kelsey said. "You'll be Tier Three in no time. Is your village going to turn you away then?

"And even if they do," she continued, "we can make a *new* home for you in Kirido. Don't tell me, after all you've seen, that you're going to be happy living in a forest again."

"What I've seen?" Tyla asked. "I have mostly seen the inside of a cage. Sleeping rough in the forest is preferable to that."

"You've seen more than that," Kelsey said. "You've seen *power*, and the abuses that those who have it make. You've seen how the rich live, off the backs of the overburdened poor. You've seen how the weak suffer, and you know that it needs to end."

Kelsey pushed the stone towards Tyla. "This is *power*, the power to correct the wrongs that you've seen."

"But why?" Tyla asked suspiciously. "I haven't even agreed to join your group."

Kelsey shrugged. "I *do* want you to join up," she said. "But that has to be your choice. If you take this and go your own way, then no hard feelings. The world will be better, either way."

"You just want to give it to me for free?"

"Sure," Kelsey said, shrugging. "It's not doing me any good just sitting on a shelf. Aris has her guns, Anton has his hero thing. Zaphar has a lot going on already, he doesn't need magic added to it. You seem like the right person, and we need a mage. So why not you?"

Tyla stared at the stone. She had felt the power of magic, of what it could do. Having the ability to fight back was tempting.

Just touch it and see. They can't make you take the class.

Nervously, she reached out. The crystal was warm under her hand, not like stone at all. And the class was . . .

Apprentice Dungeon Witch (Rare, Tier 1)
Requires: Possession of a Dungeon Core, Guidance
Stats: 5: [S|T|A|P|W]DPW (1 Free)

"It's Rare," Tyla admitted. There was Apprentice Hedge Wizard as well, but it was only Fine. "So how about it?" she asked. "Are you going to come aboard for the good fight?"

"I don't think the stone is dead," Tyla said, ignoring the question for the moment. "It doesn't feel like it."

"Once you get a few levels, you might be the only person with both the ability and the inclination to prove that," Kelsey said.

Tyla thought about putting the stone down. Part of her was appalled that she hadn't done so already. But she already felt a bond with the stone. Did it *want* her to own it? Or was that just her desires tricking her?

"Oh, fine," she said.

Are you sure you want to break your Path? [Y|N]
You have reached Level 0.
No benefits to apply.

CHAPTER THIRTY-SIX

Straight to Hell

TYLA

Kelsey urged her to get some sleep with the rest of them.

"You've had a big day, made some big changes. Some sleep, even if it's just half a night, will help you process all that's happened."

The other girls had gone to their new beds. Anton and Aris had retired. Zaphar had gone back to the inn to 'mind the fort,' as Kelsey had put it. But Tyla couldn't sleep. How could she?

"I can't," she said. "I can feel this . . . power . . . running through me. I cannot control it, I can't do anything with it, but it is there."

Kelsey grinned. "I can think of a few ways to burn off that nervous energy—but we just met! You know you're still two levels away from casting your first spell, right?"

"I know," Tyla said. "If you'd given me this opportunity before I killed those slavers . . ."

"True," Kelsey admitted. "But you hadn't impressed me then."

"Killing impresses you, then?" Tyla asked.

"Well . . . it was more about the circumstances. The whys and the hows . . . hey! Wanna go for a walk?"

Tyla raised an eyebrow. "Is that safe?" she asked. "Are we—you—not standing guard?"

"We can do that better from the outside," Kelsey said, waving a hand lazily. "It's dark, so no one is going to recognize you. We can get some fresh air and talk without worrying about waking the little'uns up."

Chuckling a little, Tyla agreed. Kelsey led her outside, carefully locking the warehouse door behind them.

Tyla sniffed the air with distaste. The warehouse district wasn't the worst part of town, but it was close to the port, and the ever-present smell of rotting fish. Here, the streets were wide and straight, unlittered by drunks and the homeless. There were plenty of narrow alleyways that such people preferred, but there were also guards, hired by the merchants that owned the buildings, to move the riffraff on.

Some of those guards were looking at them suspiciously, but from a distance. They had come out of a warehouse, so they had a legitimate reason for being here.

Kelsey took them on a circuit around their building. It was dark but Tyla's night vision was up to the task. Nor did Kelsey seem to have any problems moving around. She kept her attention on the building as they moved around it, making *tsk* sounds with her tongue.

"Too much light escaping," she muttered. "Gonna have to put up insulation, soundproofing, maybe."

Tyla ignored her meaningless words. She looked up at the stars. It had been a long time since she had seen them, and they looked different when they weren't seen through leaves.

She only stopped when Kelsey stopped talking. Tearing her gaze away from the heavens, she looked back at the strange human figure that was staring at her.

"Hey, Tyla," Kelsey said. "You want to fight?"

Tyla's eyes widened and she took a step back. Her hand found itself gripping her dagger.

"Not me," Kelsey snorted. "Something more your level. I've seen you kill, but I haven't seen you fight."

Tyla knew that the maze of a numen spirit was where elves were tested, refined into someone stronger. Wandering free as she did, perhaps the streets of this city were Kelsey's maze. Nodding, Tyla readied herself.

"I will," she said.

Kelsey nodded approvingly back. Then, to Tyla's surprise, she turned away.

"C'mon," she said. "Let's find a better part of the city to do this in."

There were not many ways in which this part of the city could be called *better*. The smell of fish had not gone away entirely, but it was drowned out by the smell of piss, alcohol, and other kinds of rotting food. This was, Tyla was fairly sure, the bad part of town. If there was a worse part, then Tyla didn't want to see it. Or smell it.

This area was more crowded than the warehouse district, but the inhabitants were much less alert. At this hour of the night, fully a quarter of the people on the street were unconscious. It wasn't easy, but Kelsey managed to find a dark alley that no one was using for crimes or sex.

"You ready?" Kelsey asked. Without waiting for an answer, she summoned an animated skeleton. For a moment, it just stood there while Tyla stared at it. Its bones glowed very slightly in the dark of the alley while its eyes glowed more strongly. It was armed with a rusty sword and wore dented metal armor.

"Bog standard Skeleton Soldier," Kelsey said. "There's a benefit for you, fighting a Tier Two, so we'll start there."

The soldier jerked forward to attack, but Tyla was ready. Slipping under its swing, she got in close, as a dagger-wielder had to. Inside the reach of her blade, she had to deviate from her training. The skeleton had no guts for her to plunge her dagger into, so she elected to make a slashing cut under the rib cage and breastplate, aiming to sever the spine.

Her blade bit in, shattering small fragments of bone, but it wasn't enough to cut through. Unwilling to stop moving and try again, she pushed the skeleton back with her blade.

She turned out to be stronger, and the monster went stumbling back, unable to strike at her as she passed back out through its reach.

"Nice," Kelsey commented. "We really should have some custom armor around the lower spine, but it looks out of place."

Tyla didn't reply.

I'm faster than it, and I'm stronger than it, she thought. *I can win this.*

She dashed in again. This time, as she ducked under the blow, she caught the arm in her off hand.

When you are the stronger one, press close, and don't let up. The advice from her mentor flowed through her mind. She pushed forward, trying to either trip the monster or force it back against the alley wall. While she was doing this, she chopped wildly at the exposed lower spine with her dagger.

Everything got confused; too much was happening at once. She focused on the important things. Her grip on the skeleton's weapon arm.

The thud of impact as she pushed the monster into the wall.

The final crunch as her sword severed its spine.

Then—pain! A sudden explosion of black and red that blacked out her vision for a moment. She staggered back, pushing the skeleton away. There was a clatter of bones as she shook her head to clear it.

The damned thing had headbutted her. She hadn't expected that. She quickly reoriented herself and then gasped in surprise.

Despite having its spine severed, the skeleton was still able to fight. Its torso was upright on the ground, slowly dragging itself towards her. Tyla thought that she could see an angry glint in its eye sockets, but its expression was, as always, grinning.

"Yeah, you need to destroy the head to stop it," Kelsey drawled. Tyla *didn't* glare at her. This was making her stronger. Kelsey was *helping.*

The head might not have been destroyed, but the fight was over. Half a skeleton was not anywhere near as dangerous. Tyla crouched down to block its strike and then stomped on its arm. Pinned, it could only grin at her as a swipe of her dagger dislodged the helmet. She thought about using the pommel, but the blade seemed heavy enough. She brought it down point first, directly into the skull.

The skull exploded into dust, and the bones all clattered to the ground. She felt the experience flow into her. Not as much as she was used to. Before, all her kills had been *hunts*, fulfilling the purpose of her class. Her new class was meant to cast spells, and this was a poor substitute.

"Nice work," Kelsey said. "Anton is better, but you can *move*, which Aris still has to work on. I didn't see any combat traits?"

"The only one I have is *Silent Shot*," Tyla said, still staring at the bones and dust that were all that remained of her opponent. "It makes my attacks silent so that I don't scare off the game."

She looked up at Kelsey, who was staring at her with wide eyes.

"Silent *Shot*?" Kelsey asked. "Wanna see if it works on guns?"

She pulled out one of the same weapons that Aris carried.

"I thought you wanted me to be a mage?" Tyla asked.

"You don't need to be a Gunslinger to use guns," Kelsey replied. "I'm not. Anton doesn't use guns because he's trained a whole lot with his sword. Anyone else, I'd recommend it."

She did something to the weapon, causing it to open up at the side. A handful of brass cylinders appeared in her other hand.

"These are what it fires," she said, slipping each one into a matching hole in the gun. She clicked it back into place and held the weapon out to Tyla. "Now you're ready to go. Six shots."

Tyla took the gun in her hand. It was heavier than she expected. Kelsey came up to her side and showed her how to hold it.

"You want to use both hands, especially when you're starting out." She guided Tyla's hands into position. It was the first time she had touched Tyla, and it felt strange. Cooler than hands should be, but still warmer than the cold night air.

"Finger slips in here, aim it where you want the bullet to go, and then you just squeeze the trigger. We'll get some zombies for you to aim at—"

"Hey, girls!" A loud, drunken, male voice interrupted. Even before she turned, Tyla could tell by the laughter that he wasn't alone.

When she did turn, Tyla saw three men at the entrance to the alley. They were unsteady on their feet, and one of them carried a wineskin. All of them had long, curved daggers at their belt. They took a few uncertain steps forward, no doubt having trouble seeing them in the darkness.

Kelsey pulled out a light-stick. Unlike the light-stones that Tyla was familiar with, this threw the light in a single direction. Kelsey shone it in the men's faces.

"Hey!" one of them cried.

"This is a private party, boys. You're not invited," Kelsey called out. Glancing over at her, Tyla could see that the spirit was sporting a wolfish grin. She angled the light down so that it illuminated the ground between them.

"Aw, don't be like that," one of the men said. He took a few confident steps forward, the others following his lead. "Can't have a party with just girls, and we can't have fun if it's just guys, you know?"

"We are uninterested, and I am armed," Tyla said firmly. The fool might not recognize the weapon she was carrying, but she had her own knives, plainly visible.

"Ah, a pretty little thing like you can't use knives for shit," the man said. "We'll get to play a bit before we have our fun, is all."

"I'm unarmed!" Kelsey said brightly.

"What are you doing?" Tyla hissed.

"They're good practice, aren't they?" Kelsey said, gesturing at the gun. "Better experience than zombies, too."

"Is this how it is done, in the cities?" Tyla asked, taking a step back. It seemed to encourage the men. "Rape and murder whenever there are no witnesses?"

"Hey, we ain't gonna murder you," the leader laughed. "Once we get started, you'll be begging for more."

"Or at least, you won't be complaining none," one of the others added. All three of them laughed.

"Well, not *officially*," Kelsey said to Tyla. "If they get caught, they'll go to jail or get a bit chopped off or something. It's just that . . . there aren't any guards here, you know?"

Tyla held the gun up. "This is wrong," she said. "Turn back now."

The men just laughed some more and kept on coming.

"Is that supposed to be a weapon, little missy?" the leader asked. "I thought you said you was armed?"

"Look at it this way," Kelsey said. "Do you want these three to survive and go on to rape other women?"

Tyla pulled the trigger.

She remembered to use her trait. There was a flash of light and a slight *whiff* sound. The lead rapist staggered and touched his hand to his bloody shoulder.

"What in Butin's name was that?" he exclaimed.

"Nice," Kelsey said. "But not fatal. Aim for the center of his chest. You're ready for the kick now, yeah?"

She idly shone her light back in the men's faces. The curses of the two partially blinded men mixed with the man who was only now realizing he was injured.

Tyla prepared herself more carefully this time, aiming lower to compensate for the upward jerk. There was another flash, and the first man fell.

"Keep going!" Kelsey encouraged.

"Jak, what's happening?" One of the men knelt and tried to rouse his buddy. Tyla shot at the one still standing.

He cried out and fell down. The last one looked up then, finally starting to connect the bright flashes with his friend's injuries.

"You can't—" he said. But Tyla could, and did, pull the trigger.

"Good work," Kelsey said encouragingly. "Almost done now."

She put a hand on Tyla's back and led her over to the corpses. The first one was the leader.

"He's dead," Kelsey said, tapping him with her foot. The corpse disappeared.

Moving over to the next, she shook her head. "This guy's still hanging on," she said. She looked at Tyla expectantly.

"He's no threat," Tyla said. "There's no need."

Kelsey shook her head again. "Remember what I said about witnesses? We can't have this guy telling tales about us. He's probably gonna die anyway. You'll just be putting him out of his misery."

Numen spirits *tested* elves, refined them. This was what Tyla needed to get stronger, to put her weakness behind her. She stepped up to the dying man.

"Final shot goes in the head," Kelsey said. "Instant death."

It almost felt as if the gun fired itself. Almost. Kelsey made a pleased noise and made the corpse disappear. The third one was also sufficiently dead.

"Feel better?" Kelsey asked.

"I feel . . . stronger," Tyla replied. She was already getting the notification.

You have reached Level 1.
Applying Benefits for Level 1
Strength + 1
Dexterity + 1
Perception + 1
Willpower + 1
Please allocate free Ability point.
Agility selected.

"You up for more training?" Kelsey asked. "Still got a couple of hours."

"I got more for killing humans than I did for killing a monster," Tyla whispered. "More than three times."

"Well, they were higher level," Kelsey said. "Still Tier Two, but closer to the top than the bottom, you know?"

Tyla nodded. Killing the rapists had taken her well past the threshold of level one. It wouldn't take much to get her to the second level.

"I want to get a trait for casting spells," she said.

CHAPTER THIRTY-SEVEN

If Trouble Was Money

Anton woke up to breakfast. Kelsey had expanded the table from last night and was serving up porridge and toast. The girls were all sitting down, marveling at the quality of their dishes and spoons. Even Soraya was sitting with the rest of them, taking dainty bites of a slice of fried meat. He took a seat, greeting all the other girls. They returned his good morning enthusiastically. Soraya gave him a nod.

Kelsey dropped a bowl in front of him. "Don't worry about washing up. Just pile them in a heap, and I'll have my people do it," she said.

"Thanks," Anton said. Aris came and sat next to him. She gave a wave and special smile to Cheia and accepted her own dish of porridge. There was dried fruit and salt on the table, along with pots that looked to be filled with sweet spreads. Anton thought that they looked like items that Kelsey had bought in the Rused and Denasti markets.

"Do we need to go buy more food?" he asked, looking at the spread before him.

"We're good for now," Kelsey said. "I don't want people to see supplies coming and going from here all the time. I can bring in what we need."

She gestured at the porridge. "I've pretty much got grain production covered, enough to cover us and help out Kirido. The rest of your complete breakfast is a little harder. The chickens proved to be . . . problematic."

"How so?" Anton asked. His parents had been rich enough to not bother with them, but Aris's family had raised some chickens and it seemed easy enough.

Kelsey sighed. "All the eggs that hatched turned out undead chickens," she said. "Something about the magical energy in there. So it doesn't look like I can raise animals. Not ones you want to eat, anyway."

Anton looked over at the meat that Soraya was eating.

"She can't eat anything else," Kelsey said. "So she gets special meat treatment."

"Didn't we pick up a load of preserved meat at the fort?" Anton asked.

"Sure, but . . . I'd rather go through our fresh stocks before we break those out."

"How much fresh stocks have we got?" Anton asked. Thinking back, he couldn't recall Kelsey purchasing that much meat. Not in bulk.

"Oh, plenty," Kelsey said. "You don't want it, though."

"Why not?" Anton asked.

"This had better not be poisoned," Soraya put in.

"Oh, no, nothing like that," Kelsey said. "It's just human meat."

Everybody froze, including Soraya. Then the courl deliberately took another bite, chewing it slowly. The pause lasted until she swallowed.

"Interesting," she said. "Human meat is forbidden in the Empire, but one hears stories."

"You can't eat humans!" Aris protested, only a little ahead of everyone else. Soraya stared them all down.

"Take it up with the cook," she said. "I am not so ungracious a guest as to refuse to eat the food served to me."

"Kelsey!" Aris exclaimed.

"What? Waste not, want not, you know? I've got a bunch of corpses that need processing, why not save some of the choice bits to feed Soraya?"

"Because it's wrong!" Anton insisted, backing up his wife.

"Is it? How?"

"In the earliest days of the Empire, the first Empress decreed that courls should not eat the flesh of sentient races," Soraya said thoughtfully. "This was a matter of pragmatism. The Empire had captured its first human city, and the Empress wished for humans to serve us, rather than be served."

She smiled at them all, a wide grin that showed all of her pointy teeth. "Over the years, there have been occasional exemptions from the rule. Now that I've tried it . . . I'm honestly disappointed that its taste is so mundane. I mistook it for pork."

"You don't eat courl, I bet," Anton said.

"Of course not! To eat one's own species would be . . . but that is not what is happening here."

"Meat is meat," Kelsey said. "There are issues, sure, with parasites and prions and such, but I've got that taken care of. Any meat that comes through me you know is safe."

She thought for a bit. "Unless I'm *trying* to spread an undead plague, but . . . I'm not! So rest easy."

"It's disrespectful," Aris tried to explain. "Eating someone that was alive like that, it's just . . . wrong."

"It was more disrespectful to murder them in the first place, I expect," Soraya replied. She thought for a moment. "Is this meat from the two guards that the elf barbarian killed in my home?"

Kelsey stopped muttering about dispersion rates and infection times and returned her attention to the conversation. "Oh . . . yeah, something like that," she said.

Anton narrowed his eyes at her evasion, but Soraya was not done talking. "The disrespect, the insult that was done, came then. What happens to the bodies afterwards matters little to the souls that have left."

"I hope you're not thinking that the souls are still in there," Kelsey said. "Take it from me, once they die, the souls are *gone*."

"Even though you can raise them again?" Aris asked. Now that Anton thought about it, wasn't *that* an even greater insult to the person that was?

"Nah. Revenants and vampires . . . they're not the person that they were before. They can *fake* it pretty well, but even if they have the same memories, it's a different thing that's remembering them."

"Where is Tyla, anyway?" Anton asked, suddenly noticing that the elf wasn't there.

"She's sleeping; she was up all night," Kelsey said. "She probably won't be participating in whatever we do today."

"That thing should be arranging for my ransom," Soraya said.

"Wait—we're not finished talking about *that*," Aris said, pointing to the remains of Soraya's meal.

"I think we are," Soraya said, languidly taking another bite. "The crime has been committed. You're not willing to condemn the murderer or the cook, so why me?"

Aris turned to Kelsey. "Just don't serve her any more humans!" she pleaded.

"Sure," Kelsey said, "As soon as you manage to explain why. You think that the alternative is more respectful?"

"You never explained what processing actually *means*," Anton said uneasily.

"Yeah, it's complicated, and not at all pretty," Kelsey warned. "Neither is what happens when you bury a poor fool. Eaten by worms and maggots? That's your idea of a proper post-death?"

"No, but . . . I—" Aris stumbled over her words. Kelsey gave her more time to speak, but she couldn't come up with anything.

"It's all part of the cycle of life," Kelsey said soothingly. "Everyone, everything, gets eaten eventually."

"You don't," Anton pointed out. "Not you, and not your monsters."

"I suppose I do have a pretty good recycling plan going," Kelsey said. "But even then . . . If I die, I imagine all my monsters and all my stores will make a nice feast for the worms."

"I have another question," Soraya put in primly. "It has been mentioned before, but why are monsters being referred to?"

"Whoops!" Kelsey exclaimed. "We've said too much in front of the Muggles! What are we going to tell them?"

Anton sighed. He looked over at the other girls, who were staring at him quietly, with similar questions on their faces.

"Right. I suppose now is the best time to explain everything."

"So *you* are a barbarian lord," Soraya said, lounging back in her chair and looking at him speculatively.

"I suppose so," Anton replied. "It doesn't feel like it, but I am. Does that matter?"

Some time had passed. Zaphar had come back and been dispatched, both to deliver some ransom instructions and to scout out the administrative quarter. No one else was allowed to leave, with the possible exception of Anton and Aris. Anton, however, didn't feel like testing his geas, and Aris wanted to stay with him. Right now, she was talking with the other girls.

Kelsey had started what she called occupational education. Most of the girls were interested in taking up a new Tier One class. Kelsey had set up a loom, of all things, and was taking them through the process of using it.

Soraya wasn't interested in a new class, and wasn't welcome in the group besides, so she had decided to converse with Anton. He was due to teach sword fighting to those interested in learning, but he was waiting for Kelsey to produce the weighted wooden swords that he'd asked for.

"Perhaps," Soraya answered. "Tiatian nobility has a certain cachet, but the barbarian kingdoms of the northern coast are not well regarded."

"You're not noble yourself, are you?" Anton was pretty sure she wasn't, but she did live in a compound that was bigger than the Baron's—than *his*—castle.

"I'm not," Soraya assured him, "But my father's wealth was such that I was hoping to marry into a noble family."

"I see," Anton said noncommittally.

"Unfortunately, my Father set his sights on the Bey's Champion, al-Kadir. A brute of a man with not a drop of noble blood."

"He sounds important, though?" The name sounded familiar to Anton. He thought back on where he might have seen it.

"Oh, he is *valued* by our lord. *Lauded* for his performances in the arena. The Bey's chief enforcer and thug. He rides the rising tide now, but his fortunes—and his family's—will last only until the first time he is defeated."

It was coming to him now, but Soraya wasn't finished.

"I don't know what Father was thinking, tying our family to that brute—giving *me* to him! Obviously, I had to take steps."

"Hang on," Anton said slowly. "Are you talking about *Salim* al-Kadir?"

"That's the one," Soraya said bitterly. "Has his fame spread even to the bar-barians? Now that I think about your murderous ways, you might even get along with him."

"I inspected him outside your house, after the auction," Anton said. "He was Tier Four!"

"Yes, he has had a certain amount of martial success," Soraya admitted. "He's considered the most powerful fighter in the city. Literally—that is what Champion means, after all."

"But because he doesn't have the right father, he's nothing to you?" Anton asked.

"In a *civilized* culture, a person's family is everything," Soraya said coldly. "Joining a noble house is the *best* way to ensure that my children will be able to rise to the destiny that they deserve. Al-Kadir can put "al" in front of his name, and he is so feared that no one will gainsay it, but his children will not be so feared. They will be cast out the moment his star fades."

"So your plan is just to take your share of the ransom, and then leave *your* family?" Anton asked. "That seems so cold."

"Well, I may consider going back to them. This embarrassment may cause al-Kadir to distance himself from my father, making the idea of engagement impossible. Otherwise . . . well, it's my father who *started* acting outrageously."

"Even so," Anton started, but he was interrupted by Zaphar's return.

"Guys! Guys!" he said, slamming the door he had let himself in by. He rested for a moment with his back to it, as if afraid someone was going to smash it in. "We've got a problem!"

"Did you make the drop?" Kelsey asked, coming over to them. The rest of the girls kept their distance. They were far more interested in the conversation than the loom, though.

"No, no, I couldn't!" Zaphar said excitedly. "Somebody was there! Waiting! The Champion of this dung-blasted city!"

"Al-Kadir? He was there?" Soraya asked.

"Wait, how do you know al-Kadir?" Kelsey asked Zaphar.

"I don't! Though I might have seen him at the auction? He looked familiar. I don't know." Zaphar shook his head, as if he were trying to shake the memories loose.

"Then how do you know it was him?" Kelsey asked.

"Because *everybody in the market was talking about it*!" Zaphar blurted out. "He's *famous*! It was very *weird* for him to be standing right in front of the post where we're supposed to post the note, so *everyone* was talking about how the most famous fighter in Denasti is going to rescue his fiancée!"

Kelsey looked over at Soraya, who drew herself up, ears going straight up.

"Well," she said, "I hope you don't think this is my fault!"

CHAPTER THIRTY-EIGHT

The Waiting

I'm telling you, I have *no idea* why he got himself involved," Soraya insisted, her voice raising as she repeated herself. "I've never even met him!"

"You haven't met your fiancé?" Zaphar asked skeptically.

"He is *not* my fiancé," Soraya said heatedly. "Father was talking about it, but nothing was decided yet! I was going to meet him at the auction, but events . . . intervened. Not that I'm complaining about that."

She grinned slyly.

"I was planning on avoiding him as best I could, but as things turned out, the whole event was cancelled before he could force his presence on me. Why he's chosen to involve himself is beyond me."

"You said that the match wasn't an advantageous one, and you didn't know why your father had made it," Kelsey said thoughtfully. "Could it be that the pressure for the marriage was coming from al-Kadir?"

Soraya stared at Kelsey. "That—why would he want to marry me?"

"It could be that he sees an advantage *to him* in joining your family," Kelsey speculated. "Or maybe he saw you from a distance and liked your looks. I'm no judge of courl attractiveness, but . . ."

"I'm gorgeous, as if you need to ask," Soraya snapped. She gave a little shudder. "I don't like the idea that he's been stalking me, though."

"It could be romantic?" Aris suggested. "If he really likes you and is going to all these lengths to save you . . ."

"He's a thug and a killer," Soraya said frostily. "I realize that may not sound disqualifying, given current company, but I don't want his bloody hands touching me."

"Awfully picky, given your father's trade," Kelsey said evenly.

"We trade in live slaves, thank you very much! Slaves for pleasure and delight, not for hard labor and combat! Our merchandise is carefully handled and kept safe—I can't remember the last time a slave died on our premises."

"Well, you've thrown in your lot with us murderous criminals now," Kelsey said cheerfully. "Unless you feel like giving up and going back to dear old Dad?"

"No," Soraya said sullenly. "If I do, I'm sure that I'll be bundled off and sold to al-Kadir before my feet hit the ground. But how are we going to send the ransom note?"

"He can't stand at the post forever," Kelsey said. "Or can he? Is that something he can do?"

"I don't think he has any traits that let him go without sleep," Soraya said. "But his Stamina is surely high enough to go a week without. He has other duties, though. He can't stay there forever."

"The fact that he just went down there, expecting to intercept Zaphar, does suggest he's a bit of an idiot," Kelsey said. "Just extremely physically capable. Do you know what his traits are?"

"Not all of them," Soraya said. "But he has used some in the arena often enough that they are widely known . . . let's see. He can make his opponent feel terror by looking at him. He has traits for striking and parrying, like most duelists. His most feared ability is *Blink Step*."

"*Blink Step?*" Kelsey repeated.

"One moment he stands in front of you, and the next he is behind you with his sword against your neck," Soraya said, shivering. "You want to hope at that point that the duel is not to the death."

"Nasty," Kelsey said. "Still, I think we can manage to nail something to a post." She looked over at Zaphar. "You're off the hook for that part, but you will have to show me where the damned thing is."

"I can do that," Zaphar said, nodding. "If, if, I don't have to get within thirty yards of that man."

"No problem," Kelsey said. "I think I want to wait for nightfall, though. The next item on the agenda is new classes!"

She looked over at the rescued girls, who had been following the conversation nervously.

"Who wants to be a weaver?" she asked brightly. "It's an honorable profession that is due to take off in Kirido."

The girls were divided into two groups, the ones that wanted to learn to fight, and the ones that didn't. Some of the latter group had already gone back to their old classes. Aurora and Elysia had gone back to Server and Servant respectively and reported that they were getting experience from cleaning up after the group's meal.

Kelsey had them all practice with the loom that she set up regardless of their current class.

"A new skill is never wasted," she told them. "I know you want to go back to your parents' inn, Aurora, but you might not get the chance."

The reddish-skinned girl nodded. She was one of two girls from the Ett Confederacy to the west of Zamarra. Well, three girls if you counted Tyla, but the elves were only loosely associated with that nation.

Kelsey showed them how to string the loom, and then left them to practice. It was the chance that Anton had been waiting for.

"Can I have a word?" he asked, indicating an unoccupied portion of the building.

"Sure," Kelsey said. "What's up?"

"I just wanted to ask about my class," Anton said. "I haven't been getting experience like I used to."

"Your old class was a beast for getting experience," Kelsey said. "Almost *any-thing* can be an adventure. You're just finding out what it's like for the rest of us."

"I get that," Anton said. "But didn't you say I'd get experience from freeing slaves? I didn't bring it up at the time, but I never got any experience when we freed the girls."

Kelsey looked thoughtful. "Huh. I would have thought . . . could it be that they're not free yet?"

"I've got to get them all the way back to Kirido?" Anton said in dismay.

"Maybe not *that* far," Kelsey said. "Think about it, though. We're just one step away from being recaptured. I'm not sure what will do it. Maybe we have to get out of the city; maybe the girls have to *think* that they're free."

"That's . . . unfortunate," Anton said. "I could really do with some more levels before we get out of the city, especially if we're up against that al-Kadir guy."

"You're not wrong," Kelsey agreed. "But there's always the old standby—killing people. How do you feel about going vigilante killer on the criminal underworld?"

"Not great," Anton said sourly. "That sounds like a way to get innocent people dead, and the city guard after us."

"Credit me with *some* discretion," Kelsey said, smirking. "I'm pretty confident that I can find some people you won't mind killing. Not that innocent or guilty makes a difference to the experience."

"It makes a difference to *me*," Anton insisted. Something about Kelsey's expression alerted him to a bigger problem.

"Have you *already* started vigilante killing?" he asked. "Was that what Tyla was doing last night?"

"It was mostly skeletons," Kelsey told him. "But there were some unsavory characters who followed a pair of girls into a dark alleyway with less than honorable intentions."

"I don't believe this," Anton said. "How is this keeping a low profile?"

"She needs levels, Anton," Kelsey said reproachfully. "And we didn't leave any evidence behind."

"Those people will have friends," Anton said. "If they saw you go into the alleyway, others will have as well. People will start to talk when the people you killed are missed."

Kelsey started to brush him off, but then paused.

"Maybe you're right," she admitted. "That's the sort of attention I used to want, as a dungeon. I'll be more careful in the future."

"Just don't do it at all?" Anton suggested hopefully.

"I don't know if I'd go that far," Kelsey said, grinning. "Tyla still needs another level before she gets actual spells to cast. When she wakes up, I'll see if meditation exercises can give her some gains."

She cocked her head to one side. "And that's a definite no for you? No heroically stalking the streets for criminals?"

Anton shook his head. "I get the feeling there will be quite enough fighting with just what we've got planned. We don't need to go out looking for fights."

Kelsey grimaced. "I just wish I had my dungeon available so you could keep grinding. All this waiting isn't getting us levels."

"Which brings us around to the new fighters," Anton said. "Are you going to . . ."

"I'll make a new room first," Kelsey said. "I don't want to panic the noncombatants by summoning zombies in their living quarters."

"That's very thoughtful of you," Anton said wryly.

It took Kelsey a while to get around to making a summoning room, as there were a lot of other improvements that she wanted to make. Mostly she provided materials and instructions and left the actual work to the penned-up humans.

She pronounced herself happy with the stone walls of the warehouse but insisted on additional "insulation" for the roof. She produced a thick, light, soft material that she had Anton hold up while the others secured it behind paneling. She made Anton wear a mask while he was holding it.

"It's non-toxic," she said. "But it's *scratchy* for anyone who doesn't have invulnerable skin, and you wouldn't want to get bits of it in your lungs."

Several of the girls reported gaining access to the Apprentice Carpenter class, and one girl who'd helped in setting up the toilet unlocked the Apprentice Plumber class, which Kelsey found amusing.

"It's a chemical toilet!" she laughed. "The only plumbing involved is straight down!"

Anton wasn't an expert on plumbing by any means, but he thought that it might refer to pipes. If so, she was right about the lack of them. The way the toilet worked was that a container was filled, which Kelsey disappeared from time to time and replaced with an empty one. He wasn't sure what the chemicals were or how they were involved.

Meanwhile, the weavers reported that they now had access to the Doffer class. No one had any idea why the weaver apprentice class was called that, not even Kelsey.

"Damn," she said when she was told. "Must be some seventeenth-century term I never heard of or something."

When she finally turned her attention to the would-be Warriors, she ran into a problem. To start with, Cheia wanted to be a Gunslinger like her sister.

"That's not going to be easy to get," Kelsey told her. "For a start, I can't have you practice firing here—it's too loud. Aris can show you how to use a gun, but you'll need to kill ten enemies with one before you qualify for the class."

"But I want to use a gun," Cheia protested. "Isn't it the best weapon?"

"What you want to do," Anton put in, using his authority as an adventurer, "Is get one kill in, take the Warrior class. Then when you get those ten kills, the experience will go towards you to Tier Two, which is what you need for Gunslinger."

"Actually," Aris said, "I think there was a requirement of not having a Combat class to get Gunslinger."

"Ah," Anton said. "Well, then, you won't get Gunslinger that way, but there will be some kind of specialist class for ten kills with a weapon."

"Kelsey set things up for me so that I could kill ten zombies all lined up in a row," Aris explained. "She can't do that here."

"I'll kill ten humans then. Or courls," Cheia said sulkily. "It doesn't matter how long it takes or if it's not efficient."

"That's the spirit, kid!" Kelsey said, ruffling her hair. "Here's your starter gun pack. You can have the ammo once you can field-strip it and put it back together, and Aris convinces me that you've got some trigger discipline."

"I don't know what any of that means," Cheia said.

"I'll explain it . . ." Aris said, whisking her away.

Next up was Lyra, the other one of the Ett Confederacy girls. She had taken back her Hunter class and wasn't interested in a gun. Kelsey found a short, curved sword for her, which she liked, and a bow, which she did not. She was also uninterested in Kelsey's spiky bow-like thing.

"Nobody likes my compound bow," Kelsey complained. "Even though the power you can get is *insane*. I had to reinforce the arrows so they wouldn't splinter."

Anton just shrugged, not really seeing what the problem was. Lyra was going to fight a few skeletons for the experience, and then she'd take part in the sword fighting lesson that Anton was holding later.

Finally, there was Syrena, who had used to work in the tavern back in Kirido.

"Should I do the Warrior thing?" she asked.

"That's the simplest," Kelsey said. "Got a weapon preference?"

"Something . . . graceful?" she asked. "I like to move on my feet."

She gave an elegant twirl. Kelsey looked appreciative for a moment, then frowned.

"Sounds like you want a rapier, but they're not good against zombies or skeletons. Thrusting is . . . ineffective."

"A rapier can slash," Anton said. "She'd likely get it caught up in zombie flesh, but as long as she goes for the joints, she can take down skeletons. If you can find a heavier one, that'd be great."

"I am quite strong for my age," Syrena offered. "Server gives Strength advances."

"Fair enough," Kelsey said. She pulled out a scabbarded rapier. Anton took it and checked to make sure it had a good edge.

"This should be fine," he said, passing it over to Syrena.

"Great," Kelsey said. "Let's get to killing!"

CHAPTER THIRTY-NINE

Happy House

TYLA

Tyla slept late, waking only when the hammering became too much to ignore. When she crawled out of her sleeping space, she saw that the warehouse had been transformed into a hive of industry. Women were fussing over a strange machine, or climbing up the metal scaffolding that had been placed against the walls, making modifications to the roof.

Kelsey was trying to be everywhere at once, offering direction and comment on what everyone was doing. She noticed that Tyla was up and came over.

"Sleep well?" she asked brightly. "You had a big night."

Tyla nodded absently, as she recalled the events of the evening. She brought up her status to remind her of how far she had progressed.

Tyla Greenwalker of the Padascar Tribe (Level 3)
Overall Level: 10
Paths: Padascar Hunter (Broken)/ Doxy (Broken)/Apprentice Dungeon
    Witch
Strength: 11
Toughness: 7
Agility: 9
Dex: 15
Perception: 16
Will: 11
Charisma: 9
Traits

Persistent Tracking
Silent Shot
Danger Sense
Sense Magic

Her path would remain forever scarred by her failures, but she was moving forward now. Level three. Kelsey had convinced her to get *Sense Magic* instead of *Cast Cantrip*.

"*Sense Magic* is going to be broadly useful for a long time, while cantrips are just for show. Make a light in your hand, fill a glass with water, that kind of thing," she'd said, and Tyla had agreed.

Kelsey had also suggested that Tyla should put her free points in Charisma. She wasn't a lone hunter anymore and would be dealing more with people as time went on.

"Plus, we don't want you falling too far behind the other girls," she muttered, which Tyla didn't understand. She ended up compromising, putting one point in Charisma and the other in Agility. For an elf, her Agility was shamefully low and was only now getting to respectable levels.

Now, Kelsey looked her up and down, evaluating her with who knew what senses.

"Good," she said. "Let's try to keep that momentum going. We don't have a monster room set up yet, but I want you to try and use your *Sense Magic*, and see if that gives you any experience."

"But . . . there isn't any magic around for me to sense?" Tyla pointed out.

"What am I, chopped liver?" Kelsey asked with a laugh. Tyla flushed. She'd forgotten. Kelsey seemed so natural sometimes that it was hard to remember that she was a creature entirely composed of magic.

"But," Kelsey went on, "what I want you to focus on is your own magic. Focus on what's welling up from that bauble of yours and try to differentiate the types."

Tyla nodded and looked for an empty corner where she could sit. Before she could go, though, Kelsey caught her by her arm.

"Wait," she said. "Where's your gun?"

Tyla blinked in surprise. "Back in my bunk," she said. Kelsey had made her clean it before she went to sleep.

"Get it, and remember to keep it with you, especially if you've got bullets. It's a dangerous weapon, and there are a few here who might see it as a toy."

Tyla nodded slowly. Kelsey had confiscated her remaining bullets last night, but it would be a good habit to get into. In the wrong hands, it could easily fire when pointed at the wrong thing.

"I will be careful," she promised and went to collect it. Then she found a spot where she could be out of everyone's way and concentrated on her new trait.

There *was* magic in the room, she realized. Anton was carrying an enchanted weapon, and there was the faintest trace of magic hanging around Zaphar. Some alchemical concoction? Or his new class? "Fae-touched" certainly *sounded* as if he had some magic to him.

Tyla had expected Kelsey to glow brightly to her new sense, but the magic she sensed from the numen spirit was muted. She clearly had more magic about her than the average human, but if she hadn't already known the answer, Tyla wouldn't have been able to say if it was a natural talent, a spell, or something completely different.

As Kelsey had suggested, the strongest source of magic in the warehouse was Tyla herself. She could feel it being drawn into her at the point where her core touched her skin. It circulated within her and then slowly seeped out of her skin. Once it left her body, it quickly dispersed, like mist on a sunny day, but Kelsey had said that it would leave a tiny bit of extra magic everywhere she went. According to Kelsey, the leftover magic from dungeons, and wizards like her, was what powered the magical traits of higher-tier individuals.

Tyla focused on the magic welling up within her. Control of it would come when she acquired a casting trait, but for now, she tried to identify the different types. Kelsey had gone over them with her last night.

The first thing that she noticed was that there were too few types. Kelsey had told her there were fifteen and she had . . . counting was hard. As she thought about it, the mana separated itself into different streams that were easier to count.

So I do have some control already, Tyla thought and then got on with her original task. There were eleven types coming from the core. Some were stronger than others, and the obvious conclusion was that some were so weak as to be entirely absent.

Tyla set aside her disappointment at the idea that there would be magic that she couldn't use and tried to identify the types that were there.

The strongest one felt black to her. There was a sense of absence, of loneliness, of death and loss. That had to be Destruction magic, Tyla felt sure. It was useful in combat, Kelsey had said. Also good at breaking through barriers and cleaning.

The next strongest was a tie between three types. Two of them seemed complex, so Tyla tried identifying the other one first. That one was hot and cold, burning and freezing at the same time. It had to be Fire. Tyla had been surprised that the two opposing concepts were the same, but Kelsey had told her that cold was just the *absence* of heat.

Having found one of the elements, Tyla decided to look for the others. She found Water, cool and refreshing, slipping through her mental grasp. It was about half as strong as Fire. Air and Water, though, she couldn't find. Two of the missing ones, perhaps.

There were three streams of mana that reminded her of water, so she started examining them. They reminded her of home, of health and vigor. Reviewing what Kelsey had told her, she realized that these must be the three types that covered living things: Plants, Animals, and People. Her Animal-type mana was the strongest of the three, about halfway between Water and Fire. The other two were about as strong as Water.

So far, I can destroy Fire, Water, People, Animals, and Plants, Tyla thought. An impressive list in some ways, but she hoped there would be more variety in what she could do. With that thought in mind, she returned her attention to the complicated mana types she had skipped over.

The first one was . . . rigid, yet moving. It's like Fire, Tyla realized. Immobility is the absence of motion, so the two are . . . actually the same?

If so, then this was . . . Motion? That wasn't a type that Kelsey had described. *What type is associated with motion?* It wasn't any of the object types. Motion was a verb and the verb was . . . Control.

This is Control mana, Tyla thought. *It controls the motion.*

Now she knew that the other complicated one had to be a verb-type. Comparing it with the three remaining verbs let her quickly guess that it was Sense. The way it seemed almost transparent didn't seem to suit Creation or Change.

Tyla had almost finished, but she was distracted from her meditation by the growl of her stomach as she smelled food. She looked around. Everyone seemed to have finished for the day, and despite the lack of a kitchen, Kelsey was handing out delicious-smelling meals. Tyla quickly headed over to claim a seat. She had woken up after lunch and this would be her first meal of the day.

The meal was full of excited chatter as everyone had new classes or skills to talk about. Tyla didn't want to talk about her own class, but she was drawn into the discussions with the girls who had become her friends during captivity. She smiled to see some of the fear fade from their faces, and they smiled to see it gone from hers.

The fear wasn't gone completely, though.

"Do you think we can get away?" Morwyn asked her. "I know they—you—got us out, but there's so much—so far to go."

"That's why you should have taken a Combat class," Syrena interjected. "That way, if they come for us, you can fight back." Her hand went to the rapier by her side.

"I think we will make it home," Tyla assured Morwyn. "Anton is a Hero,"

"And a lord!" Elysia put in.

"And handsome!" Lyra added.

"Shh! Don't let Aris hear you!" Syrena whispered urgently to Lyra. "You're not from Kirido, you don't know how she can be. And she's *married* to him now, so she's probably even worse."

"She is a fearsome opponent," Tyla agreed, and meant it. Though Aris was only at Tier Two, she wore her weapons with an ease that Tyla had not managed. And the second tier was a tier above the rest of the girls here.

"But the raiders . . ." Morwyn said nervously. "They were *all* Tier Three, weren't they? And that courl they were worried about, he was Tier *Four*!"

"The guns are a great equalizer both against numbers and higher tiers," Tyla told her. "I have . . . seen them in action, and they make killing terrifyingly easy. The odds are still stacked against us, but not as much as you might think."

She looked over at Kelsey, still producing the last dishes.

"And Kelsey . . ." Tyla said. "She is magic personified. I don't believe there is anything she cannot do."

"She is *something*," Syrena said quietly. "She made all that stuff, summoned monsters . . . I don't get how she can *be* a dungeon."

"It is a mystery," Tyla agreed. "And she is coming this way."

Several of the girls who were going to say something quickly closed their mouths as Kelsey approached.

"How's my favorite elf?" she said, giving Tyla a hug.

"Wow, you're really close," Morwyn commented. "Didn't you only meet two days ago?"

"I've got hugs for anyone that wants them," Kelsey said, giving Tyla another squeeze before letting her go. She looked at Morwyn.

"No thanks, I'm good," Morwyn said.

"Suit yourself," Kelsey said. "I just wanted to let you know that Anton, Aris, Zaphar, and I are going to post that ransom note of Soraya's."

"Can I come?" Tyla asked. "I've been sitting down in here all day."

"Or sleeping," Kelsey teased. "How's it been going?"

"I think that I have eleven types of mana available to me," Tyla said. "I've identified nine of them."

"Well, that's great," Kelsey said, "but I was asking if you got any experience for looking."

"Oh!" Tyla exclaimed. She'd gotten so focused that she had forgotten about that part. She concentrated on the sensation of leveling. She hadn't gained a level, she would have noticed *that*, but . . .

"I think I gained some," she reported. "Not much, compared to last night, but some."

"Great!" Kelsey said. "In that case, you should keep working on it. We'll be back soon.

"Oh," Tyla sighed. Kelsey giggled and gave her another hug.

"Don't sulk!" she admonished. "The whole point of this outing is to not attract attention—and that's hard enough when you look like me, without taking you along!"

"I suppose that's true," Tyla admitted. She *was* quite distinctive. Kelsey was, too, but her ears didn't give her away once she was wrapped up.

"That's the spirit," Kelsey said. "From how into it you were before, I reckon we'll get back before you notice we're gone."

CHAPTER FORTY

Ace of Spades

Kelsey summoned the skeleton before they left. Not just *any* skeleton. Its weapons and armor were missing, and she had wrapped cloth around its arm bones, shoulders, and head. Gloves had gone on the hands. Then she had draped a long hooded cloak around the whole thing.

It looked *suspicious* to Anton as Kelsey had it walk around in a circle. But it did look like a suspicious *human*, rather than a monster.

"Zaphar is with me," Kelsey announced, "Along with muggins here. You two," addressing Anton and Aris, "get to follow at a distance."

"What are we doing?" Anton asked.

"You're backup, in case things go as unplanned," Kelsey told him. "It should be a quick in-and-out, but you never know how things will go."

The walk over was uneventful enough. They split up when they got to the crowd. Kelsey's group headed around to one side, trying to get close enough to approach the post, while Anton and Aris went in the other direction, joining the crowd in the hopes of getting another glimpse of the courl in question.

The crowd was a little odd, at least to Anton's limited experience with such things. A mixture of different classes and races, they all gave al-Kadir a wide berth and never looked directly at him. At the same time, conversations were being struck up in hushed voices between strangers, commenting on the strangeness of it all.

"Is that really him—"

"—sworn to bring a killer to justice—"

"—lost a bet—"

The courl himself was leaning against a wall, about two yards from the post that was the center of all this. It was hard to mistake, covered in about a dozen folded sheets of paper that had been nailed to it. Anton supposed that it wasn't getting much use at the moment. It was mainly used by people who wanted to communicate anonymously, and they probably didn't want to be scrutinized by the glowering courl.

More than anyone else on this unimportant street, al-Kadir looked out of place. His brown fur seemed to shimmer with health and his silk robe and opulently embroidered waistcoat looked as though they were worth more than the clothes of everyone else here put together.

His piercing amber eyes scanned the crowd. Everyone looked away when his gaze passed over them, and Anton was no exception. He almost missed the words, said at a normal volume. Coming from that direction, though, they caused gasps, a sudden silence and a general motion away from him.

"Hey, you."

He had time enough to look back and see that al-Kadir was walking towards him, the crowd falling over itself to get out of the courl's way.

Anton froze. Running away would make him look guilty, and there was no way al-Kadir could know he'd done anything wrong. Could he?

Can he smell that Soraya has been near me? he wondered, panicking. It wasn't *impossible*. An advanced hunter might have such a trait. It seemed unlikely for a duelist, though. That was about all Anton had time to think of before the courl was standing in front of him.

Aris clutched Anton's arm, reminding him of her presence.

"A foreign noble and his lady," al-Kadir said, with a deep, rumbling voice. "You're a long way from home, my friend."

"I am?" Anton blurted. "I mean—yes, I am. Am I your friend, though?"

Al-Kadir smiled, a gesture that was probably meant to be disarming. However, Anton had yet to see a courl smile that didn't look cruel. This one was no exception, but Anton tried not to hold it against him.

"It's just an expression," al-Kadir said. "As a member of the Bey's court, I do have a responsibility to make foreign guests feel welcome. I—just a moment."

In an instant, he was gone. There was no sensation of movement, just his sudden absence. Looking around wildly, Anton quickly spotted where the courl had gone.

He was back at the post, holding the arm of a figure Anton recognized. The skeleton, holding a piece of paper in his hand. Kelsey had obviously taken this chance to make her approach. Just as obviously, al-Kadir was not so easily distracted.

This was still within the parameters of Kelsey's plan, though. The skeleton shivered in al-Kadir's grasp and then fell into pieces. Everyone froze in surprise, and then someone in the crowd screamed.

All around, new conversations were starting up.

"—killed him without even a blow!"

"—stripped the flesh from his bones!"

"—maybe we shouldn't be here—"

"—witness a murder—"

The crowd was starting to disperse, as curiosity warred with fear in the onlookers. Al-Kadir ignored all that. Plucking the paper out of the skeleton's grasp, he opened it up and read the contents, frowning, as Anton and the braver onlookers watched on.

Then he simply held the note out to one side. Another courl stepped out of the crowd. He was dressed much more simply, though still in silk of good quality. Taking the letter, he stepped back into the dispersing crowd as al-Kadir made his way back to Anton and Aris.

"Sorry about that, a private matter."

"Did you . . . do that?" Anton asked, pushing his guile to the limit. It seemed like the question anyone else in the crowd would have asked.

"No," al-Kadir said shortly. "It was a skeleton before I touched it. It seems I am dealing with kidnappers who are working for a necromancer."

"Necromancer?" Anton asked. He'd only ever heard the term from Kelsey, so he figured it was the sort of thing an innocent noble would not know.

"A type of mage, with an interest in raising corpses," al-Kadir said thoughtfully. "A particularly deranged type," he added. "I heard a rumor about an undead attack on the walls. . . . I will have to follow that up."

Shaking his head, al-Kadir dismissed whatever thoughts he was having and put a hand on Anton's shoulder.

"But that is no concern of yours. As I was saying, I wanted to properly greet you. Would you do me the honor of breaking bread with me?"

"Uh, sure," Anton said. "We're in kind of a hurry, though . . ."

"I know a coffeehouse not far from here," al-Kadir assured him. "The pastries are very good."

"That sounds delightful," Aris said, squeezing Anton's arm.

"Oh! Yes. This is my wife, the Lady Aris," Anton said.

"A pleasure to meet you both," al-Kadir said. "Please, this way."

Anton didn't see any sign of Kelsey as they headed off to the coffeehouse. He hoped they were being followed, but he had to admit that it seemed a bit of a risk. When they got to their destination, they were quickly whisked off to a private table in a nook overlooking the main floor. Anton wasn't a fan of the thick, sweet stuff they called coffee here, but they did serve tea, so Anton and Aris had that instead.

"I must admit, I have not been entirely honest with you," al-Kadir said, once they were comfortable.

"Oh?" Anton said in what he hoped was a noncommittal manner. The pastries *were* good.

"It's true that hospitality should be shown to foreign guests. But the court cares little for barbarian nobility that happens to wander by. My *Nobility's Privilege* showed me your title, but it also showed me your class, which I find much more interesting."

"*Nobility's Privilege?*" Anton said. To his surprise, it didn't come out as a squeak. "I . . . heard some things about you—from the crowd—and one of those things was that despite your exalted rank, you weren't a noble."

Did I say that? Anton thought. *Is that what having higher Charisma does? Makes you say things like "exalted"?*

Pulling himself together, Anton listened to the court's reply.

"I *was* a noble, long enough to get the Scion class, before my family . . . displeased the Wali. They were all killed, and I was sent as a slave to the arena. Fortunately, I had always had a talent for the blade . . ."

Al-Kadir trailed off, his gaze drifting off into the past. Blinking it away, he returned his attention to Anton. "Fighting my way up to an . . . exalted rank, as you say, was not easy. But I managed it and now I am as you see. Dishonored as a noble, the rest of the court fears and hates me, and the Bey uses me to keep them in line."

"That sounds hard," Aris said sympathetically.

"The arena was far harder, I assure you," al-Kadir said, smiling. "But thank you for your concern."

"Since you are talking to us, I've got to ask the question everyone in the crowd was asking," Anton said. "What are you doing?"

"A reasonable question," al-Kadir said. "There are those who would say I have lost my mind. While I still retain my blade, though, they must keep quiet. The truth is, I have fallen in love."

"How romantic!" Aris gushed. "I'm not sure how that follows, though."

Anton carefully didn't let himself goggle at Aris. Since when did she care about romantic gestures? That sort of thing was for nobles, which . . . they were now. He made a note to buy some flowers and to . . . ask Kelsey for ideas? That didn't sound right. He'd think about it some more. Right now, al-Kadir was talking. He'd just said Soraya's name.

"I was negotiating with her father to marry her when she was kidnapped by what I now know to be some necromancer and his gang. I'm going to have to tell her father that his slaves have no doubt been killed and turned into servants of the foul deviant. I can only hope that Soraya is still alive."

Al-Kadir forced himself to stop speaking and took a sip of his coffee to calm down. He continued after a few deep breaths.

"For the crime of laying hands on sweet Soraya, that fiend will pay with his life. I only hope he comes back, so I can kill him again."

He stared into his cup for a moment and then shook his head.

"I'm sorry, that wasn't what I brought you here to talk about," he said, forcing a change in his demeanor.

"You wanted to talk about my class?" Anton asked.

"A little, but I can see that you're new to it," al-Kadir said. "What I wanted to talk about was your fighting ability."

"I'm pretty sure it doesn't compare to yours," Anton said carefully.

"It doesn't," al-Kadir said. "I have a trait that evaluates opponents, and you're not my equal. But you could be, one day."

"You're not planning on taking him out before he becomes a rival, are you?" Aris asked anxiously.

Al-Kadir laughed. A surprised snort at first, which quickly grew into an uncontrollable belly laugh. Not sharing the joke, the other two could only wait for it to die down.

"No," al-Kadir finally managed to say. "Not that. Understand—I *live* for worthy rivals. The only time I see anything like a fair fight is when the cities vie against each other. Once a year, *at best*. The rest of the time, my fights are just executions. The blade in the victim's hand is just for show."

Al-Kadir pointed at Anton. "You. Without even trying it, I know that you can resist my *Aura of Fear*."

"I've heard that most of your opponents can't even stay on their feet when they face you," Anton said.

"You can," al-Kadir said. "You can't beat me, not yet. But when you've progressed . . . how long have you been on the first level?"

"I've . . . been having a problem with the experience requirements," Anton admitted.

Al-Kadir nodded. "Fancy classes can be trouble that way. I only get experience when I fight for the city now. Yours is a variant on Hero, correct?"

"Yes," Anton admitted. *Just how many of my secrets can this courl see?*

"Hmm . . ." al-Kadir said, thinking. "I might have something for you. First, take this." He handed Anton a paper card with writing on it. "That has my address; someone can direct you to it. I want you to come over sometime when you have time. We can have a friendly spar."

"We both already know I can't beat you," Anton said. Al-Kadir laughed again.

"Ah, but you'll get better, fighting someone better than you," he pointed out, and Anton was forced to agree.

"Now, come with me," al-Kadir said, draining the last of his coffee. He dropped a few coins on the table and strode out, dragging Anton and Aris in his wake.

He led them back to the post.

"I was pretty bored waiting out here," he said. "I took the time to examine all of these."

He carefully plucked a nail out of one of the notices and showed it to Anton. Like all of them, it was folded over, with a crude symbol drawn on the front.

"The front shows who the message is for," al-Kadir said.

"Who does a star represent?" Anton asked.

"No one I'm familiar with," al-Kadir replied. "Some of the gods have stars as part of their symbology, but this looks too crudely drawn to be addressed to them."

He opened the note and showed it to Anton.

"A bird, and . . . I can't read Elitran," Anton said apologetically.

"The kingfisher is the symbol of one of the gangs in this area," al-Kadir told him. "And the writing . . . well it's crude, possibly done by a child. It says: *Help us*."

He passed the folded note to Anton.

"If you're looking for a chance to be a hero, there it is," he said.

CHAPTER FORTY-ONE

Looking for the Perfect Beat

I thought he seemed very nice," Aris said. Soraya sniffed in response. They were all back in the hideout, telling Soraya how the ransom note drop had gone.

"You must think the world of him, seeing as he managed to spend *ten minutes* in a coffeehouse without killing anyone," she said scornfully. "Truly, my eyes are opened."

"I just . . . he said he *loves* you," Aris said. "Wouldn't it be worthwhile hearing him out?"

"Absolutely not," Soraya said. "I don't want to give him a single chance at snatching me for himself. And as for marriage, it is out of the question. There's no possible way that I could live with having my children depending on a killer's income. Not that I'd expect *you* to understand."

"You were *eating human flesh* only this morning!" Aris protested. "I don't think you're in any position to comment on my morality."

"I didn't kill it, did I?" Soraya replied. "It was served to me by your—whatever it is that Kelsey is to you. It would have been rude to refuse."

"That's not—"

"Not the time for this," Anton interrupted. "Al-Kadir is going to be a huge problem for us. He didn't make any secret of his plans to hunt down your kidnappers, Soraya."

"Well, if I should end up in his clutches, I'll be sure to mention just where they can be found and what they look like," Soraya said sharply.

"Are you sure you wouldn't like to go home, say you escaped, and try to convince your father not to marry you to al-Kadir?" Anton asked. "It didn't sound like you had a bad relationship with him."

"I don't," Soraya said wistfully. "But I'm not sure that the decision is up to him anymore. Al-Kadir may be threatening him."

"I don't think—" Aris started to say.

"You don't know his history or his reputation," Soraya said, cutting her off. "I wouldn't put it past him to kill off my entire family and then marry me, "for my protection." There are few in court who would gainsay it. Staying hidden may be the best protection I can give my family."

"What are you thinking?" Anton asked Kelsey, who had been watching the discussion quietly. She shrugged.

"It's basically double or nothing, which is a hard bet to pass up," she said. "Al-Kadir raises the stakes and makes everything more difficult, but it seems like he's already proving helpful." She held up the piece of paper from the post. "You're the local, Soraya, what do you make of this? Is the Kingfisher gang asking for help?"

"I did make some inquiries before I decided to use the post for communications," Soraya admitted. She took the paper in her hand and examined it.

"It's not from the Fishers," she said. "If it were, the symbol would be on the front. That space is reserved for either the sender or the recipient."

"How can it be both?" Anton asked. "It seems confusing."

"It's meant to be opaque," Soraya told him. "The sender knows who put the note up, and the recipient can work it out. Since the space is blank, the note is not for anyone in particular."

She unfolded the note. "Classically—the post has become much more diverse since it gets used for more than just assassinations—the inside would show the target and the price."

"So . . . the *Fishers* are the target, and whoever put up the note is asking us to do it for free," Kelsey finished for her.

"That would be my understanding," Soraya agreed. "There might be other meanings, but given it is addressed to anyone, I don't think they would have wanted to get clever with the code. The Fishers are a gang . . . on the east side? Not a nice part of the city. I don't know much more than that."

"That's fine," Kelsey said. "Zaphar can probably find out more. And, as it happens, one of the guys from last night had a kingfisher tattoo."

"I didn't see it," Tyla put in from the edge of the discussion.

Kelsey smiled. "It was under his clothes," she said. "It wasn't visible until I stripped and cleaned him."

"Are you going to bring him back to life and question him?" Tyla asked.

"No, he died outside, so I can't do that," Kelsey said as Soraya goggled at her. "But I do know what tavern he came out of."

* * *

"I don't like this," Anton said to Kelsey. She was sitting across a small table from him in a crowded tavern.

"What don't you like?" she asked from the depths of her hooded cloak. It looked suspicious, but most of the people here looked equally unsavory.

"Everything!" Anton said. He refrained from shouting it. "I don't like how my first heroic act is probably going to look a lot like that vigilantism that you were talking about before. I don't like that we're in this skeevy tavern. And this . . . wine . . . is *spicy*."

Kelsey grinned. He couldn't see it, but he knew. She took his cup and topped up her own, and then hid his in the folds of her robe.

"The difference between heroism and vigilantism is pretty thin," she admitted. "When it comes time to *act*, you'll need to go with your gut and the feelings that your class gives you."

She looked out across the room. "As for what we're doing *here*, we're making sure Zaphar doesn't run into trouble while he asks questions for us. How does your class feel about *that*?"

Anton thought about it, listening to, as Kelsey said, his gut.

"Looking out for people is heroic," he admitted. "I'm getting . . . less than a trickle because nothing has happened, but the thought . . ."

Kelsey held out his wine cup again. "And if you didn't like the wine, you should have said something."

Anton looked at her carefully, but took the cup and had a sip. What filled it now was a much more familiar vintage that tasted of home.

"That's a lot better," he allowed. Kelsey raised her cup to his in a toast.

"To each their own," she said. They nursed their drinks for a while before Kelsey perked up.

"Looks like he's finished," she said. Anton saw that Zaphar was headed to the door. He got up to follow him, but Kelsey held him down.

"Not yet," she said. "Give him a little space, see if he picked up anything."

Anton looked at her quizzically but stayed in place until two more men had left. Rough-looking men, but that applied to almost everyone here.

"Oho ho ho," Kelsey said. "Let's go."

Once they were out on the dimly lit street, Anton looked around. He couldn't see Zaphar.

"He's gotten ahead of us," he complained.

"We know where he's going," Kelsey said. "And look! Those guys are headed in the same direction!"

Sure enough, the two guys were headed in the direction of the hideout, moving at a quick pace. Anton and Kelsey hurried to follow them. They hadn't managed to catch up when a voice came out of the darkness.

"Hello, hello, you are following me, yes?"

The men came to an abrupt halt, and Kelsey grabbed at Anton again to stop him. The pair started approaching more cautiously, as the two thugs addressed the thief.

"You've been asking a lot of questions, friend," one of them said.

"I think I'd remember if I had a friend as ugly as you," Zaphar said lightly. "And what if I did?"

"Our boss is going to want to ask *you* questions, once he hears what you've been talking about," the tough said. "Figure we'll save everyone some time and take you to him now."

"Alas, I find myself otherwise engaged at the moment," Zaphar said. "Perhaps you could leave a card? Ut! Ut!" he exclaimed. "Not so close!"

Anton and Kelsey were closer now, and Anton could make out the form of Zaphar. He'd climbed halfway up the sheer wall of one of the houses and was haranguing the toughs from six feet up. The toughs seemed to have run out of patience.

"You think we can't jump that high and peel you off?" one of them shouted. They both pulled out curved blades that were about a foot and a half long. "You—what the?"

Kelsey had decided to light the pair up with her "torch." The pair of them swung around, unthinkingly making the mistake of looking directly into the bright light. Anton wasn't going to get a better opportunity.

Leaping Attack.

He didn't draw his sword. Not only did he not want to kill some nobodies in an open street, but he knew that Kelsey would want to ask them questions. So his first attack was a flying kick. When the man went down, Anton could use the graceful landing part of the trait to get on top of him.

The man didn't go down. He folded under the impact, he grunted in pain, but he didn't go down. Anton realized too late that these thugs probably had progressions that focused on strength and toughness. The one he'd kicked had felt even stronger than Anton, and the other one was probably the same.

Then he remembered that he had a way of checking for that exact thing, and he kicked himself. Before he could use it, he needed to dodge the return swipe of the guy he'd kicked. The other one was still blinking from the light and hadn't realized that he'd been attacked, but that would not be the case for long.

The swing that came at him was wild, unaimed. That seemed to be the guy's trait, though, as it moved towards Anton's head with unerring precision. Still, he had a way of dealing with that.

Uncanny Evasion.

Anton swayed easily away from the blow. They might match him for strength, but they didn't have his agility. Feeling a little more secure, he activated *Delver's Discernment.*

Esra Hatun, Level 18, Human, Thug/Bruiser/Enforcer
S: 27 T: 30 A: 10 D: 14 P: 8 W: 2 C: 5
Kemal Beyazit, Level 20, Human, Thug/Bruiser/Enforcer
S: 27 T: 31 A: 18 D: 13 P: 6 W: 4 C: 4

Anton winced. The other one, Kemal, was much closer to Anton in Agility and Dexterity. He started to question his decision not to draw his sword.

It was dumb, but a sharp whistle from behind him made everyone pause and look that way. It was Kelsey, trying to attract Anton's attention.

"If you won't use a sword," she said, throwing something at him, "Try this."

Anton snatched it out of the air. It was . . . a club? But not like any club that he'd seen before. It was made of steel, narrow at one end that was covered in some soft material. The other half was thicker and heavier, more than two inches wide. The weight wasn't distributed evenly; the striking end was much heavier.

Louisville Slugger, Weapon, Perfect Quality, Tier 2, Properties: Impact Reflection

"No more sticks," Kelsey called out to him.

Anton nodded and brought the club down on the hand of Esra, who had recovered and was slicing at him with his curved dagger. The slugger smashed into the man's hand and Anton could hear the sound of breaking bone over Esra's strangled scream.

Kemal was ready to fight now as well, but he was no match for Anton, who used *Uncanny Evasion* to avoid the thug's overhead strike. It looked strong, but it was predictable, and Anton had the reach advantage now. He swung down with the slugger, aiming for the man's knee.

Kemal tried to move it out of the way, but Anton still managed to clip it. The glancing blow sent more force into the leg than it should have, but at the same time, something absorbed the extra force. It must have been a defense trait that the man had.

"Looks like this won't be a quick fight," he remarked, taking a step back and giving the club an experimental swing.

"Yeah, I—" the man said, before quickly bolting.

Anton blinked. Esra was also taken off guard but was quick to follow Kemal. Anton looked over to Kelsey for guidance.

"Eh, let them go," Kelsey said. "It's not like you were going to torture them for information or anything."

"No. I was not," Anton said firmly. He wasn't above questioning a prisoner, but dragging those two, unconscious or struggling, back to the hideout . . . it didn't sound like a good idea.

"More importantly," Kelsey said brightly, "did you get any experience?"

"Yeah," Anton said, focusing on the feeling. "More than I would have expected for a fight where they got away."

"It's coming to the rescue of a comrade," Kelsey speculated.

"And, and, I am grateful for the rescue," Zaphar said, dropping to the ground beside them. "But, but, it seems my bait was wasted? We have let the prey escape."

"Don't worry about it," Kelsey said. "You know where they live now, right? We'll be seeing them again."

CHAPTER FORTY-TWO

Freaks Come Out at Night

TYLA

The hands came in the night, wanting what they always wanted. But this time . . . Tyla's hand found the hilt of the dagger she'd been given, concealed underneath her pillow. She whipped it up to slash at the man who'd come. Whether it worked or not was beside the point as long as he—

"Whoa, girl!"

The hand that held the dagger was caught fast in a rock-solid grip, and Tyla came fully awake at the sound of Kelsey's voice. Kyla stared, wide-eyed at the face in the darkness. Kelsey's eyes glowed very faintly.

"Jumpy, are we? You might want to work on that," Kelsey said softly. She released Tyla's hand and changed position slightly. "You can see fine in this, right? I thought I wouldn't bother with a light when waking you, but that might have been a mistake."

"I . . . can see fine," Tyla agreed. She spoke at the same volume Kelsey did . . . presumably to avoid waking the others.

"Good," Kelsey said. "Do you . . . want to talk about it?"

Tyla froze, considering the notion. Numina *were* renowned for their wisdom, having guided the tribes in times long gone. Kelsey seemed different from the tales, but she did have knowledge to share. But . . .

"I don't want to," Tyla said.

"That's fine," Kelsey said. "Do you want a hug?"

"A hug?" Tyla asked, bewildered. Numina spirits were guides and taskmasters. They didn't—

"Do elves not hug?" Kelsey asked, cocking her head to one side. Tyla just stared. Belatedly, it occurred to her that Kelsey was sharing a bed with the Hero, so perhaps she did a great deal more than hug.

"Hmp," Kelsey continued. "I have it on—actually, Mel isn't that great an authority on elves—but she seems to think that you *do* hug. So do you want one?"

"I don't know," Tyla answered honestly. Kelsey raised an eyebrow but spread her arms wide. She stayed where she was, allowing Tyla to choose if she would rise to the occasion.

After a moment's more thought, Tyla tentatively moved closer and was enfolded in Kelsey's arms. She felt . . . cool. Not cold like a corpse, but just a bit cooler than the warmth of a human or elf.

"You survived," Kelsey whispered in Tyla's ear. "I won't tell you that you're safe here, but you're strong enough to face whatever comes."

I'm not strong, Tyla thought. Her arms tightened of their own accord, and she clung to Kelsey as if she was a child. She held on for what seemed like a long time, but Kelsey just waited patiently for the storm of emotion to pass.

Tyla thought about the gun that Kelsey had given her. About her new class, and the core, and the magic it held. *I'm not strong*, she thought again. *But maybe I can become strong.* She let go of Kelsey.

"Better?" Kelsey asked. Tyla nodded.

"Why did you wake me?" she asked.

"I wanted to see if you were up for another midnight hunt," Kelsey said.

"I'm not a hunter anymore," Tyla pointed out, "and this city is not a forest."

"Once a hunter, always a hunter," Kelsey told her. "And any differences between these mean streets and a trackless forest are just cosmetic. Come on."

"Aren't they relying on you to keep watch?" Tyla asked after they'd eased the door shut and locked it again.

"The door has a lock," Kelsey said, pointing to it. "If someone tries to smash their way in, everyone should wake up in time."

"What if they pick the lock?" Tyla asked. She hadn't known that such things were possible, but she had talked to Zaphar about what he did.

"They don't take kindly to thieves in these here parts," Kelsey said. She nodded to the guards, occasionally patrolling outside the buildings they were guarding. Most of the ones they saw had ducked into shadow when they saw the pair coming, watching suspiciously as they passed. "Someone trying to pick the lock of *our* warehouse isn't their responsibility, but I wouldn't be surprised if they put an arrow in them on general principle."

"It takes a long time to pick a lock?" Tyla asked.

"Unless you're really good," Kelsey said. "Zaphar isn't great at it, which is why he prefers to use the upstairs windows."

Tyla nodded in understanding. Her one experience of an upstairs window was that it was left open and unlocked, so it made sense.

"What are we doing tonight?" she asked.

"Two things," Kelsey said. "First, we found out where the Fishers' territory is, so we're going to ask them some questions. Then, I want to rile up some priests."

"Why?"

"It's a long-term plan," Kelsey said evasively. "If we can stir up unrest in the city, we can keep the officials too busy to check our nonexistent or badly forged papers before we leave. Priests are an important part of keeping a city from getting restive."

"You're not going to kill them, are you?" Tyla asked.

"That would work," Kelsey said. "But it might be easier to scare them off. We'll try a few things. But right now, gangers. You don't have level four yet, do you?"

"No," Tyla said. "The creatures you summoned were too low a level for me to gain much. And I had to share with the others besides."

Kelsey nodded sympathetically. "I could have summoned better monsters, but then you would have needed the gun to kill them. Even if you can keep it silent, it's probably best not to fire that thing in the hideout."

"It stinks," Tyla agreed.

"Yeah. The other thing was, I had to hold some mana back for tonight." She didn't elaborate further. The pair travelled to the east side of town until they saw the symbol they were looking for painted on the walls. Tyla happened to see it first, a blue kingfisher.

"Good eye," Kelsey said. "Now, if we can find a tavern that's closing down for the night . . ."

It proved easy enough; they just had to follow their ears. This district seemed to be mostly commercial, and taverns were the only places lit up this late at night. The first one they found had the kingfisher symbol painted over the door, which seemed promising. Kelsey pushed her way through the door. Tyla followed, her hand already on her gun.

"We're closed," the bartender called out as soon as Kelsey entered.

"Aw, don't be like that," Kelsey said. "This is a Fisher tavern, right?"

Tyla looked around. It did look closed, or nearly so. There were a few people at the tables, but they were either nursing a last drink or slumped over the remains of one. The bartender seemed to be locking up his drinks, in preparation for tossing out the last of the drinkers.

"What of it?" the bartender asked.

"Well, correct me if I'm wrong, but that means these guys are all Fishers, right?" Kelsey asked, gesturing at the drinkers. "And you, you're either a Fisher or you work for them."

"Yeah, you're wrong," the bartender said. He reached under the bar for something but didn't draw it out. "What it means is, the Fishers will put your body in the harbor if you try anything here. Anything other than turn on your heel and leave."

"Nah, I've got some questions to ask about the Fishers," Kelsey said. "This seems the place to ask them."

"That's all the warning you get," the bartender said, pulling out his club. More than an ordinary piece of wood, Tyla could see that nails had been driven through it.

Kelsey didn't move, but Tyla did. "Do not!" she said firmly, sweeping the gun out of her holster and pointing it at the man's face. He sneered.

"What do you think that is?" he asked. "A weapon? You gonna hit me with a piece of metal that isn't even sharp?"

"Take the shot," Kelsey advised. "We've got plenty of spares here to interrogate."

"I won't," Tyla said grimly. "Not unless he tries something."

The bartender snorted. "Was that supposed to be a threat, little elf? You've got about two seconds to try something before I knock your teeth out!"

Swinging his club, he stepped out from behind the bar, which was all the provocation that Tyla needed.

"Silent Shot."

You didn't have to say your trait when you used it, but it felt good when you did. Satisfying. It made up for the lack of a roar when Tyla pulled the trigger. She'd heard the sound of a gun when Kelsey saved her, but she'd not yet heard the sound of her own weapon. Each time she'd used it there was just a slight *whuff* of flame and smoke.

The sound of the bullet hitting the bartender's face was also muted, the man's head exploding into gore with an eerie silence. The loudest sound came a second later, when his body hit the floor.

She became aware that everyone still conscious in the room was staring at her. The ones who had been half asleep were now fully awake. A notification popped up.

You have reached Level 4.
Please select a new Trait.
Please allocate free Ability point.

It was a little distracting, but she didn't let it stop her.

"Nobody move!" Tyla said, waving the gun to cover the room. Nobody did, but they looked like they wanted to.

"Whoo!" Kelsey said into the sudden silence. "Now, how do I get you all to pay attention to me? Oh, I know! Spider!"

Tyla didn't actually look until one of the drunks gave a high-pitched scream and tried to push himself through the wall behind him. Not everyone had looked at Kelsey when she spoke, but they did now.

There was a really big spider perched on her hand. Big enough that it was *precariously* perched.

"Yay! Everyone's paying attention to me!" Kelsey crowed. "Now, does anyone want to save us some time and volunteer everything that they know about your gang's activities?"

There was silence as the room wrestled with the question. For the moment, loyalty stood firm over terror.

"That's too bad!" Kelsey said. One of the drunks slumped over, clearly overwhelmed by terror. "Even worse, Anton said that torture wasn't heroic, and we shouldn't be doing it!"

"Um, should you be telling them that?" Tyla asked.

"It's fine," Kelsey assured her. "There's more than one way to skin a cat! You see, spiders have a lot of toxins. The one that causes incredible pain is good for torture, but it's not the only one."

All of the men were looking at her now, except for another one who had slumped over, making a soft whistling sound.

"The one I'm thinking of," Kelsey continued, "is a mere Tier One poison! It's kind of useful for taking the edge off adventurer parties, but it hardly counts as disabling. They just feel really, really *good*."

"You're saying *that thing* is gonna make us feel *good* when it bites us?" one of the drunks said, finally speaking up.

"Noooo, don't believe . . . her . . ." the man next to him said. Despite his words, he had a beatific smile on his face. He tried to say something else but then fell off his chair.

"Nah," Kelsey said. "This is a flesh-rot poison one. Don't you know the first rule of spiders? The big ones are there to distract you from the small ones."

"Small . . . what? You're . . . not . . . sleepy . . . won't let . . ." the man said before falling to the floor.

"It looks like you've got this in hand?" Tyla said. "I should check the back room?"

"Get your level done first," Kelsey replied. "No sense wasting time."

Tyla flushed. *How did she know? Well, she is a numen.*

Briefly diverting her attention, she accepted her level.

Applying Benefits for Level 4
Dexterity + 1
Perception + 2
Willpower + 1
Assign free points:

Still self-conscious of her low Agility, Tyla assigned the free point to that.

Traits available: Identify Ingredients, Cast Lesser Charm, Empower Enchantment, Empower Alchemy

She selected *Cast Lesser Charm*, as she'd discussed with Kelsey. Then, before checking the back room, she went over her status one more time.

Tyla Greenwalker of the Padascar Tribe (Level 4)
Overall Level: 11
Paths: Padascar Hunter (Broken)/ Doxy (Broken)/Apprentice Dungeon Witch
Strength: 11
Toughness: 7
Agility: 10
Dex: 16
Perception: 18
Will: 12
Charisma: 9
Traits
Persistent Tracking
Silent Shot
Danger Sense
Sense Magic
Cast Lesser Charm

"All good?" Kelsey asked. "Then let's secure this building and start asking questions."

CHAPTER FORTY-THREE

My Hometown

SULIEL

Kelsey waited all of ten minutes to deliver the bad news. Suliel was up, at least, if not fully dressed. Her people would generally wait until after breakfast to report, but Kelsey didn't care to wait.

<Someone slipped through your patrols,> she sent through the link.

Suliel scowled. *<And good morning to you,>* she sent back. *<How do you know?>*

<Because there's a team of high-level strangers delving me right now,> Kelsey told her. *<They came in last night, and they mean business.>*

"They're trying to kill you?" Suliel said aloud, shocked. She glanced at the startled maid. "Not you. Leave me for a moment, would you?"

The maid curtsied and hurriedly left the room. Suliel sighed. Word about her link had spread, but no one understood it.

<Thanks for the concern, but I've got it handled,> Kelsey said. *<You might want to check if anyone came with them that didn't enter me.>*

<Have they said anything about that?> Suliel asked. High-level infiltrators could be very bad for her. On the other hand, splitting your forces didn't seem wise when going up against Kelsey.

<No, but they spoke with Liem Tiken before coming here.>

Suliel felt a chill. *<This isn't a random raid, then.>*

<No. They've been told that there are two cores down here, and Liem is getting one of them,> Kelsey said. A feeling of smugness pervaded the link. <Not that it matters, but their information is out of date.>

<Don't let them live to be disappointed,> Suliel sent. Her ferocity seemed to take Kelsey aback.

<That . . . really is touching,> she sent. <I hadn't realized that we'd gotten so close.>

<Don't mistake this for sentimentality,> Suliel said, her mental tone approximating a snarl. <An attack on you is an attack on Kirido. An attack on me.>

<Of course,> Kelsey agreed. <Don't beat yourself up, though. You might be able to keep these guys out of a walled town. Your outer perimeter is too long and porous to keep serious intruders out.>

<For now,> Suliel promised.

<I'll keep you posted as they make it further down. I expect them to get at least as far as Cheryl. Right now, they're just finishing off the Skeleton King.>

<How long have they been in?> Suliel asked.

<A few hours. The skeletons weren't much of a challenge, but they got lost for a bit in the city.>

Suliel snorted. <Not terribly smart then, are they?>

<I think that's a given if they came after us.>

Suliel laughed out loud, her mood restored. She called for her maid and started dressing.

"Send for Captain Rynmos and Syon to attend me during breakfast," she told the maid. "It seems there are some matters that won't wait."

It took a little while for them to show up. Suliel was well into her morning meal by the time they arrived to take their seats. Places and food were set before them—it would have been rude for Suliel to leave them standing while she ate in front of them. Neither of them ate very much; they had both been up earlier than she had. Suleil started without preamble.

"A high-level infiltration team has bypassed our patrols," she said.

Both of them looked at her in alarm.

"Their main team has entered the dungeon," she added, neatly answering the question of *how* she knew this. "But we need to determine if anyone else was left outside."

Captain Rynmos nodded, his face grim. "With your permission, I'll get on that immediately, my lady," he said.

"First, is there anything to report from last night?"

"No ma'am," he said. "It was all quiet. Too quiet, it seems. There was one thing from this morning, but Chamberlain Syon already knows it."

"Go, then," Suliel said, looking expectantly at Syon.

"My lady," he said, bowing. "An Elitran ship was spotted this morning, heading towards us."

It wasn't a raider ship, at least. Those were distinctive.

<The timing is right,> Kelsey told her. <Let me see.>
Suliel opened the channel wider, allowing Kelsey to use her senses.
<Use the glasses,> Kelsey suggested and Suliel did her best to keep her embarrassment at forgetting them to herself.

It was difficult to hold the *binoculars* steady long enough to get a good look at the incoming ship, but Kelsey waited patiently until Suliel managed it.

<Yep, that's them,> Kelsey said. <Roll out the welcome wagon.>
She paused. <In other news, the intruders have reached floor ten, the Village of the Damned.>

Suliel shuddered. Many of her ancestors had died in the dungeon, and the thought of seeing her uncle and grandfather again was . . . disturbing.

<I'm thinking of re-doing that floor,> Kelsey told her, reading her emotion. <Too many people know about it for the trick to work. I would have done it already, but they make better farmers than skeletons.>
<Do you think it will stop the intruders?> Suliel asked.
<It should be more than just a speed bump, like most things have been so far,> Kelsey replied. <I've got a new trick for the next level that I'm looking forward to.>

She didn't say what it was. Suliel knew that Kelsey was looking forward to surprising the local adventurers with it as well.

To Suliel's surprise, the ship didn't immediately disgorge its passengers after it tied up at the dock. Instead, a brightly dressed courl stood at the top of the gangplank, surveying the area disdainfully.

<He's coming down to talk to you?> Kelsey said. <I didn't expect that. You're in for a treat.>

The courl stepped down to the dock, walking as if he was stepping in dung the entire way. When he got to the bottom, he glanced at Suliel.
"Is this Kirido?" he said.
"It is," Suliel said evenly. "You would be Captain Farid al-Nazari?"

The courl's eyes narrowed, and he bared his teeth. "How do *you* know *that*?" he snarled.

"Kelsey told me," Suliel said calmly. Maintaining her composure in the face of discourtesy was part of her training.

"The monkey has long lips," Captain Farid hissed. "Or you have long ears."

<At least he's not drunk,> Kelsey sent. <I guess he saves that for when he's cooped up in the harbor.>

<This was the person you chose to hire?> Suliel sent back. <You couldn't find someone more disagreeable?>

<We had a choice of exactly him,> Kelsey admitted. <And at least he got the job done?>

"Ultimately, you were hired by Kirido," Suliel told the captain. "It shouldn't come as a surprise that we were expecting your arrival. Are the passengers all safe?"

The captain glared at her, as if offended by the question. "Of course they are," he said. "I merely had to ascertain that this . . . place was the Kirido that we were contracted to deliver them to."

<I do wonder if we were above or below his expectations,> Kelsey said, <but I wouldn't recommend asking.>

Silently agreeing, Suliel addressed the captain. "Then will you allow your passengers to disembark?"

"Of course!" Captain Farid exclaimed. "I wouldn't want to stay in this hovel for a minute more than I had to."

He turned to head back up, but Suliel wasn't done.

"Actually, before you go," she said, "I was hoping to discuss the possibility of you taking a cargo of goods to trade."

The courl whirled back around. "Lady, I am not some *merchant*! If you think I have an interest in *trade*, then you are—"

"Captain!" a mournful voice called down from above. "We talked about this, remember?"

Captain Farid snapped his mouth shut, and Suliel could have sworn she was watching him count to ten.

"Talked about what?" he finally snapped.

"The ship needs money," the voice said. "Which means we need to take cargo."

"We have merchants in town willing to discuss shipping charges if you don't want to take the risk of trading for yourself," Suliel put in. "The size of your hold is considerably more than the vessels that commonly dock here."

The captain stared at her in dismay. "Go into *this* town?" he said in a horrified tone. "Talk to your *merchants*?"

He stared at her for a moment more and then started stomping up the gangplank. "You take care of it!" he yelled to whoever was on board.

"Captain," the voice came back. "We need more crew as well."

The captain stopped. "Humans?" he yelled. "You want to bring humans on board *my* ship?"

"How about Kabimen?" Suliel asked.

Captain Farid froze, then whirled around again to face Suliel. "Kabimen?" he asked.

"Kabimen," she repeated. "Most of the sailors around here are Kabimen. Crab-people."

"Kabimen," he repeated. "I don't . . ."

He trailed off in confusion and then seemed to dismiss the question with an effort of will.

"You take care of it!" he yelled, storming up the gangplank.

"So I can hire Kabimen?" the voice asked.

"You take care of it," the captain repeated. "Get these humans off my ship! The rest of you, start clearing out all that cruft that the monkey left behind!"

"Yes, sir, Captain, sir!" the voice said.

In short order, freed slaves started coming down the gangplank. Suliel made a point of greeting each of them personally. She wanted them to know who their Baroness was.

"Welcome to your new home," she said, before passing them over to Syon to handle the details of their lodging assignment. The captain wasn't the only one relying on his subordinates. At least Kelsey had sent word of who was arriving and what they were capable of.

A few of the returned slaves were Kirido residents and had family waiting for them at the end of the dock. Suliel made sure to welcome them but didn't keep them from their reunions.

The last to step down was a well-built young man. His hair had just started to grow out again, and he had an ugly tattoo that was barely visible against his dark skin.

"Tavik," Suliel said. "Kelsey thought that you might be interested in enlisting as a soldier."

If Tavik was surprised that Kelsey had spoken to her about him, he didn't show it. He stared down at her without any real expression.

"I might be," he said slowly. "Do I have to decide right away?"

"No," Suliel told him. "There's work to be had no matter what you want to do. You've got a room assigned to you. Get some food and rest, take a walk around the town. Ask to see Captain Rynmos if you decide that's what you want."

He nodded slowly, bowed as an afterthought, and then headed down the docks.

Suliel was left with one more person to see, a female courl with sandy fur and amber eyes who bowed her head apologetically.

"Sorry about the captain," she said. "He is . . . what he is. I can meet with your merchants about cargo. My name is Soraya Sandwhisper."

Suliel nodded. "That's fine," she said. "Are you sure you don't want to buy for yourself?"

The courl shrugged. "We have some money," she admitted. "We were paid well for this trip. Not so much money as to fill our hold, I think. It depends on what cargo is available."

"I think you'll be pleasantly surprised," Suliel said smugly. "We've made great strides recently in what we produce."

<Ooh, bad news,> Kelsey interrupted. Suliel didn't let her expression change as she walked the courl to the trading hall.

<What is it?> she asked.

<The next dungeon harvest is going to be delayed.> Kelsey said, adding in a rueful feeling. <Well, skipped, really. I should have recovered things by the time the one after this was due.>

<What happened?> This was bad news, but it wasn't terrible news. Even with the new residents, enough food had been set aside to avoid starvation. Kelsey's harvests were small but regular top-ups. She didn't have much space, but she could grow crops at a prodigious rate.

<The intruders didn't want to do a house-to-house fight with the revenants, so they elected to stand back and thin them out with arrows,> Kelsey said. <Of course, that's why I hid revenants in the fields around town.>

<And . . .> Suliel prompted.

<So . . . the intruders burned down the fields to clear the cover,> Kelsey said. <It's a real mess down there right now.>

CHAPTER FORTY-FOUR

Black Codes (From the Underground)

MEL

The golden fields were now a blackened husk with only the occasional burned stalk still standing. The village was just as burned and ruined. Dead bodies of revenants were everywhere. Some were burned, most were not. Humans always left devastation behind them, Mel mused. At least this scar would be regenerated once the invaders left.

Kelsey had ordered some basic tactics against the revenants. Intruders were, at first, welcomed into the village for a feast. These days, they hardly ever fell for that; these intruders were no exception. When that failed, the plan was to fall back to the defendable buildings. Get a small group to commit and then encircle them.

The invaders hadn't fallen for that either. They'd left matters to the archer, or bow-user as Kelsey insisted on referring to him. Mel didn't normally notice what *words* people used, but when Kelsey said "bow-user," it meant a different thing from when other people used "archer." A meaner thing.

The archer—Mel didn't share Kelsey's prejudices—had the party stand back and just sent arrow after arrow into the village. The ambush attempt hadn't worked. They'd moved farther back and set fire to the fields. Then, with all the remaining revenants hiding under cover of the buildings, they set the buildings on fire.

Kelsey hadn't expected them to have quite that many fire arrows, or for them to be quite that effective. The surviving revenants had tried a final charge, but it was too far, and the invaders were ready.

Now the invaders were picking through the rubble and the bodies, looking for treasure and the way down.

"Copper and silver, nothing but bloody copper and silver!" the archer called out.

"You know this dungeon's reputation, Cedric," the swordsman replied. "It's poor, with little reward for your effort. That's why we never came down before."

"I didn't think it would be *this* bad, though," Cedric complained. "I'm starting to think we undercharged."

"Just make sure you go through and check for cores," the swordsman said. "Tier Three cores are worth something and this floor hasn't been properly culled in a while. They should have grown a nice crop."

"I'm a little better at managing my mana than *that*," Kelsey muttered. "What kind of dungeons are you used to?"

The man didn't answer, of course. He couldn't see Kelsey or Mel. Instead, he looked over to where the cleric was sifting through the rubble of the town hall.

"Finnian, Holy Crusader of Butin," Kelsey told Mel. "And the mercenary guardian is called Kaelan."

"I didn't ask!" Mel bristled.

"You were about due to forget, though," Kelsey said with amusement.

"Was not!"

"What's the rogue's name, then?"

Mel looked over at the slim man in the dark cloak, slicing revenants' chests open with his enchanted dagger.

"Um . . ." she said. "Was it . . . Braven Darkthorn?"

"That's pretty close, actually," Kelsey said. "It's Draven Blackthorn."

"Dark is practically the same thing as black," Mel protested, pouting. "It should count."

Names were such a pain. They didn't have *meaning*, they were just sounds.

"Sure, sure," Kelsey said indulgently. "Now, hush, I want to see how this works."

The four men had gathered around the hole, easily clearing away the rubble of the building.

"Ugh, more tunnels," Cedric said. "I miss the open air already."

"You've had, what, three floors where you could use your bow?" Kaelan said. "The vampire floor is supposed to be pretty open as well."

"Three out of ten floors," Cedric complained. "What's down there, anyway?"

"Danger," Draven said.

"Rats, according to Tikin," the crusader countered. "Corpse rats."

"Are they worse than regular rats?" Cedric asked.

"Tier Two, but they'll swarm," Finnian said. "The higher tiers are either giant or agglomerations of rats; they'll need as much space in these tunnels as we would."

"So we'll be on even terms, then?" Kaelan said, swinging his arms to loosen up.

"It's a good point," Kelsey said. "If this test works out, I'm thinking of switching the rats with the spiders upstairs. I can tier the spiders up without the same problem."

"Don't the spiders get bigger as they level?" Mel asked.

"There are different tracks for smaller spiders—with nastier poisons," Kelsey told her.

"I don't understand why you needed to wait for the tiny things before you did this," Mel said. "Couldn't you have rigged them with, um, the fuses?"

"I could have, but this helps deal with their danger sense," Kelsey said. "Right now, they're getting a sense of danger, but it's unfocused."

Indeed, despite the rogue's warning, the crusader had unveiled a light-stone and had jumped down into the darkness.

"Do you see anything?" Kaelan called down.

"I see the rats—they're staying at the edge of the light," Finnian called back. "Tier Two corpse rats, as the guide said."

"Can't be that dangerous, then," Cedric muttered. He looked at the rogue, who shrugged.

"The feeling is still there," he said.

"Only one way to find out," Kaelan said. "Coming down!" he called. Sheathing his longsword and drawing a long heavy dagger, he jumped down into the hole.

"I'll miss you," Cedric said to his bow as he stowed it away.

"I'll leave you two alone," Draven snickered. He faded through the floor, turning into shadow.

"*That* might be trouble," Kelsey muttered. "Friggin' shadow powers. Let's go down."

The pair joined the adventurers in the cramped sewer. Since Mel and Kelsey weren't really there, they sort of stood in a space that was all their own. Helpful, as the delvers filled all of the available space.

"Now the little critters move around too much to guarantee it, but I tried to make sure the ones near the entrance were *au naturel*," Kelsey said. "And it sort of worked."

The first kill went to Draven, who was doing something with his shadow powers. He wasn't *in* the shadows, but he wasn't entirely out of them either. His daggers glinted darkly and cut through two of the rats that had gotten too close.

"Oh, they won't like that," Kelsey said gleefully. "And here comes little rat CA35."

At the first death, screeches started echoing through the tunnels, screeches that were quickly getting closer.

"Ware the swarm!" Finnian called. The group huddled together. Cold flame sprung into existence over Cedric's non-magical daggers.

Despite the warning, the first rat to arrive came alone, darting forward with a speed that belied its undead nature.

"I don't get how you can tell him apart?" Mel asked.

"His number is etched on his chip," Kelsey said. "And that number . . . when I send it the signal . . ."

She waited until the right moment, when the rat dodged under Kaelan's blow and lunged for the man's wrist, protected only by a leather gauntlet. The bite didn't get through, but Kelsey seized the moment.

The explosion was small but intense. The rat was blown into pieces. Tiny shards of bone and skin went flying in all directions, and would have proved a hazard to less sturdy combatants. The real damage was done closer to the detonation point.

"Arrrgh!" Kaelan cried. His vambrace was burned and twisted, and his hand was hanging at a strange angle.

"What the—" Draven exclaimed, but he didn't have time to process it. Two more rats were flinging themselves at him.

"Hello, D4EA and C722!" Kelsey crowed as the pair exploded. Draven had tried to stab one with his dagger, but the weapon was smashed out of his broken hand. He quickly spun, desperately turning so that his cloak took the blow from the second exploding rat. That seemed to work, much to Kelsey's displeasure.

"You're cheating again!" Mel protested. "You can't choose to explode them when you want!"

"Me? Cheat?" Kelsey said innocently. "I'm just sending a perfectly legal radio signal from the lower levels."

"This is the electricity thing all over again!" Mel complained as small explosions started to pepper the adventurers. She was so upset, she couldn't enjoy their cries of pain. "But how do the rats know?"

"Each signal is a number, and the transistors I was so excited about are for counting," Kelsey explained smugly. "When they hear their number, they detonate."

They paused to observe how the invaders were doing. Explosions were peppering them at a steady rate, but the invaders were nothing if not tough. Finnian's metal armor seemed impervious to the rat bombs, and the others were almost as well protected. Draven had lighter armor, but his shadow powers seemed to let him dodge most of the blasts.

"It's too bad I can't swarm them like this," Kelsey sighed. "If they blow up too close to each other, they might set off a cascade."

"Won't it do more damage if they all go off at once?" Mel asked.

"Maybe, but I'm worried about wasting a bunch before they get close enough to do anything," Kelsey said. "I only have limited numbers of these, remember."

Mel remembered. Kelsey had to make the rat bombs. She had a crew of skeletons that inserted them, by force, into freshly spawned rats. It didn't look pleasant, but the rats were already dead.

Now, though, they were running out. The party had weathered the storm. Not without injuries, but no one was dead.

"*That* wasn't in the guide," Draven spat.

Kaelan tried to answer, but he was in too much pain from his shattered wrist. Finnian was tending to him, his god's holy power shining on the wound.

"Dungeons change over time," he finally managed. "They adapt to adversity, as do we. I haven't ever heard of a dungeon doing *this*, though."

"It's unnatural," Draven agreed. "I didn't sense a *hint* of magic in those explosions."

"How can that be?" Cedric asked. "You need magic to do such things."

"I don't know," Draven grumbled. "Did anyone listen to the crazy things the mage was saying?"

"About the dungeon being unnatural, dangerous, and needing to be put down?" Finnian said, finishing up with Kaelan's wrist. He moved on to Draven's hand.

"Thanks," Draven said, wincing as the bones reset themselves. "Wouldn't want to get a potion to do this. He was saying the dungeon had taken over the town, that all the townsfolk were its slaves."

"Crazy stuff, like you said," Kaelan agreed, flexing his fingers. He held his vambrace, examining it. It didn't look wearable until he got a smith to fix it.

"Yeah, we agreed we were going to ignore that and just do the job he paid us for," Draven said. "One core for us, one core for him."

"Ooh, too bad," Kelsey said, unheard. "Your core is in another castle."

"And the money, don't forget the money," Cedric put in. He pulled out a healing potion and winced.

"I can get to you in a bit," Finnian told him.

"Save your strength," Cedric said. "I don't have any broken bones, and you'll be needing to heal us later." He quaffed the potion and grimaced as the pain hit.

"Well, now I'm thinking that he was right about the unnatural part, and maybe we should check out the town," Draven said.

"Nah," Kaelan said. "This might be unnatural, but it wasn't enough to stop us. We'll get to the bottom and take care of the problem at the source. Whatever it's done to the town won't matter once it's dead."

"How charming," Kelsey said. "I'm going to enjoy killing you."

The rest of the rat warren proved to be of little difficulty for the group. Once healed, they made their way through the tunnels. There were a few scares. A rat bomb that Kelsey had kept in reserve dropped on Finnian's head, but it proved insufficient to penetrate his helmet and skull.

Kelsey and Mel disagreed on which was tougher.

The rat king also proved insufficient to stop the invaders.

"That was . . . disgusting," Kaelan said when it was finally dead. "All those little tails squirming . . ."

"I thought the way it controlled the swarm was worse," Cedric said sourly. Tiny, twisted bodies were laid all around him, burning with a cold fire.

"Need a little help here," Draven gasped, clutching at his leg. Finnian stumbled over.

"What is it?" he asked.

"Poison?" Draven speculated. "Rotting at the flesh. One of the rats was special."

"Just too bad that you're all getting divine healing down here," Kelsey said. "If you went back with just potion healing you'd be spreading disease like it was 1346."

"Kelsey, I'm worried," Mel said.

Kelsey smiled at her reassuringly. "Don't be. It's too early. Delvers have gotten down to Cheryl before. No one has beaten her yet. These guys are tired, worn down, and out of half their alchemical supplies. We can take them."

CHAPTER FORTY-FIVE

In Your Eyes

MEL

It still hurts," Draven hissed, clutching at his leg.

"There's damage in there I can't heal," Finnian admitted. "Maybe a higher tier or a specialist in healing could do more . . . It's stabilized, at least. You should be able to walk on it."

Draven tried it, wincing as he put his weight down. "Should I try a potion?" he asked.

"Won't do any good," Finnian told him. "It won't heal with time either, unless you find someone who can fix it."

Draven swore while Mel giggled gleefully. "Permanent damage! I love that poison!"

"Eh," Kelsey said. "I'm still not convinced. I'd be happier if they could use a potion to fix it—they'd be down another potion."

"But this way, he's not operating at top form!" Mel protested. "He's weaker, ripe for the kill!"

"Settle down, killer," Kelsey said, laughing. "The important stuff starts now."

The party looked at the hole they'd found. The light-stone, held in Kaelan's hand, didn't extend far enough to see what was below. Draven limped forward to take a look.

"About fifty feet down, rough ground," he said. Everyone looked at Kaelan, who stroked his chin, considering.

"I've dropped fifty feet before," he said.

"On ground like this, you'd likely land badly," Draven pointed out. "Better get the rope out."

Kaelan sighed. "Once again, I'm the only one who needs it, right?"

"Once there's a light down there, I'll be fine," Cedric confirmed.

"The blessing of Butin will suffice for me," Finnian said.

Draven just smirked.

"Fine, fine," Kaelan said. "Mock the simple mercenary." He pulled a rope from his backpack, already attached to a steel spike. Not bothering with a hammer, he drove the spike into the cave wall with one hand and tossed the rope down the hole.

"I'll wait here to retrieve the rope," Draven said. "Or should we leave it?"

"I doubt the dungeon will let us keep it there once we leave the level," Kaelan said. "It might be a pain attaching it when we go up, but at least we'll still have it."

Hooking the light-stone around his wrist, he started climbing down. Almost immediately, though, there was a flurry of screeches and fluttering and yells of pain from the mercenary.

"Ow! Get off! Stop—"

"I can't make out what's going on," Finnian said, looking down into the chaos. Between the fluttering darkness and the wildly swinging light, Kaelan looked as if he were in some kind of black snowstorm.

"Bats," Cedric said succinctly. "And . . . some vampire bats."

"Just ignore them!" he called out to Kaelan. "They're only Tier One and Two—they're not going to kill you!"

"Easy for you to say, when—" Kaelan managed, just before his own antics dislodged his grip. With a strangled cry, he fell, taking the light with him.

The three stared at their leader, lying still in a small circle of light.

"I don't think he's broken his neck," Finnian said. "I'd better go down and heal him."

He stepped out and fell through the hole. Even as he started to fall, though, a golden-red light engulfed him and his plummet slowed to a gentle drift. The light seemed to repel the bats as well, so his descent was unimpeded. He wasn't halfway down, though, when the two remaining heard him cry out.

"Can someone get down there faster? There's something pawing at him!"

"Vampires," Cedric speculated. He looked at Draven, who scowled.

"Fine," Draven said and stepped into the darkness. Shortly after, there was a screech from below.

"Let's go down and take a look," Kelsey suggested.

To Kelsey and Mel, who could see through the darkness as if it were day, the twelfth floor was a huge open cavern. There was no fake sun to show off the view, which was interrupted by the rough natural towers of stone that formed a maze spreading out in all directions.

There was a large cleared area under the hole, empty except for a few boulders. Kaelan had landed on one of these, and honestly, the boulder had come off worse.

Kaelan, though, was now lying down, the gorget torn from his throat. Blood was dripping down his armor, which quickly stopped as Finnian arrived. The cause, a pale, thin humanoid, had been skewered by Draven's daggers.

"Vampires," Draven spat.

"Not too difficult, I hope?" Finnian said, his attention on his patient.

"Nah, Kaelan wouldn't have had any trouble if he hadn't knocked himself silly," Draven replied.

"Oggh, my head," Kaelan said. "What was I drinking last night?"

"It's the other way around," Finnian said wryly. "Something was drinking you."

"Really?" Kaelan asked. "Eww," he said, catching sight of the vampire. "Is that going to have any . . . effects?"

"Nothing that Butin's blessing can't kick the shit out of," Finnian said cheerfully. "The wound is healed, but if you're feeling dizzy you might want to take a potion. That will speed up your blood regeneration."

"I think I might," Kaelan said. "I have a lot of aches and pains I don't remember having. But first . . ." he held the light-stone up high, illuminating the area.

"Are you coming down, or what?" he called up. The only reply was the falling rope, the piton on the end almost hitting him. Then Cedric jumped down, landing gracefully on a boulder next to the others.

"Show-off," Kaelan muttered. Then he whirled around and drew his sword, as a hissing voice came out of the darkness.

"You've been tricked, Kaelan," the voice said. "There's no reward for you here, only death."

The party quickly arranged themselves defensively.

"There," Draven said, pointing with a dagger at the source of the voice. "It's another vampire. But also . . . there, there, and there."

"Tikin lied to you," the vampire hissed. "The core you seek is already gone."

"Did you tell them to say that?" Mel asked Kelsey.

"Of course," Kelsey replied. "Do you know how much mana psychological warfare costs? Nothing!"

"How does it know about Tikin?" Draven whispered urgently. He was trying to keep his voice from carrying, but Mel knew that Kelsey could hear every murmur in his heartbeat. And Mel didn't need to hear *words*.

"The dungeon must have heard us talking," Kaelan muttered. "Tikin said it was intelligent."

He called out to the vampire. "You're lying! There's nowhere for the other core to have gone."

The vampire made a noise like a hacking cough.

"Mental note," Kelsey said. "Never order a vampire to laugh."

"No lies," the vampire said. "Only death. Core is far, far away."

"One core is still here, though," Kaelan said grimly. "We'll take that one."

"You will never see it," the vampire promised.

Then they charged.

It was almost a fair fight, Mel thought. The vampires were close in level, but there was still a gap in the raw stats. Humans almost always had an advantage there. They had magic armor and weapons as well, so even though the vampires had more numbers, they still couldn't close the gap.

Wondering what the fight was like for them, Mel started filtering out all but the human perspectives. As a mental being, Mel didn't have any senses of her own. Instead, she shared the perspective of her host, Kelsey. A dungeon's sensorium was vast, far too complicated for Mel to process, so she had to limit it, filter it. When she first did so, she had realized that she could also share the perspectives of any person or monster in the dungeon.

Now, she limited herself to what the humans could see. Her awareness of the maze faded away, and the darkness encroached, held back only by the light-stones that they carried. She narrowed her focus further, focusing on Finnian. Since he mostly fought in the back line, he had a good view of things.

After the first wave had been dealt with, they had to start moving forward. Draven had spotted the castle on his way down, so they had a direction to move in. However, that wasn't enough. The floor of the cavern was broken up into a maze of ravines that headed in all directions. Draven had to shadowstep up to the peaks to get an idea of where the gullies led.

And everywhere, there were ambushes. Vampires popped out around corners and out of concealed caves. They dropped down from the ceiling and came out of the floor. They ambushed Draven when he was scouting, and they rolled rocks down on the party when they stopped for a rest.

The bats were particularly annoying. Many of them were normal bats. Too many to count and hardly worth the swing that would kill one. They hid the vampire bats, which were a nasty surprise, but hardly deadly. Just annoying.

Sometimes the bats would swarm around them and just disperse. Sometimes they hid another vampire ambush. Sometimes, one dropped down at just the right moment to block a party member's view or provide a distraction.

To another party, a lesser party, it would have been hell. Or death. But these invaders took it all in their stride. They endured the lesser wounds, used a healing potion when it got too much, and kept on going.

Finally, they came to the castle of the Vampire Queen. Not a large castle, as these things went, but it had high walls with an impressive door set into a gatehouse. The door was tightly shut.

"Scale the walls?" Draven suggested.

"Nah," Kaelan said. "Let's just go straight in. Cedric, you want to try your frostfire on the door?"

"Sure," the archer said. He'd pulled out his bow for this floor. The darkness reduced his range, but there had been some opportunities to use it. Now, he shot four arrows at each corner of the door. They burst into flames, which quickly spread across the wooden surface.

This fire was cold, and even as the wood burned, its temperature dropped. The door started to crack, even as its outer surface started turning into ash.

"Have you heard of frostfire before?" Mel asked. She had to step out of Finnian to address Kelsey, but the mental avatar was still right next to her, as if she'd been there the entire time.

"Can't say that I have," Kelsey admitted, her eyes on the party. "Can't say I like it, but with his strength, he could probably have punched his way through."

The doors fell with a crash, and Mel quickly stepped back into Finnian. To him, it looked as though the whole tower was just one big room, richly furnished and lit with a warm red light. Wooden panels lined the walls, and the floor was covered in a variety of red and gold rugs.

Furniture was scattered around the room, an eclectic mixture of tables, divans, and comfortable chairs. It looked as if the room was used for a variety of purposes, from feasting hall to comfortable sitting room. But rising above it all was the throne.

At the far end of the room, set on a dais, the throne drew every eye towards it. As did the beautiful lady sitting on it. Her skin was darker than that of any noble that the party had ever seen, and her eyes flashed a brilliant ruby red.

Her raven hair flowed down below her shoulders, and her cleavage was a dark mystery that the four men found themselves longing to explore.

"Welcome to my court," she purred. Her voice was cast low and husky, but they could somehow hear it clearly. "Though you have killed many of my subjects, all can be forgiven if you kneel before me. Sit at my feet, and I will show you pleasures you cannot yet imagine."

"She's using some kind of mental effect," Finnian growled. "Cedric, Kaelan, you have the lowest Will, stay strong."

The party moved forward cautiously. Not to throw themselves at her feet but in battle formation. Kaelan and Draven took the lead, Finnian in the rear, with Cedric hanging back near him. They'd advance this way until their vanguard was in melee range. Cedric was holding back on starting the fight until then.

"If you will not submit," the Queen said sadly, "then you must be subdued."

All around the room, vampires stepped out. They had been hiding behind panels and furniture. About ten of them. These, though, were armed with long, thin swords, and some of them had plate mail strapped to their arms. Good for parrying blows, while retaining maximum mobility.

The party froze, for just an instant. Then—

"Go!" Kaelan yelled, bounding forward. Draven was only a step behind. They both lunged at the Queen, lightning crackling over Kaelan's sword and dark shadows gathering over Draven's dagger.

The Queen burst into a cloud of bats after the first blow. The flock swirled around Draven and Kaelan before dissolving into mist.

Cedric started pumping out arrow after arrow, each one on fire and each one aimed at the heart of a vampire. Fennian readied himself for the charge of the survivors.

Without warning, the vampires, the lush furnishings, and the paneled walls, all started to turn into mist. Fennian felt an iron grip take hold of his face and shoulder from behind. He felt a sharp pain in his neck.

Somehow, even though her mouth was occupied, he could still hear the sultry voice of the Queen.

"Silly mortal," she said. "Don't you know that illusions are based against Charisma?"

Mel let the invader's perspective fade out. Watching Finnian get fooled had been very satisfying. Kelsey must have thought so, too; she was watching the fight start with satisfaction.

"Good girl," she said to Cheryl. Cheryl couldn't hear her, of course, not with humans in the room, but that had never stopped Kelsey from talking. "Always target the healer."

CHAPTER FORTY-SIX

Dance Me to the End of Love

MEL

The Vampire Queen danced. Lighter than air, it seemed, she twirled and pirouetted around the room, staying out of reach of poor Finnian's party members. Finnian himself was clutched tight in her grasp as she feasted on his neck from behind. One of his arms was kept outstretched, in a strange parody of a dancing position. The pair whirled around, the hapless crusader serving as a shield against Cedric's flaming arrows.

Finnian was still struggling. Something in the vampire's bite was affecting him, something more than just the blood loss. Healing himself with *Return to the Fray* was prolonging his life, but it did nothing for the powerful feeling of ecstatic languor that was slowly overtaking him. Healing himself this way was only giving the vampire more blood, something she seemed to appreciate from the way delighted peals of laughter escaped her every time she took a break from feeding from him.

Kaelan was stymied by the speed of the Queen's movement, and by the constantly changing illusions that covered the battlefield. For one moment, they were back in the throne room. Then, it all changed and they were outside in a carefully tended ornamental garden. Then, an underground cavern, and then . . .

It was *only* an illusion. The carefully placed obstacles remained where they were, even if Kaelan couldn't see them. Watching him stumble around the room, tripping over small walls and stone pillars, was quite amusing for Mel.

There was a fourth member of the team, though. He took everyone by surprise as he suddenly appeared behind Cheryl and buried his daggers in her back.

Cheryl screamed and dropped Finnian. Turning into a swarm of bats, she escaped further attacks from the Shadowblade Ranger and regrouped at a distance.

"Your shadow knows where you are," Draven spat. "And we brought lights."

She hissed at him. Her newly re-formed body didn't show any sign of wounds, but she was quickly forced on the defensive by a hail of arrows from Cedric. Draven knelt by Finnian's side.

"You okay?" he asked. Not waiting for an answer, he forced a potion between the priest's lips.

"Urmble," the priest said when he'd finished choking. "Islay . . . ninem . . . dumnt."

"Yeah, that's not making sense," Draven said, giving the man a soft slap on the cheeks. "Snap out of it!"

"Fishle . . . manan . . . . louble" was all Finnian managed to get out.

Draven cursed and stood up. He looked over at the Queen, fighting a desperate battle against his two companions. Then he spun and plunged one of his blades into the empty air.

"I told you, those tricks won't work on me," he yelled into the scream that erupted. The real Queen appeared, bleeding from his strike. She slashed at him with the razor-sharp talons that graced the ends of her fingers. Dodging back from that meant he couldn't follow up with his second dagger.

Across the hall, the vampire courtiers had reappeared. Some of them were real, some were illusions. Draven didn't have time to let the others know which was which. His fighting style depended on movement, but he was stuck protecting his fallen friend. If he let the man out of his sight for a second, the Queen was sure to finish her meal.

"Come on, then," he snarled, brandishing his daggers. "We've both got teeth, but only one of us is bleeding!"

Draven pulled the tourniquet tight, wincing.

"You thought that vampires only went for the neck?" Kelsey asked. "Guess again."

Cheryl had bitten into the leg with wild abandon, biting through bone and sinew. She preferred to take dainty sips from her victim's neck, but when pushed, she could bite off a limb and gulp from the torrent that spurted out.

Kaelan dropped to the ground next to Draven.

"Sorry," he said.

"Not your fault," Draven said, eyeing his wound. "Those courtiers were bad news. If they hadn't had their own stealth trait, I might have noticed the one sneaking up on me."

"If we'd been faster taking them out," Kaelan said. "Then—"

"So what's the plan?" Draven interrupted. "Potion to seal it up? We don't have one that will give me the leg back, do we?"

Kaelan shook his head. "Potion won't do that," he said. "Finnian might have been able to attach it again, but . . . if we get his body back to the church, they should be grateful enough to regrow your leg."

Draven froze. "Does that mean we're giving up? We're not going to cart Finnian's body into the sea, are we?"

"Won't stop me from making a revenant of him," Kelsey told them. "But hey, that's some prime biologicals there, you can't just take him."

"We're going to push on into the sea," Kaelan said. "But we can't risk the Queen spawning again behind us."

Draven cursed some more. "You're leaving me behind," he said bitterly.

"To guard Finnian," Kaelan confirmed. "The dungeon will take him if you don't."

"By all the gods," Draven swore. "You need me down there! I won't even need the leg in the water."

"We'll be fine," Kaelan insisted. "We've still got the potions we saved. Free movement, air-breathing, and darkvision."

"I hope the gods take your balls," Draven swore. "And leave you forever unable to satisfy a woman."

"You'll do it, then?" Kaelan asked.

"I don't want to leave Finnian down here, either," Draven admitted.

"How are they talking underwater?" Mel asked. "I thought humans couldn't do that."

Kelsey gave her a long look. "They're not," she said. She looked back at the humans. She didn't need to; she already knew every detail about what they were and what they were doing, but she did tend to get into the performance of having a body. Mel thought it helped.

"Do you mean," Kelsey said slowly, "the hand gestures they're making?"

"Do I?" Mel asked. She looked closely at the two men. "Oh! They are moving their hands strangely!"

"How can you know what they mean, and not tell that they're doing it?" Kelsey marvelled.

"I don't know," Mel said meekly. "I just hear the meaning, the same as always. I was also wondering why their speech got so simple."

Kelsey shook her head, laughing. Mel was glad she'd cheered Kelsey up. The thirteenth floor was proving disappointing.

The monsters—different varieties of giant undead fish—were dangerous enough. They were higher in level than the vampires, and they didn't have to waste points on Charisma or Willpower. In a competition of pure strength and speed, though, the humans still had the edge.

It would have been different if the humans hadn't cheated. The main dangers of this floor were the crushing depths, the darkness, and the lack of air. With potions to negate all of that, the invaders ran rings around the poor undead fishies.

It took them a while to find their way. The Silent Sea was large, and more than just one open area. There were nooks and crannies that needed to be explored. Small choke points that looked like areas for ambush . . . but mostly weren't.

Eventually, they found the pyramid sitting on the bottom of the ocean floor. About thirty feet high, it had a metal door, inset to be vertical, about the right size for a human.

They examined it for traps and found none. They were well aware, though, that this was Draven's specialty. Cedric had high Perception, but his sense for mana was rudimentary, and his understanding of mechanisms was poor.

It did seem, though, that the puzzle attached to the door would unlock it when solved. Mel translated the conversation that followed.

"The lock might only stay open for a limited time. Get ready to pull when I solve it."

"No leverage in this alcove. Attach rope to the handles?"

"Fine. Just one door. If you double up the rope, it should be strong enough."

"Are the gestures really that expressive?" Kelsey asked as they watched the invaders' preparations.

"Mnnn, I don't know?" Mel said. "I get the meaning that they're trying to say, I dunno how it's understood."

"Crazy," Kelsey said, but Mel knew she meant that it was good.

This was the only actual puzzle that Kelsey had placed in the dungeon. Mel had tried to convince her that the most stylish dungeons had puzzles, but Kelsey had countered that her style was "rock," not puzzles. Mel understood that Kelsey was talking about music, not granite, but she didn't really know what to do with that understanding.

Kelsey had broken from her pattern here because, as she had said at the time, "I want them to think that I *don't* want them to open the door."

From Kelsey's intent expression, Mel knew that Kelsey wanted them to open the door very much. As much as Mel did. If she had a seat, she would be on the edge of it.

The puzzle looked complex, but once you saw the trick, it was easy to solve. The idea, Kelsey had said, was to give the puzzle solver a feeling of accomplishment. Mel supposed that was a nice thing to do, all things considered.

Cedric was the one solving the puzzle. There was a faint *click* as the last piece slid into place. Mel could hear it because she was sharing Kelsey's perceptions. She didn't know if the invaders could, but she didn't have time to find out. The *click* was followed by a *clunk*, and then a *thunk*.

Mel didn't really understand it, but the different mechanisms were necessary to scale up the forces involved. If the door could be unlocked by a simple *click*, then the lock wouldn't stand up to the immense weight of the water. The invaders had thought that there was water behind the door. They'd been resigned to the thought that there wasn't, that they'd have to pull the door open against the weight of the water.

The handles were one of Kelsey's tricks. The door opened on its own, and it opened inward.

The final sound that Cedric heard was a crash, as the lock released the doors. They flew open, and the water he was floating in dragged him forward with an irresistible pull.

They were both under the influence of the free movement potion, but that had limits. It let them move as easily through water as air, but this water was moving far faster than any storm or hurricane. Cedric slammed into what proved to be a shaft, descending into the depths. Kaelan, desperately hanging on to the rope, was only a moment behind him.

Both men were too busy to notice, but Kelsey and Mel observed the second part of the mechanism activate. After a brief delay, the massive weight in the center of the pyramid descended, shutting off the torrent of water, and leaving the invaders cut off from above.

Far away, Mel knew, there was the hum of a motor as Kelsey used her electrics to open the secondary entrance. Mana pressure would build up on the fourteenth level if there wasn't somewhere for it to leak from, and it would take Kelsey a while to reset her pyramid trap.

The secondary mechanism had cut off Kaelan's rope. The rope had slowed him enough, though, that he fell after the deluge, and not with it. Cedric had fallen on the spikes below without even realizing what had happened to him, but Kaelan was able to control his fall. A bit.

"Tch," Kelsey said. "He's *still* alive?"

The pair of them watched him closely as the water drained away into the small tunnels designed for it. It took a long time before Kaelan moved. The first thing he did was crawl over to Cedric.

"You poor bastard," he whispered on seeing the spike that had punched through his friend's chest.

"Yes, it's very sad," Kelsey said. "But are you going to make us wait all day before you go off to get killed?"

Mel giggled. "What did you put down here?"

The fourteenth floor wasn't normally kept populated, aside from the worker skeletons. But Kelsey had a whole army of armed skeletons that could finish off the invader.

"Nothing," Kelsey said. "It's not necessary."

Mel looked at Kelsey in confusion. "This is the last level," she said. "There need to be monsters."

"Nah," Kelsey said. She pointed. With a hum of electrics, a large door opened up on one side of the chamber. Light, bright electric light, spilled in.

The invitation was obvious, and Kaelan didn't have any other prospects. Gathering himself, he limped over to the door.

Beyond was a corridor, of a type that Kelsey had many miles of. Smooth stone floor, smooth stone walls, painted white. It was lined with identical doors, but one of them had a red flashing light over it. As he entered the corridor, it clicked open.

Kaelan ignored it and tried the first door he came to. It was locked, but it wasn't proof against his strength. He sighed when he saw what was inside.

"Congratulations, adventurer, you've found a cleaning closet," Kelsey said.

Shaking his head, Kaelan returned to the corridor. He took a look at the lit door but decided to try one more random one. This one led to a room full of skeletons. They were all wearing white coats. Kaelan waited for them to rush him, but he was ignored.

"Well, how about that, the programming held!" Kelsey said. "Just move along, would you?"

Kaelan stood in the doorway, trying to understand what he was seeing. The skeletons seemed to be operating some kind of device set into the walls. There were dials and buttons and . . . Kaelan didn't know what.

"Is this how the dungeon is controlled?" he whispered. "I thought it was magic!"

"It is magic, you doofus!" Mel yelled at his unheeding ears. "This is . . . I don't know what this is."

"I tried explaining it to you," Kelsey said. "We settled on *it's electric.*"

"Yeah!" Mel exclaimed, remembering. "It's electric."

Choosing not to attack the skeletons, Kaelan moved on to the red-lit room. This one was larger than the last. He entered onto a raised platform that overlooked a pool, glowing with blue light. Just like the last room, skeletons in white coats were wandering around, tending to the controls.

"Is this the core?" he wondered aloud. "It glows like a core,"

"No, stupid," Mel said. "This isn't the core. It's *electric.*"

"That's right," Kelsey said. A loud Klaxon sounded, and something started rising out of the pool. It had been suspended in there and was now being pulled out.

Kelsey watched with satisfaction as Kaelan moved closer.

"That's . . . not any core I've seen," he said. "Why . . . I don't feel well."

He raised his hands to look at them.

"When did I get . . . burned?" he asked the room. No one answered him. None of the skeletons responded when he fell. It was twenty-three minutes before he finally died and Kelsey could access the floor again.

CHAPTER FORTY-SEVEN

She Works Hard for the Money

Kelsey was in an exuberant mood in the morning, humming excitedly as she produced breakfast for the girls to serve.

"Why so cheerful?" Aris asked, accepting her porridge and bread.

"I got a level!" Kelsey announced. There were some murmured congratulations from the group at large, but the girls didn't really know Kelsey and felt reticent about speaking to her. Those who *did* know her had other concerns.

"I thought you said last night wouldn't give you any experience?" Tyla asked. Anton shot a glance at her. He didn't like the idea of Kelsey acting on his own while he slept, but he could hardly stop her. Realizing he probably shouldn't take her word for it, he checked her status.

"Kelsey," Level 29, Necropolis,
S: 22 T: 19 A: 21 D: 18 P: 24 W: 25 C: 20

"It didn't," Kelsey explained. "I had some delvers come down yesterday, and three of them didn't make it." She looked at Anton knowingly. "This is the first time I've made a level since getting an avatar. Plus one to each stat, not bad, eh?"

Anton winced. "Who were they?" he asked, ignoring her question. The main crew he knew of high enough level to interest Kelsey was Rathuan's crew. They weren't exactly his friends, but . . .

"No one you know, probably," Kelsey told him. "Outsiders. Kaelan Stormblade, Draven Blackthorn, Finnian Stonehammer and Cedric Whitewood."

"The Stormguard," Anton said. "I've never met them, but I've heard of them."

"I've heard of the Stormguard," Aris put in. "They protected a lot of people."

There was some more agreement farther down the table. The Stormguard were pretty famous, and most of the girls had heard the story of how they had turned back the Darkenwolf Pack and saved the village of Alpenst.

Kelsey bristled, not liking the looks she was getting. "Well, whatever they did before, *this* time they were hired by Tikin to kill me," she said. "Suliel said it was okay to kill them."

"Wait, did you say *Magister Tikin?*" Syrena asked. "Doesn't he work for Lady Suliel? I mean . . ." she trailed off, looking at Anton. "Your lordship?"

"Not anymore," Anton said, waving her attempt at using his title away. He still wasn't used to that. "I guess we skipped what he was up to during all the excitement."

He briefly explained. "—so he *was* gone, left with Suliel's mother, back to the capital to find another core, I suppose."

"It's no surprise that he would be—well, not *back*—but back in the game," Kelsey said. "Anyway, it was all in self-defense."

"What about last night, was that in self-defense?" Anton asked knowingly.

"Actually, it was! I—"

"While the bartender *did* attack first, we *were* intruding. Against his stated wishes," Tyla put in. Kelsey pouted.

"We left the rest of them alive, at least," she said.

"We did," Tyla agreed. She bowed to Anton. "Kelsey felt that you would prefer it that way and that they were too drunk and drugged to remember much of the evening."

Anton stared at her for a moment before having the presence of mind to check her as well.

Tyla of the Padascar Tribe, Level 11, Elf, Doxy, Padascar Hunter (Broken)/ Doxy, S: 11 T: 7 A: 10 D: 16 P: 18 W: 12 C: 9

Only one level, he thought.

"Thank the gods for small mercies, I guess," Anton said, sighing. "Before I forget, one of those people Kelsey killed, Cedric. He should have had a decent bow if you're still looking for one."

"Had," Kelsey stated with a smug smile. "It didn't survive impact."

Anton wanted to ask, but didn't. Instead, he focused on what had happened *here*.

"So what were you doing in the bar?" he asked.

"Investigating the Fishers, of course!" Kelsey said. "I think we found what you're looking for."

"Oh?" Anton didn't think he was going to like what was coming.

"So the basic thing they've got," Kelsey said, "is your standard extortion racket."

"What's that?" Anton asked.

"Oh . . . Your gang stakes out a territory, and you tell anyone in that territory that they've gotta pay you money or you won't protect them . . . from all these gang members standing around."

"People pay you for protection . . . from yourself?" Anton asked. "That seems wrong."

Kelsey shrugged. "It's pretty much the same as what the nobles do, but they call it taxes."

Anton frowned. Was that what taxes were? He'd have to ask Suliel when they got back . . . but Kelsey was moving on.

"In addition, they've got a workhouse scam going on."

"What's *that*?" Anton asked again.

"Where to start . . ." Kelsey said. "Um . . . so, Denasti has got a lot of kids on the streets, same as anywhere. Orphans, runaways, abandoned . . ."

Anton nodded. Kirido was small enough that places were found for stranded children, but he'd seen how it worked in Rused.

"Now, say that you've got a building big enough to pull this off. You go to the city and say: I'm going to take care of all these children, feed and clothe them, and give them a place to sleep."

"Sounds reasonable," Anton said.

"And because food, clothes and beds aren't free, you're going to make them work, and you're going to pay them a wage, and the costs are going to come out of that," Kelsey continued.

"I guess that makes sense," Anton said.

"And because the city doesn't *check*, it doesn't notice that you're charging too much for their costs, and giving them too little in wages. By the time they come of age, they actually owe you money, enough for you to put them into debt slavery."

Anton frowned. "That doesn't seem right," he said. "Surely someone would notice."

"No one cares, because it's the best outcome for those brats," Soraya put in. She'd been quietly eating her breakfast but now she spoke for the first time. "They were just going to starve on the streets; becoming slaves will see them taken care of."

"Spoken like a true slave trader," Kelsey said. Soraya nodded, ignoring the glares from the rest of the room. "But, like most criminals, they went a bit too far."

"How so?" Soraya asked.

"Street kids are too smart to fall for that scam. They can snatch them off the streets, but the kids quickly learn what to look for. They didn't have enough bodies to be profitable, and they were already snatching kids, so . . . they just started snatching kids with families."

"That's abhorrent!" Soraya exclaimed. "Those children would be citizens. Taking away their futures like that . . . what?"

"They're looking at you like that because they're appalled at your *selective* sympathy," Kelsey explained. "But it demonstrates an important point. The Fishers are vulnerable now, in a way they weren't before. If Anton frees a bunch of kidnapped children, the hue and cry will go up and any gang members that we miss will get snapped up by the authorities."

"And too, you would be lauded as a savior of children instead of a vigilante murderer," Soraya said thoughtfully.

There was a mutinous muttering from farther down the table.

"Lord Anton isn't a murderer!" Morwyn hissed.

Soraya held up her hands. "Spare me from the wrath of your harem, Lord Anton!" she said sarcastically.

"Just keep on making friends, Soraya, I'm sure *that* will turn out well," Kelsey said. "Speaking of future debacles, have you figured out how you want to handle the ransom?"

Soraya glared at Kelsey, but she didn't take the exchange further. Instead, she modulated her tone to sound more friendly.

"I shall have to take the second option, I fear. Returning to my father does not seem wise. We shall take the money and run."

"Only now, you're talking about running from a Tier Four," Kelsey said. "Any ideas of how you're going to pull that off?"

"He's only a duelist," Soraya said. "He isn't known for any social or tracking traits. I understand that you plan to leave the city; perhaps I could accompany you?"

"So he comes after *all* of us," Kelsey stated. "I'm sure how you could see that wouldn't be ideal for *us*? Why would we take you along?"

Soraya hesitated, "Well, the money . . ."

"*That* is why you're here," Kelsey pressed. "You want to get in on our escape route as well? We need something more."

"I can't give you *more* of the money!" Soraya protested. "I need it to make a new life!"

Kelsey glanced quickly at Anton. He wanted to speak up, but he didn't want al-Kadir chasing after them. He looked away.

"You want to put our lives in danger, for nothing in return?" Kelsey said softly.

Soraya swallowed nervously.

"Um," Zaphar spoke up. "This is, it is about being useful, yes?"

Everyone looked at him and he gulped.

"I think I know how the esteemed merchant's daughter can be of use to us," he said.

"Oh? Tell me more," Kelsey purred. That seemed to discomfit Zaphar more than the stares did.

"I have, have not had much progress with the documents," he said. "I am just a thief, I do not know what is required, what is necessary for such things. Even the seals, there are many, and I do not know which is correct."

Kelsey looked at Soraya. "Do you know which is correct?" she asked. Soraya stared at her for a second and then started into life.

"Well, of course I know!" she exclaimed. "I'm not my father's daughter for nothing. In fact, I know where Father keeps examples of just the documents you are looking for. Articles of passage, registration for human cargo. . . . You would have to alter or copy the documents themselves, of course . . ."

She trailed off under Kelsey's stare before rallying gamely.

"I can show you where they would need to be modified . . ."

Kelsey held her silence for a minute more and then smiled warmly.

"I always knew you were going to be part of the team," she said.

Soraya swallowed and bowed her head. "Part of the team. I should . . . speak with Zaphar more? About where to look for the documents?"

"Great idea," Kelsey said.

"You both got new levels," Anton said, in an attempt to change the subject. "What traits did you get?"

It was a little rude to just ask, but he was fairly sure Kelsey wouldn't mind. They *were* working together, so it would help if he knew what his team members were capable of.

Tyla seemed to agree. "I can cast spells now," she told him. "Small ones. I couldn't erase the memories of the people that we questioned, but I could . . . confuse them. Make them go to sleep."

"That will improve as her levels increase," Kelsey said proudly. "As for me, I haven't decided yet. Not that it will make a difference here."

Anton blinked, and then figured it out. "Your trait will be for your real self," he said.

"Both of me are equally real," Kelsey replied. "But that's the gist of it."

She stretched out her hands to her sides. "One of the options is another avatar body, which I'd *love* to take. But Mel wouldn't hear of it."

"Does she have a say?" Aris asked. Kelsey's face fell. She put a smile right back on, but Anton had seen the lapse.

"Yeah, she does," Kelsey said. "I don't want to talk about it."

"So what are the other options?" Anton asked.

"I could get a new monster type," Kelsey said thoughtfully. "Of course, then I'd have to choose what monster. But I was thinking that the undead fishies were underperforming."

"They got that far?" Anton asked.

"They killed Cheryl," Kelsey said. "I'll respawn her as soon as that edgelord stops camping on the floor, but she won't be the same."

That fit with what Anton had heard of the Stormguard. They were—had been—powerful fighters. Kelsey saw the look on his face and decided it was her turn to change the subject.

"Let's talk about our biggest problem," she said. "We've been dancing around it, but I think you need to confront him head-on."

"Him?" Anton asked.

"Al-Kadir," Kelsey answered. "He's going to be involving himself in this ransom handover, so you need to find out just what he's going to do."

CHAPTER FORTY-EIGHT

Love Can't Turn Around

Anton sipped his tea. It was delicious, he had to admit. He held on to it, savoring the taste. The heat of the cup, the orange-blossom fragrance . . . it was the only part of this situation that he was comfortable with. As long as he was sipping tea, he didn't have to respond.

He *should* have been made more comfortable by the presence of Aris by his side, but having her here, *without* her guns, only made him worry. By contrast, the *absence* of Kelsey was a constant force gnawing at his composure.

I haven't abandoned her, nor has she abandoned me. This is part of the plan. We are working together, separately. The mantra seemed to help, a little.

The slave that had handed Anton his tea was yet another source of discomfort. He didn't wear a collar, but it was easy for Anton to tell.

Rashid Aziz, Level 13, Human, House Slave, Helot/House Slave
S: 17 T: 13 A: 10 D: 15 P: 14 W: 9 C: 10

Classes didn't impose urges, but they did provide incentives. Anton knew, if he thought about it, that freeing Rashid would give Anton some experience. Quite a lot of it, thanks to who Rashid's owner was. And yet, Anton wasn't remotely tempted. Never mind the difficulty—the impossibility—of the task, it would mean taking Rashid out of the Empire, away from everything that he'd known. Anton couldn't do that to someone who didn't burn with the desire for freedom, and Rashid . . . didn't.

Watching the perfectly servile slave, standing ready in case he should require more tea, Anton thought about incentives. Slave classes got experience from obeying orders. He didn't think about it for long, because then he would have trouble keeping his thoughts off his face. Instead, he addressed his host.

"It's delicious," he said honestly. "The best I've had. I'm astounded that someone who doesn't normally drink it can be so discerning."

Salim al-Kadir graciously inclined his head, accepting the compliment. He was drinking a cup of the same tea.

"It's not bad," he admitted. "Pleasant to the taste. It just doesn't have the kick that a properly brewed coffee does."

"I'm still not convinced that I should let a drink kick me," Anton said wryly.

Al-Kadir chuckled. "Perhaps it's for the best," he said. "I'm having enough trouble sitting still as it is. For you to accept my invitation, you must be as eager as I am to test our blades against each other."

"The best way to learn is to face someone better than you," Anton said carefully. "I only hope that you'll take it easy on me."

Al-Kadir flashed Anton a smile full of sharp teeth. "Just a little," he promised. Then he scowled. "Curse these dictates of hospitality. We should be going at it already instead of wasting time sipping tea."

Part of Anton winced to hear that al-Kadir was so eager to get to the fight. Anton quashed it down.

"I'm not familiar with your customs," he said. "There's a minimum time to spend greeting guests?"

"Indeed," al-Kadir said glumly. "If word got out that I was spending even a second less time on the proprieties . . . well, there are enough whispers about me in court already, I don't need more. I don't suppose you know any poetry?"

"My education went in a different direction," Anton said.

"Only to be expected of a barbarian," Al-Kadir said cheerfully. "If we could quote passages at each other we could go faster, but that only works if we both do it. Random small talk it will have to be."

"Then, do you want to talk about your fiancée?" Aris asked. "Have you had any luck in finding her?"

Al-Kadir frowned. "I have made some inquiries," he said, "but there are only hints and rumors of a necromancer. Nothing of who he might be, what he wants, or where he might be found."

"What sort of hints?" Anton asked, trying to sound casual about it.

"No one seems to know about the attack on the wall," Al-Kadir said. "That it was animated skeletons is not in any doubt, but there was no sign of what animated them. There is some thought that it is the work of an undiscovered dungeon breaking out. Searches are underway, but . . ."

He trailed off in thought, before shaking his head and continuing.

"That *is* the most likely explanation," he said. "The idea that a necromancer would waste so many corpses on a distraction is . . . concerning."

"Why?" Anton asked.

"It implies that he has a great many corpses to spare," al-Kadir explained. "And yet . . . armies of the undead might tread more lightly than those of the living, but they are not *invisible*. We would surely have seen some signs of such a host."

"Like footprints or dead villages," Anton said.

"Yes . . . there has been one sign," al-Kadir said thoughtfully. "We received word from Rused. Among other strange incidents, there was a garrison on the island that was . . . wiped out. Nothing was left, not even corpses."

"I guess a necromancer would have a use for the corpses," Anton agreed uneasily.

"Exactly," al-Kadir agreed. "My theory is that this necromancer came from outside the Empire, stopping at Rused to cause chaos, and has now reached here."

"That is alarming," Anton said. "But at least his army is outside of the walls . . ."

"Perhaps," al-Kadir agreed. "But I know that the necromancer himself has made it inside, and brought at least one of his skeletons with him. Perhaps the reason he was willing to waste his corpses is that he hopes to use Denasti as the source of his next army."

Is this fantasy worse or better than the truth? Anton wondered, alarmed at the direction al-Kadir was taking.

"What does the military think of that theory?" he asked.

"They do not believe me," al-Kadir said bitterly. "They say I am distraught, and they repeat the rumors that I *made* that skeleton by burning off the flesh of the man who delivered the note. They think the garrison was killed by a small elite force that took care to cover their tracks by using a nearby dungeon to take care of the bodies."

"That's . . . crazy?" Anton offered. "I mean, the making a skeleton part. You can't do that, can you?" he asked doubtfully.

Al-Kadir laughed ruefully. "Rest assured, the only way I know how to kill people is with a sword," he said.

"What about from the other end?" Aris asked. "Is her father going to pay the ransom?"

"Of course," al-Kadir said. "If he did not have the funds, I would supply them, even if he didn't wish me to. I will be making the drop-off, of course."

"You don't think your presence would disrupt things?" Anton asked.

"What do you mean?" al-Kadir asked. "I won't be taking any actions that might endanger Soraya."

"I mean, won't the kidnappers take one look at you and turn tail?" Anton said. "That might make it hard to do the exchange."

Al-Kadir shrugged. "This necromancer seems made of sterner stuff than that," he said. "As I said, I'll go along with their instructions for the handover. Afterwards, though . . . there will be nothing to save them from me."

For a long moment, no one said anything. Then al-Kadir clapped his hands. "That should do it for the idle conversation, I should think! Let's get to the fighting!"

"Steel weapons," Anton said doubtfully. "I'm more used to sparring with wooden ones."

"Rebated," Al-Kadir pointed out cheerfully. "You're getting to the stage where you need them. Wooden weapons can't stand up to the strain."

He swung his own training weapon, so fast that it blurred.

"You get tired of having to replace the damn things every few blows," the courl said. "Between your armor and your *Stone Skin*, you should be fine. I'll be holding back."

Anton nodded. Steel or not, it was blunted, and only Tier One besides. He'd be sore, but that was probably a certainty anyway.

They faced each other in al-Kadir's private training arena. Thick stone walls enclosed a circle of sand. A raised platform behind the walls allowed spectators to view. Today it was Aris and a few of Al-Kadir's servants.

"Normally, I'd let you have the first strike," Al-Kadir said. "But first, let me show you why I'm excited to spar with you."

There wasn't any change, as far as Anton could see. No dark aura, no electric flickerings of power. It was just that . . . he was facing death now. His death.

Al-Kadir smiled cruelly, and Anton knew that this was it. His end. This wasn't a spar, it was an execution. He couldn't fight it, couldn't resist it. He couldn't stop it.

He pushed through it anyway.

Leaping Attack.

It wasn't so bad, not compared to the terror he'd been living with for the last month. *Unwavering* helped him push it aside, but it wasn't like it had been on the wall.

Knowing that it would be too easy to parry head-on, Anton aimed his leap to the side. Just close enough for a slash to be dangerous. Al-Kadir parried it easily anyway, grinning the whole time.

"Nice!" he exclaimed. "Mobility and attack in one. But you see now why it's difficult for me to get opponents."

"You could just . . . not . . . use that trait," Anton managed to get out. He was desperately parrying al-Kadir's casual blows between his words.

"I could, of course," al-Kadir agreed. "But it wears at one."

He let up his attack for a moment and Anton took the chance he was given and went on the offensive. Not with *Leaping Attack*, he was too close, but with all the tricks his family had taught him.

"To spar with someone," al-Kadir continued, "all the while knowing you could end it like *that*." He snapped the fingers of his other hand, even as he activated his own offensive trait. His sword blurred, heading unerringly for Anton's chest.

Anton had been waiting for that and immediately activated *Uncanny Evasion*. His body twisted unnaturally, but it wasn't enough. He still got clipped on the shoulder. The force was enough to send him sprawling, but the blunted blade didn't get through his armor.

"That's a good trait, I have it myself," al-Kadir said, making no move to capitalize on Anton's fall. "Of course, I got it at level *seventeen*, which makes me a little jealous of your class."

"Wasn't enough, though," Anton said wearily, climbing to his feet.

"Well, *Unerring Strike* was my Tier Two capstone," Al-Kadir admitted. Anton winced. Only the even-numbered tiers had a capstone trait, a trait that was awarded at the last level of a class. Capstones were said to be better than other traits. For most people, who never made it past Tier Three, their Tier Two capstone was the best trait they ever got.

Anton was willing to bet that al-Kadir had better ones, though.

"Now, most people would have died from that," al-Kadir said cheerfully. "Most people would have fallen to their knees at the start, just waiting to die. You're much more interesting."

"You're still holding back, though," Anton said. Deciding that he'd rather attack than defend, he chained two *Leaping Attacks* to come at the courl from the side. The only difference it made was that it got al-Kadir to show him another trait. The speed of the courl's parry *had* to be a trait.

"Oh, yes," al-Kadir agreed. "But so much less than in most fights. You need to become stronger so that I don't have to hold back at all."

He turned back Anton's attacks and went on the offensive. It was all that Anton could do to hold him back, but al-Kadir still showed no sign of strain.

"Do you know, I think you're actually *better* than me, in terms of skill," he said. "It's hard to tell when I'm so much faster."

Anton didn't respond; he was too busy parrying. Al-Kadir was backing him up against the wall. Anton wasn't sure if it was deliberate or if the courl hadn't even noticed the strength of his attacks. It gave him an idea, though.

He'd been saving *Uncanny Evasion* against another casual use of *Unerring Strike*, or whatever else al-Kadir had up his sleeve in terms of attacking traits. Now he used it, both to give him breathing room against al-Kadir's relentless assault, but also to put him in the right position. He still didn't have complete control of where the trait took him, but it worked this time.

Bunched up in a ball, he reversed his trait. An attack, *then* a leap. An ineffectual swipe at the courl's legs (he jumped to avoid it) and then the launch, straight at the wall.

One hand outstretched to touch the wall, *Spider Climb* locking on. Then another *Uncanny Evasion* to *twist* just so, impossibly, so that his feet landed firmly near the top of the wall.

Momentum and a push from his hand brought him into a standing position. Standing at right angles to the ground, mind you. He caught a brief glimpse of al-Kadir's surprised face. Then he was leaping.

Leaping Attack.

Flying horizontally, from an unexpected direction, he *almost* managed to connect. At the last second, though, al-Kadir made his own unnatural twist, evading his strike.

Anton flew past al-Kadir, rolling to his feet when he hit the ground.

"I see," al-Kadir said. "You normally fight in more enclosed spaces, don't you? Dungeon-trained, no doubt. I thought *Spider Climb* was purely for utility, but you've turned it into a combat trait. Interesting!"

He grinned broadly.

"Let's go another round!"

CHAPTER FORTY-NINE

Here I Come

Was it fun?" Kelsey asked. "I hope it was fun, at least."

Anton glared at her. "It wasn't," he said. "It was a lot of hard work, and I hope you're happy with what I learned."

"Oh come on, you fighter types love that training nonsense," Kelsey protested. "Going up against a duelist twice your level? I bet your class loved that!"

"I did get a little bit of experience," Anton admitted. "And I learned a lot. I just don't think I should have done something that strenuous right before going to clear out a den of kidnappers."

"That was hours ago, you must have recovered by now!" Kelsey said.

"Bruises don't recover in hours," Anton pointed out. "Nor does muscle strain."

"Is it that bad?" Kelsey asked. "I can pull up a potion if you need one."

Anton thought about it but shook his head. "I'll be fine. I'll be feeling it tomorrow, though."

"You'll be feeling good tomorrow," Kelsey predicted, "Because you'll have earned your first Heroic trait."

Anton rolled his eyes. "And I'll have saved all those children," he corrected.

"Sure, the brats. They're important too," Kelsey agreed. "So if you're fully rested up, there's a little disagreement that needs seeing to."

"Why me?" Anton asked. He'd heard the argument starting up, and he didn't want a part of it.

"Because you're the lord," Kelsey told him. "Hard decisions like this are why you get paid the big bucks."

"I get paid?" Anton wondered aloud, but he allowed Kelsey to lead him over to where the discussion was being held.

"Quick update," Kelsey said. "I think the three girls that want to fight should come, and Aris wants them to stay."

Anton sighed. "I think I can see the motivations at play here. Aris, you'd be fine with it, as long as Cheia stays home."

"Well, yes," Aris admitted. "We just rescued her; it's too soon for her to be risking herself."

"That's not fair!" Cheia yelled. "You won't let me use a gun here, and you won't let me go out!"

"That does seem unfair," Kelsey agreed.

"Kelsey, you don't care one way or the other, you just want them to get a chance to kill," Anton said. "Is that right?"

"I'm a helper!" Kelsey agreed. "I help people!"

Anton frowned. "It was going to be the three of us, plus Tyla. Should we leave a guard behind?"

"I don't think so," Kelsey said. "We're relying on not being found. If we get raided, then one or three Tier One fighters aren't going to make much difference. Our best bet is for them to run and see if Zaphar can lead them somewhere safe."

"That makes sense," Anton agreed. He looked the girls over. Kelsey had already outfitted them in matching chain shirts. Each shirt covered a long-sleeved gambeson with boiled leather vambraces and bracers strapped to the arms.

Lyra Emberleaf: Level 4, Human, Hunter, Hunter/Doxy(broken)
S: 9 T: 5 A: 9 D: 3 P: 10 W: 6 C: 11

"You got a level?" he asked Lyra.

"I had to get *four* levels before it counted," the girl said morosely. "But thanks to Lady Kelsey and her skeletons, I'm back to where I was."

Syrena Nael: Level 9, Human, Warrior, Server (broken)/Doxy(broken)/
Warrior
S: 12 T: 8 A: 10 D: 5 P: 12 W: 7 C: 11

"Level nine?" he asked, wincing.

"Four from Server, three from Doxy, and two from Warrior," she agreed rue-fully. "I'll almost have the levels for Tier Three before I'm ready for the second."

Finally, there was Cheia.

Cheia Lucina, Level 3, Human, Doxy, Doxy
S: 6 T: 3 A: 9 D: 6 P: 4 W: 9 C: 12

"Still a Doxy, I see," Anton said, trying to keep disapproval out of his voice. It wasn't her fault, and it was—

"It's the quickest way to Tier Two," Cheia said. "I got a level killing zombies, but . . ."

It wasn't the most effective way to level up the Doxy class, but Anton didn't want to think about her doing that.

"Cheia," he said gently. "We're going to be going up against Tier Twos, at least. Maybe even Tier Threes."

She pouted stubbornly. "A gun would even out the difference."

"Sure," Anton admitted, sparing an angry glance at Kelsey, who attempted to look innocent. "But it's going to be dark and confused. I'll be in hand-to-hand combat, right in front of you. Do you want to shoot me by accident?"

Cheia didn't answer, looking away.

"Do you?" he asked again.

"No . . . what about Aris, though? She's going in with guns."

"Aris has a trait that lets her hit what she shoots at," Anton told her. "Before she got that, she was missing easy shots about a third of the time."

Cheia looked pleadingly at Tyla, but the elf shook her head. "I will be taking a gun, for emergencies, but I will be fighting with sword and magic," she said. "My magic is not yet powerful enough to injure, but it does not miss."

"You see it, don't you, Cheia?" Anton asked. "It's not that your path is wrong, but you need to walk it a little farther before it's safe to bring you with us."

She sighed. "I guess."

Anton nodded and moved on to Syrena. "You've got the abilities of a Tier Two," he told her. "No gun, but I think you'll be all right as long as you can keep your head."

She nodded and touched the sword at her side. Anton recognized the type as a common beginner's blade back home. Slightly curved and with a heavy point, it was perfect for cutting down zombies. It did fine against humans as well. "I've been practicing," she said.

"And Lyra, you're trained with the blade, right?" Anton asked the foreign girl. She nodded.

"I'm better with a bow, but tonight is going to be close-in work," she agreed.

"Then that's decided then," Anton declared. "Aris and Kelsey will be our back line, but Kelsey probably won't be doing anything unless we get into trouble."

"I'm leaving all that tasty experience for you to eat!" Kelsey said.

Aris gave him a sudden hug. "Thank you," she whispered.

Anton returned the embrace. "You can't keep her safe forever," he warned her. "Not with where we are, what we're doing."

"I know," she said softly. "But just for a little longer."

* * *

They didn't know exactly where the children were being held, but there were only a few buildings big enough to be a combination dormitory and workshop in the Fishers' territory. Zaphar had wandered through the area during the day and had spotted one such building that was heavily guarded.

He hadn't approached it, of course, lest he attract the wrong sort of attention, but it seemed worth checking out.

"Still guarded at night," he said as they approached. At a hundred yards, he could barely see the forms of the two guards in the dim light. Disquietingly, while the outside of the building was lit, the light was kept well away from the door. The guards would still have their night vision while anyone that approached would be fully lit.

"Ware," Tyla said. "Archer on the roof."

Anton looked, but he couldn't see anything. The roof of the building was flat, but there were structures up there that could hide an archer.

"Where?" Aris asked, "I can't see anything up there, it's too dark."

"I can see him," Kelsey said. "Tyla, can you take him out with *Silent Shot*?"

Tyla paused to think about it. "I do not think so," she said. "I haven't practiced with the long-range gun you mentioned. With my bow . . . I could hit him, but I doubt I could kill him with one shot."

"My bow, you mean," Lyra said. "Before you ask, I can't see him either."

"I could light him up," Tyla offered. "Only with a dim light, but enough to see him by."

"If Aris shoots him, then everyone will know . . . that *something* is going on," Anton said. "Everybody get ready. We'll keep heading for the door. Aris, get ready to shoot. Tyla, if he looks like he's getting ready to shoot, alert Aris and light him up. That will be our signal to rush the door."

Aris nodded and unlimbered her long rifle.

"Ready," she said after just a few more steps. Anton wondered what someone watching would make of it. Some kind of spear?

No one challenged them as they got closer. At fifty yards, Tyla spoke.

"He's moving. Get ready," she said.

Thirty yards.

"Now!" Tyla called. Aris whipped up her rifle and there was a flash of light and the crack of gunfire. Forewarned, all the girls had covered their ears, and Anton was glad of his hearing protection.

"Charge!" Anton yelled, and he took off down the street. The two guards were looking at him. They didn't know what they'd just seen, but they knew what to do about a charging man with his sword drawn. They readied to receive his charge.

Anton hadn't planned on fighting fair, though.

Leaping Attack.

Every point of Strength he got seemed to add a foot of height to his leap. Just before he came within reach of their weapons, he leaped straight over their heads, striking an ineffectual blow against the wall as he landed against it.

And stuck there with *Spider Climb*. The two guards stared at him in confusion, which meant that they weren't paying any attention to the girls.

Tyla had said that she wasn't going to fight with guns, but that was inside. Out here, against a pair of guards who were standing still, she could hardly miss. Anton could tell which shot was hers, because it hit the man in the shoulder, spinning him around. His wife's shot hit in the dead center of the other man's chest.

That was the second really loud noise to sound out on the street, and it didn't go unheeded by the gang members inside. The door slammed open, and a heavy-set man with a bald head and tattoos rushed out.

"What in the nine hells is going on here?" he yelled. Then he took in the two guards, one dead, one down, and froze in surprise. The perfect opportunity for Anton to descend.

Leaping Attack.

It wasn't much of a jump, or even an attack. He just dropped, sword point first. It was worth using the trait for the landing, though. With three bodies sprawled on his landing zone, he needed to do everything he could to make sure he didn't trip.

Light was spilling out of the door, but no other gang members were visible as yet. He could hear voices from within, sounds of confusion, not yet alarm.

"Come on," Anton called, pausing only long enough to make sure the others were following. He plunged into the building.

A knife skittered off the skin on the back of his neck. There had been someone else here. He'd hidden himself in a nook that seemed tailor-made for the purpose and awaited his chance.

Unfortunately for him, he only had an ordinary Tier One blade. From the looks of him, he wasn't long out of Tier One himself. Anton backhanded the skinny man with his off hand, as the angle was bad for his sword. He went flying into the wall, and for a moment, Anton thought he'd knocked the man out with one blow. But he stayed up long enough to take a sword blow from Tyla, who was following close behind.

Anton left him to her, striking deeper into the building. The shouts were rising in volume now, becoming more alarmed.

I hope the kids are here, Anton thought to himself. *I'm starting to feel bad for the gangers.*

There was no doubt that this was a gang hideout. Anton hadn't stopped to check, but enough of the guards had prominent kingfisher tattoos that Anton could be sure of that much.

Two more Fishers burst out of a nearby room and came at him with knives. In the close quarters of the corridor, that should have given them an advantage, but Anton was used to fighting in more cramped conditions than this. They didn't look as if they had the strength to take a charge.

Running forward, Anton put his sword in the chest of one of his attackers while weaving past the daggers of the other. He slammed into the remaining man, knocking him to the floor while his companion expired.

Anton felt the experience rushing in from the death. His first actual kill of the night. It felt like a lot, for someone who went down that easily.

There must be a bonus from my class, he guessed. *I guess we found the right building after all.*

CHAPTER FIFTY

That's What Friends Are For

Anton cleaned his sword on the tunic of a dead thief. The easy part was over.

Maybe not entirely. Anton couldn't guarantee there wasn't some gang member still hiding in the building. But no more were coming. Zaphar had assured him that the building only had one entrance, so it should be a while before any reinforcements showed up.

Unless they had an exit on the roof, or to the sewers. Zaphar couldn't check for that.

"Tyla, Aris—" he started. Then he coughed and cleared his throat. When had he gotten hoarse? He vaguely remembered starting to scream orders to the others in the heat of battle. Then just screaming . . . he shook his head.

"Can you check if anyone got out through the roof?" he asked. Tyla's senses and Aris's firepower. A good two-person combination. "Kelsey, can you check for a sewer exit?"

"Secret passages leading into the dark beneath?" Kelsey said brightly. "My specialty!"

"You two are with me," he said to Lyra and Syrena. The least frightening of everyone here . . . though that wasn't saying much. Both of them had more than a little blood on them, and Lyra was just now finishing off one of the fallen gang members.

"That . . . isn't a Doxy trait, is it?" he asked uneasily. The smooth and efficient way she slid her sword through the man's ribs was either a trait or a lot of training.

Lyra's green eyes flashed as she looked up at him. "Hunter's trait," she said. "*Mercy Kill.*"

"Oh, good," Anton said, unaccountably relieved that Doxy didn't provide a trait to help the class holder kill clients in their sleep. "We're going to see to the children. None of them should have classes, so try not to overreact. They'll probably try to rush us when we open the door."

Lyra nodded and carefully cleaned her sword off. Stabbing through the heart, Anton noted, greatly reduced the amount of blood spilling out of the corpse. It was the sort of thing that he should have known, but the majority of his kills had been from creatures already dead.

Syrena watched Lyra closely and then followed her example.

"Are you all right?" Anton asked her.

She nodded. "It's not that much different from killing zombies," she said. "I froze a few times back in the monster room, and threw up once. But it got me ready for this."

Anton nodded, put away his sword, and drew out the light-stone. The rooms had been poorly lit by lanterns suspended from the ceiling, but the stone cast a strong white radiance around him. Ignoring how the new light source made all the bodies around him seem more real, Anton strode to the one door that hadn't been opened during the fight.

Listening intently, Anton thought he could hear quiet sobbing from behind it.

"I'm going to open the door now," he called. "Don't panic, we're not here to hurt you."

There wasn't any response, but he hadn't expected one. The door was barred, but it was barred from this side, so it was easily opened. There was only darkness beyond.

Not willing to put himself at a tactical disadvantage, even against children, Anton tossed the stone into the room. It lit up an open area, surrounded by shadowy structures that looked like bunk beds. Four stacks on each side, looking to be about three beds high.

Anton paused to let his eyes get used to the darkness. "The first thing is, you're no longer prisoners here."

He waited for a response, but it took a while. Finally, someone spoke up.

"Yer still 'tween us un der door."

Anton blinked at the heavily accented Elitran. He struggled with it for a moment, but he got the gist.

"Just for the moment," he said. "I don't want you all running out into the night. Some of you have homes to go to."

"Na all've us."

"No. Sorry about that," Anton said helplessly. "I'm told that some of you were snatched off the street, and that you want to go back to your old haunts. Is that true?"

There were a few murmurs, but nothing that could be called a response. Anton tried again.

"Can anyone who wants to just run, to go back to the streets, come forward into the light?" he asked.

It took a while, but they came forward, in dribs and drabs. Eventually, nine kids, all boys, stood where he could see them. They looked back at him warily.

"If you want to leave now, that's fine," Anton said. "Walk, don't run. If you want to go through the pockets of the people on the floor, that's fine, too. You'll need money."

He stepped away from the door, gesturing for the girls to get out of the way as well.

"Yer just lettin' us go? Why?" one of the boys demanded.

"I want to help you," Anton said. "Whether that's finding your parents or helping you find a way to live. If you don't want my help, though, the best I can do is show you the way out."

"Can you really find Mum and Dad?" somebody said from the darkness.

"I can *help* you do that," Anton said. "You're going to have to tell me where you live."

Some of the nine looked doubtful, but one of them strode confidently forward. His gait stuttered when he got within arm's length of Anton, but he recovered and walked through the door.

Seeing that he made it, the others started walking as well. Some of them started to run, but just a cough from Anton stopped them.

Mixed shouts of dismay and delighted started sounding from outside, as the kids were shocked by the dead bodies and delighted by the treasures they held.

"Are you sure it's fine for them to be robbing corpses?" Syrena asked.

Anton shrugged. "I think that those ones have seen, maybe done, worse," he said.

"It's *our* booty, though," Lyra muttered. "Spoils of war and all that."

"Leave the corpses to Kelsey," Anton said. He turned back to the hidden kids.

"How many of you think they have homes to go to?" he asked. "Come forward."

Seven came into the light this time.

"How many of you think you could find your home at nighttime?" Anton asked gently. No one spoke up, but several of them shook their heads doubtfully.

"All right, then, this is what we're going to do," Anton said. "We're going to take you back to our hideout, and tomorrow we're going to go out and look for your parents. Is that okay with you?"

They nodded nervously.

"Come forward, then," Anton said. "Who does that leave?"

He could see a couple of kids still in the darkness, whispering to each other.

"If you just plan on escaping when we leave, you missed a prime looting opportunity," Anton said. "We won't be leaving any corpses behind."

The two kids stepped forward. "We da have homes," one of them said. "But we da want ta go back ta the street."

"You want my help," Anton said.

"Ya said you would."

"Sure," Anton agreed. "For now, food and a bed. I'll tell you about Kirido, and you can decide later if you want to come with us."

"Fine."

You have reached Level 2.
Please select a new Trait.
Please allocate 2 free Ability points.

Anton wasn't sure if the level came from the two kids accepting his help, or if it had just been waiting for him to relax. He let the girls organize themselves and the kids for the trip back while he considered his options.

Applying Benefits for Level 2
Strength + 1
Toughness + 1
Agility + 1
Dexterity + 1
Perception + 1
Willpower + 1
Charisma + 1
Assign free points:

He went with Strength and Dexterity for his free points. That wouldn't get him close to al-Kadir, but it was a start in the right direction. And having a balanced Agility and Dexterity was generally considered a good idea for an adventurer.

Available Traits: Sense Peril | Sense Degradation | Sense Destiny |
Danger Sense

Anton boggled at the options before him. The first trait for a Tier Three class was generally sense-based, but what were these?

Danger Sense, at least, he knew. This was an old standby from Adventurer.

Useful, and probably offered here as a second chance to take it. As a Tier Two trait, it was probably strictly inferior to the other three . . . but what did they do?

Peril was just a synonym for danger, so on the face of it, the two were the same trait. When that happened, Anton knew, it tended to mean that it was a similar trait that could be described by the same name. Since it was Tier Three, Anton decided that it had to be a better version of *Danger Sense*. Either it saw further in advance, or the threats it could detect were expanded somehow.

Sense Degradation sounded creepy, but when he turned it around and started thinking about what his class needed, it made sense. This sense would lead him right to situations like the one he'd just found. Bountiful sources of experience. It sounded great, but Anton was worried that while they were in Denasti, it would be going off nonstop.

That left *Sense Destiny* . . . which was probably the one that Kelsey would want him to take. Or would she? She'd admitted that she wanted to tag along with him, wherever his path took him, but she'd been coy about where she thought that would be.

If she *didn't* know, then she'd want him to take the trait, the better to lead her there. If she *did* know and was keeping it from him, she probably wouldn't want him to take the trait, the better to keep him in the dark.

Anton thought about asking Kelsey what she thought, to gain some insight into what she knew . . . but she'd probably see through that trap and choose what she *said* on how she thought he would react. She was better at that game than him. He resolved to choose without consulting her.

Thinking about Kelsey's plans put it all in stark contrast. Danger—or peril— was something that would make itself known eventually. As long as he was alert, he could see it in time. He could find his own sources of experience—Denasti wasn't exactly lacking them.

His destiny, though, was where he was completely lost. He didn't know what it meant, let alone what it was. If he ever wanted to catch up with Kelsey, then that was what he needed more information on.

I choose Sense Destiny, he thought.

He had thought there would be an immediate difference, that he'd suddenly see the way forward. Nothing changed, though. He didn't feel any tug, any call to action.

Did I dupe myself into taking a dud? He wondered. The other two options had seemed pretty good. He sighed and decided to see what the future would bring him.

"My boy, my boy, my beautiful boy! You brought him back!" Dimr's mother was monopolizing hugging the boy, which left the father free to shake Anton's hand effusively, tears in his eyes.

"Thank you, a thousand thanks, kind stranger."

"It's nothing," Anton said. "I ran into a den of thieves, and I couldn't exactly leave him where I found him."

"Please, you must stay. We will hold a feast in your honor, and give thanks for the return of our son!"

"I can't stay," Anton demurred. "There were other kids trapped there, and I have to get along and find their parents as well."

"Then money! We offered a reward, you must have it!"

"I don't need it," Anton said. "Your joy is reward enough. Keep the money; spend it on your son."

"Ha ha . . ." the man laughed, tears in his eyes. "We will, surely. But there must be something we can do for you, some way to show our gratitude!"

"Well . . ." Anton said. "You could get the full story out of your son, and then take it to the Guard."

"The Guard! Bah! Of what use are they? We went to them before, and they did nothing!"

"There's not much they can do," Anton explained. "Some kid goes missing, how are they going to find him? And it's not like the Fisher's territory is near here."

"That's true," the father said, frowning. "We have heard of the Fisher gang, but this is not their territory."

"The Fishers are still out there," Anton said. "I cleared out one workshop, but they will rebuild and start grabbing kids again."

The father growled, deep in his throat. "And we are helpless to stop them! The Guard does nothing, cares nothing for us!"

"I think it might care," Anton said, "if enough citizens complained. I'm returning seven boys to their parents today. If they all tell their friends what happened, and who did it, and *they* all complain to the Guard . . ."

"They might do something," the father said thoughtfully. "Even if they have taken money to do nothing."

"Tell your friends. Tell everyone," Anton said. "I don't know if it will work. But if the Guard set their mind to it, they can take the Fishers down."

CHAPTER FIFTY-ONE

Sledgehammer

The Poor Quarter hadn't always been the Poor Quarter. Long ago, in a time lost from the memories of the street vendors and marketgoers that Anton had talked to, it had been the ruler's palace. There had been a change of management at some point, or so Anton assumed. The people he talked to weren't at all interested in history, so all he had gleaned was that the out-of-place walls that stuck up like broken fingers throughout the quarter were part of "the old palace."

Whoever had destroyed the old palace and taken over the city hadn't bothered to rebuild from the remains, and instead left it for the poor to pick through. Much of the rubble had been repurposed for other buildings, but there were some remnants left. They tended to be the broken remains of big structures, made of stones too big for the poor to drag away.

One such remnant must have been part of the outer walls of the palace. Thirty feet high, and a hundred yards long, it didn't run straight. It bent in the middle at about a thirty-degree angle. Once enclosing the wealthy, the remains now served as one of the boundaries of the poorest quarter.

Someone, perhaps tired of constantly making a detour, had tried to tunnel through the wall at one point. Tried and failed. Some of the stones on the inner facing had been removed, and the filler rubble had been no problem, but they had been defeated by the huge stone blocks of the outer facing. They'd tried to tunnel a hole and had almost succeeded, but only by drastically reducing their ambitions.

The hole started about two feet wide on the inner side, but slowly narrowed until it was less than a foot across when it finally emerged on the other side after carving through a yard of rock.

History, at least the history that Anton had heard, did not relate why it stopped there. Perhaps the stone carver gave up or died. Or perhaps some long-dead criminal realized the use of what had been created and "convinced" the man to stop there.

Soraya had heard of the place and planned to use it for the drop-off. Now it had been included in Kelsey's plan.

"What surprised me was that there was a booking system," Kelsey said to Anton.

The two of them were sitting in one of the many of what Kelsey had airily referred to as "open-air cafes" that overlooked the clear space in front of the inner hole. All of them were much the same, a few chairs and some shade. That and a hole in the wall which served small cups of a foul brown sludge that was even worse than the coffee that Anton had been served in the past. He was taking the occasional sniff of his cup, but he had no plans to drink it.

"It makes sense, I suppose," he mused. "If two gangs show up at the same time, even if they're not feuding, they're not going to want the other one to make off with their handover."

"True, true," Kelsey agreed. Her gaze swept across the empty square.

The reason there were so many "cafes" was not the coffee they served. There were a lot of criminal factions that wanted an eye kept on this place, and their presence made the area a neutral territory, most of the time.

The wall wasn't magic. It made for a place where two people could talk to each other, and even hand over goods, without being able to lay hands on the other party. But people had friends, and rich people had hirelings. There was nothing to stop al-Kadir from sending a squad of mercenaries to the other side of the wall while he made polite conversation.

Nothing except for the sanctity of the square, run by a gang that operated on a strict first-paid, first-served basis. With all the gangs watching, any intruding force would be spotted well before they got near. Depending on the size and nature of the force, they would be seen off . . . or the criminals would run off, cancelling the meet, and no one would get what they wanted.

It seemed a precarious setup to Anton, but he supposed that was how it went in the criminal world. It was even more precarious for the two of them since they couldn't cancel and run quite so easily. Kelsey had phrased it as them having "assets deployed," but Anton saw it as having friends in vulnerable positions.

"Oh, here we go," Kelsey said.

The old man that Kelsey had paid gold to appeared out of a nearby building and made his way over to them.

"It's time. Two hours. You go," he said.

"A pleasure doing business with you," Kelsey said, getting up to leave. She strode off without further pleasantries. Anton followed.

He really shouldn't be here. If al-Kadir saw him, the courl would be . . . very angry. He would also have a lead on where to look for Soraya's kidnappers, which would be very bad. Nevertheless, Anton felt he had to be there. Aris and Cheia were safe back at the hideout, but the girls out here needed protection if anything went wrong.

He had no illusions about stopping al-Kadir if it came to that, but there were a lot of contingencies that didn't involve *him*. He threw up his hood as they approached the hole, and hung well back, out of sight from the other side.

"I hope he comes on time," Kelsey said. "A lot of wasted money if he doesn't."

"As if I would risk Soraya's life by not following instructions," al-Kadir's resonant voice came out of the hole. Despite speaking at a normal volume, his tone promised death.

Kelsey didn't seem perturbed, though. "I guess not!" she said. "Should we do introductions?"

"I see no need to exchange names with the corpse puppet of a necromancer," the courl growled.

"Wow, rude," Kelsey said. "What makes you say that?"

"I can see enough of you to use my inspection traits," al-Kadir said. "They work on people, and they don't work on you. So I know that despite looking like a human, you are no such thing."

"That's smart thinking," Kelsey said. "Most people just assume I'm using some magic to block inspection."

"One of my inspection traits works," al-Kadir told her. "The one that evaluates opponents. It tells me that should I get my hands on you, you won't last long."

"You are a scary one, aren't you?" Kelsey said. "Let's get on with it, then. Do you see this rope?"

The rope she held up stretched taut behind her and then up to the top of the wall.

"Of course," al-Kadir said.

"I'm going to redirect your attention now," Kelsey said. "When I do, pay close attention to where the other end of the rope is, and don't do anything stupid."

There was no response that Anton could hear.

"Take five steps back and look up," Kelsey continued. "Make sure to stay where I can see you."

There was a brief pause, and then an angry shout. "You dare!"

"Does that thing where your ears go back mean that you're angry?" Kelsey said. "Just stay calm. I think you've figured it out already, but if you try anything, I pull on the rope, and dear Soraya goes flying back on our side of the wall. If she doesn't choke from the noose, she'll die when she hits the ground."

"I have your money, demon," al-Kadir growled.

"Great!" Kelsey said. "Here's the other way it goes. You push the money in the hole, I let go of the rope, and Soraya takes it off her neck. There's a rope ladder she can climb down, and you can be united with your darling bride. Wait! Show me there's money in it first."

There was an angry snarl and a clinking sound. "Satisfied?"

"Absolutely," Kelsey purred. "Hand it over."

Another clinking sound as the small chest was pushed through the hole.

"Now," Kelsey said, "the rope goes slack. Can you see her taking the noose off? The rope ladder should come down any—"

A roar of rage interrupted her. "Where did she go?!"

Anton, on the other side of the wall, knew the answer. He could see Soraya and Tyla drifting down. Tyla's spells had turned a nasty fall into a gentle descent.

"I guess some guys can't take no for an answer," Kelsey said, unfazed by whatever demonstration of anger was taking place on the other side of the hole.

"I will kill you, necromancer," al-Kadir snarled. "I don't know why you made an enemy of me, and I do not care. I will find a way to trace you back through your puppets and then I will put a sword in your heart. I only hope that you come back to life so I can kill you again."

"Huh," Kelsey said. "I guess he *can* jump that high." A small device appeared in her hand, one with a single prominent button. She pushed it.

The explosion that rang out from the top of the wall was the biggest one that Kelsey had yet orchestrated. Protected from the worst of it by the shadow of the thick wall, he was still glad that he had hearing protection. Smoke and fire were spreading out in all directions, and an acrid smell filled the air.

"And we're running!" Kelsey said, grabbing at him to get him moving. Anton jolted into action. This was part of the plan. They raced over to Tyla and Soraya. They'd landed safely but had been stunned by the violence of the blast above. Not waiting for them to recover, Anton scooped up Tyla and headed into the maze of small alleys that was the Poor Quarter.

Everybody else was running, too. The blast had sent bits of wall in all directions. Some of the fragments had been large enough to do serious damage to buildings. Even without that, no one knew where the attack had come from, or why. Staying in the area seemed unwise.

They quickly lost themselves in the crowd. Soraya and Tyla stopped making shocked noises and were able to make their way on their own feet. They stayed in a close group, with Anton pushing the crowd back and Kelsey leading them unerringly to their destination. Their hideout was in the opposite direction from the one they'd fled, so they had to take the long way around, not leaving the Poor Quarter until they'd freed themselves from the frightened crowd.

It was a long, silent walk back. The silence seemed natural for Tyla. She had a contemplative look the whole way. Soraya, on the other hand, seemed to be bottling up anger. As soon as the door to the hideout closed, it burst out of her.

"What was that?!" she asked, not quite yelling.

"A successful operation," Kelsey said smugly. "Got the gold, got out, no trail."

"But the—it—" Soraya waved her hands wildly, not able to find the words.

"Explosion?" Aris asked. "That's something that Kelsey can do."

"I did tell you we were setting a trap for when al-Kadir came after us," Kelsey said reproachfully.

"The trap . . . it was those boxes?" Soraya asked.

"That's right," Kelsey said. "No need for shaped charges, just a big old airburst. Wall-burst?"

"I was sitting on those boxes!" Soraya exclaimed.

"I, too," Tyla said. "It is . . . discomfiting to know that we were treating something so dangerous so casually."

"Don't worry about it," Kelsey said, waving her hand. "They were perfectly safe to sit on. Kick them, drop them, set them on fire, you'd be fine."

"Does that mean . . . al-Kadir is dead?" Soraya wondered.

"I doubt it," Kelsey replied. "Someone as tough as he was, you'd need to concentrate the blast to kill them. Or use fragments."

She paused and looked wistful. "That would have been nice, but I had to think about the civilian casualties."

"Like the ones killed by those falling rocks?" Anton asked sourly.

Kelsey shrugged. "I didn't see anyone *definitely* killed by those, did you? Some injuries, sure. Sometimes there's more collateral damage than you expect. Setting off bombs on top of walls is new for me."

"How safe were we, then?" Tyla asked. "If you've never done this before."

"Pretty safe!" Kelsey said brightly. "You were all close to the wall, which is a bad angle for any blast *or* fragments. *Very* unlikely that you'd get injured."

"Then what happened to al-Kadir?" Soraya asked. Kelsey shrugged.

"Burned, battered, probably flung halfway into the next quarter," she said. "He'll heal up soon enough."

"I have just one more question, then," Tyla asked. "Does anything *else* in this building explode?"

Kelsey gave Tyla a wide smile. "Don't ask questions you don't want the answers to, dear."

CHAPTER FIFTY-TWO

Ain't Nothing Going on but the Rent

A storm raged through the Poor Quarter. Its rampage couldn't be stopped or slowed by those unfortunate enough to live there. Walls could not hold it back, doors were flung open or beaten down. Windows, at least ones with glass, were a rarity in the Quarter. If they had existed, they would surely have shattered with the violence of the storms passing.

Safely holed up in their warehouse, well outside of the Poor Quarter, Anton and the others listened to the reports from Zaphar. It was easy enough for him to keep an ear out for the gossip in the marketplace—everyone was talking about Salim al-Kadir.

"At least he's not killing people," Aris said uncertainly.

"Yet," Soraya countered. "As mad as he is, it's only a matter of time."

"I don't think so," Kelsey said. "He does seem *angry*, but it sounds like he's still in control."

"What part of that sounds like control to you?" Anton demanded. "Breaking into homes, interrogating people in the street . . .'"

"Two things," Kelsey said. "One, he hasn't killed anyone, as easy as that would be for him. Two, he's kept to the Poor Quarter."

"Isn't that because that's where he thinks we are?" Anton asked. "That's where we did the handover."

"That doesn't mean that's where we live," Kelsey corrected. "It's not the only clue that leads there—I dropped some skeletons off in the sewers in that Quarter a while back. Eventually, they'll find their way out or get discovered, and each one is another clue for al-Kadir."

"So we *are* trying to make him think we live there," Anton pushed.

"Sure, but he *has* to have considered that they might be ploys. A few reports of undead isn't a sure sign."

"Then why is he going through the Quarter at all?" Anton asked.

"Two reasons. For one, we *could* be there. He has to check to be sure and the Quarter is a place where he can search as savagely as he wants without repercussions."

"What do you mean?" Anton asked, feeling a little sick. What al-Kadir was doing was because of them, after all.

Kelsey nodded at Zaphar. "You heard him," she said. "People are shocked, people are outraged, but nobody is doing anything about it. Nobody cares about the Poor Quarter. If he tried this somewhere else, he'd get some pushback."

"So what happens when he runs out of Poor Quarter to search?" Anton wondered.

"He won't," Kelsey said grimly. "That's where the second reason comes into play."

"What's the second reason?" Anton asked.

"Al-Kadir is rich, you know? That means he has money. That means that he can *hire* people."

She looked over at Zaphar again. "You hear any stories about anybody else with him?" she asked.

Zaphar shook his head. "No. Some mention a single servant that travels with him, but . . ."

Kelsey nodded in satisfaction. "So if they're not with him, where are they?"

"He might not have hired anyone . . ." Anton tried, but she just gave him a pitying look. "Fine, they must be outside of the Quarter."

"Exactly," Kelsey said. "While he rages around making a big distraction and letting us think we're safe from him, his men go around quietly. Looking for us."

Anton shivered. "So what do we do?" he asked.

"We get the hell out of town, kid. Let's run like we stole something."

Anton hadn't imagined that running would involve quite so much paperwork.

"These all seem to be in order," the courl said happily, looking over the documents and at the large pouch of gold. "You are now the proud owner of the *Whiskerwind*."

"Ugh, think I'll change the name first thing," Kelsey said.

"That's your prerogative," the salesman agreed.

"Is there any chance I can make use of your dry dock?" Kelsey asked. "I need to get some work done below the waterline."

"Mhmm, we don't have a proper dry dock available right now, but the *Whiskerwind* is small enough that we can drag it out of the water and put it on blocks for you. Will that do?"

"That's fine," Kelsey said, "As long as it's out of your way. I'd like to have privacy while I work."

"I see . . ." The courl paused, and then continued carefully. "I feel that I should warn you, the harbor inspectors are *quite* thorough and well versed in spotting many of the . . . tricks that merchants use to avoid paying tax."

"Oh, it's nothing like that," Kelsey assured him. "Just some secret shipbuilding techniques from the far north."

"I see. Well, there will be an additional fee, of course,"

"I expected nothing less."

"I don't see why you put up a tent if all you were going to hide was you chopping a hole with an axe," Anton said.

Kelsey grinned at him as she drove her axe into the wood with a loud *thunk*. She seemed to be making reasonable progress at cutting a small hole in the stern. Anton would have expected it to go faster, but this part of the boat seemed to be quite sturdy.

"This is only the first part," Kelsey told him. "The secret part will come soon enough."

She returned to her work and quickly finished the ragged-edged hole.

"What do you think?" she asked.

Anton raised his eyebrows. "I think it doesn't look seaworthy anymore?" he said.

"Pftt! That's what I get for asking a layman," Kelsey complained. "Let's see what an expert has to say."

Holding out her hand, she made a skeleton appear on the platform they were standing on. This one was dressed in a bright yellow vest and wore a strange, light-looking helmet in the same color. It grinned at Anton and then turned to grin at Kelsey. Then it looked at the hole.

Somehow, despite still showing its teeth, it wasn't grinning anymore.

"Yes, there!" Kelsey said. "There needs to be a hole for the shaft to come out."

The skeleton gestured at the hole and then stuck its head in.

"Don't give me that," Kelsey said. "You can just reinforce it with steel or something."

The skeleton started counting something off on its fingers. To each count, Kelsey would respond with something like, "I've got that," or "I can get them working on that."

Finally, she handed it a tape measure. "Then let me know the specs you need." The skeleton nodded and started taking measurements around the hole and of the stern generally. Then it started climbing into the hole.

"Um, there's another way around . . ." Kelsey said, but the skeleton was already half inside. It struggled. Halfway through, it caught its vest on a jagged splinter, and Anton had to free it.

"Let's go the easy way," Kelsey said when the skeleton had dropped inside. "Most of the stuff I need to bring through is for the inside, anyway."

So the papers are coming along?" Kelsey asked.

"They are," Soraya said proudly. "It would go faster if I was able to make the applications myself, but Zaphar has made for an adequate replacement."

They were back in the hideout. The main team and a few of the girls were sitting around the table, getting filled in on the plan. The rest of the girls were making use of the new addition to the hideout, a bathing room.

Kelsey had declared that it had become an urgent necessity when the street kids had arrived. No one in the hideout was exactly clean, but the kids had been filthy. They were also, according to Kelsey, infested.

"Get them in there, use this stuff on *everything*," she demanded. "Otherwise, I'll send in the spiders to eat all the insects."

No one was sure if she was joking, but they didn't argue. The boys had been young enough that getting scrubbed down by their "older sisters" wasn't a problem, but the stinging soap put an end to a lot of the shenanigans.

That had been a few days ago, though, and the kids had passed a close inspection from Kelsey. Now they were learning to enjoy the free availability of hot water, courtesy of their friendly neighborhood dungeon.

That was another of Kelsey's phrases that Anton knew better than to talk about.

"I can't say I'm wild about becoming slave traders," Kelsey said.

"It's the easiest way for you to transport a group of, well, ex-slaves," Soraya said, her voice catching at the end. "Given that my father is still searching for them, the authorities will be quite suspicious of a passenger vessel carrying mostly Zamarran humans."

"Won't they be just as suspicious of a cargo of slaves?" Aris asked. "They don't know we freed them."

"Yes, that's why we will be forging the papers for the girls themselves," Soraya explained. "It's easy enough to apply for a permit to transport slaves—"

"Easy, she says," Zaphar said, shuddering. "It was a nightmare! All those questions . . ."

"Questions which *I* provided you with the answers to," Soraya declaimed. "In any case, assuming you can forge papers for the girls that the harbormaster will accept, we will be allowed to leave. It is only when the details are sent back to the administration that someone will make the connection between our cargo and the missing slaves."

"At which point the jig will be up," Kelsey said. "We're relying on the wheels of bureaucracy turning slowly enough for us to slip through them."

"It should take a few days," Soraya said. "By which time we will be long gone. Word will be sent to our listed destination, of course, but . . ."

"But that's not our *actual* destination," Kelsey finished for her. "So what needs forging?"

Soraya spread some papers in front of her. "These are the documents that Zaphar stole from my father's archive. As you can see, there's a covering page that lists all the girls. This part needs to stay the same, but we need to replace the names here with this list."

"I see," Kelsey said, scanning over the two documents. She made them disappear. "What's next?"

"Next is the sheet for each girl, listing characteristics and distinguishing features," Soraya said. "Here is the sample document, and here—" she said, handing over a sheaf of papers, "—is what this part should say, repeated for each of our passengers."

"That all seems pretty clear," Kelsey said, vanishing the papers away. "What papers do you—and for that matter the rest of us—need?"

"We're all listed as part of Zaphar's trading company," Soraya explained. "I'm his assistant, and you are all foreign investors. He's doing the trading, though, so all you need are the travel permits you should have got from Rused."

"We were a little busy when we left and forgot them," Kelsey said.

"Of course," Soraya said sarcastically. "Fortunately, Zaphar was able to steal this entry permit from a merchant who *did* come through Rused while following the proper procedures."

"What's going to happen to the merchant?" Aris asked.

Soraya shrugged. "He already came in on the pass, so he can probably request a new one if he reports the old one stolen," she said. "It depends on his standing with the administration."

"Zaphar can get this back to him once I'm done," Kelsey said, examining the slip of paper closely. "If he hasn't tried to leave, he might not even notice it's gone."

"Perhaps," Soraya said. "In any case, you'll need three of these, one for each of you. The only part that changes is your name and country of origin. I've listed what they should be, here."

"That all seems fine," Kelsey said. "And none of these have seals?"

"Zaphar's incorporation permit has a seal," Soraya said. "All of the others . . . they get made too often to spend wax on them. They do have a stamp on them, but you seemed certain that . . ."

"I should be able to duplicate it," Kelsey said.

"Good," Soraya replied. "As long as you can copy it, just go with the stamp that's on the sample documents. Each official has their own stamp, so it's not like inspectors can be familiar with each one."

"But I'm guessing that each stamp is registered with the central authority so that they can trace who authorized what?"

"Yes," Soraya said. "But tracing that takes time, and we'll—"

"Be long gone," Kelsey said. "Good to hear."

CHAPTER FIFTY-THREE

Straight Outta Compton

The only thing that Kelsey couldn't load onto the boat were the passengers. They were, she stated, their greatest vulnerability in terms of getting caught. To minimize the threat, she waited until the *Whiskerwind*—a new name hadn't been chosen yet—was ready to set sail before she let the girls out of the hideout.

The boys were fine. No one was after them. Kelsey claimed them as junior crew members, and they were allowed on the boat as it was getting ready to be floated. They weren't allowed belowdecks, but they practiced climbing the rigging and generally acted out.

No one batted an eye at a few kids being hired to help out. It was a common practice. There were a few questions as to where the *senior* crew were—they'd quickly clocked Zaphar, Anton, and Kelsey as not being sailors—but Kelsey managed to fob them off with a few vague statements about them arriving later.

Sooner than the dockworkers thought possible, the *Whiskerwind* was ready to be launched. Many dubious glances were cast at the metal covering the ship's stern. There were a lot of murmurs about a boat not floating if it wasn't made of wood, but Kelsey ignored them. When the boat proved that it wasn't going to sink, she blew them a smug raspberry.

"Let's tie this thing up to a dock, so we can get it loaded," she said, and the chagrined dockworkers rushed to obey.

There was another plate of metal attached to the ship. Mostly flat, with a few attachment points, it was bolted to the deck at the bow. Kelsey refused to explain what it was for, only saying that it was for "home defense."

Anton ignored Kelsey's quirks. He suspected that they were her way of releasing stress. She wasn't showing it, but this phase of "running away" had involved a lot more staying in one place than Anton had been expecting. If Kelsey wanted to have her secrets, if she wanted to hold up four fingers every time she said "set sail," that was fine.

As long as they got out in the end.

Now, there was only one real obstacle left. Their cargo had to be inspected before they were free to leave, and Kelsey was expecting some objections.

The first stage was to inspect the ship before they loaded it.

"Why is it so dry down here?" was the first thing that the courl inspector asked as he made his way downstairs. Belowdecks was lit with one of Anton's light-stones.

"I can get a bucket of water to pour on your Excellency's shoes if that makes you feel more comfortable," Kelsey said dryly. "The boat has just been launched, and it has been freshly caulked. It should hold the moisture out for a little bit longer."

The inspector stared at her suspiciously. Anton had suspected that the gunk Kelsey had him smear on the outside of the hull would be more effective than what they normally used.

"No tax on dry floors, I suppose," was all he said. Then, "What is *that?*"

That was . . . Anton didn't know what it was. An agglomeration of metal parts, shaped for a purpose beyond his understanding. He did know what Kelsey called it.

"It's an engine," she said. "An experimental method of propulsion."

"Is it," the inspector said sourly. "Didn't I see sails up top?"

"We're still testing," Kelsey said. "It would be foolish to get rid of the sails before this is fully broken in."

"I suppose," the inspector said, looking over the collection of machines. "That is a lot of metal . . . but the tax is only on ingots."

"Be assured, your Eminence," Kelsey said, "it's attached to the ship. Firmly attached. You couldn't remove the engine without sinking it."

"Very well," the inspector said. "These are the accommodations for the cargo?" he asked, looking at the bunk beds that Kelsey had installed. "Very generous. You won't make a profit that way."

"We're carrying quality goods, your Magnificence," Kelsey said with a wide grin. "The better condition they arrive in, the higher our price."

"Hmnp. Well, I hope you weren't expecting the examination to be this easy," the inspector replied.

True to his word, he poked around the cargo bay for about an hour, looking for hidden compartments. Anton was fairly sure he wouldn't find any. *Kelsey* had gone over their purchase when they got it up on blocks and had been quite disappointed when she didn't find any secret storage.

He eventually gave up looking and then subjected the crew cabins to the same careful search. Finally, he gave a disparaging snort and admitted defeat.

"You can start loading now," he told Kelsey. "You have the manifest?"

"Of course," Kelsey said, handing it to him. They walked off the ship and down the dock to where the girls were waiting.

For all the care and attention to detail that the inspector had shown before, he paid only the most cursory attention to the so-called slaves being loaded. He didn't check the names or descriptions, just counted to make sure that Kelsey had the right number. It was just as well. Some of the girls had not been keen about pretending to be slaves again. It wasn't until Kelsey had come up with the idea of breakaway collars that all of them had been convinced.

"Very well, this all seems to be in order," the inspector said reluctantly. "You can get them loaded."

"Aris," Kelsey said, her voice suddenly tight. "Take Sor and get them all on the ship."

Aris looked at Kelsey, wondering what was wrong. "Are you all right?" she asked.

"Quickly," Kelsey said. She gave Aris a look that did not match the fixed smile on her face.

"Sure . . ." Aris said hesitantly. She gestured to Soraya and they started moving the girls along.

"Now, Inspector," Kelsey said. "If everything is in order, we can get our permission slip, right?"

"Certainly not!" the inspector declared. "I have not yet verified your captain's credentials!"

"Oh, right, of course," Kelsey said. "The captain is running a little late, and I don't want to keep you—"

"He's not here?" the pompous courl exclaimed. "Unacceptable!"

"Stayed up late last night drinking, you know how it is," Kelsey tried. "We won't leave until he gets here, but there's no need for someone of your importance to wait around—"

"There is every reason, barbarian!" the courl said indignantly. "We can't have untrained idiots bumbling around our harbor! I need to verify who your captain is, and that he is qualified to take your boat out!"

"Of course, but don't you think—" A shout came from further down the docks. "Never mind," she sighed.

"What? What's going on?" the inspector asked. He looked over to where the shouting was coming from. As soon as he caught sight of the source, he paled and took a step back.

So did Anton.

"Harbormaster! Harbormaster!" al-Kadir was calling. "Do *not* let that merchant leave!"

Striding along the wharf, al-Kadir wasn't moving as fast as he *could*. He seemed to be matching his pace to the two courls that were jogging beside him. *Barely* matching, but they were managing to keep up. Incredibly, Al-Kadir seemed to be fully healed from the explosion a few days ago. Almost fully healed, that is. The fur on his face was regrowing, but it was noticeably shorter than it should be.

Anton looked at Kelsey for a clue about how to handle this, but aside from the occasional glance back at the ship, she was staying put.

"Ch—Champion!" the merchant squeaked. Under other circumstances, it would have been quite amusing to see how the pompous official had quickly turned into a frightened mouse. Under these circumstances, it was quite under-standable, and only *Unwavering* was keeping Anton from joining the courl and dissolving into jelly. "You're—you're supposed to be in the Poor Quarter!"

"I was," al-Kadir said coldly. "I received word."

He glared at Kelsey. "Where is she, flesh puppet," he demanded.

"I don't know what you're talking about," Kelsey said cooly. "I'm a legitimate foreign merchant, and your accusations are insulting."

"I may have not gotten a good look at you in the darkness," al-Kadir snarled, "But I inspected you, and I see the same blank slate now that I saw then."

He turned to face the inspector. "Harbormaster, I demand that you impound that boat and search it for stolen slaves and kidnapped maidens!"

"I—I—I'm not . . . the harbormaster!" the courl squeaked. "I'm just . . . inspector."

"It matters not who you are," al-Kadir insisted. "Just—"

"This is nonsense," Kelsey said disdainfully. "My cargo has just been inspected and consists entirely of legally obtained slaves. If you have some kind of evidence—"

"Evidence!" al-Kadir exclaimed. "You want evidence? You want to know how you slipped up?"

He laughed.

"While I searched the Poor Quarter, my men have been looking. Scouring the city and, as well, monitoring the reports that city guards make. Looking for you, looking for signs of a necromancer."

He shook his head. "They don't believe me when I say there is a necromancer in the city. But they pass on the reports to my men. And what do they find?"

"Something that confirms the ravings of a paranoid lunatic?" Kelsey said. "The ramblings of a dozen drunks?"

"A gang hideout in the Fishers' territory," al-Kadir said grimly. "Cleared out."

He looked at Anton.

"I sent you there," al-Kadir said. "Gave you the note. As soon as I heard that the workshop was cleared out, I knew it was you. But there was one other detail. All the corpses were cleared out. Nothing left behind. Does that sound familiar?"

He pointed accusingly at Anton. "You were working with the necromancer all along," he said. "You sat in my house, listening to me speak of my dear Soraya, and all the while she was held in your clutches."

"You've never even *met* her," Anton pointed out. "I don't think—"

"*SHE IS MINE!*" Al-Kadir shouted. "You *will* hand her over, and then you *will* pay with your lives for your temerity."

"Look, it sounds like we've reached the negotiation stage," Kelsey said. Al-Kadir turned on her.

"Is it the necromancer speaking behind those eyes, puppet?"

"Wow, rude," Kelsey said. "This is my body and no one else's. My pronouns are she/her and I'm not any kind of necromancer."

"Lies," al-Kadir stated. "I will go on your ship and find Soraya. We *will* be together."

"You're going to commit a crime, right in front of an official?" Kelsey asked. "This isn't the Poor Quarter. People *care* about what happens to foreign merchants. *Especially* the ones that bring in profits."

Al-Kadir hesitated. "You," he said, pointing at the inspector. "You will allow this."

"I—I—I—" the terrified courl stammered.

"Or," Kelsey said, "you could just go to hell and look for her there."

Anton barely noticed Kelsey's hands move up. Slowly, so as not to catch the eye. The guns didn't appear until her hands were in position. Anton had just enough time to think that they looked bigger than last time before she fired them.

The guns roared. These were not the silenced pistols that Kelsey had shot the Baron with. These guns blazed out, loud and fierce. Anton staggered back from the flame and smoke pouring out as Kelsey emptied both pistols at al-Kadir. Five shots, six, and then Anton stopped counting.

When she stopped, there was silence. The work crews on the other docks, the cawing of the gulls, all were stilled, shocked into absolute quiet.

Al-Kadir had fallen, his body covered with blood. His companions were clearly dead. Kelsey had found the time to spare a shot for each of them and they lacked their master's defenses. One of them had a gaping wound in his chest, and the other had lost half his head.

The inspector was also down. As far as Anton could see, he hadn't taken a shot, just collapsed from the noise and the fear.

Al-Kadir stirred.

Kelsey stood, looking down at him. Her guns were gone, back being reloaded. "Anton," she said. "Run."

CHAPTER FIFTY-FOUR

Here Comes Your Man

Anton ran. He knew his life depended on it. Kelsey was running right next to him.

"Why is he still alive?" he gasped.

Despite going at full pelt, Kelsey didn't seem to have any trouble talking. "He's *wounded*," she said. "I saw my shots getting deflected. I think he's got a trait that turns any fatal injury into a flesh wound. Kind of useful for a duelist, no?"

Anton felt a chill at the thought that al-Kadir had twenty traits, all of which were optimized for one-on-one hand-to-hand combat.

"Can he even *be* killed?" he asked.

"Not sure," Kelsey said. Then she called ahead. "Cast off! Untie us! We're leaving!"

The girls on the boat mostly milled around, not understanding what she was saying, but the street kids had been around the docks long enough to understand the basics. They started unhooking the heavy ropes that were holding the ship to the dock.

One of the kids tried pulling in the gangplank. It was a job for someone with adult strength, though, and it didn't work out. It splashed into the harbor at just as Anton and Kelsey were arriving.

Neither of them needed it. Anton used *Leaping Attack* to make a deft landing on the ship's deck. His sword, drawn while he was in the air, came down on the last remaining rope, severing it.

"Nice!" Kelsey said, making her own leap, less graceful but no less effective. She raced to the pedestal that she had installed in the stern and started barking out orders.

"Anton, get to the front and push our nose away from the pier! Aris, get on the roof and start shooting Soraya's boyfriend! Use the rifle! The rest of you, hang on or get below!"

She did something that Anton couldn't see, and a rumbling sound started from below. It sounded similar to the moterboat engine from before, but deeper and muffled by the deck. It seemed that they would be able to talk, this trip.

"We did test it," Kelsey said with some relief, "But it's nice to know that it worked first time."

Soraya had taken Kelsey's advice and was holding on to a line tied to the side of the boat. She was staring down the dock at the blood-covered form of her would-be husband in horror.

"Can't we start leaving faster?" she called out plaintively.

"We're pushed out as far as I can go!" Anton called back. The dock was hanging just six inches away from his outstretched foot. He'd seen dockworkers use long poles for this purpose, but they didn't have any.

A *crack* came from the roof of the crew's quarters, as Aris took a shot at al-Kadir.

"It's not working!" she called down. "I think he's . . . batting them out of the air?"

"You're slowing him down," Kelsey called back. "Keep firing!"

She did something that Anton couldn't see and the ship lurched forward.

There was another *crack* from Aris's rifle.

"He's getting closer!" Soraya called out urgently.

"Going as fast as I can . . ." Kelsey said as she eased her way past the other tied-up ships. There were a few crew members aboard them, looking on with amazement as the *Whiskerwind* moved without sail or oar.

There were thirty feet between them and the dock now, a gap that Anton couldn't have crossed, but he wasn't prepared to say that al-Kadir couldn't. He was just reaching the end of the pier. He wasn't running—he seemed to need to keep his guard up against Aris's constant barrage, but he would take a few steps and then *blink*, about fifteen yards closer.

He got to the edge just as Kelsey found a clear line to travel. The engine beneath the deck roared and they jumped forward again.

Al-Kadir waited for Aris's shot. He wasn't swatting the bullets out of the air, Anton could see, he was blocking them with his forearm. Blood spurted out where the bullet hit, but the wound didn't look debilitating.

Then he leaped. The dock cracked under his feet as he flew through the air. It was a prodigious leap, far in excess of what Anton could do, even with his trait. It wasn't going to be enough, though. Then he blinked.

Leaping Attack.

Anton's foot smashed into al-Kadir's chest. Anton didn't know why he did that. He didn't know that he *could* do that, leap to a target that *wasn't there yet*. But something inside him told him that he needed to do it. He listened.

Al-Kadir was much, *much* stronger than Anton. But they were both in the air. This encounter was about momentum and mass, and al-Kadir was about the same weight as Anton. The kick shoved Anton forward, and al-Kadir *backward*, cancelling his momentum. For a brief moment, Anton feared that al-Kadir might grab his leg, putting them both in the drink. The courl champion grabbed at him, but he was just too slow. Maybe it was the surprise or the pain of his wounds, but Anton's leg was just outside of al-Kadir's reach when his hands closed.

From that point on, their trajectories diverged. Anton fell back on the deck, getting the breath knocked out of him by the impact. al-Kadir fell into the water with a mighty splash.

Kelsey stared down at him as he lay on the deck, recovering.

"Nice trick," she said. "Does anyone know if courls can swim?"

"We don't like the water," Soraya said haughtily, "but we're certainly capable of swimming."

She looked at Anton, who was groaning and peeling himself off the deck. "Thank you," she said in a much humbler tone. "If he'd gotten on board, I don't know . . ."

"Think nothing of it, princess," Kelsey said. "You're part of the team, now, aren't you?"

"Of course, yes," Soraya agreed. She bowed her head in Kelsey's direction. "Part of the team."

"Anyone got eyes on loverboy?" Kelsey asked.

"I see him," Aris called out. Her rifle cracked again.

Looking at the splash, Anton saw that it went wild. He could see the small dark dot that was al-Kadir's head, making its way back to the docks.

"I can't compensate for the waves," Aris complained.

Anton looked at her in surprise. He didn't think that Aris would try to finish off a helpless opponent.

"What?" she asked. "We're still trying to kill him, right?"

"Please don't stop on my account," Soraya said.

Kelsey cackled gleefully. "Don't worry about it, I think we're done with him for now."

"We will see him again, though," Anton said.

Kelsey gave him a long look. "Is that coming from your *Sense Destiny* trait?" she asked.

"Um, maybe?" Anton replied. "I'm not sure why I'm so certain."

"Well, it doesn't take a semi-mystical trait to know that he's going to come after us," Kelsey agreed. "Hopefully, *Sense Destiny* will provide some insight that isn't quite so obvious going forward. Take the wheel."

"Uh, sure, why?" Anton asked as he stepped forward to take Kelsey's place.

He'd taken a turn manning the tiller during their first trip with the Kabimen. This ship had started with a similar tiller arrangement, but Kelsey had replaced it with a wheel like the bigger ships had. "Are you sure we don't need a captain to get out of the harbor? The inspector seemed pretty certain."

"That's 'cause he's used to sailing," Kelsey said scornfully. "You need a lot of skill to pilot a sailboat. The wind blows one way, and you almost always want to go in another. You gotta worry about currents, and how your sails are set—"

"Galleys don't have to worry about those things," Soraya interrupted.

"They have their own problems," Kelsey said. "Coordinating all those slaves . . . just being so long makes it hard to turn. We don't have to worry about any of that."

She pointed at the wheel. "Just turn that in the direction you want to go. When you're heading in the right direction, bring it back to the center."

She pointed at a lever to the side. "Move that forward to go faster, back to go slower, and farther back to go backward. Simple."

Anton nodded his understanding. He immediately spun the wheel until their course changed about thirty degrees and then restored it to the center.

Kelsey looked at him and then scanned the harbor ahead of them.

"Anton," she said pleasantly. "Why did you do that?"

"It . . . felt like the right direction?" Anton said.

"We were already headed out of the harbor," Kelsey pointed out.

"We still are," Anton returned. "It's just . . . better this way."

Kelsey blinked. "Whatever," she said. "I don't have time for this now; we'll break out the Zener cards when this is over."

"What's wrong?" Soraya asked. "We got away from al-Kadir, didn't we?"

"So it seems," Kelsey said, making her way forward. "But we've got ninety-nine more problems. We never got a pass to leave."

"But you need one!" Soraya protested. "Why did we do all that work if you weren't going to get one?"

"*For starters*," Kelsey said as she reached the bow. She was talking loudly but Anton could barely hear her. "We were lacking a credentialed captain."

"We don't have a captain?" Soraya said. "Oh, you were just saying . . . Father always had a captain. Their credentials never came up."

"Right. Live and learn," Kelsey said. "The other part was your boyfriend showing up before we could sort that out."

She started attaching long metal rods to the attachments on the steel plate.

"I'm sorry, this is all my fault, isn't it?" Soraya said. "But we need a pass. They check just about everybody at the entrance."

"It's a risk," Kelsey agreed. "As is the risk that the inspector wakes up and tells anybody who will listen that we're rogue traders that need to be stopped at all costs. I doubt our little battle with Al made a good impression on him."

The rods all came together into . . . something. Something complicated. Anton wondered what it was for, but it soon became clear.

"But then . . . they'll definitely send ships after us!" Soraya exclaimed. "What are we going to do?"

"I have some hope of outrunning them," Kelsey said. "But *this* is the other half of that plan."

The complicated thing, it turned out, had the job of supporting another thing that Kelsey summoned. *This* looked more familiar. It looked a lot like Aris's rifle, only more . . . complicated. More like an engine. And bigger.

"Kelsey?" Aris called out. She was still on the roof. "There's something happening ahead." She pointed.

The Bey's ship, that massive, opulent excess of a ship, was pulling out of its berth.

"That's just a coincidence, surely," Kelsey said. She looked back at Anton. If they'd taken their original heading, they would be passing much closer to the barge.

"A coincidence?" Soraya said. "Do you know the Bey?"

"Can't say I've met him," Kelsey said, "But he might have read reports about me."

She took out her twin spyglasses and examined the ship closely. Then she swore, loudly and at great length. It was in a language that Anton didn't know, but he was still pretty sure that she was swearing.

Then she stomped back to where he was.

"Take a look," she said. "I'll keep the heading."

Anton steadied himself against the steering pillar and took a look. He still couldn't control it well; his gaze wandered all over the faraway ship.

"Oh," he said. "Is that?"

"You see it?" Kelsey asked.

"I'm not sure," he temporized.

"Don't try to tell me all courl look alike," Kelsey said with grim amusement. "That's racist, that is."

"Well . . . I didn't get a good look at him before, but I recognize the uniform," Anton said. "But there must be others with the same fancy coat?"

"Use *Discernment*," Kelsey suggested.

Oh, right, Anton thought.

**Orhan al-Demir, Level ???, Admiral, Midshipman/Reckless Pilot/Ship's
    Captain/Admiral
S: ?? T: ?? A: ?? D: ?? P: ?? W: ?? C: ??**

"It *is* him," he said despondantly. Just how many Tier Fours were they going to have to face? "Why is he on *this* ship, though? He wasn't before."

"The Bey must have brought him back to report on our previous naval battle," Kelsey said thoughtfully. "Our gunfight earlier must have attracted some high-level attention."

"What are we going to do?" Anton asked.

"You have to ask?" Kelsey said gleefully. "It's time for round two!"

CHAPTER FIFTY-FIVE

Bring the Noise

Y eah, he's cheating again," Kelsey complained. "There's no way that tub would move that fast normally."

What are we doing then? Anton wondered, but only to himself. Without even having their sails unfurled, the *Whiskerwind* was moving faster than he thought a ship could. It was moving so fast that it was creating its own wind, which made it hard for Anton to tell which way the real wind was blowing.

Sailors were always going on about the importance of the wind direction, but Anton didn't *think* he needed to care about it. As Kelsey had said, the engine made piloting the boat a matter of point and go. Simple enough for him to get his head around.

"They have some method for long-distance coordination," Tyla called down from the roof. She had gone into the hold with the other girls but had quickly exited, claiming the conditions were cramped. Kelsey had told her to climb up the mast and act as a lookout. There was a perch up there for the purpose, a sling of sailcloth to hold a sailor in place. It looked precarious to Anton, but Tyla seemed comfortable.

"More cheating? I *thought* tubby came out earlier than he should," Kelsey said. Anton wasn't sure who she was talking about. He'd seen a heftier and richly dressed courl on the other ship's deck, but the Admiral himself was whip-thin. Or she could be talking about the ship? If ever a ship could be called overweight, that one could.

"More than that," Tyla called. "There are two galleys outside the harbor that are moving to intercept. Some sort of signaling method?"

"Are we going to use the torpedoes again?" Anton asked.

Kelsey looked at the waters over the boat's side. They were much higher up than they had been on the motorboat. "Have you gotten stretchy arms while I wasn't looking?" she asked.

"No, but we could lower them from a rope or something?"

Kelsey shook her head. "Maybe if we had time we could rig something, but that design is meant to be launched by hand. And it barely rates being called inaccurate."

"I hit both times, though?" Anton protested.

"Sure, but that was all you, boyfriend. That and the close range and the fact that they had no idea it was coming. And even then, it didn't sink that guy's boat."

She glared out over the water at the luxurious barge that was headed for them. Even with its unnatural speed, it didn't look as though it was going to cross their path. The galleys, though, were further ahead. Anton didn't think they could avoid engaging them, which would give the barge a chance to catch up.

"That tub," Kelsey said, "is going to be even harder to sink. It will have internal walls and supports and who knows what else with that guy at the helm. No, we're trying a different method this time."

She nodded at the contraption at the front of the boat. Anton thought to use *Delver's Discernment* on it.

Deck Sweeper, Weapon, Good Quality, Tier 4

"How did you make a weapon with a higher tier than yours?" Anton asked. "It doesn't even have any enchantments!"

"I didn't *make it*, make it," Kelsey said unhelpfully. "My skeletons did. *They're* just Tier Two. Some of my more advanced stuff just gets tagged with a higher tier. It's a pain."

"Is it?" Anton asked. "I know Tier Two smiths back home who would kill to be able to forge Tier Four weapons."

"They will be," Kelsey promised. "Once they get up and running with the new tools I'm providing. For me, though, having it be Tier Four means that I can't just magic up another one. I have to build them all the hard way."

"That must be limiting . . ." Anton said. He was a bit dubious about how limiting it was, though. He'd seen how quickly Kelsey could produce mechanical devices.

"It is what it is," Kelsey said. "Now, I'm going to man the gun for this next little bit, but I've got a few pieces of advice for you, my captain."

"You're not going to have Aris shoot?"

"I wish I could," Kelsey said reluctantly. "I'd like for her to get the experience.

But it's a little trickier than what she's used to, and we don't have the time to bring her up on the learning curve."

Anton just nodded as Kelsey veered into unintelligibility, as normal. "Some advice?" he prompted.

"Right. First of all, you'll have noticed that we aren't at max throttle. There are reasons for that."

Anton looked down at the throttle control. He hadn't needed to change speed, so he hadn't looked at it, so he hadn't actually noticed. He nodded anyway.

"The first reason is that it damages the engines if it's on full throttle for too long," Kelsey said. "The second reason is so that you can put on a burst of speed if you *need* it."

"Got it," Anton said. That was pretty good advice.

"The other thing is," Kelsey continued, "and I'm sure this has occurred to you . . ."

She gestured at the front of the boat.

"I've got a pretty good field of fire where I am," she said. "But I can't fire backward. If you want me to fire on something behind you, you're going to need to turn the boat around."

Anton felt his cheeks go warm. That *was* pretty obvious.

"Got it," he said. "Can the boat go as fast backward as it can forward?"

"Good thinking!" Kelsey praised. "But no. About a fifth as fast."

Anton nodded. "What's the range on the . . . deck sweeper?" he asked.

"Unsure," Kelsey said. "The bullets should go two, three times bow range, but accuracy under these conditions has yet to be determined."

"I guess that's it then," Anton said. "Unless you've got more advice?"

"Nope!" Kelsey said. "I'm leaving our strategy to you, Captain!"

She ran up to the front of the boat. She was still close enough for a shouted conversation, but he already felt her absence. He looked around at everyone who was still on deck.

"The rest of you should get below," he said. "We're sure to take some arrow fire."

Most of the girls nodded and headed below as fast as they could. One of the street kids protested, but he was dragged away by his elder "sisters." Not everyone went so easily.

"I'm staying," Aris said. "I *can* shoot behind us. My accuracy isn't great with all the movement, but I can still contribute."

"What about Cheia?" Anton asked.

"She's below, being held down by Seryna and Morwyn. I know she wants to learn to fight, but this isn't the time."

Anton felt his stomach churn at the thought of Aris taking a random arrow, but he knew he wasn't going to stop her. He looked up at Tyla, still in her sail-cloth hammock.

"I think that if I focus, I can deflect an arrow before it hits me," she said. "I will remain on lookout."

Anton almost asked if she could protect the whole boat, but he knew her magic wasn't powerful enough for that. Yet. He looked over at the last remaining noncombatant.

Soraya looked back at him, green eyes flashing. "I am not going to meet my fate cowering in a ship's hold," she said. "A Malik's place is on the bridge!"

"What bridge?" Anton asked, confused. Soraya stared at him blankly.

Kelsey's voice floated back from the front of the ship. "The bridge is the part of the ship where you command it from, doofus! You're standing on it!"

Anton felt his face get warm again. *How was I supposed to know that?* He noted, though, that Kelsey could hear him just fine from the bow. *See, I know some ship names.*

"Fine," he said. "If you want to risk yourself like that, I can't stop you."

"Didn't Kelsey say her gun had a longer range than bows, though?" Aris said.

"Ordinary bows," Anton said. "They'll have Tier Three archers on some of the ships. They can use *Longshot* or *Arcing Shot* for longer range. They didn't bother before because we were small and heading right for them. They won't make that mistake again."

"Then," Aris said, looking ahead to the galleys that were quickly getting closer, "I'd better get ready then."

"Find some cover," Anton advised them both. Then he took a deep breath and considered their situation.

They were trapped in a triangle of three boats. If he'd been trapped like this on foot against skeletons, Anton would have spun and dropped back, to take out the one at the rear. Boats, though, did not spin around so quickly. Momentum counted, and so Anton changed course to aim directly at one of the intercepting galleys.

His instincts stayed quiet, so he assumed that he wasn't making a fatal mistake, at least. He watched as the ship he targeted reacted, turning to face them directly.

That reminded him of something. "Kelsey, can we ram ships?"

Soraya gasped, but it was Kelsey's reply he was listening to.

"We'd lose!" she called back cheerfully, "But coming at us head-on like that, they make a nice target!"

"You don't have a ram, you fool!" Soraya berated him. "They do. They'll crack our hull like an eggshell and take no damage themselves."

"Right," Anton said. "What's a ram?"

Laughter came from up front, but Kelsey let Soraya continue to educate him.

"It's a weapon," she said impatiently. "It extends out from the front of the ship, about three yards underwater. You can't see it, but it means you'll sink before you hit it."

"Understood," Anton said. "I'm keeping this heading for a bit!" he called out to Kelsey.

"Got it!" she called back.

Arrows were starting to fly. Long, arcing shots that travelled immense distances. *Arcing Shot*, Anton knew. It didn't get much use in the dungeon, but he was familiar with it from books. He was less familiar with arrows that were on fire.

"Is that going to be a problem?" he called out.

One of the fiery arrows came close to the crow's nest. As promised, Tyla did manage to deflect it into the ocean.

"Not as much as it would if we had our sails out, but still. Make yourself useful, Soraya!" Kelsey tossed a metal bucket back towards them. It landed with a clatter on the lower deck. Somehow, Kelsey had managed to tie a rope to the handle.

"I'm not—" Soraya started, but Kelsey cut in.

"Part of the team, Soraya! Part of the team."

"Very well," Soraya said and climbed down to get the bucket.

One of the arrows landed in a sail, wrapped around the cross-mast. Anton looked at it with concern, but Tyla was on the case. She looked at it and the fire went out.

"I don't have the range to do that unless it's near the mast," she told him.

Slowly, and grumbling the whole time, Soraya pulled up a bucket of water and drowned the flaming arrow that was stuck on the deck, spluttering fitfully.

"How many times will I have to do that?" she asked.

"As many as it takes," Anton said grimly. "Kelsey!"

"Returning fire, Captain!"

Then the world ended.

BRAP-DA-DA-DA-DA-DA-DA-DA-DA-DA-DA-DA-DA-DA-DA-DA

The sound went on forever. It ran through Anton, bypassing his ears and shaking his bones. He started to feel his spirit float away . . .

Then it stopped. Anton was still behind the wheel, still on the boat. The sound had just been Kelsey's weapon. She was doing something to it, removing a box and replacing it.

Anton noticed that she was wearing something round and bright red over each of her ears. She looked back at him.

"Ready to fire again, Captain!"

Anton pointed down at the deck where Soraya was lying, twitching slightly. Anton and Aris had hearing protection. The others, not so much.

"Oh . . . that's my bad. I'll fix it!" Kelsey said, jumping down to attend to Soraya. She produced another pair of the red round things and tried to affix them to Soraya's head. It didn't work until she put them on upside down, with the connecting band under Soraya's chin. Then she fed the girl a healing potion.

"Are you okay?" Kelsey called up to Tyla. Anton could see that the elf girl still had her hands over her long ears. He had to leave that to Kelsey, though, as they were getting into arrow range of the first galley.

He looked ahead to see what effect Kelsey had had on the intercepting ship. At this distance, he couldn't see any damage, but it hadn't gone unscathed. A lot of the oars were pointed in the wrong direction, and the top deck, which should have been filled with deadly archers, was a morass of cowering and wounded victims. No one seemed interested in firing arrows at them, despite the shouted orders from the ones in charge.

"Um, Anton, are we still planning on ramming it?" Aris asked. Neither ship had changed heading. The galley had stopped rowing and was quickly coming to a stop, but the *Whiskerwind* was still bearing down at speed.

"No," Anton said, "but we are going to get a lot closer."

CHAPTER FIFTY-SIX

Critical Beatdown

Soraya limped back onto the bridge. "I'm fine," she said, looking anything but. "I just tripped when the sound came."

Anton nodded, but couldn't spare much attention for the courl girl. He was focused on the two galleys he was engaged with. One was dead in the water, and the other was moving in fast. Soraya looked forward, to where they were heading.

"I thought I told you that we couldn't ram!" she yelled. Anton ignored her. After Kelsey's attack, the archers on the first galley were in no condition to fire on them, and while the second galley was in arrow range, the first was too close to their line of fire to risk it.

Anton tried to figure out where each ship was going to go and frowned. If he was right, the second captain had not only worked out what he was going to try but had also worked out a counter to it. Still, there wasn't much else for him to do.

The first galley was starting to loom over them as Kelsey finished tending to Tyla and ran forward.

"Kelsey!" Anton called. "We're pretty sure the oars are manned by slaves, aren't we?"

"Spoilsport!" she called back. Anton took that to mean she'd grasped his meaning. "The top deck is fair game, though, right?"

How is she going to shoot the top deck? Anton wondered. The galley was a full three yards taller than their boat's top deck. That hadn't mattered at a distance, but now that they were closer, Anton's view of the archers was already blocked. He would have left it to her to decide, but then he remembered her reloading time.

"No! Wait until we come out from behind, and target the second ship!" he yelled. Then he spun the wheel so that his boat swung to the side, no longer on a ramming course. Then he swung back so that they would pass the ship and have it block the sight of the second galley.

It might not have worked if the galley had been fully operational. As it was, they tried to reorient the ship but failed. Too many of the oars were hanging limply in the water, getting in the way of the working ones.

This is exactly what the other captain expected me to do, Anton reminded himself. He hoped he wasn't overestimating the galley captain but he felt confident about his assessment. The captain did this for a living; there was no way that Anton was going to outsail him.

But Kelsey had left him with one surprise to pull. He jammed the throttle to the maximum. The pitch of the engine rose higher and the *Whiskerwind* jumped forward.

"Look out for oars!" he called as Kelsey whooped in glee. They sped past the galley, not close enough to touch, but close enough that any oars left in the water got splintered against the *Whiskerwind's* hull. Most of the still-working oarsmen saw them coming, and raised their oars high, out of danger. One enterprising team tried to bring their oar down on Kelsey, but she laughed and shot it to pieces with her handgun.

Aris started taking shots, using her pistols to shoot at targets of opportunity, as men and courls started looking over the side of the galley at them.

Now that they were closer, Anton could see the damage that Kelsey had done to the ship. Her bullets had punched holes right through the hull and had gone on to injure those behind. He couldn't see into the lower decks, but, based on the number of inactive oars, they must have been awash with blood.

It was only a few moments more, and then they were past the first galley. As Anton had predicted, the second galley captain had lined himself up perfectly.

They must practice these maneuvers, Anton thought. *One ship shielding the other, so when it moves out of the way, the other is poised to strike.*

If Anton had kept at his previous speed, the second ship would have been perfectly placed to slam into him from the side. It must have taken great skill to get it exactly right—or maybe the captain had a trait. Too fast, and he would have rammed his ally; too slow, and Anton would have slipped out of reach.

He'd gotten it right, but Anton had arrived early. Which meant the *Whiskerwind* was sliding past the deadly underwater ram, just out of reach. The second galley wasn't out of reach of Kelsey's deck-sweeper, though.

"And it isn't even my birthday!" she exclaimed. Then she fired.

BRAP-DA-DA-DA-DA-DA-DA-DA-DA-DA-DA-DA-DA-DA-DA-DA

This time, Anton noticed more than just the overwhelming sound. He felt the way the entire ship shuddered with the recoil. He saw the puffs of smoke and splinters as the bullets smashed their way into the hull. As he'd requested, Kelsey directed her fire slightly upward, shooting through the hull to rake fire across the entire top deck.

Anton didn't know how a galley was arranged, but he was fairly sure that the top deck was where the archers were, where the captain and the important officers were. They were all targets of Kelsey's fire. Maybe a Tier Four like al-Kadir could dodge or block bullets. For the rest, survival was purely a matter of chance. Kelsey couldn't see who she was aiming at, and they couldn't see the bullets coming.

This time, when Kelsey stopped firing, they were close enough to hear the screams over the sound of the engine.

"Yeah! Take that, capitalist pigs!" Kelsey called. She left her position and headed back to the stern deck.

Anton pulled the throttle back to what it was before. He fought the urge to turn around and offer help.

Those are the enemy, he reminded himself. *Those are the ones who raid Zamarra whenever they feel like getting a few more slaves.*

Aris was looking equally somber. She stepped closer to him, and he pulled her in for a one-armed hug.

Soraya was looking back across their wake with a stricken look on her face. "How . . ." she said.

"That's the power of modern engineering!" Kelsey said brightly. She clapped Soraya on the back. "You're on the winning team now, kid."

They stared back in silence. It was fortunate that the boat didn't need any input from them. It just kept on travelling on the same heading, out into open sea.

Finally, Tyla called out from above. "The barge is stopping to render assistance," she said.

"Does that mean we've gotten away?" Anton said. A notification and a surge of experience was his answer.

You have reached Level 3.
Applying Benefits for Level 3
Strength +1
Toughness + 1
Agility + 1
Dexterity + 1
Perception + 1
Willpower + 1
Charisma +1
Please allocate 2 free Ability points.

"We did," he said, answering himself. "I'm getting the experience from free-ing the slaves."

Almost without thought, he put the free points in Strength and Toughness. He had a long way to go before he could catch up with al-Kadir, but it was a start.

"There might be some in there for your awesome job at captaining," Kelsey said.

"It was pretty heroic," Aris said. "I thought we were going to die when that second ship came at us."

"That weapon, though," Soraya said nervously. "I knew guns were . . . dan-gerous, but I had no idea they could get that powerful."

Kelsey pouted. "I just wish I'd had time to train someone on it so the experi-ence wasn't wasted," she said. "Can you imagine if Cheia had made all those kills?"

"I'm not sure I want Cheia being . . . that comfortable with killing so many peo-ple," Aris said. "I'd much rather she transitioned into a lady-in-waiting or something."

Anton blinked. Now that he thought about it, Cheia was the sister-in-law of the Baron, that is, himself. Did that make her noble? He wasn't sure, but he resolved to ask Suliel when they got back.

"*You* took up guns," Soraya said, and Anton could hear a hint of disapproval in her voice.

"I did what I had to, to save Cheia," Aris said, her voice hard. "I'd do a lot more if I had to."

"Soraya," Anton said carefully. He knew better than to interfere, but he also knew they didn't need a fight right now. "Can you go below and let everyone know that the fighting's over? They must have been worried with all the noise."

"I—" Soraya started, and then visibly reconsidered. "I can do that, yes," she said and headed for the cargo hatch.

Kelsey watched her go, expressionless. Then she turned to Aris.

"Well, loath as I am to stand in someone's path," Kelsey said, "there are a lot of new classes opening up in Kirido. Not all of them are combat oriented. We can see if she's interested in any of them."

"There shouldn't be any need to fight now, though?" Aris asked. "We can just sail back to Kirido and Cheia will be safe. I can let Mum and Dad convince her to stay a baker."

"There's a bit more to do yet," Anton told her. "We still have to go after the third group of slaves."

"Oh," Aris said, disappointed. "I'd forgotten about those. Where did they go?"

"They were bought by Dragan Vorin, from Verheti," Kelsey told her.

"Can't we go home and drop everyone off and then go back to Verheti?" Aris asked.

"The longer we take to get there, the more likely it is that they've been sold, and the harder it gets to track them down," Kelsey said. "We've got a pretty defensible mobile base now; we can keep them safe while we travel."

"I suppose," Aris said. "I just really want to get back now."

"Anton promised to save everyone," Kelsey said. "And to be honest, rescuing slaves is great experience for him."

The others were coming up from below decks, filled with questions.

"We made it?"

"What was that noise?"

"What's happening now?"

"Where're all our supplies?"

"I need to go to the toilet."

Kelsey clapped her hands together, attracting everyone's attention. "Ladies and decidedly-not-gentlemen!" she called out. "Let me try and answer your questions in order of urgency! Yes, we have escaped."

She looked at Aris. "Aris, I'm sure you've noticed the sling and sailcloth tucked away in the corner. You can show anyone who needs to go, how we do it on board ship."

Aris looked where Kelsey was pointing. "Ugh, we have to go over the side again?"

"We're a little cramped for space," Kelsey told her. "I'll see what I can do about setting up an onboard toilet, but I don't like our chances."

She turned back to the crowd. "What's happening now is a celebratory feast! We'll get the tables and food out in a minute."

This got a half-hearted cheer from the group, but a few of them put up their hands.

"I don't feel like food right now," Syrena said. "I've been feeling ill since I got on the boat."

"That will pass," Kelsey told them. "Stare at the horizon until you get used to the motion. Those of you who are feeling all right can help me with the tables and food. Then we'll start allocating cabins. And all of you, leave our gallant captain alone. He needs to pilot the ship."

Anton watched as the lower deck evolved into a bustling hive of activity. Once things had settled down, Kelsey brought a plate up for Anton and Aris to share.

"So," she said. "We're headed for Verheti?"

"Yeah," Anton agreed. "Sorry, Aris."

"It's all right," Aris said, leaning against him. "You need to save everyone in the town, not just Cheia."

"We'll keep her safe," he promised her. *All of them*, he promised himself.

He turned to Kelsey. "So which way do we go?" he asked.

"Verheti," Kelsey said.

"Right, but which way is that?" he asked.

Kelsey looked at him, puzzled. "You don't know?" she asked. Then her eyes widened. "Did we . . . forget to get a map?"

CHAPTER FIFTY-SEVEN

On the Road Again

SULIEL

<I'm pleased to report that Kirido has won its first naval engagement.>

Suliel didn't freeze at Kelsey's message. She was walking in front of a detachment of her troops and didn't want to get trampled. Instead, she gave a mental sigh and marshalled the numerous objections she had.

<First of all,> she sent back, *<Kirido doesn't have a navy. If we did have a navy, it would be a Zamarran one, but we don't.>*

<Why doesn't Zamarra have a navy?>

<We're too small. Both the Tiatian and Elitran navies take a dim view of armed ships in what they consider their waters.>

<Oops,> Kelsey replied.

<Furthermore,> Suliel continued, *<having a navy is something that sovereign states do. For Kirido to have its own navy would go against what we're trying to convince the King of—that we remain a loyal and subordinate demesne.>*

<Well . . . at least no one knows you have a navy?> Kelsey tried. *<We're not flying a Kirido flag or anything.>*

<Thank the gods for small mercies.>

<Do you . . . have a flag? Anton didn't know.>

Suliel let an impression of blistering scorn flow down the channel. *<Second of all,>* she sent, *<didn't you already win a battle at sea?>*

<Eh,> Kelsey sent. *<We can't really count that one. An inflatable motor boat and the torpedoes were handheld. We'd get laughed out of the naval annals*

if we tried to get that one in. We've got a proper boat this time, and we didn't have to get whisked away by a friendly fae.>

<Is everyone all right?> Suliel asked. She was pretty sure Kelsey would have let her know if that wasn't the case, but it was best to be sure.

<Everyone's fine,> Kelsey assured her.

<Then can we focus on the matter at hand? We're here.>

They had reached the entrance of Kelsey's cave. In the light of late morning, it looked quite innocuous, but no one here was fooled. Holding her hand up for quiet, Suliel thought she could make out a few faint growls and gurgles.

<He won't be long,> Kelsey told her. <Those zombies aren't slowing him down at all.>

Suliel nodded. Kelsey couldn't hear that, so she allowed the dungeon access to Suliel's senses.

<Lovely day,> Kelsey commented. <I really should do something with this entrance; it needs sprucing up.>

Suliel didn't respond, waiting for Kelsey to notify her of the man's arrival. Finally, it came.

<Here he comes. This will be his final jump,> Kelsey sent. <Arriving . . . now.>

"Now," Suliel echoed. Thought was faster than her voice, but Kelsey was adept at adjusting her timing to account for that. She was annoyingly good at such details, Suliel had found.

The man appeared as soon as the word left Suliel's mouth. Her men were impressed but were not distracted from leveling their blades at the intruder. At first glance, they hardly needed to.

He didn't look like a dangerous Tier Three adventurer. The black leather and cloth that he wore matched his dark skin, making it difficult to tell where one began and the other ended. Adding to the effect was the thick coating of grime and dust that covered him from head to foot. Suliel had been told that he'd dragged himself at least part of the way up from the twelfth level, and he looked it.

The reason for his difficulties was, of course, his missing leg. A blood-soaked tourniquet was still in place, but he'd used healing potions to scab the wound over.

He must have been on the edge of his endurance because he took one look at the waiting guards and collapsed back to the ground.

"Stredyn's blood-soaked teeth," he groaned.

"Secure him," Suliel replied.

They'd been expecting this, so the guards knew what to do. Two of them sheathed their swords and came forward, dragging the man into the light. Kelsey had said that most of his traits were shadow-related, so they made sure to drown him in sunlight. Before manacling him, they searched him, cutting off his backpack and belt and feeling under his clothes for the hard shapes of concealed blades.

<Don't forget his cloak,> Kelsey sent. <It's Tier Three.> Suliel passed the information on.

Throughout all this, the man did not resist. He barely seemed to be conscious. Finally, they were done.

"Calling on the God of Murder," Suliel said. "I can't say I'm surprised."

With great effort, the man looked up at her. "I figure he appreciates a heads-up when one of them is going to happen. Can't hurt to have a god feeling grateful when you're about to pop off."

"You're not going to die today, Draven Blackthorn," Suliel said. "I have questions."

"Reckon I might," Draven disagreed. "Got bit a few times going up, got a few poisons running through me that the antidote didn't take care of." He paused for thought. "Maybe they were diseases or curses, I dunno. Lost our cleric, you see."

"I'm aware," Suliel said. She gestured for Therin to come forward. His maroon and gold robes identified him clearly as a priest of Tiait. "We can arrange for healing."

Draven looked at the priest without any kind of hope. "Healing, and then what, the rest of my life in a cell?"

"I'm not under any illusions about my ability to keep someone who can shadowjump locked up," Suliel said dryly. "That's why you'll answer my questions now, *then* get healed. After that, you'll spend some time in a cell, yes. I should think you'd appreciate the rest. A month or two, then you're free to leave."

His eyes narrowed. "You want to keep me from letting anyone know what I told you."

Reasonably certain of what she'd find, she activated *Nobility's Privilege* on him.

Draven Blackthorn, Level ??, Family: None, Loyalties: None

"As I thought," she said. "You don't have a loyalty to anyone. I'll wager that you used to have one towards your teammates. The Stormguard wouldn't have the reputation they did if you weren't a close-knit team. But they're gone."

Draven's jaw clenched. "Aye, they are," he agreed. "And who's to blame for that?"

"You can blame the dungeon if you like," Suliel said. "She welcomes your hate."

<I do!> Kelsey agreed.

"*She* might say that you were trying to kill her and it was a fair fight to the death, which your companions lost," Suliel said.

<Well, except for that bit about fair,> Kelsey commented. Suliel sent a bit of her irritation back down the connection.

"*I* say it was Magister Tikin who sent you to your deaths," Suliel said, ignoring the interruption. "Blame him, if anyone."

Draven glared at Suliel for a bit longer, before dropping his gaze.

"We all knew what we were getting into," he admitted. "Risking death is part of the job."

He looked at the ground for a moment more. "Do I get my stuff back when I've served my time?"

<Oooh . . . I know someone who could really use that cloak,> Kelsey wheedled. Suliel ignored her.

"If you cooperate fully, yes," she said. "If only to stop you sneaking around looking for it when we let you go."

He chuckled. "Fair point," he admitted. "But since you can't stick me in a cell to rot until I change my mind, what are you going to do if I say no?"

"We'll just throw you back in the dungeon," Suliel said coldly. She pointed, and the guards parted so that Draven could see the entrance.

Standing right at the entrance to the cave, two zombies were waiting, drooling hungrily. Suliel wasn't sure what made the tableau more concerning: the presence of the zombies themselves, or the fact that *something* was holding them back.

Draven shivered at the sight. "I didn't really believe Tikin when he said the Baroness was in league with the dungeon," he said. "I mean, how?"

"I'm asking the questions," Suliel said.

The adventurer looked at her. She saw the hard look in his eyes. He was over twice her level . . . but he bowed her head. Her class thrilled to see it, and some more experience trickled in.

"Aye, your ladyship, that you are. Ask away, even if it seems you know all the answers."

"To start with then, who were Tikin's backers?"

"Backers?" Draven asked.

"Tikin escaped from here with the clothes off his back," Suliel said impatiently. "He had no magic, his connection with the Rose Circle died with my father. Where does he get the money to outfit an expedition for the Stormguard?"

"God's teeth, girl, your father was a member of the Circle?" Draven said in alarm. "Why are you telling me this?"

"What do you know of the Circle?" Suliel asked, her eyes narrowing.

"I know that talking about it is a good way to get killed!" Draven retorted. "Are things different out here?"

"I trust all the men here," Suliel said confidently. "What do you know about them? Their goals? Anything that they've done?"

"That cell is starting to look awful welcoming," Draven muttered. "All I know is that they're for nobles only. That, and there's a standing contract out for anyone who talks about them."

"A contract with who?" Suliel asked. Draven hesitated.

<I bet it's the Shadowblades,> Kelsey said. <It's in his class.>

"The Shadowblades?"

"You know about that, too?" Draven groaned.

"It's hardly a secret when it's right there in your class," Suliel pointed out. "Are they some kind of assassin guild?"

"A loose one," Draven said. "You're right, it's not much of a *hidden* secret. It's more like, *most* people are smart enough to *not* poke their nose in their business."

"I'm afraid I'm just an ignorant country noble, with no idea of what I should or shouldn't be doing," Suliel said with a little bit of amusement.

Draven looked askance at her. "Whatever it is you are, lady, it ain't that."

Suliel gave him a thin smile. "Back to the subject at hand. There is a contract with the Shadowblades to kill anyone who mentions the Rose Circle."

"Right. If one of us hears about someone asking questions about them, we pass it up the chain. Soon enough word comes down that the hit is sanctioned and we'll get paid for it."

"Did your companions know that you were a hired assassin?" Suliel asked.

"I'm mostly retired," Draven told her. "Once you get to a certain level, it's a very loose association."

"Hmm. Back to the original question. Tikin's backers?"

"I dunno. At least, I couldn't tell you if they were where he was getting his money. But I did check him out."

"And?"

"We had three meetings with him, hashing out the details. I followed him after, to see where he went. After two of them, he met with another group."

"And they were?"

"I only knew one of them to look at. Kalren Voss, he's a mage at court. I figure him and Tikin go way back."

"The others?"

"I didn't recognize the other two, but they were nobles from the look of them. No one important at court, not wearing any heraldry."

"And the other time you met?"

Draven grinned. "He went straight to a brothel."

"And that's all you know?" Suliel asked. "You didn't follow the others?"

"It isn't wise for the likes of me to get involved in nobles' business," Draven said. "Or mages, for that matter. A bit of extra information can help, but I didn't want to dig too deep."

"I see," Suliel said. She nodded to the priest. "Heal him."

She started heading back down. Half her detachment went with her, the other half remained to guard the prisoner. Halfway down, she was met by Syon, her chamberlain.

"My lady! We're late! The coach has arrived!"

Suliel nodded. Part of her wanted to break into a run, but his Majesty would wait a few minutes more.

"Is everything ready to go?" she asked. **<On your end, as well?>** she sent to Kelsey.

"Yes, my lady, all packaged and prepared and loaded onto the carriage," he said.

<What he said,> Kelsey replied. **<We're all ready to go. Oh, there was one thing . . .>**

<What,> Suliel sent. It was a bit late for last-minute requests.

<You wouldn't happen to have a map of Elitran waters I could look at, would you?>

<I don't think so,> Suliel sent, **<but I could probably find one in the Capital.>**

<Don't worry about it,> Kelsey replied. **<We should have found one by then. We'll just muddle through in the meantime.>**

About the Author

Christopher Hall, also known as Maxlex, is the author of the Dungeons Just Wanna Have Fun and Phantasm series. Hall started writing his first novel while sailing the Tyrrhenian Sea one summer, the salty night air flavoring and enriching his worldbuilding. Since then, he has continued to hone his craft while holding down diverse jobs in metalworking, marketing, perfume sales, and briefly, modeling. In addition to writing, Hall's interests include illuminated lettering and artisanal brewing. He endeavors to convey a sense of l'esprit in all his creative pursuits.

Podium

DISCOVER
STORIES UNBOUND

PodiumAudio.com

Milton Keynes UK
Ingram Content Group UK Ltd.
UKHW040403111224
452348UK00004B/384

9 781039 465206